THE SHARPENED FANGS OF LUPINE SPIRIT

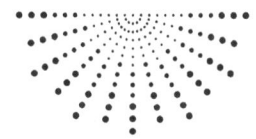

H. G. SANSOSTRI

Copyright (C) 2021 H.G. Sanostri

Layout design and Copyright (C) 2021 by Next Chapter

Published 2021 by Shadow City – A Next Chapter Imprint

Edited by Terry Hughes

All Illustrations Copyright © Adam Pickering 2021

This book is a work of fiction. Names, characters, places, and incidents are the product of the author's imagination or are used fictitiously. Any resemblance to actual events, locales, or persons, living or dead, is purely coincidental.

All rights reserved. No part of this book may be reproduced or transmitted in any form or by any means, electronic or mechanical, including photocopying, recording, or by any information storage and retrieval system, without the author's permission.

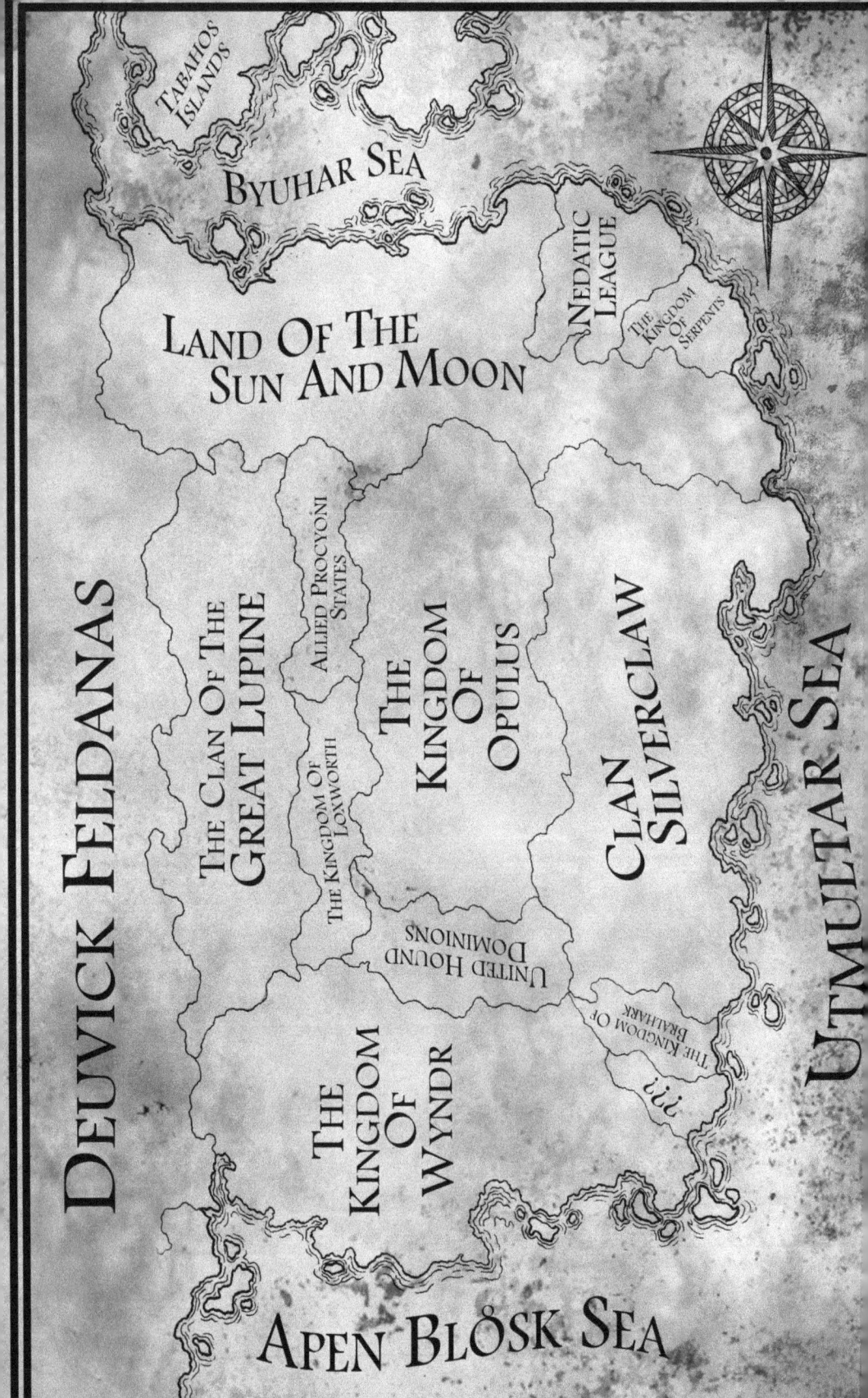

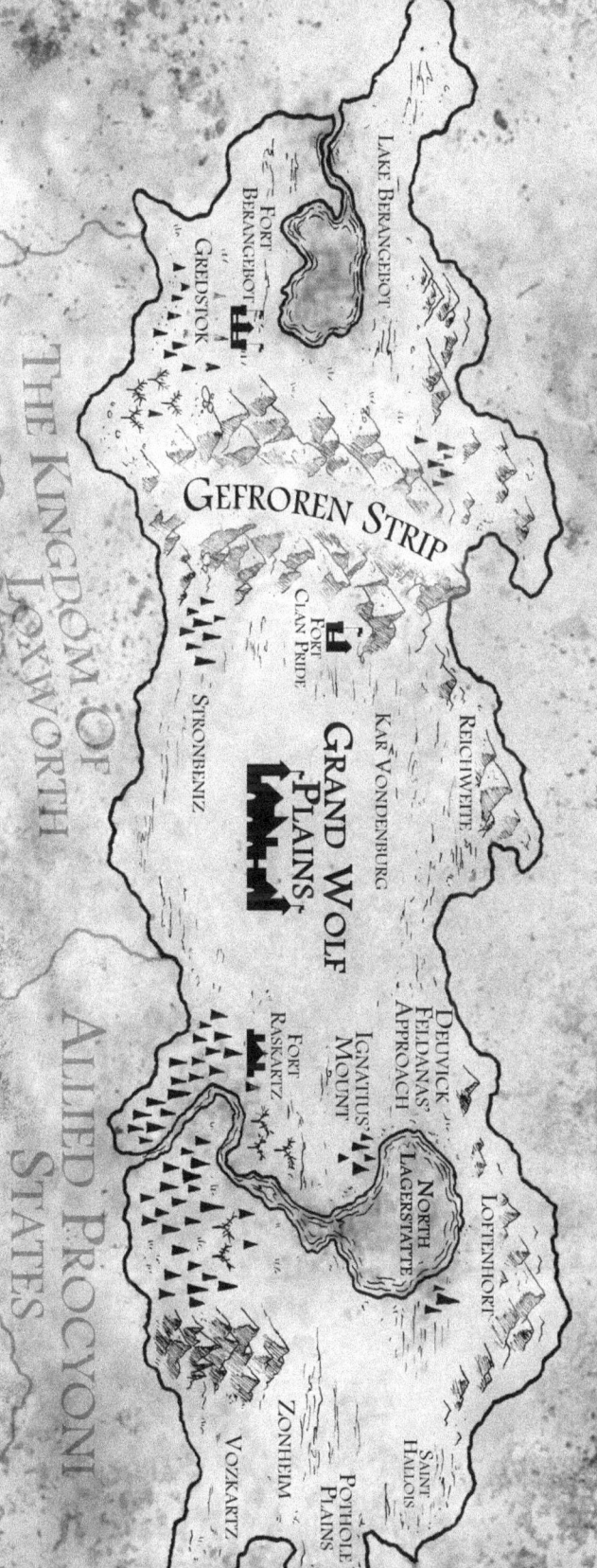

VICK FELDANAS

THE KINGDOM OF LOXWORTH

THE ALLIED PROCYONI STATES

LAKE BERANGEBOT

FORT BERANGEBOT

GREDSTOK

GEFROREN STRIP

FORT CLAN PRIDE

STRONBENIZ

KAR VONDENBURG

REICHWEITE

GRAND WOLF PLAINS

DEUVICK

FELDANAS' APPROACH

IGNATIUS' MOUNT

NORTH LAGERSTATTE

LOFTENHORT

FORT RASKARTZ

SAINT HALLOIS

ZONHEIM

POTHOLE PLAINS

VOZKARTZ

AUTHOR'S NOTE

The Sharpened Fangs of Lupine Spirit has been a personal project of mine for about three years. I started the *Vos Draemar* series back when I was 16 in 2017, writing a chapter every day after I'd completed my daily studies. It's been through re-edit after rewrite after redo, alongside the subsequent books in the series, but I am now finally at a point where I am happy enough with Corsair's story to share it with you.

There is a group of people I'd like to thank for their unrelenting support, not just in regards to *Vos Draemar* but in my pursuit of writing books as a whole. They have all played their part in getting me to where I am today – whether it be through illustration, publishing or their support.

Thank you to Adam Pickering, my illustrator, who designed the jacket and map for this book. Adam also illustrated the book covers of *The Chronicles of Derek Dunstable* and *The Little Dudes Skool Survival Guide.* While this may be a very different genre, the talent is still up there. I am looking forward to working with Adam again in the future.

Thank you to Next Chapter for taking me on and helping me

publish not just this book but the *Vos Draemar* series as a whole. They have given me the opportunity to share my stories with all of you and, for that, I am nothing but appreciative.

Thank you to the author Stewart Bint for guiding me through my writing journey since *The Little Dudes Skool Survival Guide*. Your help and advice have been of immeasurable value to me and I am honoured to have your ongoing support.

Thank you to my siblings, Christian and Charlie, for being there for me when I needed it. I can't even put into words how thankful I am for something as immeasurable and priceless as the bond we have.

Thank you to my dad – Francesco Sansostri – for being the man I want to be. He's kind, he's strong, he's caring and has always been there for me. There's no person I admire more. There's no person I'm more proud of than him.

Thank you to my mum – Deborah Sansostri – for being the ninja warrior she's always been. She has always shown nothing but love and care towards me. I love her to the moon and back.

Thank you to my fans, wherever you are, from *The Little Dudes Skool Survival Guide* and *The Chronicles of Derek Dunstable*. I know it's been quite the wait for the next book to come out but I am grateful for your patience. I hope this has been worth the wait!

And, finally, thank you to you – the reader. Without you, the tales of Corsair Sedrid would be unknown. Without the reader, there'd be no need for the writer. I cannot thank you enough for your interest and I hope you'll be looking forward to the next book in the series.

Grazie di tutto,

HG Sansostri

'Eternity began at the precipice
of destruction.
The fields, mountains, deserts, seas, forests and
winter plains witnessed unending chaos and
bloodshed.
Barbarity and perpetual war purged the
land and preyed on the innocent.
Existence was a grim torture all were forced to
endure.
But a light shone across the darkness,
emanating from the land's centre.
The beacon of hope was none other than Silas Opulus,
a hero of pure heart and soul.
Surrounded by those like him, he cleansed the land of
the barbaric and savage, the wicked and cruel.
Those born of evil fell before them and, in their place,
rose civilisation that reached to the beaches and out
into the seas.
The People's Kingdom, born from adversity, ruled with
Silas at its throne. He divided the land among the
races. The four great nations formed.
To the canine and lupine went the winter plains of the
north for their bravery and steel against evil.

To the rabbits went the sun-kissed fields and hills of the east for their intelligence and sophistication.
To the deer went the thick forests and swamps of the west for their undying faith.
To the felines went the scorching deserts and soothing tropics of the south for their devotion and cunning.
All those who enjoyed peace were welcomed to the centre of the People's Kingdom, regardless of their allegiance or race.
Silas chose his own people, the felines, to serve as the realm's sworn protectors and formed the mighty Opulusian Legion.
The Kingdom of Opulus entered the world and, holding its paw, a newly-found era of peace followed.'

'The Origins of Vos Draemar', 22 (*Adgrediom*)

PROLOGUE

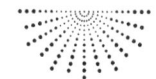

The sands of the Venada desert stretched out to the horizon, endless.

For tens of miles, nothing but dunes could be seen. Nothing could be heard. Other than a faded stone road that led on for miles towards nowhere, all that remained were the hills of sand, the sun's unending glare and the occasional scorpion scuttling along minding its own business. A bird of prey flew high above, looking down on the world below.

All was calm.

All was still.

And then, as if revealed from the fanged mouth of hell, chaos spread.

"For the Clan of the Great Lupine!"

"Look out! Incoming!"

"Help! Apothecary! Apothecary!"

"I'll kill you all! I'll slaughter you!"

Dozens of soldiers tumbled down the side of a sand dune, knocked away by the combat raging around them. Ictharr steeds,

1

wolves, hounds and felines rolled to the bottom while yelling out, weapons flying from their paws.

Arthur Sedrid, helmet flying off, grunted as he arrived at the bottom of the slope in a heap.

Dazed, he pushed himself up on to all fours. He had rolled down into a depression between two dunes, coming to rest at the base of the first and left metres away from the base of the second. Sand clung to his fur and slipped through into his armour, making the Krosguard suit far from comfortable.

But, as he stood, he knew that was the least of his worries.

Soldiers screamed from all around him. Allied and enemy ranks blurred into one mess, losing all semblance of cohesion and unity. Opulusian legionnaires tackled felines with short swords and daggers, struggling against them and kicking sand into the air. Royal Order knights bellowed orders in New Opulusian to their soldiers, trying to rebuild their formation. Wolves wielded their swords and shields, turning on the enemy and swinging at them with snarls and growls. Others took their chances with their maws, flinging themselves at the enemies and sinking their fangs into their throats.

He looked around, drawing his sword.

His ictharr was nowhere to be seen.

"Reginald? *Reginald!*"

A battle cry sounded from behind and, before he could turn, someone tackled him to the ground. His sword fell from his gauntleted paw and landed in the sand, out of his reach.

A paw wrapped in leather straps grabbed his shoulder and wrenched him on to his back. Arthur saw a hooded Silverclaw soldier straddling him, one paw holding him down while the other yanked a curved dagger from his belt and raised the blade. With a cry of Sikkharan he stabbed the blade down at Arthur, thrusting it at his throat. His paw flew up and caught the attacker's wrist, resisting with all his power.

"Reginald! Reginald, help!"

There was no sign of him.

The soldier applied greater pressure, forcing the dagger down as hard as he could. Arthur struggled, growling and snarling, before he overpowered the soldier. He pushed his arm away and punched him across the face, his metal paw sending the soldier stumbling to one side. Arthur scrambled to his hind paws and scooped up his longsword, turning around as the soldier charged him again shouting in Sikkharan.

He lunged, stabbing forwards. Arthur darted to the right and, with one swift move, slashed downwards. The blade tore through the metal cuirass and the dark desert clothing beneath, drawing blood. The soldier yelped and fell on to his side, hurrying back to his hind paws, but Arthur stopped him rising. He thrust his sword down into the soldier's side, penetrating the cuirass and summoning a wail of pain. He pulled his sword out and turned, blood staining the blade.

Two Silverclaw soldiers rushed forwards, both wielding steel *Kabar* sabres. Arthur twirled his sword on either side of him, taking up face-on stance.

"Come on, then! Kill me!"

One stepped forward, *Kabar* sabre swinging back, but came no closer.

A streak of grey shot out in front of Arthur and, with a snarl, tackled the soldier. He stood no chance against the ictharr, who sank his fangs into the screaming Silverclaw warrior and shook his head wildly. The second soldier staggered back in shock, cursing in Sikkharan as she watched the beast tear her comrade's neck apart.

Arthur seized the moment. He charged forwards and swung with his sword, cutting downwards as he moved. The soldier came to her senses and evaded the swing, slashing through the air with her nimble sabre. Arthur deflected the attack, stepping back. Lunging, the soldier swung for his throat. Arthur darted right and swung at her stomach as she attacked, the broadside of his blade striking the cuirass with a *clang*. The force brought the enemy to a stop, knocking her to his knees.

Arthur raised his sword and swung at the Silverclaw warrior's side, cutting into her ribs. She gurgled, going taut with pain, before the wolf kicked her off the blade and left her corpse bleeding in the sand.

Arthur turned.

"Reginald, Reginald! Are you OK?"

His steed turned away from the bloodied corpse of the soldier, crimson droplets falling from the darkened fur around his maw. He growled in the affirmative, ignoring the peripheral slash across his right flank, and rallied to his master.

"I can always rely on you."

"*Come on then*! I'm right here!"

Both his and Reginald's ears stood in response to the familiar voice. He turned to see a hulking white-fronted brown wolf fending off a trio of Silverclaw soldiers, blood dribbling from the stump of his left ear. His dented helmet and two Opulusian legionnaires lay dead at his hind paws, slain by feline blades. One attacked and the lupine warrior knocked away the swing with his shield, kicking his adversary into the sand with a growl.

"That's the best you got?"

Arthur sprinted towards his comrade, Reginald bounding beside him. He barged past the warring canines, lupines and felines, focused on the brown wolf. Slashing with his sword as he went, his blade cut through the side of a soldier's neck. The soldier gargled and choked, dropping his sabre and clutching his bleeding throat as he slumped to the ground. A fellow soldier turned to avenge his dying comrade but met the sharp fangs of Reginald, wailing in pain as he was torn to shreds.

The brown wolf dispatched the third, stabbing her in the stomach and knocking her down with his shield.

He looked at Arthur, panting with tongue hanging from his maw.

"Thanks, Arthur... I thought I was a goner."

"Your ear, Duncan."

Either delirious from the pain or the adrenaline, the wounded Duncan just scoffed.

"At least it's not my head."

Arthur looked around for an apothecary, scanning the dunes above and the chaos below him, but saw no available wolves to aid his friend.

"I'll get you help."

"I'm okay Arthur."

"Apothecary! Apothe-"

A mighty howl sounded from above, one that he recognised immediately. It cut through the battle like a blade through flesh, drowning out the deafening sounds of war all around him. He cast his gaze up to the dune.

On its peak stood Winter Baron Elias Sedrid, mounted on his trusted ictharr. Krosguard armour clung to his body, the resilient plating and extra chainmail layer beneath the suit providing excellent protection against blade and arrow. He slashed away at three Silverclaw soldiers, sending their corpses rolling down the slope into the depression. The winged Winter Baron helmet sat upon his head, a combat version that came with a protective metal mask covering the snout and face. He thrust the banner of the Clan of the Great Lupine into the air in triumph.

"Victory shall be ours! Fight on! *Fight on!*"

This rallying cry summoned strength to the wolves and hounds battling the enemy, driving them to victory in the brutal conflict. Arthur looked around him and saw the Silverclaw soldiers beginning to retreat up the opposite dune, leaving behind their dead comrades.

And then he saw him.

Among the retreating ranks scrambling up the dune, one feline was aiming a crossbow. He knelt and brought the weapon up to his shoulder, closing one eye and pressing a gloved digit of his paw against the trigger.

Too far away to intervene, Arthur could only warn his father.

"*Dad, look out!*"

The Winter Baron heard the despairing cry of his son and -immediately - found him among the chaos. He saw his son standing there, blood dripping from his sword and spattered over his armour.

He noticed the crossbow aiming at him too late.

Arthur Sedrid's soul was cleaved in two as the crossbow bolt whizzed up the slope and struck his father in the right eye.

Elias Sedrid slumped down from the saddle and fell, disappearing in silence.

A decade later, Arthur Sedrid found himself in a hurry.

The whole of Grand Wolf Plains had gathered around the Sedrid residence. The crowds occupied all of the main pathway and stretched through the gaps between adjacent houses, held back by the perimeter of servants and soldiers in front of the door.

His second cub was on the way.

On his right was Reginald, his personal ictharr. The grey beast padded alongside him, the fur around his snout turning silver with age. His seniority did not damage his status or ability, however. Nearby ictharrs looked on in awe as he strode along with youthful vitality, looking straight ahead with a determined look in his eyes.

On his left was his firstborn, Ragnar Sedrid. Arthur dragged him along by the paw down the snowy path to the house. The snow mingled with his white front while other snowflakes stood out against the coal-black fur across the rest of his body like stars against a night sky. The cub was bewildered, wide-eyed, and lacked any knowledge of what was happening. A cloak several sizes too big covered his shoulders. It verged on engulfing him.

"Daddy? Daddy, where are we going? Why is everyone around our house?"

"It's a surprise, Ragnee," he said, using his nickname. "It's a surprise for everyone."

"A surprise?"

"Yes, yes. We've got to hurry though, okay?"

"Is it a good surprise?"

"Yes, it's a very good surprise."

He could hear the yells and shouts of good will to his wife, Ophelia, from the crowd. Army soldiers patrolled past the gatherings, forming a barrier between them and the house. Krosguard soldiers repeatedly circulated among the crowd, able to see over everyone from their elevated positions on their ictharrs.

The weather was kinder at this time; the snow fell softer and the temperature had ever so slightly increased. Arthur smiled.

"Stay strong, my dear. Stay strong."

"What did you say, Daddy?"

"Nothing, Ragnee. Just talking to myself. Come on, let's be quick now."

As he waded into the crowd, he saw people turn and yell to one another.

"*Make way!*" the guards yelled.

"*Move*, the Winter Baron is coming!" the crowd bellowed.

The sea of bodies parted before him. He kept a tight hold of his son's paw as he slowly guided himself through the maze of bodies. The onlookers waved and cheered, wishing the Winter Baron and his wife good luck. Paws reached out and petted Reginald on the sides. The ictharr thanked them with growls of approval. Ragnar looked up and scanned the faces of the people, still maintaining his bewildered expression.

Arthur stopped as the wall of soldiers parted for him to step through. As he did, he saw the head servant turn and open the front door before stepping to the side.

"Thank you, Peter," Arthur said, stopping before the door. "How is she?"

"In labour, Winter Baron," Peter said. "I would hurry inside."

"Of course. Keep an eye on things out here, please."

"Of course, Winter Baron," he nodded.

"Reginald, stay."

The ictharr growled in agreement, turning to face the other way and sitting beside Peter. The head servant petted him.

Entering the spacious lobby of the house, Arthur let go of his son's paw when he heard the door shut behind him. Three servants, all eager to give him details on the birth, rushed forwards.

"Winter Baron, Winter Baron!" cried one, taking his helmet from him and placing it on the dining table. "We are reaching the end of labour. Your wife is on the verge of giving birth!"

"You'll need to come with me if you wish to be present, Winter Baron," another said.

"Of course," Arthur nodded, hastily turning around and placing his grey paws on his son's shoulders. "Ragnee, Daddy has to go get the surprise ready. Be good and wait here with Klaus and Gertrude. I'll let you know when it's prepared, okay?"

"What's the surprise?" he asked.

"Not right now, Ragnee. Be good and you can ride Reginald with me later, okay?" Arthur said, turning and racing upstairs with one of the servants. "Look after him, please!"

Moving quickly across the wooden landing to the bedroom door, Arthur could hear his wife's cries of pain coming from inside. In addition, he could hear the sounds of the doctors working their hardest to facilitate the birth perfectly, talking frantically to one another in medical jargon.

"Here we go, Winter Baron," the servant said, pushing the wooden door open.

Before him, the bedroom was a madhouse – tables had been brought in on which to place medical equipment and at least 10 wolves were buzzing around the room. Two doctors, both highly esteemed practitioners of medicine, instructed their subordinates on what to do.

"Ah, Winter Baron," one of the doctors said. "You might want to take your wife's paw."

Arthur didn't question her – he quickly walked over to his wife's bedside, her white and black fur matted with blood on the lower side, and he held her paw.

"Oh my God, Arthur! *Oh my God!*"

"Come on, dear. It's the second time around – the second time is always easier."

She screamed.

"Okay keep pushing!" the doctor yelled.

"Come on, Milady! You'll be done soon!" the other doctor yelled.

"Ophelia, deep breaths, all right?" Arthur said.

"O-okay... okay."

"Push!" the two doctors yelled.

With a mighty scream and a sharp clench of Arthur's paw, she closed her eyes and began to push.

"Come on, Ophelia!"

"Come on, Milady!"

"Keep going – not too long!"

"Think of how beautiful he will be afterwards!"

"Harder!"

"Come on!"

"What are we going to call him?" Arthur asked Ophelia, trying to take her mind off the pain.

Ophelia had her eyes tightly closed and was too busy dealing with the pain to respond immediately. She punctuated every second with a grunt of pain, body trembling from the ordeal.

"Dear, open your eyes."

One red-rimmed eye barely opened, looking right back at him.

"What are we going to call our son?"

"We're... we're going to call him... C-Corsair."

"Say it again, dear, come on."

"Corsair! We're going to call him Corsair!"

"I... I can see a head!" one doctor yelled. "I can see him!"

The news reverberated around the room, one wolf passing it on to the next.

"They can see Corsair!" Arthur said. "What's his full name going to be?"

"Corsair Sedrid! Son... son of Arthur and Ophelia Sedrid!"

"Who is he going to be brother to?"

"Ragnar Sedrid!"

"I've almost got him! Keep going, Milady!"

"And what's he going to grow up into?" Arthur urged her.

"*A beautiful, brave and wonderful wolf!*" she screamed at the top of her lungs.

One doctor recoiled from Ophelia, a bloody bundle in his arms.

"I've got him! I have him, I have him!"

Arthur froze and stared at what was now his second cub.

Before him, cradled in the doctor's arms, connected to his loving wife by a red cord, was his cub. He whimpered and gasped, his body matted in crimson. The doctor shushed him as he began to cry, letting the second doctor lean in for observation.

"Hold on to my wife's paw," Arthur said to a nearby servant.

"Yes, Winter Baron."

Arthur let go of his wife's paw and walked towards the doctors. One inspected the cub in her arms while the other prepared a warm cloth in which to wrap him. Arthur approached with apprehension, not wanting to grow optimistic too quickly. She looked up and made eye contact with him, smiling.

"Winter Baron, our predictions were correct. I am currently holding a perfectly healthy son."

Arthur sighed with relief and smiled. He looked down at his joy.

Our joy.

"Corsair Sedrid."

"That's him, Winter Baron. A fine name too. I imagine he'll grow up to become a wonderful wolf."

"My pup," Ophelia whimpered. "Is my pup okay? Is he hurt?"

"No, no, Milady!" the other doctor comforted her. "He's quite all right. Winter Baron, may we show Milady the pup?"

"Of course," Arthur said, walking back over to his wife.

He knelt by her bedside as she held Corsair Sedrid, their second son, in her arms. Wrapping an arm around her and gently bringing her into him, he looked down at the pup and smiled.

"Corsair," Ophelia said. "I love it. It suits him so well."

"It does."

"Ragnee is going to love him," Ophelia sniffed. "Corsair and Ragnar. They'll be inseparable. God, they'll be such troublemakers."

"They will."

"We believe your son to be in good health, Milady," one of the doctors reported. "Can we proceed with cutting the umbilical cord now?"

He looked at his wife, who was busy looking at their new-born son, and then looked back.

"I'd say a few minutes. Thank you so much."

"Of course, Winter Baron," he nodded, turning away.

Hours later, Arthur walked down the landing towards the stairs holding a basket between his paws.

Ragnar sat in front of the fire, a book of fables in paw while Gertrude and Klaus conversed quietly at the dinner table. Arthur shook a silent 'no' when they noticed him, gesturing to his oblivious son by the fire, and they understood.

He stopped behind Ragnar, who turned and looked up at him.

"Daddy? Is the surprise ready yet?"

"It is, Ragnee, it is," Arthur smiled.

He placed down the basket facing the other way, hiding its contents.

"Now, listen to me closely. I'm going to show you the surprise but only on two conditions."

"Okay, Daddy!" Ragnar agreed excitedly, putting down his book.

"First, you need to be very quiet. If you're loud you will upset him, okay?"

A very enthusiastic nod.

"Second, you cannot touch him. You can look and sit with him but you cannot touch him *whatsoever*."

Another nod.

"Good. Well then. Say hello to... Corsair Sedrid, your little brother."

He turned the basket around to display the sleeping cub in the basket. Ragnar gasped in response before clamping his small paws over his mouth. Arthur smiled, beaming with pride, and put a paw on his shoulder.

"Good job on not being loud because he's sleeping right now. We both know how important good sleep is, right?"

Ragnar nodded, paws still clamped over his mouth.

"All right, Ragnee. You like him?"

His son went to answer but held his tongue.

"Ragnee, you can speak, but not too-"

"I love him!"

Arthur shushed him and rolled his eyes.

He has to show his excitement somehow.

"You two will get along well. He hasn't opened his eyes yet but when he does we'll see what they look like."

"Daddy?"

"Yes, Ragnee?"

"Why doesn't he open his eyes? Can he not see?"

"No. It's because when you're born your eyes stay shut for a while. That happened to you as well when you were born."

"But *why* does that happen?"

"I think one of the doctors would be happy enough to explain it to you in Daddy and Mummy's room. You want to go and say hello to Mummy?"

"Is Corsair coming with us?"

"Of course he is. Come on, let's go."

His son leapt up with joy, racing up the stairs and down the landing to the bedroom long before Arthur even reached the foot of the stairs.

"Winter Baron," one of the servants asked. "The crowds outside are restless. Do we tell them the news?"

"By all means. Let the soldiers and Peter know to spread the word. Have one of the Krosguard lieutenants go to the aviaries and have the news dispatched across the clan."

"Of course, Winter Baron," one nodded, rushing to the door with their co-worker.

As Arthur climbed the stairs, he could hear his family name spreading like wildfire amongst the crowds outside.

"*Long live the Sedrids! Long live the Sedrids! Long live the Sedrids!*"

Upon reaching the top of the stairs, Arthur looked down at his son sleeping soundly in the basket. He smiled.

"Welcome to the world, Corsair Sedrid. Welcome to Vos Draemar."

CHAPTER ONE

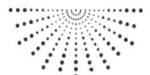

*N*othing stirred in the maze of snow-covered trees.

Within the confines of the woods, only the snow was daring enough to move. It floated down from the heavens, white specks swinging to and fro in the chilling breeze, adding to the white blanket over the ground. Undisturbed, the vast pillow looked plump to the woodland creatures that wandered between the trees.

From a hole excavated into a trunk, edging out from its shelter, came a creature. It was tiny, with one curious eye scanning the surroundings and a small nose sniffing the air. A hazelnut-coloured coat covered its body, small white stars beginning to nestle in its fur, and shielded it from nature's cold breath.

It stepped out. Sniffing the air again and blinking away the snow from its single eye, it cast its gaze up to the canopies. The branches above strained with the weight of the snow, every so often letting out an annoyed creak, but they held firm. The creature glanced left, then right, and then stepped out into the open. Wading through the white carpet, the creature kept its eye forward, hoping to burrow another home into a tree farther along its journey.

It stopped.

It heard a noise. A rapid padding through the snow, something propelling itself at great speed, but it couldn't pinpoint where it was coming from. Frantically looking around, it sought the source of the noise but failed to see it.

The sound grew louder.

It turned to retreat to its home, trudging through the snow at a brisk pace. With every step the noise grew closer, increasing in volume.

"*Hyah!*"

From the array of foliage to the left leapt a streak of white, blending in with the surroundings and making it difficult to discern its shape. With a high-pitched squeal, the creature dived inside the safety of its home and cowered in the corner, watching the beast shoot past the entrance and kick the snow up into the air.

Sprinting through the dense forest was an ictharr. The four-legged beast pounded across the ground, propelling itself forward with every push. Its purple eyes focused ahead on its path. A shaggy fur coat covered its body, fur sprouting up in places while forming streaks in others. A leather saddle hugged its midsection.

On that saddle sat Corsair Sedrid.

The wolf leant forwards, his paws clutching the reins as he directed the ictharr through the trees. His front fur was white, claiming the area around his green eyes and the sides of his snout, while the rest was black. A dark, hooded cloak billowed behind him, blown back by the wind, and exposed the thick winter clothes beneath.

"*Hyah!*"

He snapped at the reins and directed the steed to the right, steering it past a tree. The ictharr zoomed across the snow, air blowing in and out through the black leathery nose at the end of its snout, weaving through the obstacles of the forest.

"Left!"

Corsair pulled the reins left. The ictharr planted its paws in the snow and turned, skidding, before propelling itself in that direction.

It followed the rider's instructions to the letter, following every touch of the reins and verbal command.

"You can go faster, come on!"

The ictharr offered a protesting growl between breaths but didn't defy its master. Agility prevailing, they evaded tree trunks and rocks, disrupting the even surface of the snow and causing it to explode into the air. They left in their wake a trail of large pawprints and uneven mounds.

"Left!"

Yanking the reins to the left, Corsair guided the beast through the forest. Woodland animals peeked from their homes as the rider and his steed shot past. The wolf spotted a formidable bulge in the carpet of snow, shaped like a long tube running from left to right. It lay metres ahead, tall enough to trip up the accelerating ictharr.

"Leap!"

His steed complied with his command. It leapt up into the air and soared over the fallen log. They continued on their course unhindered, Corsair glancing back at the obstacle.

"You're doing good, keep it up!"

The ictharr managed a grunt of approval, its pink tongue hanging out from the side of its mouth, eyes focused on the path ahead. Corsair looked up to see a lone branch hanging out from the side of a tree, positioned to strike him in the stomach and knock him from his saddle. Knowing that the branch was too low to duck beneath, he drew his longsword from its sheath on his belt and swung.

The blade tore through the branch with ease, causing it to fly off with an audible *snap*. He threw his free arm up in front of his face to protect himself from any debris but none of the splinters struck him. Lowering his arm, he saw his companion looking back to ensure he was okay.

"I'm fine, keep your eyes forward."

Both ictharr and lupine looked ahead and saw the treeline stop. The woodland failed to continue, the ground disappearing, and both pairs of eyes grew wider.

"Stop!"

Corsair yanked on the reins and the ictharr pushed its paws out, yowling in panic. They skidded towards the edge, the wolf pulling back on the reins hard as the brink rushed towards them.

To his relief, his companion's paws stopped just short.

The ictharr, its eyes wide, scrambled back with such frantic haste that it pushed back on to its hind legs and flopped over on to its side. Corsair hit the ground with a grunt and fell from the saddle, rolling away from his steed. He came to a stop and remained still, sprawled out on his back with green eyes looking up to the grey sky.

They both lay there for a moment.

Blinking the snow away from his eyes, Corsair pushed himself up and grimaced. His clothes clung to him in a wet embrace.

"Great. Soaked."

He felt something push against him and he turned. His ictharr was nuzzling him, his warm breath against his face, and Corsair smiled. He placed a paw on the side of his companion's head and stroked him.

"I'm fine, Quickpaw, I'm fine."

As if suddenly possessed, Quickpaw drew his head back from him and shook his coat. Corsair shrank away as the snow was flicked across him, raising an arm to shield his face. When Quickpaw had finished, Corsair lowered his arm and looked down at himself. His clothes were clinging damply to his legs and torso. He looked over his shoulder to see the fur on his tail ruffled and knotted. He sighed.

"Thanks, Quickpaw."

Quickpaw sat and let his tongue hang from his mouth, resting between the numerous fangs inside. Corsair looked back into the treeline, spotting the trail they had left during their run, and nodded in approval.

"You ran pretty fast today, Quickpaw. Good run. I pushed you hard."

Quickpaw yapped.

"But... next time? Eyes forward."

Corsair approached the edge and peered over the side. A slope stretched out from the top of the hill. It was hardly the sheer or deadly drop it appeared to be when one approached it.

Still wouldn't be fun to fall down.

He looked up.

Hundreds of metres beyond the base of the hill, reinforced by three fortified stone walls, was a city. Houses and cottages lined the snowy pathways winding through it, the tiny dots of inhabitants moving back and forth between the buildings. He could see the marketplace in the centre, hundreds of wolves hurrying from stall to stall. The Lupine Halls of Justice were visible to the north, lonely except for the soldiers around it and the jail opposite. The Clan Iggregom Vaults stood to the west, its doors open as groups of people walked in and out to manage their savings. The woods returned at the base of the hill and bled into the south of the city, the only side without a wall. Other than the south's thick foliage, there was nothing but snow beyond the walls.

As always, Grand Wolf Plains was bustling with life.

"There it is," Corsair said as Quickpaw arrived by his side. "There's home."

Quickpaw growled in response.

"Can you see our house from up here?"

He watched his steed jerk his head in the direction of his home. There, to the east, he could see the distant shape of the Sedrid house.

"I bet you're looking forward to seeing Mum, huh?"

At the mention of his mother, Quickpaw pawed at the ground in excitement.

"Maybe we'll have some leftovers tonight, huh?"

He sat and yapped, looking at him with excited eyes.

"Well... if Peter ends up cooking..."

Both snarled in disgust, shaking their heads. He could almost taste the stale food.

"Well, either way, let's hope we have something nice tonight."

Quickpaw nodded in agreement, looking down towards the city.

Corsair did the same, eyes focused on his house – and that's where he saw them.

Two figures stood behind the building, one mounted on an ictharr while the other stood to the side. A third figure lingered metres away, watching everything unfold, and Corsair squinted at them. Quickpaw watched his master, registering the frown.

"What are they doing?"

Then he remembered the conversation he had with Peter as he left that morning.

You're up early today, Sir.

Taking Quickpaw out for a ride.

Right. Remember, Sir, training is going to start in an hour.

I'll be back, don't worry. Just say that I'm out riding.

I'll do so.

Corsair gasped.

Training.

"Training!"

He was late.

Again.

Quickpaw sensed urgency in his master's voice and stood. Corsair turned and rushed towards his steed, pulling himself up on to the beast and snapping the reins.

"Hyah!"

Grunting, Quickpaw turned and rushed away.

Corsair reined in his mount at the front of his home and dismounted, stumbling as he landed. The Sedrid household was almost identical to the structures around him, made from the same dark wood and constructed in the same format. He could see windows installed in the upstairs bedrooms, with one large window allowing someone to peer out from the kitchen. Wolves dressed in grey uniforms moved back and forth from the counters and tables, talking to the two cooks who held boxes of ingredients in their paws.

I guess that means we're having Peter's food tonight.

"Come on, Quickpaw."

They hurried around the side of the house, the wolf stumbling through the snow.

"Put more force behind it, come on!"

The thundering voice of the instructor echoed from the back of the house, growing louder with every step. Corsair slowed and crept forwards, peering around the corner.

In the snow, standing beside his ictharr, was Ragnar. His brother was considerably taller than Corsair, with broader shoulders and an intimidating physique. He was dressed in thick clothes to battle the cold (which only worsened as the seasons passed), a leather training vest drawn over his torso and his helmet dangling from the saddle of his steed. Standing upright beside him was a steel lance, its wooden shaft leading up to the metal head. Along the circumference of the head's base were numerous engravings. Corsair could see his own resting against the wall.

"Let me show you what I mean, Ragnar."

A wolf with dark brown fur took the lance from the trainee. He brought the lance back, handling its hefty weight as if it was nothing, and thrust it forwards towards an imaginary target. He repeated the motion, Ragnar watching and nodding along.

"You see? The momentum you have when charging headfirst towards your opponent is your weapon. If you use it correctly, you will knock your opponent from their saddle. At the very least, a good hit will stun them."

Alpha Dominik Tiberius was a behemoth of a wolf. About the same height as Ragnar, maybe a few inches taller, the lupine was a tower of sheer muscle beneath his brown coat. A stern expression always sat on his scarred face, one that commanded discipline and respect from those he instructed or so much as walked past. A pair of bright streaks of red paint cut across his left eye, often mistaken for scars as they blended in with the myriad of other wounds on his face. They were accompanied by a thick line of red running from between his eyes, down the bridge of his snout and to his black nose.

"Let's do it again. Saddle up."

Ragnar took the lance back from the instructor and turned to mount but stopped as his blue eyes fell upon his brother. The alpha noticed and turned to follow his gaze, spotting the younger sibling.

That's when Corsair saw his father standing around the corner.

Winter Baron Arthur Sedrid stood with arms folded, eyes focused on his younger son. Corsair's ears flattened and his tail curled between his legs, lowering his head.

"Come here," his father growled.

He trudged forwards. Quickpaw went to follow but Corsair told him to stay where he was. As Corsair stopped before his father, he raised a paw to the left side of his neck.

"You're late."

"Sorry, father."

"Do you want to know what Peter told me you were doing? He told me you were out riding *that*."

Arthur jabbed a digit of his paw past his son and towards Quickpaw. Eyes wide and ears collapsing, the ictharr shied back away from them and sat down, averting his gaze as he whimpered.

"I just wanted to take him out for a bit, father."

"And go on another one of your adventures? Waste the day?"

Corsair didn't answer.

"Alpha Tiberius is sacrificing his time to train you two. There are places he might need to be or more important things he could be doing but he's here training you. If you want to waste your time on your stupid rides with *that*, do it when it doesn't come at the cost of someone else's time."

Corsair didn't dare answer back.

"Arthur," Alpha Tiberius said, "he hasn't cost me much of my time. I'm sure he gets it."

The Winter Baron looked back to his son, who didn't dare make eye contact with him. He gestured to his lance.

"Get your things. Don't waste any more time than you have already."

Corsair didn't hesitate. With Quickpaw following him (giving his father a wide berth), he approached his array of equipment leaning up against the wall. A leather training vest was beside his trusty lance. His lance was similar to his brother's – a long wooden shaft with a steel head. It bore different inscriptions and symbols along the head's circumference. Each one was a testament to a victory he had achieved throughout the years he had been fighting, a trophy case he carried in his paws.

A trophy case far emptier than his brother's.

He knew he had no time to gawp at it. He pulled his leather vest over his torso and strapped it down around the waist, wincing as he felt it press his clothes into his sides. Jostling it into a more comfortable position, he stepped towards Quickpaw with lance in paws. His steed stood ready by his side, allowing his master to check that the saddle was correctly fastened around his midsection.

Corsair caught a glimpse of his brother. Ragnar stood beside his own beast, a stoic black-furred ictharr named Harangoth. Ragnar shot Corsair a warm smile, one he appreciated, before looking away again.

He looked back at Quickpaw. The ictharr's eyes were focused on Harangoth in admiration of his physique and attitude. He looked down at himself, ears wilting in disappointment.

Comparing the two was as easy as comparing day and night. While the formidable Harangoth looked as if he could take on 50 maugs, the scrawnier Quickpaw looked as if he'd have a fair fight against a baby vorsair. While Harangoth's stoic face never faltered, Quickpaw was busy amusing himself with a lone insect forging a path through the snow.

Corsair stroked the scruff of his neck.

"You're fine as you are, Quickpaw. That's what matters."

Something landed metres away in the snow with an audible *piff*.

Both heads snapped to the left, large eyes fixating on the leather ball lying in the snow. Their long ears stood to attention and they tilted their heads, maws partially agape.

"Go get it!" Alpha Tiberius yelled.

Corsair stepped back from Quickpaw, watching as he bounded towards the ball with energy in every step. Harangoth was slower to react, turning to lunge, and was beaten as Quickpaw arrived by the ball. Scooping it up into his mouth, he turned to rush back to his master.

A yelp came from Quickpaw as Harangoth rammed him, knocking him aside with his immense strength. Corsair winced as he watched his companion slide through the snow, promptly scrambling back up. Quickpaw dived for the ball, now in the opponent's maw, and wrestled against Harangoth. Despite his best attempts, Quickpaw was unable to do more than knock the ball from Harangoth's mouth before he was shoved aside again.

Come on, Quickpaw.

His supportive thoughts could not aid his steed. Harangoth bounded from his opponent and scooped the ball up into his mouth. His hulking form rushed over to Ragnar, a sight terrifying to anyone who did not know the steed personally, before sitting and dropping the prize. Ragnar picked it up and passed it to Alpha Tiberius, whispering praise to his companion.

"Exercise over!"

Quickpaw pushed himself on to all fours, shaking his fur, ears down and tail curled. Head hung, he padded over to Corsair and grumbled in defeat, casting his sad gaze over to the victor.

"Hey, you did great. You tried. You'll beat him some day, don't worry."

Ragnar gestured to Quickpaw. Harangoth nuzzled against Ragnar's head before turning and approaching his companion. He stopped before Quickpaw and lowered his head to make eye contact. He grumbled in concern. Quickpaw looked up and his face grew brighter, a sight that made Corsair smile.

"All right, enough downtime," Alpha Tiberius said. "On your saddles, let's continue. We've got a lot of things to go through."

"Yes, Alpha."

He mounted Quickpaw and glanced at his father.

His father stood back with arms folded across his chest, glaring at Quickpaw.

"Corsair, come on! No time to daydream!"

The alpha's thundering voice jolted him back to reality, forcing him to snatch the reins and spur Quickpaw forward after Ragnar.

CHAPTER TWO

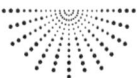

*C*orsair and Ragnar lasted three seconds inside their house before their mother reprimanded them, seeing her two sons drenched and sodden while standing by the door.

"Oh, here we go," Ragnar said, rolling his eyes.

"Ragnee, Corsair, you're both soaking!"

A white-fronted wolf in red silk robes stole forwards from the dining room table, two servants rushing after her with combs in paws. They looked flustered, as if they had been tending to the wolf's fur for the past hour, and that was exactly the case. Corsair could see his mother's tail swishing behind her, all her fur streaking in one direction and forming a smooth dark wave. The fur around her neck and atop her head (between her small ears) had been combed thoroughly, not a single hair out of place. The black leather pads at the bottom of her paws had been washed and cleaned, fur brushed out of the way to display them.

"Were you two training or playing out in the snow again?"

"We don't play out in the snow, Mum," Ragnar scoffed. "Training."

"And what is Arthur having you do? Roll around in it? Look at you! You're dripping wet."

"So, I'm guessing you don't want us coming in, then," Corsair said.

"Until you two clean yourselves up, you are *not* going upstairs to your rooms. Ingrid and Sebastien spent a long time cleaning them – especially yours, Corsair – and I will not have them tiring in there again."

"We'll find somewhere to dry ourselves," Ragnar said. "We could head down to a tavern."

"To Mr Duncan's place?" Corsair asked.

"Mr Duncan's place sounds good. He has those washing stalls. We'll just dry ourselves there and come back."

"We can't dry off here, Mum?" Corsair asked.

"I don't want you stomping around with your wet paws."

"Oh, Mum..."

"Otherwise no dinner for you two tonight."

Corsair went to open his mouth to protest but, realising what her words implied, shut it again. He stared at his mother with widening eyes.

"Mum, you're cooking?" Ragnar asked, tail flicking.

"I am. Dressing up some fine meat this evening but if you two are going to be so insistent on not drying off, then..."

"No no no that's fine, it's fine. We'll dry up quickly. Isn't that right, Corsair?"

"Oh, yeah, no doubt," Corsair said.

"Why is it so important that I'm cooking?"

"Mum, have you tasted Peter's food?"

"Of course I have."

"Then you know *exactly* why we're making a big deal," Ragnar chuckled.

"Peter's food is fine."

Corsair and Ragnar both gave their mother an exasperated look.

"Well... it isn't exactly perfect, but it's decent."

27

"Less than decent."

"Whatever his cooking ability, I'm cooking tonight. If you two want any chance to get your paws on my food then you need to go and dry off. Now."

"Okay, okay, we're going," Ragnar said. "'Bye, Mum."

"'Bye, Mum," Corsair said.

"See you in a bit! And you'd better be *dry* when you come back!"

Denied entry until they returned dry, the two siblings turned and pushed back out through the door. They faced the cold with indifference, the idea of a good evening meal motivating them, and

looked right to face their companions. Corsair's eyes went to Harangoth, sitting patiently. The ictharr was focused on something beside him, blinking as he watched.

Ragnar followed his gaze and, a moment later, smiled.

"Well, he's having a good time."

Quickpaw rolled on the ground, his white fur blending with the snow as his legs flailed in the air. Harangoth growled in exasperation and shook his head as the younger ictharr played like a pup, ignoring the snow that hit his side.

Corsair sighed.

"Oh, come on, Quickpaw. I'll just have to clean you again."

Quickpaw scrambled up on to his paws and shook the snow from his coat, flinging it across Corsair's front. He grimaced, sighing as his brother chuckled.

"It just isn't your day today, is it?"

"It's all getting wet and covered in snow right now. Come on, let's go for a walk."

The duo started down the main pathway towards the city centre, their ictharrs walking beside them. Quickpaw continually sniffed the ground, turning his head left and right, whilst Harangoth walked with eyes forward.

"Tough training this morning, huh?"

"You bet. Tiberius loves giving us hard work."

"He's definitely a clan alpha, that's for sure."

A silence fell between them. The only audible sounds were the crunching of snow beneath their hind paws and the distant chatter of traders farther along the pathway that ran from east to west. Up ahead, the city got busier, more and more wolves sauntering back and forth past them.

"I know it's probably not what you want to hear but... you need to be turning up to training earlier."

"Thanks. Didn't think of that."

"Come on, don't be like that. You're always up there in the hills riding Quickpaw. Is it that hard to be on time?"

Corsair looked at Quickpaw. He continued to sniff the snow, distracted. Corsair shrugged.

"I forget. A lot, granted, but I forget."

Ragnar opened his mouth before reconsidering his words, taking a moment to rephrase what he was going to say.

"I'm not trying to lecture you. I don't see a problem with you spending time with him up there, you know I don't. You bond with him, you learn how to ride better... I don't see the problem. But Dad, for whatever reason, does. If you want to avoid these things every morning then you've just got to turn up on time."

"Even if I turned up on time, Ragnee, he'd be just the same. He always has it in for Quickpaw. Anyway, I don't want to talk about him right now."

"Fine. I'm just trying to help, nothing else. Just letting you know."

"I appreciate that but... it's routine. It's nothing special."

"It doesn't have to be routine."

Corsair gave him a tired look.

"Fine, fine, I'll back off."

"Let's just forget about this morning and get washed so we can eat Mum's dinner later."

The mention of the wolves' mother's cooking was enough to rouse Quickpaw from his investigation. He craned his head up from the snow, ears standing, and gave an enquiring grumble.

"Yeah, you heard me. Mum's cooking tonight."

With excitement in his veins, the ictharr bounded around the back of the wolves to walk beside Harangoth. Drawing beside him, he relayed the news through yaps and growls. Corsair could see a flicker of excitement in Harangoth's steely face as he looked to his master.

"We'll make sure both of you get leftovers," Ragnar said. "Only if you're good when we're inside the tavern though."

"So no wild yapping, okay?"

Both ictharrs signalled their agreement and faced forwards, not making a sound as they approached the centre.

"Speaking of Mum's food, what do you think she's doing for us?" Ragnar asked.

"It better be good."

"You think it's maug meat?"

"If someone in the market was brave enough to hunt one, sure. Either that or vorsair meat. Probably gerbeast."

As he said that word, a flock of white birds flew across the sky above. Corsair looked up and watched the vorsairs – he could see some of them had prey in their talons, carrying them off to their nests to feed their young.

"No matter what, it'll still be good."

Ragnar hummed in agreement. Both the ictharrs poked their tongues out and swept them across their mouths.

"Mr Duncan's food is pretty good, though. For tavern food, anyway."

"*Nothing* is as good as Mum's, Ragnee, *nothing*. If you even suggest anything is, then that's the worst type of blasphemy I've ever heard of."

Ragnar's eyes focused on something behind him.

"Even worse than 'duck'?"

Corsair frowned.

"Duck? What do you me-"

Piff.

He yelped in surprise as a snowball struck him on the back of the head, making him reel forwards. He spun, trying to maintain his balance, but only fell into the snow with flailing arms.

"Nice shot!" Ragnar called to the attacker.

Quickpaw and Harangoth both turned and leapt to their masters' defence, standing before the assailant and baring their fangs, before recognition dawned. Corsair sat up to see them both bounding towards the culprit.

"You two are excited to see me today, huh?"

Standing metres down the pathway, petting both ictharrs as they sat before her, was a black wolf. She was shrouded in a dark cloak that draped over her blue skirted tunic and dark trousers, hood lowered. Her fur coat was entirely black, almost the same as her cloak, except for the few spots of white fur. Both her paws and hind paws were white, easily mistaken for gloves and hind-paw socks. A single thick stripe of white fur ran along her snout, stretching from between her eyes down to her black nose. Her brown eyes sparkled as she fussed over the two beasts, reducing even the stern Harangoth to a mere pup by petting him.

What made her particularly recognisable, though, was the lower part of her face. Along her jawline, leading to the base of her snout, tufts of her coat were neatly tied off with string to produce six evenly spaced sprouts of black fur.

"OK, that's enough. Come on," Ragnar said.

The two ictharrs lingered by Rohesia's side for a few additional seconds before they turned and retreated to their owners, standing beside them. She walked forwards, smirking at Corsair.

"Hilarious," he grumbled.

"Come on. You've got to admit that it was a good shot."

"I thought it was a good shot," Ragnar said. "I'm sure Harangoth and Quickpaw did too."

"Yeah, well, it's hard to agree when I've got soaked for the third time today," Corsair said. "You couldn't just say hello?"

"Eh. Not my style."

Ragnar scoffed and helped Corsair to his hind paws.

"You lost today. I'd just accept it. It makes it less embarrassing."

"I'll find a way to get you back for that. Both of you," Corsair said.

"I'm trembling, Corsair. *Really* trembling," Rohesia said.

He sighed, pushing snow off his shoulders

"Where are you going anyway?" she asked.

"To Mr Duncan's place. We were going to dry off in one of his wash stalls, maybe get a drink or something to eat," Ragnar said.

"Want to come?" Corsair asked. "As much as I hate you right now."

"Sure. Sounds good. Sounds like you need a bodyguard from the snow, anyway."

"Shut up."

The trio took off towards the city centre, Harangoth and Quickpaw maintaining their promise to behave well by remaining silent. A minute passed before they arrived upon the east side of the city market.

"Sure is busy today," Rohesia said.

Stalls upon stalls were lined up on either side of the numerous pathways, curving with the roads and following them to the other side of the market. Through the walls of market stands, Corsair caught a glimpse of the square. It was a large stretch of land cordoned off from the rest of the city, the ground made of snow-covered paved stone. In the centre of that square resided a stone statue of a lupine figure heroically standing tall and peering off into the distance. A shield stood at its hind paws, a sword in the right paw, and a pair of unblinking eyes glared ahead as they watched over Grand Wolf Plains. Snow dared to form mounds around the elbows and on the shoulders, creating pillows over the bridge of their snout, but it did not deter the strong gaze of the wolf.

Winter Baron Julian Krosguard.

Across from the square and to the north, through the hundreds of market stalls, stood a stone building that made the nearby houses look as insignificant as insects. Four grand stone pillars held up the overarching roof from the front, evenly spaced out across the stone steps.

Seeking refuge beneath the roof, a pair of wooden doors sat at the top of the steps with two wolf soldiers dressed in armour standing beside them. More soldiers were positioned at each pillar, scanning the crowds for any suspicious activity, but Corsair doubted they would find any. Measly crimes such as petty theft were rare among the city community, a fact that acted as one of the few warming things on the winter plains.

"Bustling as always," Ragnar said.

"No surprise there," Corsair agreed.

They waded their way past the bodies of wolves, all gesturing to each other as they debated prices and confirmed transactions. Bags of Iggregom coins were passed from paw to paw, exchanges going on every second. Traders referred to their abaci often, glancing between them and the customer as they worked.

"Hello Sir!" a trader said, gesturing to an array of meat. "Fresh maug meat up for a low, low price! Hunted by the best archers of the clan. Interested?"

"We'll pass, thank you," Ragnar said.

"Ah, I bet you two are looking for some new cloaks!" a rabbit trader said, cocooned in multiple layers of clothing. "Why not browse my new wares? I'm sure you'll appreciate a look! They're made from cloth imported from the vast crops of the Land of the Sun and Moon!"

"No thanks," Corsair said.

"I know you three are searching for some hind-paw socks!" a fox trader said, shielded from the cold by numerous layers. "These are freshly made and imported from the clan's friendly neighbour; the Kingdom of Loxworth. Available at a bargain price!"

"Not interested, thank you," Rohesia said.

They pushed through the barrage of offers and loud voices, fending them off with polite tones, before they arrived outside the tavern. A set of stables stood before it, most of the wooden structures filled with ictharrs except for a pair of opposite-facing stalls at the back.

"Come on Quickpaw," Corsair said.

They led their companions to their stalls, stepping past wolves who were withdrawing or depositing their steeds. No guard was stationed to watch over the stables, confident in the honesty of the citizens.

"In you go," Ragnar said.

Corsair watched Harangoth pad into the stable and turn, facing out into the aisle as the door was shut and locked. Ragnar patted him on the head before stepping aside for his brother to come forward.

"Come on."

Corsair took two steps forward before wincing at the sound of Quickpaw whimpering, turning to see his ears flattened and tail curled. Rohesia waited at the end of the aisle, observing his interaction.

"I know, I know, but I won't be long. You can get some sleep while you're at it. I know this morning's training made you tired."

Quickpaw didn't make eye contact.

"Come on."

Refusing, Quickpaw sat down and grumbled.

He looked over his shoulder to Ragnar. His brother waited in front of Harangoth's stable, eyes on the stubborn beast.

"Ah, well... I guess I can't convince you to just go inside the stable, can I?"

Quickpaw grunted.

"It's a shame. We were so looking forward to having a pint for lunch, some good food on the side maybe."

Quickpaw mocked him with a series of grunts and grumbles, tilting his head left and right to mimic him.

"And now we can't dry ourselves off to go back home, can we, Ragnee?"

"I guess not," his brother said.

"And because we can't get dry, Mum won't cook for us."

Quickpaw's head turned, ears standing upright.

"And we were so looking forward to tonight, too. We would have had such a good dinner. All that *succulent* maug meat to feast on. There'd be so much that, surely, there'd be *no way* we could eat it all."

Quickpaw mewled with uncertainty.

"But, seeing as we can't dry off, we should just go home now. No maug meat tonight and *definitely* no leftovers. Oh well... come on, Quickpaw."

He turned to walk back out of the stables but, as he did, Quickpaw finally surrendered. With an annoyed expression, purple eyes narrowed at his master as he stood up, he trudged past and into the stable. Corsair stepped forward and shut the door, watching his steed turn and glare at him.

"Good ictharr."

He ruffled the fur atop his head. Quickpaw ignored him, standing there with an annoyed expression, until his master leaned in and whispered in his ear.

"Extra leftovers tonight."

His annoyed expression fell in shock at the promise of the reward, tail flicking back and forth in anticipation. Corsair smiled and petted him again before turning and walking out of the stables.

Inside, the tavern was a scene of goodwill and camaraderie. As they entered, Corsair's ears were filled with the familiar sound of metal pitchers clanging against one another, accompanied by the laughter and jeers of those who indulged in drinking en masse. Many were sitting around tables with friends and comrades while some crowded the bar, sitting on the stools positioned before the countertop.

"Let's get a place by the bar," Ragnar said. "Mr Duncan will be happy to see us."

"To see you, sure," Corsair said.

"He's not that petty, Corsair."

The trio waded through the tight aisles between seated wolves, Ragnar clearing a path while Corsair and Rohesia followed behind him. Some wolves muttered greetings as they passed and the two Sedrids returned them.

They approached the bar and Ragnar found a weakness in the wall of wolves surrounding it, pushing forward and waving his paw to get the attention of the bartender.

"Hey, Mr Duncan!"

"Ah, Ragnar!" a deep voice responded. "How are you doing?"

Corsair drew up behind Ragnar and his eyes fell on Mr Duncan. A giant of a wolf, the figure's front was covered in white fur while a brown coat covered his back. His eyes sparkled with the bright energy of youth that belied the more advanced age of his body. His lack of a left ear helped to identify the barkeep, although it wasn't too hard to notice the giant in the first place. One massive paw held a metal pitcher while the other held a cloth, paused in the process of polishing it.

"I'm good, I'm good. How are you?"

"Me and the missus are doing fine. I see you brought Corsair with you."

"Hello, Mr Duncan," Corsair returned, waving.

Mr Duncan met Corsair's gaze with a more hardened expression, although he saw some affection hiding behind it. The younger Sedrid met it with an awkward smile and looked away, leaving the conversation to Ragnar.

"Mind if we get three pints of mead and use one of your washrooms to dry off? Mum wants us clean before we go back home."

"Ah, Ophelia being her usual self?"

"More than ever, yeah."

Mr Duncan gave a hearty laugh and offered a paw, giving Ragnar a firm shake. What would have made most wolves cringe in pain did not work on Ragnar, who endured the mighty shaking of his arm and kept a smile on his face.

"One of the stalls should be freed up. I'll get your drinks – on the house!"

"That's too kind, Mr Duncan, but I would feel bad if I didn't..."

"Nonsense! I want to do this. Take it while you can or I'll just charge you double, eh?"

"Well I just can't refuse now, can I?"

Mr Duncan smiled and turned away, preparing the group's drinks. Surrendering to the kindness of the large wolf, Ragnar turned to face the two other members of his party.

"Do you want to go first?"

"No, I'm okay. I can wait."

"You sure?"

Corsair nodded. Ragnar accepted.

"All right. Just hang around here until I come back."

"Got it."

Ragnar disappeared from sight, heading off towards the washrooms to free himself of the water that clung to his fur. Corsair was left with Rohesia by the bar. A single stool remained unclaimed, open for someone to seize.

He gestured to it.

"After you."

"Are you sure?"

"Yeah, of course, go ahead. I'll just get it wet anyway."

She took him up on his offer and sat in the stool.

"How noble of someone who just got hit in the head by a snowball."

"I'm planning my revenge. I'm officially warning you to sleep with one eye open."

Amused, she laughed. They both waited in silence for a moment before Rohesia turned, opening her mouth.

"Mr Duncan really seemed to hit it off with Ragnar."

"He loves Ragnee."

"I can tell. Why does he know you two, though?"

"A few years back, Dad wanted us to help out around town. Mr Duncan's really close friends with him so he said we could help out at the tavern. We both worked here for a few months."

"How does Mr Duncan know your father?"

"They were friends in cubhood. They were in the army together during the whole thing with Silverclaw."

"Right. Must be a strong bond between them."

"Yeah, probably. Mr Duncan doesn't like me as much as he likes Ragnee, though."

"I heard you say something as we walked in. Why?"

"I, uh... tended to mess around when I worked here, goofing off with other people when I was supposed to be serving drinks and food. Ragnee did everything he was told and more. If he wasn't a prince, he'd make the perfect barkeep."

"He still likes you, though?"

"Yeah, he does, but he definitely prefers Ragnee."

A lapse in the conversation formed, one that was well timed as Mr Duncan arrived with the drinks. He placed them down on the counter by the two wolves and walked off to tend to another customer, someone yelling for him to fetch them a specific drink.

"I don't like taverns," Rohesia said.

"Why?"

"They're pretty loud. Gets a bit annoying."

"I think they're warm and charming."

"*Warm* and *charming?*"

"Yeah – like me."

She chuckled.

"The name Corsair Sedrid and the word charming do not go together."

"But you admit I'm warm?"

"After I hit you in the head with a snowball you're as far away from warm as you can be."

Rohesia reached for one of the pitchers and lifted it up to her mouth, Corsair watching with interest as he slowly lifted his. She tilted it back and managed one mighty glug before her eyes widened and she slammed it back down, raising her free paw to her mouth to prevent any mead from spilling out. Urgently, she swallowed down the strong alcohol, coughing as the final drops of the liquid disappeared down her gullet. She shook her head and wiped her eyes, looking at Corsair.

"Revenge works in mysterious ways, Rohesia," he said as he took a casual swig of his drink.

"That is strong! What is this?"

"Stronbeniz mead."

"There is no way this is mead. This is way too strong."

"Aw. Could little Rohesia not handle an adult drink?"

"I hate you so much."

"I wouldn't have it any other way. Cheers."

"Cheers."

Sighing, Rohesia lifted her pitcher and clinked it against Corsair's.

CHAPTER THREE

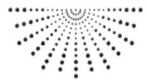

*C*orsair was so bored that he would have had no quarrel in reaching for his sword across the room and ramming it through his chest.

An hour or so after the two brothers had dried themselves off and taken a moment to enjoy their mead, they said goodbye to Rohesia and returned home to prepare themselves for their history tutorial. The area in front of the fireplace was cleared for two wooden chairs with a small table placed in front of each seat for writing. They faced away from the front door towards the dining table.

Before him stood the dreariest person he could have ever imagined.

Mr Klement was a grey wolf, the hairs of his fur coarse and rough. He was dressed modestly with only a dark coat over a white shirt and a pair of loose slacks. None of this hid the formidable bulge of his stomach, which Corsair had watched him maintain for all the 15 years Mr Klement had been teaching them.

The way he cultivated its growth seemed almost like a talent.

"...and the war brought about a change in modern policy," Mr Klement rattled on. "As a result of the First Rabbit-Lupine Clan war, resources were being heavily invested into the manufacture of weaponry, particularly the blacksmith industry. They assured this prioritisation of war didn't develop into a clan-wide famine by a policy known as what, Ragnee?"

Corsair looked over at Ragnar.

The older Sedrid had many words written down on his parchment, the quill held expertly in his paw as if it was nothing more than an extension of his body. Corsair could see how fluid and sophisticated his writing was, how the final letter of each word curved off at its end. Ragnar wouldn't have looked out of place if he had been sitting among the scholars of the Land of the Sun and Moon.

He looked down at his own work.

His parchment had a title scrawled at the top.

It had already been half-an-hour.

"Uh... I don't know the name, but it was a method of increasing exports to nearby smaller countries in order to get food."

"Indeed it was. The Outsource and Reap policy, or *Lofstok non Vedick* as it was dubbed by the Winter Baron's council, was a method of buying allegiance from nearby territories by sharing supplies for them in return for surplus food. Corsair, tell me – what language does the phrase *Lofstok non Vedik* hail from?"

"Our language, *Lanzig*."

"Invented by?"

Memory failing him, he froze. He opened his mouth to answer but no words followed and he, momentarily, became a statue.

"Uh... it was, uh... Winter Baron..."

Mr Klement looked unimpressed.

"Anytime this century, Corsair."

"I... I don't know, sorry."

"Fine. Ragnar. Care to answer?"

"I think it was, uh...Winter Baron Harangoth?"

"Indeed, yes. Winter Baron Lloyd Harangoth developed the *Lanzig* tongue during the days of separation between us and the hounds. The Origins of Vos Draemar, written by ancient rabbit scholar John Luxzancque during Adgrediom of the 22nd year, spoke of both wolf and hound being given the north to inhabit. After events in 139, they migrated south and settled in free territory on the border with the Kingdom of Opulus. Throughout the centuries, they underwent a lot of internal conflict, changed their names, language and governments *a lot*, but eventually stabilised in around the fifth century. They are now known as...?"

"The United Hound Dominions," Corsair said with Ragnar, trying to hide his boredom in both his face and voice.

"Exactly, yes."

Corsair rolled his eyes. He could not imagine how those who attended clan academies could sit and listen to old wolves ramble on and on without withering away from boredom. How they could sit there and write for an hour without losing the will to live.

There's a whole world out there and I'm stuck in here listening to him talk about dead people.

"I would like to focus on the First Rabbit-Lupine Clan war of 396, Gelidiom, until 403, Adgrediom. Obviously, we know four seasons equal a year – Adgrediom, Aestiom, Auxiom and Gelidiom – so this war lasted about *six years*. It was one of the first devastating conflicts of early Vos Draemar and it is important we know about it. Now... any questions?"

Corsair was not daring enough to ask the tutor to go through the last half-an-hour's worth of material in order to compensate for his lack of interest so he let Ragnar raise his paw instead.

"Do you think we'll be looking at the Silverclaw war?"

Mr Klement paused, blowing out air in thought.

"Uh... well, it is a very interesting field to look at. It is a rather integral to our understanding of modern Vos Draemar so I would say at some point we will learn about it. But it is difficult to gather material on the war, considering it transpired only three decades ago. I was your age when conflict broke out. By historical standards it is still rather new."

Ragnar nodded. Mr Klement, as if he couldn't talk enough, continued.

"But the Urremond Travesty of 551, which I know we have looked at, is a big factor that led to the war's commencement. The lack of an heir was all it took to jeopardise the stability of the Kingdom of Opulus and, arguably, Vos Draemar. That is something we will revisit soon."

Ragnar nodded again.

"Okay, now we shall advance in our learning. In regards to the events of the war, the first major battle that occurred was the Battle of Verundri. It was fought between the Clan of the Great Lupine and the then Sun's Eastern Alliance, formed of snakes, rams, rabbits and members of the..."

Corsair drifted away.

He was *so* bored. What even was the point in learning the battles? He was none the wiser as to the answer of the question. Cultural enrichment? What aspect of what he was learning enriched his culture or that of the people around him? No one cared about the First Rabbit-Lupine Clan war. That was hundreds of years ago.

The world moves on.

He longed to be out in the open again. To be riding with Quickpaw and preparing for his next tournament. Sword competitions were easy but, with how agile Quickpaw was, races were twice as easy.

Mounted fighting, however, proved to be the most difficult discipline.

His ictharr was, in his eyes, the best he could ever ask for. Funny. Loving. Loyal. Endearing. Fast. He loved every quality about him; from his best to his worst. But the riders he faced did not value the same characteristics as much as he did. He faced monolithic ictharrs that could knock Quickpaw on to his side with a single kick or ram. Being agile did nothing against that.

The fact his father would only glare at Quickpaw did not help.

He's not strong like a lot of the others, sure, but I don't care. Why should I? He's my companion and I like him. That's my decision. I'm 20. I'm not a pup anymore.

"Corsair, who were allied with the Clan of the Great Lupine during this period of conflict?"

Jolted from his reverie, he looked up at Mr Klement.

"Uh... Opulus?"

Mr Klement scrutinised his face for any indication that he was unsure of himself. Corsair held strong.

"Yes, the Kingdom of Opulus. Ragnar, who was the King of Opulus at the time?"

"King Samuel Nordvasar. A lion."

"Very good. King Samuel Nordvasar offered to assist the lupines in their war and send troops to reinforce them. They arrived to monitor the front line while the wolves recovered from the Battle of Verundri. Now, the..."

To some it would seem interesting. It would to Corsair, too, but Mr Klement often forgot himself. He took the opportunity of teaching to almost parade his own knowledge rather than educate them. It drove him away from caring.

He glanced over at Ragnar's dense notes again and realised what a poor excuse that was.

"When the counterattack came against the Opulusian Legion, they did not expect to see deer Skullmongerers charging their lines."

Corsair frowned. Ragnar looked puzzled.

"Deer Skullmongerers?" Ragnar asked.

Mr Klement's face softened in realisation as if he had come across a great revelation.

"Ah, of course. We have not looked at the Kingdom of Wyndr much, have we?"

"No. Why?"

"Well, the Kingdom of Wyndr has kept itself isolated from the issues affecting Vos Draemar for a long time. After the First Rabbit-Lupine Clan war and a few smaller conflicts with their southern neighbours, they chose to keep to themselves. They do not involve themselves much with the world so, naturally, they would not be very evident in clan history. Interestingly enough, most of what we know about their history is from accounts written in other countries."

He continued.

"Anyway, deer Skullmongerers were fearless warriors of the druidic religion. A lot of details about such matters are kept away from prying eyes by the Kingdom of Wyndr and nothing is specified in the Origins of Vos Draemar but we know for sure that they were soldiers from one of the many different tribes that occupied the forests and swamps of the west in order to fight our clan."

The two princes nodded along.

"Actually, I might have a copy of a drawing... one moment."

He turned back to his leather satchel and rummaged around inside with his paw, muttering to himself as he did so, and Corsair took the opportunity to turn to his brother. He caught Ragnar's eye, who turned his head to look at him, and Corsair put both paws together as if holding a sword and violently thrust them towards his chest. Ragnar snickered before dismissing him with a shake of the head, writing more notes.

That reminded him.

I still haven't written anything.

He sighed.

I guess I'll just have to scribble down some random stuff.

"Ah, here we go!"

Corsair and Ragnar both looked up as the tutor approached with a scroll in his paws, kept rolled up by a thin red ribbon. Undoing it delicately, Mr Klement unravelled the scroll.

"Wow," Ragnar said.

Glaring out of the page was a deer, its outline and details etched in ink. It was expertly drawn, verging on the sort of masterpiece that would be up on display in a manor, but the two Sedrids did not focus on that. Their eyes scrutinised every feature of the warrior and Corsair felt a pang of fear as he gazed at him.

Over the warrior's face, masking the identity, was the skull of a fallen deer. The antlers of the warrior grew out from behind the mask, points sharpened, and his body was naked except for a leather kilt. Numerous scars and patterns adorned his body, thin lines drawn across the torso and limbs. One hand held a spear, its shaft adorned with numerous etchings and carvings, while the other held a circular wooden shield. A sword was tucked away in a sheath on his belt, ready to be called upon in case the spear failed him.

"These warriors usually fought with their torsos bare to show off the patterns, scars and tattoos that represented their tribes and druidic orders. Some wore sashes diagonally across their chest while others wore religious robing, especially during the cold days of Gelid-iom. This was because..."

Corsair wasn't listening. His eyes were focusing on what was before him, analysing the features of the terrifying warrior. He found himself engrossed somehow. He felt intimidated before he had even come into actual contact with the figure. He dreaded thinking of the idea that he could ever fight such an adversary.

"*Corsair!*"

Jumping, he looked up at his tutor. Mr Klement met his gaze with a face of utter horror and he was aware of Ragnar staring at him from his right. Corsair looked from one to the other, confused.

"W-what?"

"My parchment!"

He looked down.

He had been holding his quill against the parchment for so long that a large black dot formed at the centre, an abyss that reached downwards forever and sucked in light. He immediately yanked the quill from the parchment and stood, raising it with one paw.

"Sorry, I'm so sorry!"

Mr Klement snatched the parchment from him and glared at the damage, eyes wide.

"This is 10 Iggregoms' worth! And now it's ruined and..."

He leant in, eyes narrowing at his lack of work.

"N-no notes? You failed to write a single note?"

Corsair stood frozen, mouth left open.

"What have you been doing for the past 40 minutes, Corsair?"

"I've had enough of these antics."

Corsair stood on the landing, back against the wall. His tail curled. His ears fell. His eyes lowered. One paw covered the left side of his neck, hiding the flesh beneath it.

His father stood before him, half a metre away, with one paw raised up and holding the ruined parchment in question. The black spot had dried on to the material, a permanent stain on the soiled writing sheet.

"How much do you think I pay for Mr Klement to come here and tutor you both on clan history?"

Corsair was silent.

"Answer me."

"A lot, father."

"A lot, yes. A lot of Iggregoms to ensure that you two should be able to become leaders who know what the hell is going on in Vos Draemar. So the clan can prosper and survive."

He gestured to the blank ruined parchment.

"But you clearly think this isn't worth your time, don't you?"

"I..."

"Why do you insist on acting like a *pup* all the time, Corsair?"

He hesitated, unsure.

"I asked you a question."

"I... I don't really like clan history..."

His father stepped forward so his snout was inches from his. Corsair pressed his back into the wall, unable to retreat further.

"This isn't about your interests. This isn't about what you like or don't like. *You're* 20. If you ever want to be Winter Baron, you need to start doing things because you have a duty to your clan instead of doing things for selfish reasons like *you don't like it*. You have a duty to this clan, to *these people*, not to frolicking in the fields and woods with that thing you ride."

"I just feel as if Ragnee is..."

"What have I told you about using that nickname? What have I told you about talking like a pup, Corsair?"

His son bowed his head as far as it could go, looking down at the floor. Silence fell between him and his father, each quiet second increasing the tension in Corsair's head. He pressed harder and harder on the left side of his neck, closing his eyes.

He heard his father step back.

"You're a prince. Start acting like one."

His father turned and stormed down the stairs, leaving him alone on the landing.

"Where is Ophelia, Peter?"

"She went out with Ingrid to visit the market, Winter Baron."

"I need to speak to her when she gets back. Have her come see me as soon as she's home."

"Of course, Winter Baron."

Corsair opened his eyes and looked up. His father had disappeared downstairs, conversing with Peter about his mother's return.

In moments of anger, others would have complained. They would have argued back. They would have defended themselves. They would have defied their father to prove they were not in the wrong.

But, instead, he just let the moment of defiant anger pass and accepted his punishment.

I'm an idiot. What am I doing? I need to focus and stop being such a fool. I'm 20. Be an adult.

Repeating that to himself, he returned to his daily routine.

CHAPTER FOUR

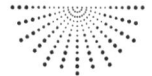

"It has been ages since I cooked and I'm looking forward to seeing how you all enjoy it," Corsair's mother sighed as she sat down, taking a seat beside her husband.

The dining room shared the same space as the living area before the fire. It was all one large hall, stretching from the front door to the back wall. The table was positioned beneath the landing above, a rectangular panel of wood placed on a thick supporting block. Arthur and Ophelia Sedrid sat on one side of the table, holding paws, while Ragnar and Corsair sat on the other.

"We've been looking forward to it all day," Ragnar nodded. "Haven't we, Corsair?"

"I'm having to stop myself from drooling right now."

"You drool on this table and I'll give your food to Ragnar," his mother said.

The two sons chuckled. Corsair's gaze shifted across his father's face, making eye contact with him, and he could only hold it for a second before he averted it. He could feel his father's gaze pass over him every few seconds, sweeping back and forth, and he was reluctant to look up and risk eye contact again.

"How was training today, Corsair?" his mother asked.

"It was good. We got soaked but it was good."

"I saw this afternoon. Arthur, dear, can you not find an alternative method that doesn't get them so wet?"

"Dominik sees to their training regimes. I watch."

"Well, you really must tell him to ease up. These two came in soaking wet earlier."

"Dominik is more than experienced. His teaching gives them resilience."

"And they have to be soaked in order to understand that?"

"It helps the process."

"Well, if they were soaked, I don't even want to know how Harangoth or Quickpaw were."

"They were fine," Corsair said. "He was rolling around in the snow when we went to Mr Duncan's."

"Oh, Duncan! How is he doing?"

"He's doing well. His tavern seems to be doing pretty good."

"We must invite them around soon, Arthur. It has been months since they last came for dinner."

"It would be nice for me to talk to him again," his father said. "How was he with you two?"

"Oh, really nice. Gave us three pints and everything," Ragnar said.

"Three pints?" his mother said.

"No, I didn't have them all, Mum. Rohesia came with us, we had one each."

"Oh, thank goodness. I'm not having my son grow up a drunkard."

"Agreed," his father said.

"Mr Duncan probably wouldn't have let me, anyway. Not in the middle of the day."

"Duncan is very kind. When did you meet him again, my love? In the army?" his mother said.

"No, years before. A lot younger," his father said.

"And then you went to fight in Silverclaw, didn't..?"

Ragnar trailed off.

"Sorry. Didn't think about what I was saying."

Corsair didn't hear his father accept the apology. A silence fell between the family members, filled with the sounds of the servants preparing the food in the kitchen, before his mother swooped in to save the dinner.

"So, Corsair, how is Rohesia?"

"She's fine."

"I haven't seen her in ages. She should come around to our place soon. She's a delightful wolf."

"I do find the fur decoration around her jaw to be a weird statement," remarked Arthur.

"It is not a weird statement, Arthur, other wolves do it all the time. I'm sure Duncan used to have those things on the back of his head."

His father mumbled something in response. Ignoring him, his mother turned her attention back to her two sons.

"I've never seen her parents, though. Have you ever met Rohesia's parents, Ragnar?"

"No," Ragnar said. "I haven't. She does live on the other side of the city."

"Did you ever go to play at her house when you were younger, Corsair?"

"No. She always came here or we played in the woods."

"And she doesn't have an ictharr?"

"No. Harangoth and Quickpaw might as well be hers, though," Ragnar said.

"They go crazy for her," Corsair said. "Have you seen them around her, Mum?"

"No, I haven't. What do they do?"

"We were walking to Mr Duncan's and she came up behind us.

Both of them were walking by our sides but the next minute they rushed towards her to get petted."

"I'm guessing Quickpaw was the first one to run towards her."

"They both went," Ragnar said.

"Harangoth?"

"Yeah, Harangoth."

"I don't believe that for a second. Quickpaw I can see running towards her but Harangoth? Never."

His father grumbled something but his mother ignored him. Corsair always marvelled at how well she dealt with him. There was no doubt that she loved him with all her heart and was devoted to her marriage, but behind her loving and caring exterior there was a fiery and firm side to her that seemed impossible to conquer. His father rarely challenged her on anything.

As Ragnar went to open his mouth to continue the conversation, the door opened behind them and the two brothers turned in their seat. Standing in the open door was Peter, a senior grey wolf dressed in the grey servant attire. A sprout of fur protruded from the back of his head, tied off at the base. He bowed upon greeting the Winter Baron's family.

"Winter Baron, the food is ready. May we bring it in?"

"Of course."

He nodded, turned back to face into the kitchen and beckoned with his paw for the culinary servants to enter. Four wolves walked in, each holding a metal plate of food in their paws, and stood beside each of the four occupants of the table. They leant down in unison and bestowed a plate of food on each member of the family, stepping back as Peter approached.

The family waited in silence as he tasted each portion of food, assuring that none of the meals were tainted with poison, and Corsair watched him roll the dice on his life without a falter in his hardened expression. He seamlessly tasted each meal, standing up straight after each one, and nodded seconds later.

"The meals are safe, Winter Baron. Enjoy."

"Thank you, Peter."

He nodded and walked backwards towards the wall next to the kitchen door, remaining observant as the rest of the team disappeared into the kitchen. Corsair looked down at the food, examining the meal, and resisted the urge to tuck in immediately and disregard the family prayer.

Sitting on the plate was a fine slab of red meat, its exterior glistening from the layer of sauce that thinly veiled it. A small and neatly-arranged portion of vegetables was clustered on the right side of the meat, transported from the slightly warmer south, and Corsair was barely able to resist the enticing meal set out in front of him.

"Paws together for the prayer," his father ordered.

Corsair complied, placing his paws together and bowing his head.

His mother began to pray. He listened to her soothing voice, eyes shut as she recited the words. It was calming, sitting in silence with nothing but the fire crackling. He remembered all the songs she would sing when he was a cub to comfort him during the night.

"Amen."

"Amen," the rest of the family said.

Raising his head and opening his eyes, Corsair heard the forever fateful words that sealed the fate of the meal in front of him.

"You can tuck in."

With restrained desire he picked up his cutlery, sliced away a small, thin piece of meat and placed it on his pink tongue. Closing his mouth and chewing, he savoured the sweet taste of the food, marvelling at how hugely different it was from Peter's dinners. He made a mental note to save half of his meal for Quickpaw, despite the urge to bolt it all down.

"Wow, that's good," Ragnar said.

"Five seconds in and you like it already?"

"It's great," Corsair said.

"Don't talk with your mouth full," his father said.

He covered his mouth with his paw as he ate, shielding his family from seeing the grotesque sight of meat being mashed into fleshy debris.

"It is very good, Ophelia."

"Thank you, dear."

The married couple briefly held paws, lasting a few seconds, before his father gently eased out of the connection and continued to eat.

"How did you even cook this?" Ragnar asked.

"As it has been a while since I have cooked, I did ask Ingrid to help me prepare the meat."

Both young wolves gave exaggerated gasps.

"You cheated."

"Cheater."

"I did not cheat. I still cut the meat and finely cooked it. She just helped me with the recipe, that's all."

"I don't know, Mum. That seems really deceptive," Ragnar said.

"How about, next time, you go into the kitchen and cook instead?" his mother retorted. "Maybe your food will be better than mine."

Ragnar fell silent.

"I thought as much, darling, so continue to eat your food before I threaten never to cook for either you again."

This was enough of an ultimatum that Ragnar immediately returned to eating, smiles growing on both their faces. Corsair shovelled another piece of meat into his mouth.

"So, father, when is our next tournament? It's been a while. We've been training hard," Ragnar asked.

Corsair looked up to see his father answer the question but saw movement in the corner of his eye and turned his head. There, he saw his mother's crestfallen face and he winced at the sight.

His father finished his mouthful and spoke.

"That will be it for the time being. It's time that we advanced from the sporting career for now and began to focus on how you two contribute to the clan. In times like this, the Winter Baron's sons need to serve in order to display leadership and loyalty to our people."

Corsair looked at Ragnar and, while the young Sedrid didn't understand what he was implying, his older brother's face showed that he did.

"Surely, it can wait a few years," his mother said. "They're young..."

"I was 20 when my father had me enlist in the army."

Corsair, hearing the plan his father had for them, choked on his food and spat it out. A wet clump of meat came up from his throat, coated in saliva, and the whole family recoiled from the table.

"Sir, is everything okay?" Peter yelled, rushing forwards and assuming a position to resuscitate him.

"Y-yeah," he nodded, nursing his throat with his paw. "I'm fine."

"God, Corsair, how quickly were you eating?" his father said. "Chew your food or you'll choke."

He nodded. With a sigh, his father turned to Peter.

"Can you clean up this mess, please?"

"Of course, Winter Baron. Right away."

He hurried off to the kitchen, disappearing through the door and calling out to the other servants.

"Are you okay, Corsair?" his mother asked.

He nodded, hiding the dread that had mounted up inside of his gut.

"I'm fine."

"As I was saying before we were interrupted," his father said, "it is time for you two to go into the military. I wanted to discuss your entry into the Krosguard."

"Krosguard?" Ragnar said.

"Yes, the Krosguard. Your fighting ability is far beyond that of the regular army. In order to display your ability to lead you must be a member of the foremost elite. Now, as I was saying, the Krosguard requires recruits to enter with their own ictharrs. Ragnar, Harangoth is perfectly suitable for this."

Corsair knew what he was going to say before he even made eye contact with him.

"Quickpaw isn't prepared for military service. There are plenty of stables only a few miles away from here that have adult ictharrs for sale. I'm sure we could find one-"

"Dad-"

"Don't interrupt me when I'm speaking and call me 'Father' when you address me, Corsair. As I was saying-"

"Father, that's not fair."

His father sneered.

"You are not a cub. This isn't about it being 'fair'. This is about what works in reality. It's about your people."

"Quickpaw is fine. I'm not leaving him."

"What did we just talk about upstairs?"

"I'm *not* leaving him."

Corsair fought the urge to submit when he saw his father's thunderous face.

"I don't appreciate that tone. Watch how you speak to your father."

"Quickpaw is fine. If I... I have to go to the Krosguard, then he's coming with me. I'm his rider."

"The hills to the south are not reality. This is military service in the *Krosguard*. This isn't a game."

"I'm not replacing him."

His father opened his mouth to continue but his mother swooped in once again to intervene.

"Arthur, dear, let him take Quickpaw with him. They've known each other for so long – you can't expect him to leave him behind."

"I'm his father."

"And I'm his mother. I hope you haven't forgotten that."

Corsair watched his mother and father glare at each other from where they were seated, silence falling over the table again. Seconds of quiet agony passed, the two siblings exchanging uncomfortable looks, before their father looked away from their mother.

"The recruitment drive is in four days. I expect you to be down at the Great Hall of Wolves then."

$\sim$

Doomed, the leftovers from Corsair's meal plummeted from the plate and towards the floor of the stables. They hit the ground with a wet *thud*, lasting a second before Quickpaw's head shot down to the ground and tore it to shreds. Corsair watched his steed enjoy his surplus meal, petting the back of his neck.

"Good ictharr."

Quickpaw lifted his head to nuzzle his paw before returning to his meal, a gesture that made him smile. He looked over to the neighbouring stable to see Harangoth consuming his dinner in a more reserved manner. Ragnar watched him, leaning over the stable door.

Corsair looked to the right. Beside Quickpaw's stable was another stall, one that was once occupied by Reginald. It stood empty, last filled with his presence years ago. He contemplated his last memories of the beast before looking back to his own companion.

He was a kind ictharr, Reginald. He lived a long and good life. That's all you can hope for.

Amid the low-level munching of the ictharrs, Ragnar spoke.

"Hey... I'm sorry about what Dad said tonight."

Corsair sighed.

"You shouldn't be the one apologising."

"I know, but..."

"Seriously, why would he say that? He is always looking for an excuse to insult Quickpaw all the time, every day, every week. He's a good ictharr. He's loyal. What else does he want to see?"

"I don't know."

"He never takes my word for anything."

Silence. Corsair sighed again, rubbing his face.

"It's... it's not even that, you know? It's mainly us going into the

Krosguard in the first place. It's so sudden. He said it like it was nothing."

"We've got to contribute."

"And we can't do another few months in Mr Duncan's place? It has to be war?"

"Corsair..."

"I've been fighting in tournaments for the past 10 years and *now* I have to kill people?"

Ragnar turned and placed a paw on his shoulder.

"Corsair, *relax.*"

The younger Sedrid took deep breaths.

"We are safe. We're not at war with anyone. There's nothing to worry about. We'll be serving for a year and then that's it – we're out. Back down here eating Mum's food and riding in the hills. It'll go past in no time."

Corsair looked unsure. Ragnar noticed and gestured towards Quickpaw, who had finished eating and was peering out from his stable.

"You said he's loyal, right?"

"Yeah, he's loyal."

"And you trust him?"

"Of course. With my life."

"Then you're fine. You'll have him with you every step of the way and he'll keep you safe."

Providing evidence to his statement, Quickpaw pushed his snout against Corsair's face. He smiled and pulled his head away, scratching the back of his ears.

"And I'll be there, too. I'll look after you."

Corsair gazed at his companion. Quickpaw gave a low growl, one that promised to stand by him always, and he stroked the bridge of his snout.

"Are you reassured?"

"I think so."

His brother stepped forwards and hugged him, an embrace the

younger Sedrid welcomed. They held one another there, the two ictharrs watching.

"I love you," Ragnar said. "I'll always be there for you, okay?"

"Okay."

"We'll be fine. You'll be fine. One year will pass in no time."

CHAPTER FIVE

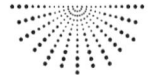

*C*rack.

The head of the axe came down hard on the wooden block, perfectly slicing the log into two chunks. The pieces fell off either side of the chopping block, landing in the soft white pillow of snow covering the ground. Corsair leant down to pick them up. He threw the firewood into the basket and placed down a new log, raised his axe up and brought it down again.

Training had been going normally that morning. Corsair had arrived on time and began practice with Alpha Tiberius, alongside his brother, when a soldier rushed forwards and urged the alpha to make his way to the Great Hall of Wolves. Both the alpha and his father left, ordering the brothers to prepare firewood in the meantime. Ragnar kindly volunteered to scour the woods at the back of the house while Corsair took up the easier duty of chopping them into smaller pieces.

Quickpaw sat in the snow, watching his master work away, but Corsair ignored him.

Three days.

The shadow of recruitment loomed in the distance, drawing closer and closer by the second.

After another axe swing, he gave himself a moment to draw his cloak closer around him. The morning's snow was quite harsh, a peak in its usual capacity to hinder those who ventured outside. Corsair would have been lying to himself if he did not admit that the interior of his house and the warmth of his cosy bed appealed more than chopping wood in the cold. Quickpaw seemed unbothered, his thick white coat shielding him more than the wolf's cloak.

He looked to his left. Four guards stood vigilant by a tree, longswords in scabbards and heads held high. They were positioned to defend him if anything happened. They had offered to deal with chopping the wood but Corsair turned their offer down. The work would at least keep him warm and he didn't want his father coming back to the sight of him not following orders.

"Good morning."

He looked up, expecting to see his father or Alpha Tiberius, but instead saw Rohesia standing there with her usual attire draped over her. Quickpaw spotted her and leapt on to all four paws, bounding past his master and rolling over before her. He watched as his steed abandoned him.

"You love appearing out of nowhere, don't you?"

"At least I didn't hit you with a snowball – that's got to be a bonus."

He didn't answer. Looking over his shoulder, he saw the guards staring at the black wolf.

"It's okay. She's a friend. Give us some privacy, please."

"Yes, Sir."

They turned and walked in the opposite direction, stopping several metres away. Quickpaw rolled on to his front and rushed off behind a group of trees, throwing himself into the snow and thrashing around in it.

"He's very energetic today."

"I couldn't take him on a run this morning. I had training."

"You have training every morning."

"I wasn't late this time."

She looked at the graveyard of wood by the chopping block.

"And part of your training is... cutting wood?"

"Dad and Tiberius rushed off to the Great Hall of Wolves for something important. This is our work in the meantime."

"Trying your paw at carpentry?"

He ignored the joke, bringing the axe up and slamming the head down against the log. It splintered and fell into two, joining the pile of its comrades. Rohesia's eyes focused on the axe in the block, thinking.

"Are you okay?"

He hesitated at the idea of answering. Seeing this, she sat down on a nearby stump of a fallen tree and tucked her tail between her legs, leaning forward to listen. He contemplated telling a lie.

Why should I lie to her? She's my friend. I can trust her.

He tore the axe out of the block's surface and placed it by its side, sitting down on top of the block and facing his companion. Quickpaw shot past behind him, throwing himself into a mound of snow by the base of a tree.

"Dad's sending us to the Krosguard."

Rohesia didn't respond. She waited, expecting more, until she blinked and said a single word.

"Oh."

"Yeah, 'oh' is a word to describe it."

"I thought you'd be going into another tournament."

"That's what we both thought. Dad made this revelation last night, so wise and insightful that I brought up some of my din-"

"Too much information, Corsair."

Quickpaw ran past Rohesia and skidded, crashing into a tree and falling on to his side. He got up, shaking his head and sniffing the offending tree.

"Fine, sorry. Then, next thing, Dad starts trying to convince me that I should get a replacement for Quickpaw because he doesn't think he's ready for it."

On hearing the word 'replacement', the white ictharr padded over to his master and whimpered. Corsair felt him push his snout against the side of his head, making him lean away and raise his paws up to pet him.

"I won't replace you, don't worry. You're my best friend, aren't you?"

He yapped while being stroked, satisfied with the treatment he was receiving.

"Do you think he's ready?"

Corsair hesitated.

"I don't understand it, Rohesia, I don't. We're being pushed from years and years of experience into something we haven't seen before. It's... scary. I don't think I could... you know..."

She understood.

"I've been raised all my life to try and make sure I don't badly injure someone and now that's all out the window."

"It sucks."

"It does. You know what else sucks? Dad trying to push Quickpaw out of the way at every opportunity."

Quickpaw tilted his head, long ears standing, before he looked to the right. He skulked off towards a tree, sniffing around its base.

"He tries to convince me to replace him, to put him up for adoption, to keep him but only train with a new ictharr from a breeder. He has a grudge against him and he doesn't understand that he can't just expect me to leave him. I've had him all these years. I love him."

She didn't say anything. She listened, wanting her friend to get it all out.

"I don't care if Harangoth is a prize ictharr. I love Harangoth and I love Ragnee, you know I do, but I also love Quickpaw."

"So do I."

They both watched him bounce around in the snow, yapping and growling playfully as he slid through it. His fur was specked with white dots and he shook them off with every romp only to add new ones to the ranks.

"He's not like Harangoth. He's not from a breeder. He's not this strong hulking ictharr like he is. And as much as I love him and want to leave him behind so he's safe... I can't. I can't leave him back here for a year."

"It's not right to expect you to do that."

"It's not. So I don't know why Dad can't understand that."

Quickpaw's head shot up as a bird fluttered past, nesting in the tree above. He bounded over to the tree it was resting in and stood, placing his front paws against the trunk and yapping at it. Proud of himself, he looked to his master, tongue hanging out.

"I see it, don't worry."

The bird, annoyed, flew off into the distance. Quickpaw dropped down from the tree and sat down, watching it fly away.

"I can join with you two," Rohesia said.

"You haven't got an ictharr."

"I don't need one. The army accepts anyone who can use a weapon. I have my bow."

"But... you'll be killing people."

Rohesia fell silent.

"See? I don't understand why we can't do another month or two at Mr Duncan's. That's contributing, isn't it?"

"Maybe your father is thinking of something more impactful. More applicable to leadership."

Corsair wanted to argue but he knew she was right, as much as he didn't want to admit it. Being barkeeps would hardly teach the siblings the skills they needed to face the problems of the clan. Even if he never became Winter Baron, he could still move on to be some kind of leader.

But he still didn't like it. His paw moved up to the left side of his neck, gently rubbing it.

"You do that a lot, you know."

He looked up.

"What?"

"That."

She pointed to the paw over his neck. He dropped it down so it dangled between his legs.

"Just a habit."

"Is your neck all right?"

"Yeah, it's fine. I do it when I'm nervous."

"If there's anything you need to say, you know I'm-"

"*Corsair!*"

Both wolves and the distracted ictharr turned their heads to face right, spotting Ragnar and Harangoth sprinting through the woods towards them. Corsair got up to his hind paws as Quickpaw hurried to his side, ears standing. The four guards, hearing Ragnar's yells, rushed over with paws on the grips of their swords.

"What is it? Did something happen?"

Ragnar arrived, out of breath.

"What is it?" Corsair asked.

He shook his head.

"It's... it's Dad. He just declared war on the Land of the Sun and Moon."

The Great Hall of Wolves was a sight to behold.

Inside the grand hall, full of fine wood carvings and supported by stone pillars, all important and political meetings affecting the clan were held. Wooden benches ran from the left side of the hall down to the right, split into two sections by a middle aisle. The front rows were usually taken up by important figures in the military and members of the Winter Baron's council. Above were two balconies, one placed behind the podium facing the wooden seats, the other above the entrance way opposite. Behind the lectern from which the Winter Baron was speaking, a stone wall ran from left to right on which sat many gold plaques. Each one commemorated a leader from the past. It formed a timeline of Winter Barons and Winter Baronesses, a sacred and eternal legacy reaching back to the clan's birth.

Now, however, he couldn't care less about it.

With a meeting being called so urgently, only a few wolves sat in the rows of seats and they were dressed in their everyday clothes. He could see Alpha Tiberius seated along the front bench among the Winter Baron's council, eyes forward towards the podium.

He shifted his eyes to his father.

Standing behind the lectern was the grey wolf who had hurried away from practice that morning. Atop his head sat the Winter Baron's helm, a steel helmet with golden angel wings projecting from each side. It was the prestigious mark of the clan's leader – the one wolf they could rely on to protect them and maintain prosperity. He was addressing the small assembly that had mustered together that morning.

"We have received word via messenger birds from the east that the rabbits have invaded Pothole Plains. This kind of invasion can only be met, and resolved, with force. As much as I dislike the idea of propelling the Clan of the Great Lupine into another conflict, we cannot allow the rabbits to interpret our inaction as indifference, leniency or tolerance."

A white wolf raised a paw.

"I fully agree with your thinking and reasoning, Winter Baron. We must act and demonstrate to them that their actions will not go unpunished. But do you not have doubts about stepping into conflict immediately?"

"If we do this, we could possibly be propelling ourselves into a third war with the rabbits," another wolf agreed.

"This is not interfering in foreign conflict like Silverclaw," his father said. "The issue is on our doorstep. The rabbits, under orders from their Supreme Chamber, swept through the settlement and removed any lupine citizens from it by force. While they were thankfully not harmed or killed, this is a way of testing our boundaries to see what they can get away with. They are defying the 400-year-old legacy of the Raskartz-Amien Pact. It clearly states that rabbits and wolves will live in harmony within one of the many interracial town projects such as Pothole Plains. They have treated our trust with contempt and, for that, action must be taken."

"And risk a third war, Winter Baron?"

"I am willing to postpone military action to use diplomatic methods but I do not intend to rely heavily on them. The Land of the Sun and Moon is stubborn – if they want land, they will take it and keep taking it regardless of other opinion. I will have one of the members of my loyal council write a letter to the Guild Premier warning him that if they do not vacate Pothole Plains and formally apologise to the wolf inhabitants of the town, there will be military action."

He gestured to the group.

"Does anyone disagree with this approach?"

No one disagreed.

"Good. There is a recruitment drive coming up in three days. Send messenger birds to all towns to convince as many able wolves as possible to enlist on the day. New soldiers will be trained for a month before we launch a counterattack against their invasion while our current forces cordon off the town from the rest of the clan and other interracial projects on the border. This also gives us enough time to attempt to disarm the situation before any action is taken. Before this assembly ends, I would like to speak to Alpha Tiberius and Alpha McVarn – the rest of you are dismissed."

Some of the wolves began to get up, already moving to leave the hall, while Tiberius and a black wolf approached his father. Corsair ignored the meeting they were having and marched towards him, Ragnar following.

"Corsair, no! You can't just rush into a meeting and interrupt it!"

He ignored the warnings and pushed on, the conversation of the trio getting louder.

"I'll be here for the recruitment drive in Grand Wolf Plains," the black wolf said. "My officers will see to other settlements before we bring back the candidates to Ignatius' Mount. The Krosguard will be more than prepared to deal with the Land of the Sun and Moon, Winter Baron."

"So will the army," Alpha Tiberius said. "We'll drive them out of our land and remind them what the consequences are for this aggression."

"I have no doubt. We'll see to this..."

His father trailed off as he saw his son storming up the aisle, stepping around the two alphas and confronting him.

"What's going on?" Corsair said.

"You were told to collect firewood."

"Ragnar told me that you declared war on the rabbits."

"That is none of your concern."

"*None of my concern?* I'm joining the Krosguard in three days! I'll be fighting-"

"You do not march into here and start interfering in matters that are not your own."

"But-"

"*Be quiet,*" his father growled, fangs bared, and it was instinct for Corsair's paw to move to the side of his neck. Ears going down and tail curling, he averted his gaze as all his bravado died within a fraction of a second. He felt his father's gaze linger over him, no one daring to speak, before his father eventually looked back to the two alphas.

"I know you two have a lot to see to, especially now. You can go."

"Thank you, Winter Baron."

Both the alphas shook the Winter Baron's paw, bidding him farewell as they walked down the aisle and out through the doors. The Great Hall of Wolves was left empty, except for the three guards stationed in the viewing galleries.

"When I ask you to collect firewood, you follow my instructions. You do not dare to interrupt my meetings, clan-sensitive or not. Is that understood?"

"Father, he was-"

"I'm not speaking to you, Ragnar."

Corsair was silent.

"Stop acting like a cub and look at me when I'm talking to you."

Apprehensively, he looked up.

"Do you understand?"

"I... I understand."

With no more than an annoyed grunt, his father removed his helmet from his head and walked past them. The guards hurried from the viewing galleries and down the set of stairs to the right, glancing at the two siblings before pushing through the doors.

Silence.

The younger Sedrid sat down in the front bench and leant against the backrest, a look of defeat on his face. Ragnar sat down next to him.

For a moment, neither spoke. The only sounds were the muffled chatter of the market and whirling snow outside the windows.

Ragnar opened his mouth and shut it. He paused, eyes flicking from his brother to the wooden floorboards. He spoke.

"We... we can make this work."

"How? How can we possibly..."

Corsair was choked with tears, eyes reddening.

"Come on, don't cry."

"I'm not crying." He growled, trying to steel himself, but he couldn't hide the tears brimming over. He wiped them away, sniffling and shaking his head. "Ragnee... I don't want to die."

"You're not going to die."

"I don't want to kill anyone."

Ragnar hesitated, unsure of how to comfort him with that thought.

"I'm not prepared for war. I wasn't... even prepared for fighting any criminals. I can't do this. I can't go."

His brother put an arm around him.

"A-and Quickpaw... oh, God, Quickpaw. I don't want him to get hurt. He's not ready for it and I can't just..."

"Hey, shush, it's okay."

"It's not okay!"

"Calm down. Deep breaths."

Heeding his brother, he focused on his breathing. He brought in a shaky breath and pushed it out, blinking away the tears as he did so.

"Nothing bad is going to happen to you or Quickpaw, okay? *Nothing.* I'm here to protect you. No one will hurt you or Quickpaw, *no one.*"

Corsair didn't answer.

"I promise you. Trust me."

With a surrendering sigh, Corsair nodded.

"Okay."

"Do you believe me?"

"I believe you."

They drew into one another, united in their brotherhood. Corsair's snout rested on his sibling's shoulder.

He could only pray that nothing bad would befall him, Ragnar, or Quickpaw.

CHAPTER SIX

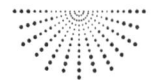

*J*t was only three days before Corsair found himself in a line outside the Great Hall of Wolves, Quickpaw's reins in paw as he stood beside him.

News of the outbreak of war had swept throughout the clan like wildfire. Dozens of messenger birds had come and gone from the watchtowers, relaying information back and forth. Countless recruits and veterans arrived from nearby towns to enlist in the army, forming a line that stretched from a temporarily requisitioned tavern all the way to the east wall. There was an eager atmosphere surrounding them all, many lupines conversing in an excited tone. Corsair couldn't believe it. They were all lined up to fight a horrible war – what was there to look forward to?

Is there something I'm not understanding about this?

The line to enlist in the Krosguard was noticeably shorter, drawn parallel to its longer counterpart and separated by the sea of bodies that was the city market. Traders and customers often glanced at the long queues, smiling at the brave wolves who volunteered to defend them from the rabbit menace in the east.

"You okay?"

Corsair looked forward. Ragnar was standing in front of him, Harangoth to his side, and looking over his shoulder.

"Yeah," Corsair said.

"There's nothing to worry about."

"I know."

There was plenty to worry about but he didn't want to force his brother to give another reassuring lecture. Ragnar had his own worries to confront, which he did with a stronger face than he could. Corsair felt embarrassed about the tears he shed three days ago, scolding himself for acting like a cub.

I'm stronger than this. I'm stronger than this.

"Next!"

The line shifted forwards. He was not too far away from the front.

Peering around Ragnar, he could see that an inspection area was positioned in front of the Great Hall of Wolves. A few soldiers were conversing casually by the base of the stairs, watching as their comrades waved Krosguard hopefuls through. They inspected their ictharrs while asking the riders numerous questions.

He felt the reins tug in his paw and looked back to Quickpaw. He was gently pulling away from his master, whimpering with head hung and eyes aimed at him. He shushed him, stroking his head.

"It's okay, it's okay."

Quickpaw was satisfied, glancing around himself. Corsair looked over his shoulder at the recruits behind him. His eyes fell upon a line of stoic ictharrs, a range of different colours but all bearing the same hardened expression as their masters.

At least he's not running around and annoying them.

"Next!"

The wolf was rejected, sent back in the opposite direction, as another came forward with beast in tow. She faced a series of questions as relentless as the day's snow, giving answer after answer, until her entry was declined. She walked away, mumbling to herself as her ictharr padded behind her in shame.

"Next!"

Ragnar gave a smile to his brother and patted him on the shoulder before stepping forward.

"I remember you. You came into the hall three days ago, right?"

"I did with my brother, yes. I'm Ragnar Sedrid."

"Ah, I *definitely* know you then, son. I'm Jonah McVarn, alpha of the Krosguard. The pleasure's all mine."

Corsair caught a glimpse of McVarn's face as he stepped around the side of Harangoth. He was the same black-furred lupine from three days ago, the one summoned to the podium alongside Alpha Tiberius, except he could now see three large sprouts of fur protruding from the back of his head. Thick string was knotted around the bases, holding them in position. The same streaks of bright red that Alpha Tiberius wore across the eye and down the bridge of his snout were on the face of Jonah McVarn.

"And you're Corsair, right?" he said, pointing to the younger Sedrid.

"I'm Corsair, yes."

"Well, nice to meet you, son. I'll be right with you after I've seen to your brother."

The leader of the Krosguard moved towards Harangoth, examining his flank as he walked. Two soldiers followed, dressed in full suits of armour, longswords slid into scabbards.

"So – what brings a champion rider like yourself down here, son? Did you get bored with tournament life?"

"Our father wants us to contribute to the clan. More than serving drinks at the local tavern, Alpha."

"You're definitely helping the clan when it needs it most. Your presence here is noted."

He eased his paw on to the bridge of Harangoth's snout, eyes level with the beast's. The ictharr didn't even flinch, eyes staring forward.

"A few entry questions, son. Have you ever fought in a war before?"

Ragnar frowned.

"I'm 24, Alpha. I haven't lived long enough to serve in anything."

"I know, I know. Dumb question. I have to ask them. Have you ever served in the army before?"

"No, Alpha."

"You've held weapons before?"

"Yes. Lances, swords, javelins, shields."

He paced around to the other side of the ictharr, nodding.

"What's his name?"

"Harangoth."

"Right. Commemorating one of the earlier Winter Barons, son?"

"He shaped the clan to be what it is today. I don't think that's something to be forgotten."

"Not at all. How old is he? He's male, right?"

"He's male. Eleven years old, Alpha."

"I would ask you if he follows commands well but that'd be like asking a champion archer if they can aim with a bow."

Ragnar chuckled.

"Show me how you hold a sword, son."

Corsair watched as his older brother drew his longsword from its sheath and held a face-on stance – sword held horizontal, high enough that it was parallel with his snout, and his hind paws shoulder-width apart. Harangoth waited patiently as his master's stance was scrutinised by McVarn's vigilant eyes, muttering to himself.

"Good. A few tweaks here and there but they're minor. It looks good."

Ragnar relaxed from his stance as he drew around to Harangoth's front, making eye contact with him.

"Are you prepared to face an enemy in combat, son? Are you ready to put your life and the life of your ictharr at risk for the Clan of the Great Lupine?"

"Yes, Alpha."

McVarn offered his paw and Ragnar took it, met with a smile.

"I think you're welcome into our training course, son. Meet us at the east gate tomorrow morning."

"That quickly, Alpha?"

"Usually there'd be a transition period of a week. Considering what's happening, a day is pushing our luck. It's your responsibility to be there if you're serious about joining the Krosguard – no one will be waiting or looking for you. If you don't turn up, you don't turn up. Understood?"

"Understood."

McVarn gestured in the opposite direction for Ragnar, patting him on the back as he went, and turned to face Corsair. His brother stopped a metre away, turning to watch his brother's inspection.

"Next!" one of the soldiers yelled.

Quickpaw gave another whimper. Corsair stepped forward with him in tow. They stopped before McVarn and his entourage, feeling all eyes on them.

"Pleasure to meet you, son. I'm Jonah McVarn, alpha of the Krosguard. I've worked with your father for a long time."

Corsair, for a few seconds, failed to notice the paw held out towards him. He nodded and muttered, unsure of how to respond, before he spotted the lonely paw held out before him.

"Oh! Sorry."

He shook it and let go. The alpha, to his relief, overlooked the awkward interaction and immediately turned to face Quickpaw.

"Another tournament rider out to join the Krosguard?"

"Yes, Alpha."

"Your presence this morning is appreciated. How old are you?"

"Twenty."

"Okay. Have you ever fought in a war before?"

"No, Alpha."

"Have you ever served in the army?"

"Uh, no, Alpha."

"You've held a weapon, I'm guessing?"

"Yes, Alpha."

"What kind of weapons?"

"Lances... uh, swords, too, Alpha."

McVarn hummed to himself. He moved to Quickpaw's flank and stood there, examining him. Corsair met his steed's worried eyes, placing a paw on his side.

"It's okay. He's just looking at you, that's all."

Quickpaw was distracted by his master's reassurances so much so that McVarn resting his paw on Quickpaw's snout was completely unexpected. The moment Quickpaw felt the weight on his snout he shook it off and rounded on McVarn, baring his fangs and giving a defensive growl. McVarn stepped back, drawing his paw away from him. The two guards stepped forwards, paws on the grips of their swords.

"Whoa, easy, easy!" Corsair said, stepping in front of him. "Relax, okay? There's nothing to be scared of."

Quickpaw gave a protesting moan, nuzzling him.

"Stay still for a few minutes. I need you to do that."

Wary of the wolves inspecting him, Quickpaw gave a growl of agreement. Corsair turned his head to meet the leader's eyes.

"He's a bit nervous, sorry. He's not usually like this, Alpha, I swear."

He could tell that the alpha was unimpressed. McVarn came forward again and muttered to himself as he rounded the beast, the two soldiers chuckling with eyes focused on Quickpaw.

"What a runt," one said.

Corsair winced, hurt by the harsh tone they put behind their words, and was thankful that Quickpaw was too distracted to hear. McVarn came back around to the front and stopped, his warm expression replaced with a stern look.

"What's his name?"

"Quickpaw, Alpha."

"Age?"

"He's 11, Alpha. Male."

McVarn sighed.

"Son, from what I've seen, this ictharr is not prepared to be in the Krosguard. He doesn't possess the same ferocity the others do and he doesn't display any form of faith or discipline."

Corsair was speechless, mouth agape.

"You... you can tell all of that from one small thing?"

"I've done this for 30 years, son. I'd appreciate it if you didn't question my judgement. War isn't a suitable path for this ictharr. Thank you for your presence but we can't accept you. Army is always open."

McVarn patted him on the shoulder and turned before Corsair could answer, one of the soldiers stepping forwards to guide him away.

"Next!"

A moment passed where Corsair was content with the outcome. No Krosguard service. No war. No danger to him or Quickpaw. But then it subsided. He remembered his father and the scowl he aimed at Quickpaw constantly. He remembered how they had clashed four nights ago, his father determined for him to replace Quickpaw.

Those memories filled him with fear.

"Aren't you even going to look at my stance? How I hold my sword?"

"Hey, he said beat it, *cub*," the soldier said.

"What's the hold up?" a wolf from the line yelled.

"The alpha is done with you. *Beat it*."

"If you're going to send me away, look at my stance, too!" Corsair yelled.

"He said-"

"Let him have his way."

The two soldiers turned, confused. McVarn stood there, an exasperated look on his face.

"I'll humour him. We've got the whole day to inspect the arrivals. We're in no rush."

"What about me?" the next wolf asked.

"You can wait," the soldier said, changing his tune.

McVarn approached him. Corsair held his ground, placing a paw on his sword's grip, ready to demonstrate his fighting capability.

"Let me see your blade, son."

He drew his sword from its home and passed it to McVarn, who examined the broad side of the steel blade. He turned it back around to display to the owner, revealing the numerous symbols and insignias engraved there.

"You have a lot of commendations."

"Victories, Alpha."

Humming to himself in thought, he passed the blade back to Corsair.

"Face-on stance. Go."

Corsair immediately took up the stance as the alpha walked around him, bringing his blade level with his snout and staring ahead. His hind paws were shoulder-width apart, perfect to the millimetre, and the end of his sword did not waver. Holding it straight, he waited for the alpha's remarks.

And waited.

And waited.

What is he doing?

He could see the two guards walking away, approaching the base of the stairs. The inspection area was left empty, with even the group of distracted soldiers relocating. Lowering his sword, he turned.

"Are you going to-"

There was a flash of steel and, on trained instinct, Corsair brought up his sword to block it. McVarn's sword struck his with a crystal *clang*, driven with enough force behind the blow to send Corsair staggering backwards. Flustered, he could see the alpha moving towards him, sword held across his body. Quickpaw snarled, taking a step forward towards the alpha, but the nearby guards held their weapons up to deter him.

"Hey, what the hell are you doing?" Corsair yelled.

"Come on, son! The enemy isn't going to let you know they're attacking – you've got to be ready for it! I thought you were a champion fighter!"

Yelling out, McVarn charged and stabbed for Corsair's chest. Corsair weaved out of the way, fear keeping his own blade at bay, and he could only backpedal away from the alpha. Everyone in the marketplace watched, invigorated by the commotion.

"You're going to kill me!"

"You're free to drop your sword at any time and go home, son! All you have to do to win is get my sword off me, easy! Simple tournament rules!"

Corsair's eyes swivelled in his sockets, moving from every corner and inch of his body to the next, looking for an indication that he was making a move. McVarn jerked forwards to fake an attack and Corsair's overattentiveness to detail made him believe it, dodging to the left as the alpha swung the other way. Reacting quickly, he tucked into a ball and rolled, moving underneath the swing and arriving behind McVarn. He brought the sword back and swung it at the black wolf's hind paws with the sword's broadside, hoping to knock him down, but McVarn was quick to react. He jumped up and turned, landing once the sword had swept past him, and sliced downwards from above. Corsair blocked the blow, keeping McVarn's blade away from him, and stabbed forwards at the hilt of his sword. McVarn darted back, moving out the range of his swing.

"I was expecting a lot more, son! A *lot* more!"

Corsair knew that wasn't the truth from the sound of the alpha's heavy breathing. He could see McVarn had bitten off more than he could chew, having underestimated his capabilities, but he still hid it well behind his confident attitude. The cheers of his soldiers drove him on.

"He's easy, Alpha, get him!"

"He can't be that good, Alpha!"

"Come on! He's just a rookie, Alpha!"

"Don't beat the poor prince too hard, Alpha! Don't want him running home to tell Daddy!"

The crowd laughed. McVarn swiped at Corsair, trying to hit him in the side, but Corsair saw it coming and parried with a crystal-clear *clang*. He pushed the sword from left to right, shoving him away.

Corsair had him where he wanted him.

Coming forwards shoulder-first, he crashed against the alpha. The driving force behind the shoulder barge caused McVarn to stagger, on the verge of falling backwards. Corsair took the opportunity available to him. With remarkable accuracy, the wolf swung down and struck the hilt of the blade, knocking it from the alpha's paw. Before McVarn could even register that he dropped his sword, Corsair stepped forwards and pressed the side of his blade up against his throat, eyes staring into the alpha's.

Silence.

Corsair stood there, nostrils flaring as he drew breath in and puffed it back out. He was as shocked as McVarn was, blinking as if to deny the reality of his victory.

"You... you can put your sword down now, son."

Corsair lingered for a moment before he pulled the blade away, sliding his sword back into its scabbard. Unease raced through the ranks of the spectators and circulated the makeshift arena.

McVarn stared at him, bewildered.

"I... I would like a moment inside, son."

"I want you to know that I had every intention of sending you away from the Krosguard minutes ago."

The Great Hall of Wolves was vacant, the podium left without a speaker and the benches unoccupied. McVarn stood on the stage, Corsair beside him.

"We're only as good as we are because it's not an 'everyone-is-welcome' club. A big factor in whether or not you qualify is the ictharr that turns up on recruitment day. I also didn't want to deploy a hesitant soldier to a war zone under the leadership of a unit that faces the worst of the worst. I was ready to turn you down."

Corsair nodded.

"But when you kept asking to show your stance, I thought: 'I'll give him what he wants and show him up in front of everyone. That way he'll stop begging for another go.' As scary as it might seem suddenly to be attacked by a wolf with a sword, I had no intention of hurting you. I had full control over my weapon."

"I understand, Alpha."

"The first sign was when I saw the symbols on the side of your sword. There were a *lot* there, son. I started to put some evidence to the seemingly impeccable record of yours. Still, I have to admit, I was expecting to send you away with your tail between your legs."

McVarn chuckled.

"Then you just went and showed me up in front of the capital. That's damn good sword-wielding, son."

"Thank you, Alpha."

"After a display of skill like that, I'm thinking of allowing you into the Krosguard training course. If you're interested and would like a chance to join our ranks, be at the east gate tomorrow morning. We won't wait for you."

Corsair blinked.

"You're accepting me?"

"I'm chalking up what I saw from your ictharr as just nerves from being in front of so many people. You're his rider, after all – you know his limits better than anyone. If you think you and your companion are up to the challenge of selection then I'd be happy to welcome you into the ranks. But one thing, son."

McVarn stepped closer.

"This isn't a game. This isn't a tournament fight where losing means you miss the chance to get another engraving on your sword. Losing in war means your brother will have to bury you. The Land of the Sun and Moon's army won't hesitate to kill you. So I'm warning you - the Krosguard is the most ferocious fighting force in the history of this clan and Vos Draemar. If you know you or your ictharr can't handle our intense training or the war we face, *don't turn up tomorrow*."

Corsair didn't answer.

"Tomorrow morning, east gate. Maybe you'll appear, maybe you won't. That's for you to decide. Go home, get some rest, think about this decision. I have more inspections to see to."

Alpha McVarn shook his paw.

"Have a good day, son."

With that, he walked down the aisle and out through the doors, Corsair's eyes following him as he left.

CHAPTER SEVEN

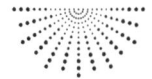

eart thundering in his chest, Corsair stood by the gates of the east wall with his family.

Delivering the news of his acceptance into the Krosguard was an affair of both happiness and woeful tears. His brother congratulated him with endless hugs and pats on the back in celebration of his achievement while his mother wept for the brothers' upcoming departure. Both young wolves spent the evening coaxing her and trying to help her relax, to relieve her of the worries that plagued her mind.

His father, stone-faced, didn't utter a word.

The night before, he had lain in bed, staring up at the ceiling with the moonlight streaking across his nightmarish mess of a room. McVarn's words repeated in his head, bouncing off the walls of his mind, confronting him again and again.

If you know you or your ictharr can't handle our intense training or the war we face, don't turn up.

For a fraction of a second, Corsair decided that he was not arriving at the east gate. He would curl up into a ball in his bed and wait until the time passed, no matter the repercussions.

A moment later, his defiance receded and he couldn't believe he had considered being so rebellious. His father would torment him with that perpetual annoyed expression, patronise him with his scolding, and would never let him hear the end of his grand betrayal of his family and his clan.

His paw had, on reflex, moved to the left side of his neck.

I need to go. Quickpaw and I will be fine. Ragnee is with me and we'll be fine. We'll be fine.

And that's how he found himself by the east gate that morning.

The Sedrids stood patiently as they awaited a Krosguard official to direct them to their new home during their training. Before the open gates was a herd of ictharrs, their owners walking between the beasts and conversing with others they knew. Corsair could sense how apprehensive Quickpaw was, standing behind him, and rested a paw on the scruff of his neck.

"Easy, Quickpaw, easy."

He nuzzled him in response, thankful for the reassurance. He glanced over to Ragnar to see Harangoth standing beside him, not requiring any comfort from his master. His mother stood between them, with Peter standing on one side and a second servant on the other. A squad of guards formed a perimeter around them, facing outwards and focusing their gazes on the passing citizens of Grand Wolf Plains.

She was holding her sons' paws. She squeezed them regularly, trying to reassure herself they were still there, muttering under her breath.

"Mum, hey," Ragnar said, "relax."

"Relax?" she said. "When I see you two raise your own cubs, then you'll understand *exactly* how I feel right now."

"We'll be fine," Corsair said. "We don't want you to worry."

"You two don't understand that I am your mother – worrying is a big part of my job as a parent. No matter what, I will *always* think of you as my cubs."

The two wolves rolled their eyes and groaned, Quickpaw

contributing with a tired growl of his own. Corsair even noticed a falter in Harangoth's steely gaze, giving a low moan as if he was sighing.

Finally, after moments of silence, Alpha McVarn made an appearance at the front of the herd.

"*Shut up!*"

Everyone fell silent, turning to face him.

"We will be riding east to Ignatius' Mount where you will do your training. If you're part of the Krosguard training course, then I'm giving you a minute to mount your ictharrs and ready yourselves to travel. It'll be a long journey so pair up with someone you can talk to – there's not a lot to do on the way. Move it!"

The riders hurried to their ictharrs and mounted, sliding weapons into sheaths and compartments attached to the saddles. Corsair saw his brother's paw slip from his mother's.

"You two need to go now," she said. "I'll have you in my thoughts all the time, OK?"

"Mum, come on."

Corsair could see the tears in her eyes, her face beginning to crumple, and the two brothers immediately leaned in and hugged her. She held them, sniffling and wiping away tears over their shoulders. She eased them away and shook her head.

"I-I'm fine. Just... promise me you'll stay safe, okay? You'll come home safe?"

"We will," Ragnar said. "Promise us we'll get some more of your great cooking when we get back, though."

"I'll make the best dinner you two have had in your life. Now go, hurry!"

Peter and the servant waved as the two wolves turned to their steeds, snatching the reins up and joining the back row of the group. Corsair pulled himself up into the saddle and settled in his seat, making sure he was comfortable for the long journey ahead of them. Ragnar was on his left side, mounted on Harangoth. Riders were positioned on their left and right, eyeing the two princes on their beasts, muttering to each other.

"Goodbye, my loves!"

Corsair and Ragnar both waved back to their mother, ignoring the chuckles of the few soldiers up ahead. A part of the younger Sedrid felt as though he did not belong among the ranks of these hardened lupines, their steeds grunting and growling to themselves. Quickpaw grew uneasy, shifting from paw to paw and glancing left and right.

"Easy, easy. We're okay. Everyone is friendly here."

He grumbled, unsure of his advice, before looking left. His gaze froze over the sight before him, peering around Harangoth to catch a glimpse. His purple pupils bloomed and he almost gasped in awe.

"What's wrong?" Corsair asked.

He looked left.

A white wolf sat on his steed, countless bags and sacks strapped on his back filled to the brim with items Corsair could not discern. A white braided tail draped over one side of the saddle, a decoration that caught his attention immediately. He knew, however, that the lupine's tail was not the point of interest for Quickpaw. Lowering his gaze, he saw the ictharr beneath the wolf, a sleek creature that held itself with an elegant poise. Bags dangled from hooks on either side of the saddle, carrying hefty luggage as its rider did. Its fur was white, with hundreds of black splotches and one jagged dark patch over the right eye. Its tail was braided in the same way as the rider's and was flicking back and forth. Its orange eyes stared forwards, an expression much like Harangoth's on its face.

Corsair laughed.

"In love, huh?"

Quickpaw demonstrated the intensity of his feelings by darting back out of the formation, almost throwing Corsair from his saddle.

"Whoa!"

"Corsair, what's wrong?" Ragnar asked.

"I don't know – hey, stop!"

Quickpaw rapidly rounded the rear of Harangoth and arrived beside the black-spotted beast. He drew alongside the creature and gave a playful yap, mouth hanging open and tongue flopping out from one side. The rider's head shot to the left, eyes focused on Corsair, his steed showing surprise at Quickpaw's sudden greeting.

"Uh."

"Sorry, sorry! He's a bit excited to be here, uh..."

To his surprise, the serious attitude of the black-spotted ictharr somewhat eroded away. There were no playful yaps offered in response but it tilted its head, amused at Quickpaw's friendly approach. It was a stark contrast to the usual growl he received from ictharrs that weren't as sociable as first thought.

"Wow. Corsair Sedrid, right? The Winter Baron's son?" the white wolf said.

"Yeah, I'm him. Look, I'm sorry about this. I'll move..."

"No, Sir, honestly it's fine. Arwenin gets excited easily, too. She's just feeling a bit stroppy today."

Arwenin grumbled, looking down at the snowy ground.

"See, Sir? This is what happens when you don't let your ictharr sleep in."

"You don't have to call me that, you know."

The white wolf frowned.

"Oh, you sure? I just don't want to be disrespectful to you. I mean, you're a prince!"

"No, it's fine. Just Corsair."

"Not even 'fighter'?"

Anxious, he didn't detect the jovial tone.

"I mean, if you want."

"I'm joking, I'm joking. I wouldn't want to annoy you."

He offered a paw forward.

"The name's Axel. Army apothecary."

Corsair hesitated, taken aback by the sudden greeting.

"You're uh... supposed to shake it, you know."

"Y-yeah, right."

Corsair shook Axel's paw.

"Nice to meet you, too."

"Is your brother here?"

Axel looked to his right to see the older Sedrid waving, Harangoth silently greeting Arwenin. She mimicked his serious expression, holding her head up high and nodding to him.

"Hello," Ragnar said.

"Oh, u-uh, hi," Axel said, flustered. "Wow... never thought I'd be beside the jousting champion and prince of the clan himself."

Ragnar chuckled.

"I'm flattered."

"You're flattered? *I'm* flattered. I can barely speak!"

Corsair chuckled. Ragnar smiled and looked back towards the front, distracted from the conversation.

"So... what's his name?" Axel asked, pointing to Quickpaw.

"Oh, he's Quickpaw."

"Nice. He seems like a pretty jolly ictharr."

"He has ups and down. Right now he's in the middle of an 'up', as you can probably tell."

"It's normal. Arwie's guilty of getting excited over a bundle of rope loads of times. Favourite chew toy."

She whimpered, wincing in embarrassment and shooting Axel a scowl. Quickpaw teased her with a yap, which received a snarl in response.

"Easy, Arwie. Who's the bruiser you have, Ragnar?"

"Harangoth."

Axel whistled.

"Wow. You must be feeding him bone and gristle to get him that big."

"He came from a good breeder. He's friendly – I know he doesn't look it that much."

"He'd rip me in two, by the looks of it."

Axel opened his mouth to continue the conversation but was interrupted by the sight of the front ranks padding forwards, following Alpha McVarn's ictharr at a steady walking pace. The crowd began to shift, waving goodbye to the many wolves that came to bid them farewell.

"Well, looks like it's time to go. Come on, Arwie."

Still sulking, Arwenin rolled her eyes and began to follow the crowd. Quickpaw looked up at his rider, giving a growl as if to ask for his approval to proceed. He was eager to follow his new friend.

That same feeling came back to Corsair – that momentary defiance he felt the night before. The temptation to abandon the Krosguard and stay at home was overwhelming, burning inside of him, causing him to look back towards the saddened smile of his mother.

"Corsair?" Ragnar said.

Then the moment was gone.

"Huh?"

"The crowd's going."

Quickpaw whimpered again, gazing after Arwenin. Shaking himself from his doldrums, Corsair snapped at the reins.

"*Hyah!*"

Without hesitation, Quickpaw shot after the crowd. Harangoth followed him rather more slowly. Corsair waved goodbye to his mother, making eye contact with her for one last time before the stone arch of the gate blocked his vision and he was forced to look forward.

Before him lay a lone trail in the snow, the group of Krosguard hopefuls padding along it while murmuring to one another. He could see woods further along the path they were following, several hundred metres away, and knew it would be at least a few minutes before they trudged underneath its canopy.

He caught up to Axel, drawing beside him.

"For a moment I thought you changed your mind. Glad to see we still have you with us."

"Just saying bye to Mum," Corsair said as Ragnar joined them.

Quickpaw overtook Arwenin by a few steps, putting himself in her vision, but she grumbled and looked away.

"Come on, give her some space," Corsair said. "She's not in the mood."

Giving a disgruntled growl of agreement, Quickpaw retreated a few steps before maintaining a steady trudging speed, hanging his head and grumbling to himself.

"She'll be brighter tomorrow," Axel said. "I'll find her a chew toy tonight and then she won't be so grumpy."

They rode on in silence for a minute. Corsair looked over his shoulder and watched as Grand Wolf Plains shrank with every step, knowing that he was putting distance between himself and home.

We'll be fine. We'll be fine.

"We're not annoying you by riding beside you, are we?" Ragnar asked.

"You kidding? I'm riding alongside Ragnar *and* Corsair, both heirs to the Winter Baron's helm and top sports fighters. I am the furthest from annoyed right now."

"Quickpaw kind of imposed," Corsair said.

"Doesn't bother me. He was just being friendly. Besides, I'm not going to be bored for the whole trip now, am I?"

The two Sedrids nodded.

"So... what's the reason for your sudden change from tournaments?"

The true reason behind the sudden change of setting for the brothers was eager to throw itself out of Corsair's mouth but he restrained it and put another excuse in its place.

"Needed a change of pace. Bit nervous, though."

"So you chose war?" Axel frowned.

Corsair stammered. Ragnar swooped in.

"We're the Winter Baron's sons. We have a duty."

"Suppose you're not wrong. I don't know what it's like to be a prince, right?"

Corsair saw Ragnar smile at him from behind Axel, a way of trying to calm the younger wolf down. Corsair smiled back, looking away.

"God, sometimes I wish we lived somewhere warmer," Axel said, pulling his clothes tighter around him.

"I like the cold," Corsair said.

"Same here," Ragnar said.

"You two do?"

"Well, not all of it, but it's nice."

"Nothing can beat some warm sun. I went to the Land of the Sun and Moon once. Once you feel the sun on your fur you never want to go back. Isn't that right, Arwie?"

A grumble.

"Right. Forgot you were in a mood today."

Axel shook his head and looked at Corsair.

"One day these guys love you to death. Other days they act like they couldn't care less. Unless you have food."

"I was about to say that."

"Does Quickpaw love eating meat?"

"Well, ictharrs are carnivores," Ragnar laughed. "It'd be weird if he didn't, right?"

Axel faltered but composed himself.

"R-right, yeah, that makes sense. I just meant like what kind?"

"He enjoys maug the most."

"Arwie is exactly the same. And she gets really sleepy afterwards."

"So does Quickpaw," Corsair said.

Axel chuckled, turning to face Ragnar.

"Let me guess with Harangoth. Maug meat? Sleepy afterwards?"

"To the letter," Ragnar said.

He laughed.

"Was Arwie secretly a triplet or something?"

The trio chuckled. Corsair appreciated Axel's laid-back attitude. It was pleasant to have someone with a friendly nature to ride beside in the cold of the territory, the conditions made only more vicious by the harsh attitudes of the soldiers around them. With one sweeping glance of the warriors riding ahead, he saw that many were older than him. They were possibly in their thirties and forties, all veterans of past conflicts and engagements, with a variety of scars and wounds as trophies.

Corsair looked back at Axel and saw someone akin to him and Ragnar in personality, youth and vitality. If he were older it couldn't have been by any more than five years.

"You brought a lot of bags with you," Ragnar commented.

"I'm more bags than wolf, yeah," Axel chuckled. "It's 50 per cent of the job."

"The other 50 per cent?"

"Carrying the bags."

"It sounds hard."

"Being an apothecary? God, yeah, it can be. Still – it's something I'm good at. I think, anyway."

"That's worrying for an apothecary to say," Corsair said.

"Trust me, you're safe in my paws... probably."

"Did you say 'probably'?"

"Maybe. Maybe not. Got no choice but to trust me, right?"

Corsair chuckled. Ragnar looked ahead at the wolves before him.

"What is it?" Axel asked.

"Some of these wolves are huge."

"Oh, I know. I'm kind of surprised their ictharrs can carry them. Don't feel intimidated, though. Most of them are nice people."

"Most of them?" Corsair asked.

"Well, not *all* of them. But what matters is they're on our side and not against us. They're tough."

"They look like it. Are you friends with any of them?"

"Some people I know from the army came to the drive with me. None made it in though. McVarn was pretty serious about training."

Corsair nodded. He noticed that the woods were growing closer and closer, not as far away as he anticipated, and they would be within the maze of trees in seconds. The snow-topped woodland loomed over them, beckoning them. He was somewhat unnerved.

"It'll be a long ride," Axel said. "Good thing you guys like the snow 'cause we'll be seeing a lot of that and little else."

"It shouldn't be too bad," Ragnar said. "Right, Corsair?"

"No, it shouldn't."

He already felt homesick. He looked over his shoulder again and saw the diorama of Grand Wolf Plains in the distance, with tiny specks walking back and forth on the walls and watchtowers. Quickpaw continued forwards, causing the size to keep decreasing, and Corsair knew there was no going back.

We'll be fine.

He faced forwards, rolled his shoulders, and followed the group into the woods.

CHAPTER EIGHT

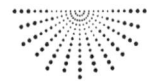

*I*t was a laborious trek.

The journey wasn't a problem for the ictharrs and Corsair knew it especially wasn't a problem for Quickpaw. As rider and beast, the duo had both endured long runs through the woods and even longer training sessions during the day. This was no shock to them.

But, unlike the adrenaline rush of weaving between the trees and making sharp turns every few metres, it was boring.

An hour had passed by. Conversation died between all members of the group, leaving the herd with only the sound of snow crunching beneath the ictharrs' paws. A trail of pawprints stretched out behind them for miles, the snowfall too light to conceal them quickly.

He glanced to his left. He was greeted by a view of the trees for the hundredth time, mounds of snow holding position at the bases. Woodland creatures peered out at him from their nests and burrows, wary of the ictharrs that plodded past.

He glanced right. Axel and Ragnar were focused on the road ahead, Arwenin and Harangoth puffing out clouds of mist with every few steps. Corsair scratched Quickpaw between the ears.

"Shouldn't be too far now. You're doing well."

Quickpaw gave a growl of appreciation, turning his head to look back at his master.

"Eyes forward. We don't want to get close to falling off another cliff."

Corsair looked ahead to gauge how much further they had to travel and was relieved to see that he was approaching a town. Through the tree trunks, he caught a glimpse of a stone wall, most likely the perimeter defence of a settlement.

"Finally," Axel sighed.

They pushed forwards and spotted their destination. At the end of the path cutting through the forest, wide enough for a single-file convoy of carriages to drive along, was a settlement at the top of a hill. Some huts and houses ran around the perimeter of the village, smoke puffing up from chimneys, and Corsair could see a single stone church spire rising up into the sky.

"This is Ignatius' Mount!" Alpha McVarn yelled from the front. "No need to stare at it so hard – you'll get sick of this place after a month!"

The group reached the top of the mount, arriving by a gate monitored by two Krosguard soldiers in suits of armour. They stood with longswords sheathed and shields standing upright by their hind paws. Both had the metal visors of their helmets raised, allowing Corsair to spot the singular red scar-like streak of paint across their right eye.

They continued into the town, crossing the vast paved courtyard before the church. Many more riders were already present in the town, candidates from other cities and settlements. Many buildings and homesteads were dotted around the settlement, villagers walking back and forth, but the town lacked the numerous taverns and markets of Grand Wolf Plains.

"Dismount!" Alpha McVarn yelled. "Form a line against the church wall, now!"

Everyone dismounted from their saddles and Corsair followed suit, throwing one leg over before dropping down and taking hold of the reins in one paw. He hurried over to the wall, bringing Quickpaw in beside him, and was thankful that Ragnar and Axel took position on either side. Arwenin made eye contact with Quickpaw. He yapped. She grumbled and shook her head before looking away.

"*Lieutenant is present!*" a soldier yelled.

All the nearby Krosguard soldiers stood upright and faced forwards, forming a line before the trainees. This sight silenced any nervous murmuring that circulated the recruits, causing them to all look left.

The lieutenant wore a suit of armour, standard among the soldiers, but his helmet was tucked under his arm. His fur was grey, the same shade as the stone on which they were standing but silvering around the snout with age, and he possessed a stern face identical to Alpha Tiberius. One red streak cut across his cruel right eye.

Behind him trailed a sight that caused the ictharrs, all except Harangoth, to whimper and lower their gazes.

Around the corner crept a gargantuan ictharr, its fur as black as coal and with multiple gashes and scars left on its flanks like a wound trophy case. One harsh eye glared at the line of beasts as it padded after its master, its legs mangled and scarred horribly. It followed the lieutenant to his position before the line of recruits, snarling at them and baring its fangs. It stopped beside the lieutenant.

"Introduce yourself already, Lieutenant," Alpha McVarn said, glaring at him.

He merely grunted, his gaze sweeping across the faces of the wolves. Moments of silence passed before he came forwards and began to walk parallel to the line, inspecting every recruit present.

He stopped in front of Ragnar.

"Ragnar Sedrid?"

"Yes, Sir."

He nodded, murmuring to himself. Moving along, he stopped in front of Corsair. Corsair's ears flattened and tail curled but he forced himself not to look away.

"Corsair Sedrid?"

"Corsair Sedrid, Sir."

"And this?"

He gestured to Quickpaw, who shrank away from him.

"Quickpaw, Sir."

He shook his head and chuckled. Corsair looked confused.

"Is... is there something wrong, Sir?"

"I'm wondering how this mess passed selection."

Quickpaw winced. Corsair peered over the lieutenant's shoulder, trying to make eye contact with the alpha for help, but Alpha McVarn didn't intervene.

"He's good, Sir."

"He looks like he'll be eaten up and spat out by an adeun."

Some of the soldiers chuckled. Quickpaw whimpered but Corsair nudged him with his hind paw, telling him to stop.

"I'd bet 100 Iggregoms that he wouldn't last a day."

"I, uh... think he will, Sir."

"Move along, Lieutenant," Alpha McVarn said, staring.

The lieutenant grumbled and continued down the line. Quickpaw whimpered again, looking at his master with a saddened look accompanied by lowered ears. Corsair consoled him.

"Don't worry about him, all right? You'll be fine. I'm here."

Harangoth gave a low growl, trying to reassure his friend. Quickpaw responded with a mewl. Arwenin sympathised with him, trying to make eye contact from where she was, but he refused to look up.

"Pay him no mind," Axel said. "He's just vindictive and miserable."

Corsair looked forwards as the lieutenant returned to the front, standing beside his ictharr.

"My name is Maximus Verschelden," the grey wolf said. "I'm the lieutenant of the Krosguard. You are going to address me as 'Sir' from now on, is that clear?"

"Yes, Sir," the line chorused.

"You will be training here for a month. If you are falling behind, if you don't display the values we want from someone working in the Krosguard, if you're late, you go home. No second chances. Is that clear?"

"Yes, Sir."

"I will lead your training every day, which will be overseen by Alpha McVarn. Thornfang will make sure your ictharrs stay in line and don't dare step over it."

She growled, snarled, and then bared her fangs. The ictharrs shrank away from her again as they caught sight of her teeth, chiselled and cut down so the front curves formed serrated blades inside her maw. Corsair stroked Quickpaw on the side of his head, staring at the brute.

"Your training will end with a finale where you will demonstrate your ability to serve to an audience of your family and friends, out here in the courtyard. Most of you won't even make it – that's a guarantee. If you want to do us a favour and lighten the load, pack up your things and go home. No one is stopping you, is that clear?"

"Yes, Sir."

"The Krosguard is the greatest fighting force Vos Draemar knows and, most likely, has ever known. We're very selective about who we pick and I can already see who won't last a day. You know who you are and you're out of your depth."

He held his gaze over Corsair for a few seconds longer than anyone else.

"Training starts tomorrow morning. If you're smart and know your limits, you'll leave tonight."

Lieutenant Maximus turned to face his superior.

"How many do we have, Lieutenant?" Alpha McVarn asked.

"One hundred, Alpha."

"Divide them into 10 barracks, with one of them in the church attic. Let them have the first day to rest."

"You heard him – divide into groups of 10, now!"

Immediately, the line broke apart. Wolves turned to unite with those they knew, others gesturing for the lonely to come and join their group. Corsair moved towards his brother, Quickpaw behind him, and Axel followed. A group of other wolves joined, bringing the total to ten.

"Your ictharrs will spend the night in the stables," Lieutenant Maximus announced. "It's your job to clean and feed them regularly. If your little sweetheart flops over dead because you forgot to feed her last night, then that's your problem and you're out. Soldiers, get them to the stables."

The soldiers watching stepped forwards and began to guide the groups towards the stables. Corsair could feel Quickpaw was reluctant to move away from him, whimpering and grumbling.

"Hey, it's okay. I'll come down and check on you regularly. I'll see if I can take you on walks as well."

Harangoth nudged one of Quickpaw's legs to get his attention. He gave a deep growl of encouragement. Quickpaw hesitated but, prompted by another growl, stood upright to impress his master.

"No time to daydream, come on!"

The soldier waved them through, guiding them down the side of the church wall. Corsair led Quickpaw forward, walking behind Axel and Ragnar.

"Where do you think you're going?"

Lieutenant Maximus stepped out in front of him, arms crossed over his chest. Thornfang padded over to his side, glaring at Quickpaw. Ragnar and Harangoth turned to stop but were forced to keep moving by a soldier, leaving his brother alone to face the lieutenant.

"You're coming across to me as pretty stupid for a prince."

"What?"

"I said people who don't belong here should go."

Corsair froze.

"Are you going to answer me?"

"B-but... Sir, you haven't given me a chance-"

"I don't need to give you a chance to know you won't get far. Just because you're a prince doesn't mean I wouldn't kick you out of here if I could. You and your brother get no privileges."

"But..."

Aware that Alpha McVarn was still in the courtyard, he leant in and growled.

"And I also heard about that impressive trick back at the capital where you beat McVarn. Some people seem to think it's because of your experience in the arena but I don't think so. He's not a tough fight. He's an old timer. You're not special."

"You didn't say anything to my brother."

"Your brother has an actual ictharr with him."

"Quickpaw is just as much an ictharr as Harangoth."

Thornfang snarled, baring her serrated fangs. With a yelp of panic, Quickpaw frantically tugged on the reins, whimpering and whining. Lieutenant Maximus grinned.

"I wouldn't be so sure, Sedrid."

Before Corsair could answer, Alpha McVarn stormed over.

"Lieutenant, leave him alone," Alpha McVarn said. "You've had your fun."

Lieutenant Maximus chuckled to himself before turning and walking away, Thornfang in tow. Corsair watched them leave. Quickpaw whimpered, almost trying to hide behind his master.

"Let's get your ictharr to the stables," Alpha McVarn said. "Then we'll get you to your dormitory."

"Here you go."

Corsair peered through the doorway as Alpha McVarn held the door open, stepping into the room. He had been led to the dormitory above the church hall, an attic converted into quarters for the soldiers. Ten beds were pressed lengthways against the walls, five on each side, forming a decent-sized aisle between them. The wolves already escorted up there had the benefit of first choice, picking the cleanest beds and leaving the final bunk in the right corner free for him to take.

"Have a good day of rest, son. Training starts early tomorrow and will continue for the rest of the month."

The door shut behind the prince, leaving him with the other nine wolves in the room. Everyone, apart from one wolf who was frantically packing her things, glanced in his direction. For a moment, all eyes were on him, before they disregarded the prince and returned to unpacking. Thankful, he made his way to the back of the attic, looking up to peer through the skylight. It was covered by a blanket of snow, leaving nothing but an eternally white view.

"Corsair."

He looked down to see Ragnar place a paw on his shoulder.

"Are you all right? Did he..."

"I'm fine, I'm okay."

"If he laid a paw on you, you tell me right now. Did he?"

"No, Ragnee, he didn't. He scared Quickpaw to death with that... Thornmouth thing."

"They should really put a disclaimer out when you join," Axel said, not looking up from his unpacking. "Lieutenant Maximus clearly isn't the person you want to have a heart-to-heart with. Especially not with his hell-spawn Thornfang around."

"She's terrifying."

"How someone can have an ictharr that big is beyond me," Ragnar said. "She's bigger than Harangoth."

Corsair dumped his bag on the last available bed. It was adjacent to Axel's, across the aisle from his, and Ragnar's was directly in front. The older Sedrid unpacked his things like everyone else, folding his clothes and arranging them on the bed.

"So... do you know a lot about Maximus?" Ragnar asked.

"Not a lot. I got a glimpse of him once a few years ago and nothing more. I kind of forgot he existed until I saw him again today."

"Lieutenant Maximus is insane."

The three wolves turned to see a brown-furred veteran facing them. A panicked face met their gazes, belonging to the trainee he'd seen packing her things. Her belongings were stowed away in bags and placed at the base of the bed.

"Insane seems to be the right word," Ragnar said.

"The wolf's a *criminal*," she said. "I've heard that he only got into the army as punishment for killing someone."

"Who?" Corsair asked.

"I don't know."

"How do you know this?" Axel asked.

"People talk. The soldiers told me. I served alongside him during the war in Clan Silverclaw. That thing he rides? It tore those cats apart in Venada. Someone told me it only takes one bite from those teeth and then you're in two pieces."

"And, after all that, he's a lieutenant in the Krosguard? I don't believe that," Ragnar scoffed.

"You don't believe they'd put a killer in charge of killers? Fine. Be stupid. It's your safety on the line. I'm out of here."

"Whoa, let's relax here," Axel said. "Seems a bit drastic when it's only the first day."

"He's called the Butcher of Tomskon for a reason, okay? He *massacred* those cats. After all the screaming, there was nothing left of them. He's not someone you want to be messing with. If you idiots want to stay here, fine, but I'm gone. I know better. I'm not training alongside that lunatic!"

Without another word, she grabbed her things and rushed out of the barracks. All the trainees watched as she barrelled through the door and slammed it behind her. They exchanged disturbed expressions with their counterparts, unsure as to whether staying was a good idea. Ragnar faced Corsair.

"If you want to leave, I'll come with you. I saw him giving you a hard time. If you don't feel safe we can go."

Corsair was confronted with another momentary lapse. He didn't want to be trained by a criminal. He didn't feel safe. It wasn't like they'd stop him leaving – they wanted him to go. They would leave later that night and not have to think about it anymore.

But then the consequences reintroduced themselves. Condescension. Mockery. Emotional attacks from all sides.

Or worse.

"No. I can do it."

"Are you sure?"

"I'm sure. He was trying to scare me, get inside my head. It's something they do, right? Try to weed out the weak from the strong?"

Ragnar hesitated before giving in.

"Okay. The moment something goes wrong, though, we're going. I don't care about the consequences."

Corsair nodded, turning to look at Axel.

"That thing can't really bite people into two, can it?"

"A maug? Sure. An ictharr? No way in hell. She's paranoid. Those fangs are just for show."

Axel didn't look too sure himself.

Quickpaw stood in his stall within the stables, peering down at the snow-covered concrete beneath him.

Dusk had fallen over the town of Ignatius' Mount. His master had come to visit him an hour before he turned in for the night, rubbing his side and scratching the backs of his ears. He enjoyed the moments he had with him before he left, promising to see him first thing in the morning.

Now he waited.

The ictharrs in the neighbouring stalls gazed out into aisle, growling and yapping to one another in excited conversation. Many were hardened beasts of war, with scars and wounds decorating their flanks and faces. Some were missing teeth, others had lost ears, and a few had shortened tails. The sight made his tail wilt.

Harangoth was in the stall next to him. He stood in silence, blinking every so often when snow got in his eyes, waiting to be told to go to sleep. Quickpaw stared at his friend in admiration of his unyielding courage.

Quickpaw puffed out air and looked across the aisle. Arwenin was in the opposite stall, looking towards him, tilting her head to the side as she made eye contact. When he recognised her, he yapped.

She didn't respond, tilting her head in the opposite direction, and he opened his maw again when the ictharrs on the left side of the stables fell into silence. The only sound he could hear from that direction was paws crunching through the snow.

He leant out and looked left.

The shadowy hulk stalked the aisle, sending out a shockwave with every step, throwing nearby ictharrs into panic as they tried to retreat into the back walls of their stalls. Quickpaw heard Arwenin whimper and bow her head behind the stall door, hiding from sight.

Before he could do anything, Thornfang stopped in front of his stall. She turned her head, her body still facing towards the end of the walkway, and gave a low growl. Quickpaw tried to step back from her but could go no further, forced to stay in the presence of the beast. Others peeked out from their own stalls, watching the confrontation.

She stopped growling and puffed out air into his face. He flinched, shaking his head in response, watching as the behemoth pulled just ahead so her rear stopped before the door.

He tilted his head as her tail stood up.

He was struck across the snout twice by the tail in alternating directions, making him flinch and shake his head again. The other ictharrs yapped and growled, belittling the runt. Arwenin peeked up over her door, furious eyes glaring at Thornfang.

Satisfied with the humiliation, the proud ictharr continued on her patrol. Harangoth peered out to check how his friend was, offering a growl of sympathy. Quickpaw gave a sad answer before retiring, lowering himself down behind the door and closing his eyes.

CHAPTER NINE

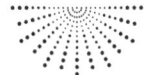

"*R*ise and shine, recruits!"

Corsair's eyes shot open, body taut from the shock of hearing the booming voice. Others in the dormitory hurried out of bed, throwing their covers back and standing to listen to the officer.

"I said *rise and shine*, Sedrid!"

Realising that he was being addressed, he reached for the sheets. He was too disoriented to notice that he was dangerously close to the edge of the bed and found his paw closing on air. He felt himself lurch over the side and yelped as he plummeted to the floorboards, scrambling up to his hind paws with his sheets still draping from his shoulders. A few snickers came from his counterparts, accompanied by Axel covering his eyes with one paw. The officer looked less than amused.

"For the Winter Baron's son, I expected a more self-aware wolf."

"Sorry, Sir."

The officer turned to address the dormitory.

"Training starts in 10 minutes. Lieutenant Maximus doesn't like wolves who are late, so you'd better get dressed and head down to the stables."

The wolves stared at him.

"Did I stutter? Get dressed, now!"

None of the training cohort hesitated to turn and dive underneath their beds, rummaging around for the sets of clothes that were given out the night before. Corsair shrugged off the lethargic grip of the sheets, threw them back into a heap on the bed, and reached underneath. He felt his paw close on the fabric of his clothes and dragged them out, turning.

Axel met his gaze and smirked.

"You're not that good at this whole 'first impression' thing, are you?"

"Shut up."

"Next group, get your ictharrs and head to the courtyard!"

Corsair entered the stables with his group, walking down the aisles of the stables in search of his companion. Other wolves bustled past him, muttering 'watch it' as they did so, but he ignored them.

This is the one.

Marching down the aisle, he looked to his right and analysed the faces of the ictharrs as he passed. His eyes scanned face after face until he came across Quickpaw.

His steed sat within his stall, body facing towards the door, but his head was hung. His ears were down and tail curled as he waited.

"Hey."

Quickpaw looked up and, within a fraction of a second, changed his attitude completely. Leaping up on to all four paws, he tried to push through the door as if it weren't there and barked, leaning his head out and licking him across the face.

"Ugh, come on," Corsair muttered, wiping away the slobber. "Now I'm going to stink for the rest of the day."

Ignoring his annoyed tone, Quickpaw yapped again and shifted from paw to paw.

"You're really excited to see me this morning. Was everything all right?"

He removed the latch from the door and pulled it open. Quickpaw padded out and turned to face his master, giving a playful growl.

"We can't go on a run right now. We need to go to the courtyard."

Begging, Quickpaw whimpered and pushed his snout towards his face. Corsair leant out of his reach and placed his paws on either side of his snout, holding him back.

"Not right now. I promise we'll have a walk in my free time, okay?"

If I even get any free time.

Corsair reached for Quickpaw's harness, saddle and reins from the hook fixed to the frame of his stable. Years of experience allowed him to tack up his steed within two minutes, securing and reviewing every strap and buckle. Steering him out of the stables with his helmet tucked under arm, he led him to the courtyard. A line of wolves and their companions formed by the church wall, one that he joined immediately when he spotted Lieutenant Maximus beside Alpha McVarn. Thornfang stood a few metres before him, scanning back and forth across the line.

Minutes passed and the rest of the training cohort arrived, congregating by the wall. He could see Ragnar was one of the first at the far end of the line while Axel was towards the opposite, Arwenin standing by his side.

He noticed that the line was shorter than the previous day.

The lieutenant turned to face them.

"Welcome to your first day of training. I can already see we've had some of our trainees make it easy on themselves and leave early. If any of you still feel like this isn't for you," he went on, gesturing to the wide-open gate on the opposite side of the courtyard, "then no one's stopping you. You'd be doing me a favour."

Silence. Some wolves looked down the line to see if anyone would leave, glancing left and right. Corsair stared straight ahead.

I'm not going. I'm not even going to be tempted.

"Well, seeing as you all think you've got guts, let's start training. Mount your ictharrs."

All turned to hop into their saddles. Corsair did the same, pulling himself up on to Quickpaw's back, and straightened himself in time to see Lieutenant Maximus mount Thornfang. The horrid beast trained her gaze on the line. Alpha McVarn and two subordinates mounted their own ictharrs and sped away through the gates, taking a right down a path and disappearing.

"Follow me," Lieutenant Maximus said. "Don't fall behind. If you get lost, I'm not coming to find you."

They rode along for 10 minutes, following the same path McVarn and his entourage had, when Thornfang came to a stop and turned. The lieutenant didn't need to say anything – the front rank followed a few metres behind the beast, their steeds refusing to go any closer, and then backed away a few when they saw her turn on them. Even the guards who rode beside him flinched in anticipation.

"We're starting with a race."

He gestured behind him and Corsair gripped the reins harder.

Along the left side of the snowy path cut into the trees ahead was a slope, steeper than the one south of Grand Wolf Plains. Trees, both fallen and upright, dotted the hillside. At the bottom it met the road, not too far away from their destination, but was separated from the mount's base by an abyss.

"Navigating in dangerous terrain is an important skill to master if you want to be considered one of us. We'll send you off in groups of 10 – follow the path all the way down to the clearing where the alpha is and stop there. If you're feeling lucky, try your own route, but no one will come to find you if you get lost on the way or fall down into that pit."

The lieutenant, without another word, turned and led Thornfang away from the front of the group. One of the soldiers pointed to the front line.

"You 10, you're up!"

Corsair scanned the group's faces as he saw them approach the impromptu starting line and was thankful that he didn't see Ragnar or Axel amongst them. He looked about him – he was at the back of the group, separated from those he knew, and he began to ease Quickpaw through the ranks to look for his sibling.

"Corsair, what are you doing?"

He looked right to see Axel there, atop Arwenin.

"Have you seen Ragnee?"

"Ragnar?"

"Yeah, Ragnar?"

"He's in the second row, I think. I thought you were eager to get up to the front."

"Not a chance in hell."

"Just stick to the right of the path and you'll be fine. We have to get it done, right?"

He hesitated. This was insane. He was going to risk death to evade his father's scolding? No way. He knew this wasn't right – he felt obliged to quit and return home. His brother would agree with his reasoning and follow him back.

But he couldn't face that scowl.

"I need to find Ragnee."

"I'll follow."

He nodded and directed Quickpaw past the ictharrs, listening to the nervous and excited murmurs of the Krosguard trainees. He glanced left and right, leading his steed forwards to the front, when he saw his brother within the first line on the right side.

"Ragnee?"

His brother looked over his shoulder and Harangoth glanced behind him, nodding to Quickpaw.

"We need to do this together," Ragnar said. "I don't care if we come in last place – I'm not letting you near that hill."

"You think I want to go near it?"

He opened his mouth to speak but saw movement in his peripherals, turning his head. The guard stepped forward, pointing to the front line.

"You 10, get ready."

"No," Lieutenant Maximus said, riding forwards. "Switch these two out. Sedrid and I will go instead – we'll see how they do against Thornfang."

The riders within the first line shot nervous looks to one another, with only a minority grinning at the idea of a challenge. Ragnar brought Harangoth forwards, giving his brother a reassuring nod.

"Not you. *Corsair* Sedrid."

Corsair's ears stood to attention.

"What?"

"You heard me. Join the line. You're in the next race."

"But, Sir, I only came forward to-"

"In line, Sedrid, now."

Thornfang growled, glaring at Quickpaw. Corsair felt his steed back away. Intimidated by the menacing gaze of his superior, he looked to his brother for assistance. Ragnar opened his mouth.

"Sir-"

"If I wanted both brothers, I'd have asked for both brothers. I want the younger Sedrid on this race, not you. If I hear anything else out of either of you, you're both going home. *Got it?*"

Driven by fear of the disgrace of being sent home, Corsair reluctantly directed Quickpaw to the starting line. Quickpaw dug his paws into the snow and refused, whimpering.

"We have to. Please, Quickpaw. Be strong for me."

Quickpaw looked to Harangoth for aid, whining. The black ictharr nuzzled him and growled, telling him to be safe. Corsair made eye contact with Ragnar.

"Stick to the right," Ragnar said. "Stay safe. Forget about winning."

Thornfang snarled, urging the latest additions to hurry up.

Surrendering and giving the lieutenant a wide berth, Quickpaw padded over to the starting line and waited.

Okay, stay calm. Stay calm.

"Nothing to worry about. It's a normal race, Quickpaw. It's just a normal race."

"Get ready!" the Krosguard soldier yelled.

All 10 ictharrs leaned down on their front legs, ready to propel themselves forward and down the road. Corsair blinked away the snow as he clutched the reins, his paws beginning to hurt.

"Go!"

"*Hyah!*"

All 10 riders snapped at the reins and the ictharrs barked in response, shooting off down the road. Quickpaw bounded forwards and his rider directed him, glancing left frequently to see how close his competition was. The snow bombarded his face, constantly getting in his eyes. He cursed under his breath and furiously wiped them.

"Left!"

Quickpaw dug his paws into the snow and skidded to a halt, turning and shooting off again down the mount. He cut in front of one rider and forced him to manoeuvre away from him, the snow kicked up behind Quickpaw blinding the rider momentarily. A quick glance at the competition to his left and he knew that he was starting to create distance between him and the other riders.

We're in the lead.

And then, following the *snap* of jaws closing on air, he felt Quickpaw fall away from him.

Yelling out, he was flung forwards and landed on his side in the snow. He rolled and rolled until he came to an eventual stop against the bank on the side of the road, covered in white specks and left with soaked clothes. He scrambled to his hind paws to see Thornfang shoot past him, now leading the charge amongst the group as they hurtled down the road.

Quickpaw.

"Are you all right?" he yelled, rushing back towards his steed.

Quickpaw eased himself up, shaking his coat and flinging snow through the air. Corsair stopped short of the barrage.

"Did Thornfang try to bite you?"

Quickpaw confirmed it with a growl. A second-long inspection told Corsair that the beast had fortunately failed to injure him.

"Okay, we haven't got a lot of time. We have to catch up with them. Come on!"

He pulled himself back on to the saddle and snapped the reins, propelling his reluctant ictharr down the path and around the turn. After a few seconds he pulled back on the reins and came to a stop.

The group was hundreds of metres ahead, almost at the next turn. There was no chance he could close the gap in time, considering that he had been barely pulling ahead from them.

He'd be in last place.

I'll get kicked out. I could get kicked out.

He felt his paw move to the left side of his neck.

I can't go back. I can't get kicked out.

Then he saw the slope.

No, I can't. It's too dangerous. I could fall and die.

But his fear made him reconsider the idea of irrational behaviour. He could travel close to the left and cut a few metres off his route. At least he'd have a greater chance of intercepting someone if he tried that instead of running the whole course.

"Forward, Quickpaw."

He directed his companion towards the left side and he wasn't surprised to feel Quickpaw refusing to move.

"Please – if I lose, I get thrown out. I can't go back to Dad like that. I need to make it in."

Quickpaw whimpered.

"I'll keep us safe. It's just to cut a few corners. Trust me."

Quickpaw hesitated, looking back to the top of the slope, before agreeing to the dangerous plan. With a snap of the reins, he took off along the left side of the road, taking his master in the direction of the group.

"Come on, faster! We can catch up!"

Quickpaw grunted and pounded across the snow, weaving past trees as Corsair yanked the reins left and right.

"Keep going, you're doing great!"

They continued to travel this close to the top of the slope for minutes more, darting back and forth between the trees, leaping over fallen trunks and evading the standing monuments. Corsair felt that he was gaining on one of them, clinging to the idea that he wouldn't finish last if they maintained their pace.

"Come on!"

And then he saw it.

A formidable bulge in the snow lay ahead, cutting across his path as they moved left to evade an incoming tree. He saw it rushing towards them, about to strike Quickpaw's legs, and he realised that he was half a metre away from tumbling down the slope.

"*Stop!*"

There was nothing he could do.

With a yelp, Quickpaw tripped over the fallen obstacle and flung his rider from his saddle. Corsair yelled out as he flew from his seat, landing in the snow and rolling, before he felt his body lurch over the edge. He tried to grab on to something, anything, flailing with his arms, but felt only snow under his paws as he clawed at the ground.

With a scream and a terrified howl, both Corsair and Quickpaw tumbled over the brink and down the slope.

"*Oh God oh God oh God!*"

Corsair slid down the slope on his back, speeding towards the ravine at the base. Quickpaw was metres to his left, desperately trying to slow himself down by rapidly clawing at the hill, but it did nothing.

"*Help! Someone help!*"

His voice echoed across the plains and down the mount but he knew that, even if someone heard him, it was too late. The gap was too wide for him to attempt to jump – only Quickpaw's legs would be strong enough to cross that distance.

Looking left, he saw his companion in a fit of pure terror. Yelping and yowling, whimpering and howling, the ictharr was unable to stop himself sliding towards his death.

"Move towards me!"

No response other than terrified yelps and howls.

"*Quickpaw!*"

He couldn't be reasoned with.

I can't die I can't die I can't die–

Time was running out. With nothing to stop himself from hurtling to his death, Corsair began to copy his companion and try to grab on to anything he could while moving. Nothing was close enough to aid him, all the trees too far away to be grabbed.

"*Ragnee!*"

He turned back to face his doom and saw it – a single fallen tree lay before him, pointing diagonally towards Quickpaw's route. It was right in his path.

If I grab it I'll get trapped there and Quickpaw will still die–

Then it came to him through his panicked thoughts. If he timed it just right, he could run across the fallen trunk and jump on to Quickpaw as he travelled.

I could miss I could miss I could miss–

There was no time to think of the consequences. It was this or die.

Angling himself towards the log, he prepared to leap for his life. The trunk drew closer and closer, his one chance of saving them.

It arrived.

With the momentum he had gained, he almost fell flat on his face when his hind paws hit the tree trunk. He stumbled but maintained his speed, rushing towards the end, looking left to see Quickpaw approaching.

He leapt.

For a moment, he thought he had overshot the jump. His eyes

went wide and he anticipated the pain he would feel when he plummeted into the abyss and struck the hard ground at high velocity, shattering every bone in his body.

But he didn't.

He landed on Quickpaw on his side, yelling out as he did so. With adrenaline helping him ignore the pain, he hurried into a sitting position and snatched up the reins. He had a second to look up at his impending doom, his ictharr still panicking.

The chasm was metres away and closing.

Do something!

"Leap!"

The command drew Quickpaw out from his bout of hysteria and, knowing it was his last chance of survival, he jumped. Time slowed as the wolf looked down into the ravine. They sailed over it, Corsair's eyes wide and mouth hanging open in an endless scream of terror.

Then he felt Quickpaw land on the opposite side.

Still driven erratic by adrenaline, Quickpaw dashed down the road. Corsair snapped at the reins, trying to speed them away from the ravine, panting with tongue hanging out from the corner of his mouth.

They rounded the corner and he saw them.

Alpha McVarn stood beside his ictharr, a few Krosguard soldiers standing behind him with the first racing group resting behind them. All turned to see Corsair and Quickpaw speed towards them, yelling as they threw themselves out the way.

"Halt!" Alpha McVarn yelled.

Corsair yanked on the reins and Quickpaw skidded to a stop before the alpha. The beast was panting, plumes of his misty breath pushing out from his gaping maw, while Corsair blinked at the reality that he was still alive.

"You almost trampled us, son."

"I... I made it."

"You did, son. First place. Impressive."

He marvelled at the fact he was alive, raking breaths in and out, before he realised what the alpha said.

"Wait... wait, first place?"

"First place, son. No mistake."

"But..."

Hearing rapid crunching through the snow, he looked over his shoulder to see Thornfang dart around the corner. She powered towards the destination before her eyes fell upon Quickpaw, causing her to skid to a halt. Others raced around the corner and spotted the halted rider, yanking back on their reins.

"*What?*"

Lieutenant Maximus dropped down from Thornfang and stormed towards Corsair, eyes trained on him.

"How did you overtake us? How?"

"I-"

"*Answer me*, Sedrid!"

"Lieutenant, you calm yourself down *right now*," Alpha McVarn growled.

Lieutenant Maximus stood there, fury brewing behind his harsh eyes. Corsair continued to pant, meeting his glare.

He made me do that. He tried to make me come last and that made that happen. I almost died.

But, as the lieutenant stormed back to Thornfang, he found that his anger was diluted by the relief of still being able to draw breath and not lying dead at the bottom of the ravine. It was his idiocy that almost brought about his demise, regardless of the lieutenant's cruelty. As he dismounted, he staggered from the shock of the victory against death and turned to face Quickpaw.

"We're... alive."

A moment of stunned silence passed before Corsair became the first to fall. He groaned in shock before he tipped backwards and collapsed in the snow, sprawled out across the ground with eyes shut. The ictharr wobbled, groaned, and then flopped on to his side beside his rider.

CHAPTER TEN

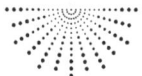

"*L*et me get this straight," Axel said. "You raced against the lieutenant of the Krosguard, fell off Quickpaw because Thornfang tried to bite him, tried to catch up by riding next to the top of the hill, fell and slid down the hill towards your death, leapt off a fallen log, landed on Quickpaw, told him to jump across, took a *massive* shortcut because of that, and won the race."

"Kind of."

"And then fainted?"

"Yeah."

Axel blinked, astonished.

"You're... going to need to give me a few minutes on that one."

Hours after the first session of training, the lieutenant finally permitted them a measly 20-minute break back at the settlement. They all had traipsed back to the town of Ignatius' Mount, the marginally smaller group splitting up to spend their precious time on different activities. Corsair and Axel found themselves in the stables among numerous others, feeding their exhausted ictharrs.

"I'm still trying to come to terms with what happened."

"Understandable. It's not every day you barely escape plummeting to your death, is it?"

"I guess not."

"Does anyone else know?"

"No. I haven't told anyone other than you. Ragnee would kill me."

Corsair turned his head back to look into Quickpaw's stable. The beast lay on his front, tearing through a bowl of meat like he hadn't eaten in years.

"You're enjoying that."

Quickpaw lifted his head from the bowl, small morsels of meat attached to the fur around his maw. He grunted and turned his nose up at his master, pushing the bowl around so he didn't have to face him. Axel whistled.

"Someone's got a bit of attitude today."

"He's not that happy with me."

"Can you blame him? What you did almost killed both you, as hard as it is to believe it actually happened on your first day."

"I don't think it would have been any less of a spectacle if it happened a week later, Axel."

"What you did was stupid. Let's be honest. It was a race – you didn't need to kill yourself over it."

"I didn't want to get kicked out. You saw what happened to everyone who came last."

"I value my life over this, Corsair. This isn't worth dying for."

"So why are you here?"

"I'm an apothecary – I'm trying to stop others from dying for something that isn't worth it."

And that's what made him freeze in another moment of sudden defiance.

He's right. I'm putting my life on the line for... what? Dad's approval? I'm going to fight a war just so I can hear him say, 'Well done,' and pat me on the back? No – I'm done. I'm not going out there for just because he says. I'm 20. I'm an adult. I make my own decisions.

But then it died as quickly as it had been born. He didn't answer, watching his steed eat his meal, happy that they had both made it out of the situation alive. As he shifted his position ever so slightly, a dull pain bloomed from his left side and he winced, placing a paw over it. A large bruise had formed where he had taken the brunt of the landing. Despite that, he couldn't complain – he was lucky even to have lived, let alone get out without any serious injuries.

"So... you missing the tournament life yet?"

Corsair considered telling the truth about his thoughts of being in the Krosguard but, after a moment, decided against it.

"The Krosguard life isn't so bad."

"Apart from sliding down death hills?"

"We could miss that part, yeah."

"You know, I gotta ask. Did you ever lose? In your tournaments?"

Corsair took a moment, thinking.

"Uh... I lost quite a bit in jousting and mounted fighting tournaments. Ragnar and Harangoth were always the better out of us two on that. I never lost a race and never lost at all with sword fighting. Oh, actually... I think I lost once."

"Only once? Bragger."

"Shut up," Corsair chuckled. "Seriously, only one. It was against a doberman. Someone from the United Hound Dominions. I was 15 and...I think he was around 25. Can't remember."

"*Fifteen?* Seems like a bit of an age gap to me."

"I was good enough to fight in that age group. Like I said, I only ever lost to him in a longsword tournament. No one else."

"Impressive. I consider myself to be quite the fighter, too."

"You do?"

"Yeah. I fought my trio of demon sisters a few times. I don't think my record is quite as good as yours."

"Why not?"

"I lost every time."

They both chuckled. The conversation lulled into a comfortable silence for a few moments before Axel changed the topic.

"So... anyone back at home you're missing?"

"Oh, yeah. I've got Mum and... Dad and stuff. You?"

"Same. A mother, father. Those three hellish sisters."

He looked down at his tail.

"They convinced me to do this stupid thing with my tail. It's 'family tradition', according to them. If anything, it's an excuse to torture me."

"I think it looks fine."

"Yeah. *Real* masculine, Corsair."

"Who cares about that, right? Wear what you want. You're not harming anyone."

Axel smiled, looking back at it.

"I... I suppose you're right. Thanks."

"And what about your parents? Where are they?"

"They run a library up north. My sisters moved down to the capital to live together and, like a fool, I decided to join them."

"Sounds fun."

"If you're a masochist, sure."

Corsair chuckled. Axel glanced to him.

"What about you?"

"Hmm?"

"Any friends waiting back at home for you?"

And, for the first time in a while, Corsair realised he hadn't thought about Rohesia. She was off training in the army. His ears drooped slightly, the guilt of forgetting about her settling in.

I hope you're all right.

"You drawing a blank on me?"

"No, sorry... I have a friend."

"One? For a prince, I'd thought you'd have a few more."

"I kind of do. They're not as close, though. Went our own ways."

"Right. Well, what's his or her name?"

"Rohesia."

At the mention of his friend's name, Quickpaw shot up and turned, forgetting the near-death encounter they'd undergone a few hours earlier. He approached the open stall door, tongue hanging out from mouth and panting with excitement, eyes focused on his master.

"He changed his tune," Axel said.

"He's a big fan of Rohesia. The moment she turns up both he and Harangoth run towards her like pups."

"You're kidding? Harangoth?"

"Yeah."

"I've only known your brother for a day but... his ictharr is scary. I cannot imagine him being excited about anything."

"It's a miracle. You need to see it."

"Maybe one day. You two get on well?"

"Yeah, we do. Cubhood friends."

Axel grinned. Corsair took a moment before he realised why.

"Wait-

"Hey, I didn't say anything."

"No, but I know what you're thinking. We're *just friends*."

"Sure. If it helps you sleep at night, pal, have at it."

"Shut up."

Axel laughed. Quickpaw spotted Arwenin across the aisle, facing him while seated and tilting her head in the same confused-but-amused way. Corsair stepped out in front as he went to bound across, resting a paw on the sides of his neck and holding him there.

"Easy, easy. Arwenin's tired. We all need some rest after this morning."

Quickpaw grumbled, pleading to be let out.

"Nope. Back in, come on. You haven't even finished your food yet."

Growling, Quickpaw turned and flicked him in the face with his tail.

"Hey, come on, Quickpaw!"

Axel chuckled as Quickpaw sat down and sulked in the corner of his stall, facing away from the door. Corsair cursed under his breath, shaking his head.

"He's coming and going today, isn't he?"

"When he doesn't get his way, he throws a little tantrum. Whenever I try to get him to wait in the stables, to go somewhere he doesn't want to, he complains. Sometimes he listens..."

He glanced back at Quickpaw.

"...but other times he sits down and sulks like a pup."

Quickpaw mimicked his master with growls and grunts, mocking him.

"He must have been a real terror with his breeder."

"We'll never know. He didn't come from a breeder."

"He didn't?"

"No, he was a stray."

"Stray? Where did you find him?"

Nine-year old Corsair Sedrid sulked as he sat on the step to the farmer's home, the bottom of his snout resting on both paws. The snow seemed to sympathise with him, delicately filtering down from above, but he was too upset to notice it.

His brother was infatuated with the ictharr pups rushing around in the yard, all swarming him when he entered and making feeble attempts to stand on their hind legs. He admitted they were adorable to watch run around and play but he didn't like any of them. He imagined that he would feel some sort of connection to the one he wanted. It was what everyone said about selecting his own ictharr, who would be his companion for at least 60 years.

But nothing resonated with him. They'd exhausted every farm, every breeding settlement, every market. None offered any connection.

Daddy said I'd know when I found the one I wanted. Why haven't I found one? Is something wrong with me?

He sighed. Dad would eventually force him to pick one and then he'd be stuck with it.

Rising from his seat, he traipsed down the steps and walked through the snow. The guards posted outside kept eyes on him while talking, giving him a glance every few seconds to make sure he didn't stray from sight, but they weren't worried about any danger.

He walked over to the line of ictharrs on the side of the road. The beasts were busy eating their food, heads bowed to reach into the depths of their warm bowls. Reginald was amongst them. As Corsair approached, he spotted the prince in his peripheral vision and focused his eyes on him.

"Hello, Reggie."

Reginald mewled and craned his head down, nuzzling against the prince. Corsair giggled, stroking the soft fur around his neck, before he stepped back and let him go on eating.

When he went to stroke an ictharr, he always had to look up. They towered over him. Even while sitting, they had a significant height advantage over the small cub.

One day I'll be as big as them.

Then he heard it.

He whipped around and scanned the trees.

Nothing.

Then he heard it again.

What?

Even though he was among armed soldiers and brave ictharrs, he felt scared. He looked toward Reginald to see if had heard the noise but he was happily munching away, distracted and oblivious. He took a step back and wondered if he should report the noise to one of the guards, have them search the trees for any sign of danger.

He turned and took a step towards them before he heard it a third time and finally knew what he was hearing.

A whimper.

It was a distressed sound, as if the source of the noise was calling for help. Corsair felt torn, unsure whether he wanted to bring the issue to the guards at the risk of them disregarding it and returning him inside.

He looked back.

A wolf could be in danger!

Making sure the guards weren't looking and the ictharrs were preoccupied, he hurried over to the trees as fast as his small legs would carry him. Stepping over a fallen branch, he crunched into the snowy woods and scanned the area ahead. Nothing but the warped forms of the trees leered back at him. His ears flattened and he whimpered, taking a step back.

Then he heard the call for help again.

I can't leave them.

Defying his fear, he pushed on into the woods. The sound got louder with every step he took, causing him to question his choice every time, but the cub was brave. He picked up a twig from the ground and, glancing left and right, he prepared himself to swat away any terrors that might attack him,.

He was so apprehensive that he forgot to look at the ground and tripped over the snow-covered root of a tree, yelling out as he fell. He dropped the twig and threw his arms out to break his fall, grunting as he did so. Moaning and with tears in his eyes, the cub pushed himself back up with a cold and soaked front.

Mummy is going to be so angry.

He decided, finally, to retreat. There was no point in going on. The fall that had got his clothes soaked deprived of him of whatever weak determination he possessed to keep going.

But then he heard a growl to his right.

He whipped around and stepped back, eyes wide and ears standing, before he realised that he was staring at an ictharr pup. It was curled up by the base of a tree. Its fur was white, tangled and knotted over its frail body, a pair of terrified purple eyes staring at him while it bared its tiny fangs.

"A puppy?"

He took a step forward and the ictharr snarled, pulling its mouth back further. He noticed that a large splotch of crimson stained the white fur over its left hind leg. Corsair trembled, unsure if he wanted to move closer, and contemplated going back to tell the soldiers.

It could run away if I go. It's hurt – it needs help.

"I-I'm not going to hurt you, o-okay? Please don't hurt me."

Corsair took a step forward and the ictharr growled but he could see that it was now hiding its fangs. He still felt its eyes fixed on him, watching for any indication that he was going to harm it. He made sure to not make any sudden moves.

His small heart thudding away, he knelt down in front of the ictharr. He met its gaze, seeing fear in its eyes, and then looked down to the wound on its leg. Blood stained the fur around the laceration, more crimson trickling from it, and he noticed a trail of red droplets stretching back into the woods.

"You walked a long way."

Corsair moved a paw towards the ictharr and it growled again, making him withdraw it.

"You're hurt – I-I need to take you to Daddy. He'll help you get better."

He reached forward again and the ictharr growled.

"Please. If I don't take you to Daddy, you might die. I don't want you to die – I want to help you."

He tried a third time and, despite a barely-audible growl, the ictharr didn't react. It watched as he reached for him with both paws and prepared to lift him into his arms, drawing breath in and out.

"I-I'm going to lift you, okay? Don't bite me, please. Don't bite me."

The ictharr continued to stare. With a flinch of anticipation, Corsair lifted the pup up and turned, rushing back towards the house. He could feel the blood oozing from the wound wetting his thin chest but he didn't care – his mind was focused on running at a good speed yet being careful not to jostle the ictharr enough to make it bite him.

He arrived in front of the house and raced towards the doors.

One of the guards glanced at him and saw a pup in his arms, stepping away from his counterpart.

"Master Corsair!"

The wolf threw open the door and rushed into the hallway, darting through to the living room. He could hear the voices of his parents negotiating with the breeder. Ragnar was still out in the yard playing with the pups.

"Winter Baron, I can assure you, I am the best breeder in the clan. When people of high standard like yourself come to me, I will never sell an ictharr unless they know it's right for them. Your son will find his companion right here – guaranteed."

"I hope so. We've been travelling from town to town for days. I have work to get back to and Ophelia is getting exhausted from these visits."

"Arthur, I am telling you, I'm..."

"Daddy, Mummy!"

Corsair darted into the room, holding the wounded pup in his arms.

"Corsair, darling, what's wrong?" she said as they all rose.

"I found this ictharr pup out in the woods! He's really hurt!"

"Pass him to Mr Gregentop," his father said with urgency in his voice.

Mr Gregentop took the pup from him, making sure to not upset the beast, and took him into the back room. Minutes later, after many yaps and yowls of pain, the breeder walked back out with the ictharr in his arms, bundled up in blankets and with bandaging wrapped tightly over the wound on its leg.

"It was a nasty cut across his leg, most likely from a sharp branch or a bad fall. He must have become separated from his mother somehow. He's very tired but you did the right thing bringing him here, Master Corsair. I don't know if he would have lasted another night out alone in the woods."

Corsair smiled as his mother patted him on his head, drawing him in close.

"What will happen to him now?" his father asked.

"I will notify my colleagues and see if any of them would be interested in passing him on to someone else or raising him themselves."

And then Corsair felt his eyes sting. The idea of leaving that pup for someone else tugged at his heart. He felt bound to it, somehow. It was as if his encounter in the woods had captivated him. His ears drooped and he stepped forward, pulling out of his mother's embrace and pointing to the white ictharr.

"Daddy, can I have him?"

"Oh, I don't think so, Corsair. He's feral. He might be dangerous to have in the house."

Corsair's mouth began to tremble.

"B-but... Daddy..."

"I'm sorry, Corsair, but we need one that'll be strong and loyal."

"Arthur, dear, let's not be harsh," Ophelia said, wiping away a tear from her son's face. "We came out here to find a companion for both Ragnee and Corsair."

"We did, but one that we know won't hurt them."

"Come on, it's only up to his knee! There are plenty of breeders in Grand Wolf Plains that can help train him to be just as good as any other ictharr."

Unsure, his father looked back at his son. The wolf cub stared into his eyes pleadingly, sniffling and whimpering, hoping his father would accept.

"Mr Gregentop, you're the expert here. What do you suggest?"

"Well... Winter Baron, I understand your son is struggling to find his own steed. If he feels like this one is important to him out of the hundreds he's seen already, then I shouldn't be the one to deny him it. And I doubt he's aggressive – he was only growling and snarling because he was scared and hurt. It's a natural reaction even for bred ictharr pups."

Corsair's face lit up.

"Okay, then," his father said. "For Ragnee's choice and the pup –

how much?"

"Five-hundred Iggregoms for Master Ragnar's selection but none for Master Corsair's. I'd feel like I'd be cheating you if I made you pay for an ictharr your son discovered and rescued. Please, he's all yours, Winter Baron."

Mr Gregentop held the pup towards the Winter Baron. His father gestured to his son.

"Please, Mr Gregentop. Let my son have him."

He nodded, turning to face the prince, and knelt. He gestured for the Winter Baron and his wife to step back, unwrapping the pup from the wad of blankets.

"If he's not able to walk well, I'll pass him to you. Let's see how he is first."

Corsair stood there, eyes focused on the pup. The tiny ictharr scanned every face in the room, a low growl coming from him.

"Come, Master Corsair. He's just uncertain. Put your paw out. Let him know you're there."

The prince, anxious, nodded and knelt.

"This is safe, yes?" his mother asked.

"I'll pull him away if I think he's becoming aggressive. Right now there is no reason to be fearful, Milady."

Corsair extended one small paw and saw the pup turn, eyes focused on him.

"Hello. I'm Corsair."

The pup's growls grew in volume. Corsair's resolve faltered, drawing his paw back an inch. His mother gave a worried look to Mr Gregentop and, acknowledging her concern, he prepared to intervene.

But then, as quickly as they had grown, the growls died.

Corsair ears stood and his eyes widened, confused about the reason for the sudden change in mood. The pup was sniffing the air around him, as if he recognised him, and he felt calmer now that the growling ceased.

The pup took one step closer. He hobbled slightly, his injured leg hindering him, but he was determined. After another cautionary sniff, he took another step.

Corsair was entranced by the sluggish approach of the pup, shuffling forwards gently to close the distance. The pup kept advancing, the time between each step decreasing, and Corsair didn't dare move in case he frightened him back into growling.

He stopped right before Corsair's paw.

Corsair watched, enraptured as the pup leaned forwards and sniffed the black pads beneath his paw. The prince looked up at his mother and father, who smiled at him with nothing but love in their hearts, and then looked at Mr Gregentop. He had shuffled forwards silently behind the pup, still within range to snatch him if he grew aggressive, but the soft smile on his face told Corsair there was nothing to fear.

The prince looked back down.

A further second of silence passed. The pup sniffed his paw, making his final inspection, before he took another step forward.

He watched the pup lean in and lick his paw. He felt the small feeble tongue touch the pads, tickling almost. He gasped and looked up at his parents, who watched in amazement.

Following the lick, the ictharr then pushed the side of his head up against his paw and mewled. Corsair giggled and gently placed his second paw on his tiny side, feeling his frail heart patter away.

"Well, it's safe to say that he likes you, Master Corsair," Mr Gregentop said, standing. "I recommend that you have him weaned by a breeder in the capital while he's growing but, other than that, he should be all yours. Winter Baron, would you like to come through with me and confirm our transaction?"

"I would be happy to."

"I'll stay with Corsair, dear," his mother said.

His father strolled out of the living room with the breeder while his mother sat down and watched the pup with her son. Corsair continued to stare, thankful for his encounter in the woods, and knew that the ictharr in front of him was the one he had been looking for.

CHAPTER ELEVEN

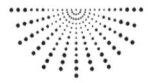

"*Y*ou saved his life," Axel said. "He should be more thankful."

"It's a mutual thing. I've saved his life, he's saved mine."

"Like sliding down a death hill?"

"Team effort."

Corsair noticed something move in his peripheral vision and turned his head, Axel following his gaze. At the end of the aisle stood a Krosguard soldier.

"Training starts again in a couple of minutes! Move to the court-yard and line up against the church wall!"

"Welp, break time's over," Axel said, turning to face Arwenin. "Come on, Arwie."

Standing, she padded out from her stall as her master shut the door behind her. Axel looked over his shoulder as he walked ahead, leading his steed by the reins.

"You coming?"

"I'll be with you in a second."

He turned to look back at Quickpaw as the apothecary walked

on. The white ictharr had been peeking over his shoulder before his master turned to face him, making the beast grumble and look away.

"I know you're angry with me, Quickpaw, I know. We have training now, though, and as much as you don't want to do it, we have to."

Quickpaw refused.

"I'll take you on a really nice walk tonight."

Intrigued, he looked over his shoulder with one long ear standing. He gave a cautionary growl in response, asking a question.

"No, we won't go near any more hills."

Quickpaw looked away again, grumbling, before he gave in and turned around. Corsair stepped back to allow his steed room to exit before shutting the door behind him and taking his reins.

"You ready?"

He grunted.

"Come on, then. Let's go."

Minutes later, Corsair found himself among the cohort against the church wall, standing beside Axel and Arwenin. He couldn't see his brother in the crowd no matter how hard he searched the vicinity and he abandoned his efforts when he saw Alpha McVarn and Lieutenant Maximus, accompanied by a growling Thornfang, walk out in front of him. Behind the leadership stood a group of Krosguard soldiers beside a large war drum. It was played by a lupine adorned with red streaks across his body and face, dressed in nothing but trousers and hind-paw socks.

"Welcome back to training," Alpha McVarn said. "I'm sure that 20-minute break was enough for you to all recover from this morning's work. You've probably noticed that your numbers have dwindled a bit since you returned. If you maintain your high standards during training, you'll have nothing to worry about. Any questions?"

No one raised a paw.

"Lieutenant Maximus, they're all yours."

The alpha of the Krosguard retreated a few steps, watching on with numerous onlookers by his side. All eyes, however, were focused on Thornfang as she drew nearer.

"Races are a rare luxury around here," Lieutenant Maximus said. "We won't be kicking out as many people as we did today but don't slack. Clear?"

"Yes, Sir," the recruits chorused.

"Good."

Lieutenant Maximus turned and climbed on Thornfang, shifting in his saddle.

"Each of you will be fighting against me."

Immediately, nervous murmurs passed around the cohort, some wolves turning to exchange anxious gazes with their counterparts. They fell silent as the lieutenant looked to his superior, following his gaze to where the alpha was pointing.

For a terrifying moment, Corsair thought Alpha McVarn was pointing at him.

Then he saw Axel's shocked expression.

"Me, Alpha?"

"You, son. Come out here and fight the lieutenant."

He froze. All the other recruits looked his way, both surprise and relief upon their faces. Axel stared at Thornfang.

After that terrified moment, Axel collected himself and rolled his shoulders back. He looked to Corsair.

"Wish me luck."

"Be careful, Axel."

With a calm and collected demeanour, Axel readied himself and stepped forwards.

The next moment, Arwenin contradicted his fearless attitude.

Corsair jumped as he heard Arwenin frantically scramble back away from the direction Axel was pulling, shaking her head. Pleading yelps of fear came from her as she thrashed against the apothecary's pull, eyes focused on the snarling beast waiting for her.

"Hey, Arwie, what the hell? Come on, we haven't got time for this!"

Everyone but Corsair took a step back, only highlighting the struggle Axel was having with his steed. Quickpaw watched his friend try her best to resist fighting Thornfang, desperate to rush to her aid. Axel tried to position himself in front of her gaze.

"Please, Arwie, we can't be doing this."

"What's the problem, Auryon?" the lieutenant called with a smirk. "Busy braiding your tail?"

The onlooking soldiers laughed.

"Just... having some difficulty! Give me a second, Sir!"

"I don't think we have a lot of time to spare. We have a tight schedule."

"I hear you, Sir, just one moment!"

Arwenin sat down and Corsair knew, at that point, Axel had lost. He tugged and pulled, furiously trying to bring her into the court-yard, but she wouldn't budge. Abandoning his physical efforts, he began to reason with her, stroking the side of her neck as he whispered comforting words.

"I don't think you have good control over your ictharr there, Auryon."

"One moment, Sir!"

"Son, reel in your ictharr," Alpha McVarn said.

"She's nervous, that's all, Alpha!"

Driven to do something by the sight of his friend so terrified and panicked, Quickpaw darted out of the crowd. Corsair's grip on the reins had loosened while he was distracted by the ruckus and he turned to see his companion diving out into the open.

"Quickpaw, hey!"

He rushed out after him and found himself exposed. Quickpaw stood metres away from Thornfang, growling and with paws spread out in a fighting stance. Corsair stopped by his steed's side, looking over at the terrifying ictharr.

He made eye contact with Lieutenant Maximus and felt his ears flatten when he saw that excited expression on his face.

"Sedrid," he said, grinning. "How noble of you to volunteer."

A few of the soldiers chuckled, arms folded across their chests, but Alpha McVarn remained stern and unimpressed.

"N-no, I wasn't..."

"That was an order, Sedrid. Defying a superior will get you removed from the course."

"Alpha, let me fight!" Ragnar yelled. "I volunteer!"

"Shut it, Sedrid. Wait your turn."

Corsair looked at Quickpaw. His companion was glaring at Thornfang, a glimpse of his fangs showing. He cursed his bravery. Feeling his heart race, he climbed on his ictharr and prepared himself for combat.

"Swords!" the lieutenant yelled.

Two Krosguard soldiers rushed forward bearing swords with dulled blades and blunt tips. One of the soldiers stopped by his side and passed him his weapon.

"You don't have a chance in hell," she muttered.

She walked off, happy with herself, and Corsair clenched his paw around the grip of the sword. Lieutenant Maximus swung his blade through the air, pointing it at his opponent.

"Begin when the drum sounds!" Alpha McVarn yelled.

No one moved.

Corsair stared at the lieutenant.

The Butcher of Tomskon stared back.

Then the single low *thud* of the drum sounded.

"*Begin!*"

Without warning, Quickpaw shot forwards as if he had no rider in his saddle. Corsair almost fell off backwards from the shock of the sudden movement, rebalancing as he rushed towards Thornfang and the lieutenant.

"Quickpaw, stop!"

He didn't listen to his commands. He lunged for Thornfang, swinging a large paw at her face.

"Back!"

The Butcher of Tomskon yanked her back out of the way of the swing. Quickpaw came forwards again and frantically tried to hit Thornfang, missing swing after swing and bite after bite. Corsair looked up to see a flash of steel and threw his sword in the way, feeling a blade strike his own. He was unable to coordinate a counter-attack, distracted and thrown off-balance constantly by Quickpaw. In a desperate attempt to defend himself, he swung wildly at his opponent, trying to get him to back away.

The Butcher of Tomskon didn't attack again, a grin on his face as he watched the prince flail about in panic.

"Quickpaw, come on!" Corsair yelled.

Quickpaw didn't listen. Corsair yanked on the reins with one paw but he refused to obey, ignoring the command and advancing on Thornfang again. She merely observed the attempts to hit her as if she had better things to do.

Then the Butcher of Tomskon struck.

He swiped at Corsair and hit him in the side of his head with the broadside of the sword. Corsair yelped and felt himself lurch over one side. He reached for the saddle but was unable to do so as Quickpaw darted away from him, lost in his battle against Thornfang. World spinning and ears ringing, the wolf grunted as he landed in the snow and rolled through the mounds.

He came back to his senses. He looked up to see Quickpaw looking back, distracted from the paw about to hit him directly in the face.

"*Watch out!*"

Quickpaw turned before Thornfang swiped him hard across the snout, knocking him down with astonishing strength. He landed on his side and yelped, scrambling to get back up on to all fours, but Thornfang rested her two front paws on his side and pinned him there. He struggled, eyes wide and yelping in terror, trying to wriggle free from her grip.

"Get off him!"

Thornfang craned her head down to Quickpaw and opened her maw wide, displaying the sharpened fangs ready to tear through flesh.

"No!"

To his relief, she was not intent on killing Quickpaw.

But what she did instead was no less terrifying.

She unleashed a hellish roar into Quickpaw's ears, her open serrated maw held inches from the side of his head. He struggled and writhed, whimpering in panic, all his courage driven from him.

"Back."

The Butcher of Tomskon drew back on the reins and eased Thornfang off him, allowing the white ictharr to shoot up to his paws and rush over to Corsair. Due to his sheer terror, he tripped over his own front legs and fell forwards on to his face, summoning a groan from many and a chuckle from some. Finally, Quickpaw arrived by Corsair and threw himself down into the snow, covering his face with his paws.

"That's enough," Alpha McVarn told the soldiers. "Lieutenant, get him up and back in line."

Corsair continued to lie there, still somewhat dazed from the blow, and saw Thornfang pad over to him. She stopped a metre away, allowing Lieutenant Maximus to drop down from his saddle.

The prince looked up.

The lieutenant knelt.

"You don't belong here, Sedrid. I'm the alpha around here, you understand? Me. Not McVarn, me. Learn your place. Don't try to show me up again or I will tear you and that *thing* into enough pieces to send everyone in Grand Wolf Plains a souvenir."

"Lieutenant, that's enough!"

Lieutenant Maximus, reprimanded by his superior, immediately offered a paw and helped Corsair to his hind paws. The lieutenant glared at him, reinforcing his message, before gesturing for him to return to the line.

Corsair Sedrid, tail between legs, did as he was told.

CHAPTER TWELVE

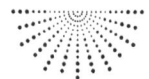

*I*n the grand nave of the small church, the two princes sat in the middle of the pews. Corsair's head was down and his eyes were focused on the backrest of the bench before him, his brother's paw rested on his back. Silence filled the air and nothing stirred, everyone in their dormitory having retreated to their beds for the night.

Corsair sighed and rubbed his face.

"I don't know what he was thinking."

"I don't either, Corsair. It was brave."

"I don't care if it was brave. I'm out. Tomorrow morning I'll wake up, head down to the courtyard, and then that's it. McVarn will tell me to pack my things and I'll see that... *stupid*... grin on Maximus' face. And now you're leaving too because of me."

"I'm doing it because I want to. You're never a burden."

"But this wouldn't have happened if... God, all he had to do was stand there and wait and we wouldn't have been picked."

He paused, reconsidering what he said.

"I mean... I know Axel was in trouble and I feel like a coward for standing there and watching but... I could have done something else other than have Quickpaw drag us both out there to get humiliated."

"You were like everyone else he fought. You all lost. You're no different."

"I'm going to have to explain this all to Dad, Ragnee. He'll give me that annoyed scowl he always gives me and then he'll ask me why I'm back, even though he can guess why, and force me to answer. He'll know it's because of Quickpaw and then..."

Corsair shook his head.

"We can't go back, Ragnee."

"I know Dad's been rough-"

"*Rough?* I almost died."

"Trust me, I know. But we just need to be cal-"

"I can't calm down, all right? I can't stop thinking about what'll happen when I get sent home because *stupid* Quickpaw decided to be a hero and get us both beaten up!"

The ancient wooden door of the church creaked open and Corsair looked over his shoulder. He found his impending doom there, staring at the two Sedrids as it shut the door, taking a step down the aisle before stopping.

"Ragnar, I'd like to speak to your brother for a moment," Alpha McVarn said.

Corsair looked back to his brother. Ragnar nodded at the alpha before patting his sibling on the back and standing.

"You'll be fine."

He turned and walked towards the stairs. Corsair watched him walk out of the pew and down the side aisle, turning left and climbing the staircase. After three steps he was out of sight.

"May I sit, son?"

"Of course, Alpha."

He slid over to allow his superior access into the row. The black wolf stepped inside and sat down, groaning with relief as he leant back.

Not a word was uttered.

Corsair waited for the verdict to be delivered, to be told he was no longer wanted in the ranks of the Krosguard. McVarn never spoke. He kept staring ahead in thought, helmet resting on his lap.

Corsair decided to get it over with.

"Alpha-"

"It's been a long day, hasn't it?"

Corsair frowned.

"Uh... yes, Alpha."

"It's not easy."

"No, Alpha."

He sighed and turned his head, meeting Corsair's eyes.

"You know, son... I don't like to boast... but I feel I am a good judge of character. Trust me, when you get to my age and you've been doing this for 30 years, you start to really know the characters that come through selection. You get the jokers, the aggressors, the overconfident – you get a wide range of people."

Corsair didn't interrupt.

"I was impressed by your training today. After the race this morning, your expertise with the sword shone through during those exercises, and it matched the skill you displayed when you kicked my sorry behind out of the capital."

Corsair chuckled.

"Then came this afternoon."

He let that hang in the air.

"I don't want to force you to dwell on what happened because I'm sure you're not proud of it. I won't focus on the details. It's your ictharr, Quickpaw."

"Yes, Alpha?"

"I won't lie to you, son. When I saw that starting group yesterday, I saw *beasts*. I saw ictharrs that would die beside their masters and defend the Clan of the Great Lupine until they had no blood left to shed. I saw riders who would command their companions and they wouldn't hesitate to follow orders. But when I saw you there..."

He paused with maw open, trying to phrase his words correctly.

"It didn't seem like you fitted in. Not you, specifically, but Quick-paw. He may be an adult now but all I can see is a pup out of his depth, son. I don't see a warrior in him like you do."

"He does listen to me Alpha."

"I'm sure he does when you're out on a walk or going for a ride. All ictharrs listen to their riders after they've got attached. He clearly loves you, son, but..."

He stopped.

"You remember what I told you back in Grand Wolf Plains? After you embarrassed me?"

This isn't a game. This isn't a tournament fight where losing means you miss the chance to get another engraving on your sword. Losing in war means your brother will have to bury you.

"Yes, Alpha."

"This applies here. This isn't a tournament fight. Sure, when you're out and about he's obedient, but how can we both be sure that when there's people dying around you and arrows flying, he'll be able to stay calm and listen to you?"

"I... I know him, Alpha."

"And you can tell me, while looking me dead in the eye, that you know he won't panic out there?"

Corsair didn't answer.

"You know, we have plenty of ictharrs without riders. If you feel like you'd do better-"

"No!"

Corsair froze, seeing the unimpressed look on the alpha's face.

"I mean... no, Alpha. I'll see to Quickpaw. I'll make sure this never happens again."

The stern look faded, forgiving the outburst.

"Tell me why you're here, son."

"What, Alpha?"

"Tell me the reason you're here, in the Krosguard, giving up the comfortable life of both the Winter Baron's son and a champion fighter."

Corsair opened his mouth to answer. The words refused to come out.

"Did your father send you?"

"I..."

He couldn't answer.

"Look, son, I don't have to be up at this hour doing this. I could be asleep right now and I could kick you out in the morning. At least make the effort worth it and tell me why you're here."

Corsair didn't speak for a moment before he stammered out a response.

"I'm just... stressed out, Alpha."

"Let's not be vague, son. Tell me."

"Honestly, Alpha, I'm..."

"Just stressed out? You really want me to believe that?"

He was caught by the alpha and he knew it. McVarn's stern expression showed it all – he was not biting.

Finally, Corsair spoke.

"I want to do my father proud, Alpha. I want to do the clan proud. I don't want to be a disappointment to them both by getting sent back."

Relieved, he saw Alpha McVarn's expression soften.

"You don't want to disappoint him."

"No, Alpha."

"I can see that, son. And I know being the Winter Baron's son isn't the easiest thing in the world – many things aren't. Feeling an obligation to do well on the behalf of someone you look up to can be both a relief and beyond stressful."

"It is, Alpha."

McVarn nodded.

"Son, I've made mistakes in these kinds of situations. It's inevitable, given the amount of time I've been doing this. I've sent away wolves that would have served this clan to their dying breath and I've allowed wolves to continue and sent them to their death. This time, son, I want you to choose."

He stood, taking a step out of the pew.

"You're free to leave tonight, as always. I understand if you and your brother decide to leave and return home. If you think you're able to carry on, though... I'll be seeing you tomorrow morning."

Corsair didn't answer.

"Regardless, I've had a word with Lieutenant Maximus and asked him to restrain himself."

"I understand, Alpha. It's just-"

"He's a piece of shit?"

Corsair laughed.

"I... I guess, Alpha."

"I don't like him any more than you do... but it's beyond my power. Killers make good soldiers, I suppose."

He turned to leave.

He turned back.

"But while I don't like him, I like you. Out of some of those self-righteous veterans who have their snouts up their own backsides, and even in comparison to some of the soldiers already in the Krosguard, you seem like the most tolerable. Up until now, anyway."

Corsair gave a small smile.

"Thank you, Alpha."

"I have a duty to the clan and the Krosguard, son. If something like this happens again and you are unable to control your ictharr, you're gone. There'll be no other chances, no opportunity to get a new ictharr, no pleading. Being a prince doesn't change anything. Understood?"

"Yes, Alpha."

It was a chilly night, to say the least.

Corsair drew his cloak around him tighter, trying to shut out the snowy bombardment, but shivered with every step. The warmth of the church kept calling him back, its temptation growing as he got further away, but he couldn't abandon Quickpaw. He needed to comfort him after the terrifying experience they had both had. He needed to be there for him.

He'd be there for me.

The snow crunched beneath every step, leaving a trail of small pawprints leading to the church door. His black pads felt cold, numb, and he wondered if the snow was starting to get through his hind-paw socks.

Hopefully Axel's feeling okay back in the attic.

There had been a moment of fear from the apothecary. He confronted it well, but Corsair sympathised with him. Being singled out to fight two monsters was not an engagement anyone wanted to be a part of.

He took a left, walking by the perimeter wall. The gates were closed and some guards were walking back and forth along the walkway, the orange auras of their lanterns like floating dots in the darkness.

I'd hate to be on patrol at this time.

He stopped.

His ears stood.

Was that... laughter?

He could hear casual conversation emanating from a hut farther down the pathway, the door wide open with light pouring out from within. Checking behind him, Corsair eased his way towards it, making sure not to alert whoever was in there by stamping through the snow.

"It's the first day and already 10 of them have gone," someone said.

"You're doing a pretty good job of terrifying the new recruits," another one said. "You must be enjoying yourself."

"It's easy. Like you said – it's only been a day. I wouldn't be surprised if we had no one left to send to Pothole Plains."

Corsair recognised that voice.

Maximus.

"Your turn, Gregor."

A momentary silence hovered between them, followed by the sound of dice clattering on wood. One of them groaned.

"This game is rigged," the other complained.

"You're the idiot placing Iggregoms on it," Maximus said. "Should have thought of that, shouldn't you?"

"You asked me to play."

"Shut up, Levin," Gregor said. "I got a fair roll."

"Knowing you two, this dice is weighted."

"You cashing in next turn or what?" Maximus asked.

"Yeah, whatever."

Another moment of silence. Corsair waited, straining his ears for any more information.

"Wow," Levin said. "You really want that money, huh?"

"I'm on a winning streak," Maximus said. "Win the fights, win the games."

"Nah. You got lucky in those matches – *especially* against Sedrid," Gregor said.

"He's pretty terrible for a sports fighter, let alone a prince," Levin said.

"I couldn't care less. Sports fighter or not, prince or not, he's learnt his place."

"How did he even cut in front of you?"

"The idiot probably slid down the hill and jumped the gap or something. He definitely didn't come past me."

"I'm surprised the thing he rides can even walk, let alone run."

Another roll of the dice.

"Cough up," Maximus said.

"Sure, whatever," Gregor said, followed by the clattering of metal coins against wood. "You think he'll last through training?"

"Who? The idiot or the mutt he rides?"

"Both."

Maximus scoffed. "He might last another day. Maybe two. After that? He'll get kicked out."

"You think he's leaving tonight after what happened?"

"No. That idiot McVarn has a soft spot for the runt. He's not going to be kicked out."

"You know, I got to ask," Levin said, "is there an actual reason you don't like him?"

"At first? Just didn't like him. But when he crossed me and came first? Then I had an even bigger issue."

"Seriously? That's it?" Gregor asked.

"Do you want me to fly off into some monologue?"

"No, but... come on. You make the trainees cry and piss their beds but that's standard. You do that with everyone. But I can tell you *especially* hate his guts."

"I hate most of their guts. They walk in here thinking they own the place 'cause they fought in a war or killed someone. Very cute."

"But Sedrid specifically?"

"Look, idiots, I came here to play a game and forget about stupid McVarn being too soft on them and telling me to calm it down with Sedrid. I have my reasons for hating him and his stupid pet that he brought with him."

"But nothing..."

"If he was smart he would go home with his brother tonight. If he had anything up in that thick skull of his he would go home. If he was *half* the wolf he thinks he is, he'd go home. But he won't. I know he won't because he's got his snout up his arse from being the Winter Baron's son. I could beat him any day, with or without Thornfang, and I'll make him hurt so bad from training that him and his twiggy ictharr will have to crawl all the way home. Now shut your maws and paw your coins over already, I haven't forgotten."

"Whatever you say," Gregor said. "God. You ever relax?"

"Shut up."

Their chatter returned to silence before Levin began talking about another subject, steering the conversation away from Corsair. The prince stood there, astounded by how viciously the lieutenant spoke of him, before creeping around the back of the hut and towards the stables.

...

Corsair walked down the stables, passing the loud snores and grunts of the dozing ictharrs in their pens. He glanced down at the sleeping forms in the stalls, lost in their dreams, until he found him.

Quickpaw lay in his stall, eyes half-open and with a defeated expression on his face. His ears hung down and his tail lay limp. He looked up at the silhouette above and realised it was his master.

"Hey."

With a soft growl of sadness, Quickpaw turned his head to look away.

Corsair kept his green eyes on him, feeling his own ears flop down at the sight of the downtrodden and ashamed ictharr. Undoing the latch to the door, he pulled it open and stepped inside, shutting it behind him before sitting.

Quickpaw turned his head back and gave a confused growl.

"Don't worry, I'm not angry. You're not in trouble."

He reached forwards to pat his companion on the head and Quickpaw obliged. He gave a low growl, one of apology, and the wolf smiled.

"I know, I know. You were brave. I was a coward."

The ictharr felt slightly more chipper, inching over to his master to be closer.

"Why did you do it, though? To save Axel?"

Quickpaw responded with another growl and jerked his head towards the door.

"You... did it for the door?"

Annoyed, Quickpaw shook his head and did it again. Corsair tried to think of what he could be referring to, looking down at the wooden floorboards in thought, before he realised.

Arwenin.

He remembered her terrified expression and wide orange eyes, struggling as if she was fighting for dear life.

"You didn't want her fighting Thornfang, did you?"

Quickpaw growled in agreement.

"I'm sure she'll be really appreciative tomorrow. Well done."

As he continued to pat his head, comforting Quickpaw as he mewled along, he realised that he still had a choice to make.

Stay or leave.

When he knew what possible fate was coming to him after that fiasco, a part of him had been overjoyed. It would have been an excuse to be sent home. He wouldn't have to face Lieutenant Maximus's cruelty. He wouldn't have to prepare to rush into a bloody war. He'd be back at home.

But, within seconds, that idea quickly receded.

He knew leaving would only have him enrolled into the army instead, and it would lead him back to his father. Back to the annoyed scowl. Back to the patronising attitude. Back to the questions and the disappointment and the shame.

He moved his left paw over the left side of his neck.

I can't go back.

But was staying an option?

Looking into Quickpaw's purple eyes, he didn't see a warrior. He saw his best friend. He saw the pup he rescued in the forest. He saw the pup that edged towards him in Mr Gregentop's home. He saw one of the only things he could rely on. He didn't see a killer.

He could die.

He wouldn't be able to bear seeing him die out in the battlefield, slain by a blade or arrow, crying out in pain as life fled from him. There was the chance he would panic. There was the chance he would charge forwards to defend Arwenin and throw them both into peril.

But I can't go back.

He knew that, if he stayed another day, he'd have to face Maximus again.

He's got his snout up his arse from being the Winter Baron's son.
He doesn't belong here.

I could beat him any day, with or without Thornfang, and I'll make him hurt so bad from training that him and his twiggy ictharr will have to crawl all the way home.

Corsair wanted to leave. He wanted to go back home and leave the terrifying lieutenant to toy with the others who stayed on. He wanted to spare him and his brother the torment for the remaining part of the month.

But he knew the lieutenant would win.

Leaving would mean seeing his father again and knowing that Lieutenant Maximus was sneering about it to his friends miles away, satisfied with his victory.

And he'd be leaving Axel alone.

He could be the next target.

Corsair looked back at Quickpaw.

"I know that the last thing you want to do after today is face them again. Part of me wants to just go home and forget about Maximus."

Quickpaw tilted his head, ears standing.

"But I can't let him chase me out of here. Even if it would let us be free of him and whatever horrible thing he rides, he *won't* beat us. We'll join the Krosguard and show him and McVarn and Dad that I belong here. That *you* belong here. That we are warriors, just like them, and that we can face this war like a proper wolf and ictharr. What do you say?"

Quickpaw gave a yap in agreement. Corsair shushed him.

"Don't do that, you'll wake the others."

He leant his head down and gave a soft yap, as loud as a whisper.

Corsair smiled. "Glad to hear you're on board."

CHAPTER THIRTEEN

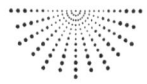

What followed Corsair's decision was a brutal month of relentless training and exhaustion. The snowfall only worsened day after day and it was excruciating when coupled with Lieutenant Maximus's ruthless regimen. Quickpaw was pushed beyond his limits, forced to ride that extra metre, urged to drag the burdening load one more step. They both wavered continuously, often tempted by the idea of surrendering to defeat and packing their bags, but they endured. Numbers dwindled around them every day, more beds and stables becoming vacant as time marched on.

And, after four weeks, they made it to the final day.

Ignatius' Mount was bustling with life in a way Corsair had never seen it before. Throughout the month, he saw lonely villagers making their way from their humble homes to the town square, meagre in comparison to Grand Wolf Plains. Life seemed bleak and tedious, with even the snowfall beginning to find itself bored, until now. Businesses flourished in the centre, selling their wares to the swarm of new arrivals. Clan flags hung high in the air, billowing in the wind, displaying the clan insignia. Wolves guided the onlookers to the many seats erected in the courtyard, offering them beverages and meals for a small price.

Corsair could hear the voices from the stables, which were a fair distance away from the centre of Ignatius' Mount. The air around him was filled with the bustle of his remaining trainee comrades, preparing their ictharrs for their final test before they became official Krosguard soldiers.

Quickpaw grumbled, irritated.

"I know, I know," he said. "When this is over, you won't have to wear that for the rest of today, all right?"

From afar, his steed could easily be mistaken for a beast of steel. Hardened steel plates covered his body; they were clasped over his lower and upper legs and stretched upwards, spreading across his body and covering the scruff of his neck. A helmet covered the top and sides of his head. Strapped around his torso was an armoured saddle, a protective layer of gerbeast leather with the odd metal plate embedded into it over vital areas. On the sides were handles and grips to hold Corsair's weapons ready for quick switching – his lance took up the space of the entire left flank while spare blades and javelins were arranged on the right.

Quickpaw whimpered, trying to scratch at his ears with his paws, but was unable to free himself from the helmet's grasp. Corsair's determination immediately evaporated at the sight of his friend in distress.

"Here, let me help."

He undid the strap beneath Quickpaw's jaw and removed the helmet, stepping back to allow him room to scratch his ears. He did so with a grin on his face, relieved of the annoying itch, and gave a yap of gratitude.

"You need to keep this on now. I'm not happy wearing all this stuff either but it's what we have to do."

Quickpaw nodded and didn't complain as his master eased the helmet back on to his head and fastened the strap again.

"All trainees – report to the courtyard in five minutes!" a voice yelled.

Corsair stepped out into the aisle and peered into Arwenin's stable, seeing Axel as he finalised the preparations. Looking left, he found his brother standing there, the hulking form of Harangoth clad in similar armour beside him. Ragnar was plated and ready to go with helmet tucked under his arm and sword slid into scabbard.

"Today's the day."

"Yeah, it is. You look like a real Krosguard soldier."

"So do you."

Corsair looked down at himself. Despite how itchy it felt, scratching against his fur and skin, it was comforting to have substantial armour over him. Interlocking steel plates covered his arms and torso, his helmet held by the rim in one paw. His legs were covered by black slacks to allow free movement, with metal plates clamped down over his shins and plated hind-paw socks over his hind paws. A white garment was draped over him, a single strip of fabric with a hole for his head and running down both his front and back from his neck to between his legs. In the centre of the tabard was the Clan of the Great Lupine's insignia – a side view of a black wolf's head thrown back in a howl.

"You ready?" Ragnar asked.

"I'm as ready as I can be."

"We've got this, all right? There's no Lieutenant Maximus, no Thornfang – just us and the others who are still here. We're better than them. *You're* better than them."

Corsair looked back into his stables, seeing Quickpaw pad out. His steed gave a growl of comfort, agreeing with his brother's words, and he smiled.

"It's been a hard month. This is the last obstacle, Corsair."

"I'm worried about Dad."

"Don't worry about Dad. Forget him. Just do your best."

"I understand. Focus on the fighting."

And forget Dad's even there.

That was easier said than done.

"All right!" a soldier yelled. "Move to the courtyard as we practised!"

"Well, that's our cue," Axel said, bringing Arwenin out from the stable by the reins. "You two ready?"

"Yeah. Let's go," Corsair said.

Reins in paw, the wolves led their ictharrs down the aisle towards the door of the stables. Axel led the way with Ragnar and Corsair walking alongside each other. Harangoth gave Quickpaw a growl of reassurance, telling him he was okay, and he returned it.

"Part of me can't believe it's been a whole month," Axel said.

"Neither can I," Ragnar said. "It feels like we've been here a year."

"More like a decade."

"Or a century."

They both chuckled and took a left at the end of the aisle, ignoring the orders of the officer to move more quickly. They passed huts and houses, navigating their way towards the tall church spire that rose above the rooftops. Corsair saw some cubs stop and point at the armoured wolves, shouting excitedly to their parents.

With every step they took, the sound from the impromptu arena grew louder. As they rounded the front of the church, every step seemed to take longer, and the distance to reach their destination felt as if it had doubled. Corsair rolled his shoulders back, exhaling to relieve the nerves, and heard Quickpaw give a concerned growl.

"I'm fine. Let's focus on doing well, okay?"

Finally, they came around to the courtyard.

In front of the gates, through which they had all traipsed a month earlier, were rows upon rows of wooden benches. The rows were tiered, climbing upwards to allow those at the back to see over the heads of those in front. Krosguard soldiers, with helmets on and metal visors down, patrolled back and forth. Vendors continued to prey on potential customers with their wares and meals, shaking a pouch at them that caused the Iggregoms inside to *clink* with every jostle.

And then, to the left, was his mother and father.

A wooden stall had been erected to the left of the benches, separated from the crowds of the village people and families of the trainees by a wooden frame and a security detail of armoured guards. His mother scanned the faces of the recruits and spotted her sons, beaming at them as she began to wave.

His father just stared.

Don't worry about him. Ignore him.

Murmurs hovered over the crowds as they joined the line, turning to face the audience. Alpha McVarn was positioned off to their right, conversing with his dreaded lieutenant, gesturing towards the stables. Lieutenant Maximus nodded and walked across the courtyard that would become Corsair's battleground soon enough.

Corsair felt Lieutenant Maximus glare at him as he walked past.

I'll prove him wrong. I'll show him we're better.

Alpha McVarn cleared his throat and stepped out into the centre. The conversations immediately ceased as the crowd saw him waiting to address them, turning their heads away from the people they were talking to.

"Hello, citizens of Ignatius' Mount, Winter Baron Arthur Sedrid and his lady, Ophelia Sedrid. I welcome you all to the final training day of the Krosguard, our prestigious cavalry that is prepared to conquer any foe it meets. Today, they will be demonstrating their mettle and prowess in trial by combat."

He turned and performed a sweeping gesture towards the remaining cohort of the Krosguard. Corsair glanced left and right to see how the month had trimmed them down – only 70 trainees remained, and he was sure they'd undergo a final cull.

"We will cycle through multiple combinations of combatants for the next two hours before we conclude our finale today. Participants will have to strike the enemy or the enemy's steed three times to claim victory. Please welcome our first combatants, Ragnar and Corsair Sedrid!"

Corsair's ears stood up. Before he could ask for him to repeat, the crowd began to applaud and the sound drowned out his voice. Quickpaw turned his head to look at Harangoth, who looked equally surprised.

"It's us two," Ragnar said. "Come on, I'll let you win."

"No, it's fine."

"Corsair-"

"Hey," one of the guards yelled, "you two are up first! Move it!"

Knowing time was limited, the brothers didn't say another word. Corsair watched as Ragnar led Harangoth out into the arena, the black ictharr casting an apologetic gaze back to Quickpaw.

"It's all right, Quickpaw. He won't hurt you and you won't hurt him. You'll both be fine."

Although hesitant, he led his companion out into the arena and stopped opposite his sibling.

"Mount your ictharrs!" a soldier yelled.

Both brothers mounted their ictharrs at the same time, shifting in their saddles to become as comfortable as possible.

"Helmets!"

Corsair pulled his helmet on, crushing his ears. It covered all of his head. The visor was up away from his face and allowed him to look out.

"Visors!"

He pushed the visor down, swinging it into place with a metallic squeak, and clicked it closed over his face. The mask gave him two ports over the eyes to peer out from and covered his snout in metal. The underside remained exposed so he could speak. He began to feel uncomfortable, ears squashed against the helm, but ignored it.

"Ready!"

A shirtless wolf, covered in red streaks and symbols, approached the war drum beside the benches. He readied his baton-like drumsticks and waited for his cue. Corsair and Ragnar both lifted their lances up and readied themselves, the older Sedrid holding both a shield and the reins in his other paw.

Quickpaw whimpered.

"It's all right," Corsair's voice sounded muffled. "You won't hurt him. He won't hurt you."

It was with that sentence that the soldier yelled.

"*Begin!*"

The drummer struck the drum, creating a slow rhythm.

"*Hyah!*" Ragnar snapped at the reins and sent Harangoth speeding towards him, lance ready to be thrust forwards.

"Away!"

Corsair yanked the reins and darted Quickpaw to the side. Ragnar's strike was sloppy and would probably have missed even if he had remained still. Corsair hurried away from his brother, making a quick turn at the opposite end, before yelling out and thrusting his lance at him. Ragnar weaved out the way and created distance between them, giving him time to switch to his sword, before he came forward and swung.

Clang.

Corsair yelped as he felt the sword strike him.

"One hit!" the soldier yelled.

Corsair drew his sword, hastily placing his lance back against Quickpaw's flank, and swung back at Ragnar. His brother made a feeble attempt to deflect the hit and it struck his arm, making him grunt.

"One hit!"

Quickpaw drew back. He and Harangoth repositioned themselves opposite one another before both riders charged. Corsair and Ragnar swung at the same time, their blades meeting in the middle with a crystal-clear *clang*. Both deflected and parried swing after swing, accompanied by the sound of blades swiping through the air and the occasional *clang* of metal striking metal. Corsair backed off, distancing himself from Ragnar. His brother pursued, lifting his sword up in an attack that a blind wolf could have seen coming.

"Duck!"

Quickpaw lowered himself to the ground, allowing Corsair to evade the swipe at his head and jab up at his brother. Ragnar grunted as the blade struck his side, leading Harangoth away from him.

"Two hits! Final warning, Ragnar!"

To make the battle seem authentic, his brother unleashed a swarm of attacks to overwhelm his brother. Each attack was equally punctuated by a pause long enough to allow Corsair to prepare for the next swing, but not so long that the others would realise he was going easy on his brother. Corsair blocked each one, yanking back on the reins and bringing his steed away. Ragnar prepared a swing, holding it back long enough so his brother could interrupt him.

"Lunge!"

Quickpaw, confronted with the idea of attacking his friend, hesitated. This lapse in determination meant Corsair couldn't interrupt his brother's swing and, instead, felt the sword knock against the side of his helmet. On reflex, he grabbed for the saddle and prevented himself falling over the side, groaning.

"Two hits! Final warning, Corsair!"

Drawing back, Corsair arrived at the opposite end of the arena and exchanged his sword for his lance. His brother, positioned at the other end, copied him and both wolves stared at each other for a moment.

Ragnar gave him a delicate nod, one only he could notice. The crowd was silent in anticipation.

Finally, they both snapped at the reins.

"*Hyah!*"

"Go!"

Yowling, both ictharrs charged towards each other, each rider aiming his lance at his opponent. Ragnar was aiming to miss, looking to career past his brother and swing around for another joust, but Corsair made sure he would strike his target. Guilt tried to avert his aim but he could feel his father watching him.

Staring at him.

I need to win this.

With a cry, Corsair thrust the lance forwards as the two ictharrs met. The tip of the dulled lance struck Ragnar and the force, accumulated from both the momentum and Corsair's strength, knocked him backwards off Harangoth and sent him plummeting to the snowy ground. He grunted as he landed, lance rolling away from him.

"*Finish!* Corsair Sedrid is victorious!"

The crowds applauded furiously, excited by the spectacle, but he didn't care about them. He brought Quickpaw to a halt and dropped down, rushing over to his brother and falling to his knees.

"Ragnee? Ragnee, I'm so sorry..."

"It's fine," Ragnar said, removing his helmet. "We'll both make it in now, for sure."

He offered his paw and Corsair took it without hesitation, helping Ragnar to his hind paws. Corsair dusted the snow off his brother's armour and then lifted his own visor, thankful to feel the cold breeze against his face.

"Hey!" a soldier yelled. "Back to the wall, no delays!"

Not uttering another word, both brothers took their reins and led their companions back to the wall. Quickpaw drew up next to Harangoth and mewled, apologising for defeating him. He growled back, telling him not to worry, and both masters petted their steeds on the side of the neck.

Corsair arrived beside Axel.

"Good fight."

"Thanks. Ragnee went easy on me."

"That's a sign of a good brother if I've ever seen one."

Corsair looked right and cast his gaze over to Ragnar. He was tending to Harangoth, muttering reassurances and praise to him. He and Quickpaw both gazed at their counterparts in admiration.

"Yeah."

"You know what my sisters would have done?"

"What?"

"Claimed the glory like the unforgiving monsters they are."

Corsair laughed and looked back to the box where his parents were sitting.

His mother beamed, as always, proud of her son being able to hold his own in the arena. She gave a small wave and he only smiled in response, not wanting to be scolded for interaction by the soldiers.

But then he saw his father's face.

He wore his typical scowl, eyes focused on him, arms crossed as he reclined in his chair. His ears twitched, maw held firmly shut.

Corsair placed a paw over the left side of his neck.

Did I not impress him?

He shook himself free of his worry and focused on what was ahead. The next two wolves were summoned and he waited, knowing that soon he would fight again.

"Corsair Sedrid."

Lieutenant Maximus Verschelden stared towards the arena from the stables, peering through a gap between houses that gave him enough of a window to see the prince standing beside the idiot Axel Auryon.

He had won the first fight.

Then the next.

And then the next.

He was on a winning streak. Every single opponent he faced failed to bring him down. There were close calls and moments where Lieutenant Maximus was sure he'd be defeated, but he always came through to victory at the last moment.

"So... you decided to stay on for a month and still make it into the Krosguard, huh? I thought of you as a coward who would give up the moment something hard got in your way."

Corsair was talking with Axel, watching the fight rage in front of them.

"But you stayed on. Maybe in some people's eyes that's impressive but I know you're bottling up all that fear. You're still the little pup I know you are."

He smirked and looked behind him. His armour was arranged within the stable, waiting for him to don it, and beside it stood Thornfang. She was sitting there in silence, fearsome eyes staring down at the ground.

"If he keeps this up, he may end up at the top of the ranks. And he'd definitely make it into the Krosguard."

Thornfang looked at him as he approached.

"At this rate, he'll be fighting me."

He smiled. He stroked the side of her neck.

"So, when we fight Quickpaw... I want you to tear out his throat."

Thornfang flashed her serrated fangs in understanding.

THE ALLURE OF RIVALRY

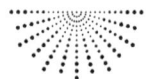

(1139, AESTIOM)

*O*phelia Sedrid winced as one of the riders was sent flying off his steed by a well-placed hit, making the crowds groan in sympathy.

"Hit! Final warning, Thomas!"

Thomas grunted and threw himself back on to his ictharr, rushing away as his opponent gave chase. Everyone's eyes followed them, appreciating the intricate and fluid dance of combat in the arena, but her eyes lingered on her sons.

Corsair and Ragnar had slowly moved towards each other throughout the tournament, both watching the fight while clad in armour. Their helmets were laid by their hind paws. Every few seconds they would murmur something to each other, drowned out by the cheering of the crowd and the sounds of combat, but she didn't care.

I love you two so much.

She knew that this was possibly the last time she would see them. It pained her. The fact her sons would be at the risk of death during their time on the front was unfathomable and she felt nothing but guilt for allowing them to be placed in harm's way.

But it was their duty as the Winter Baron's sons, as Arthur said.

All she could do was pray they would be safe. That God was watching.

She saw movement to her left and noticed Alpha McVarn approaching. He slipped through the blockade of guards and stopped by the Winter Baron's side, saluting.

"Winter Baron."

"Yes?" Arthur said.

"I wanted to make sure you were comfortable, Winter Baron. Anything to eat or drink? I didn't want the townspeople trying to bother you for a quick Iggregom."

"I don't want anything."

Alpha McVarn looked towards Ophelia.

"And you, Milady?"

"I am quite well, thank you."

"Of course, Milady. Winter Baron?"

"Yes, Alpha?"

"I wanted to speak about your sons. They had a slightly rocky start at the beginning of this month but... they've progressed well throughout the course–"

"I'll believe it when I see it. Leave us, Alpha."

Alpha McVarn looked towards Ophelia, holding her gaze, and gave a polite smile despite the discourtesy of her husband. He walked back to the group of officers he was deliberating with, all focused on the match.

Ophelia looked at her stone-faced and almost disinterested husband.

"Arthur?"

"Yes?"

"That was rude. He wanted to talk to you about how well Ragnar and Corsair are doing."

Her husband ignored her. He kept staring into the arena, that familiar scowl upon his face, and Ophelia followed his gaze to find it training on Corsair. Her son was oblivious, lost in conversation with a white wolf beside him.

"Why are you staring at Corsair like that?"

"Not him."

She revaluated where her husband was looking and saw where his gaze was truly directed.

Quickpaw stood beside Harangoth, highlighting their significant height differences. While Ragnar's companion continued to stare ahead, glancing every now and then down at Quickpaw, the white ictharr was not so disciplined. He lay on the ground, staring up to watch the snowflakes fall. Once his eyes were focused on a specific snowflake, he would follow it down to the ground with wide eyes and attentive ears, waiting for the right moment before throwing his front paws up to catch it. A look of disappointment followed before he was distracted again with the next snowflake, already devising a scheme.

"It's *that*," Arthur said.

"Arthur, we've talked about being harsh towards Quickpaw."

"It has no discipline. Look at the line – all these ictharrs, when I look at them, look as if they belong in the Krosguard. They have discipline. Then you look at... *that*–"

"Arthur!"

Her husband, ignoring her, jabbed an accusative digit at the ictharr. Quickpaw attempted to capture a snowflake again, somehow managing to lose his balance and roll on to his back. Harangoth looked down at his friend, seeing him lying belly up, tilting his head in confusion. Their masters noticed this and gave a quick tug on the reins, urging their steeds to return to their positions.

"Trying to catch snowflakes, Ophelia, *snowflakes*. It has the attention span of a dumb-minded maug. No, a maug is too smart for *that*. Most probably a gerbeast waiting to be slaughtered."

"Arthur."

"*Ophelia*."

Her name was delivered in a growl, one that ordered her to silence herself.

"I know what I'm saying. Corsair found him hurt in the woods. For all we know he was the runt of the pack and got left behind because he was weak. He isn't trained and he isn't properly bred. We made a mistake taking him in. It's softened him. He isn't an ictharr."

Arthur looked away, returning his gaze to Quickpaw. Ophelia continued to stare, a part of her wondering what made her husband so hostile towards him.

She looked back at her son.

I love you, my cub. I will always watch over you. God will always watch over you.

"*Grrrah!*"

The fighter swung his dulled sword and struck his opponent on the side of the head. The crowd yelled as he fell off his ictharr, roaring in celebration of the warrior's victory.

"*Finish!* Thomas is victorious!"

Corsair watched the opponents gather up their things and lead their ictharrs back to the wall, the victor bathing in his glory while the loser traipsed back with an ashamed ictharr. Quickpaw watched them walk past, tilting his head as he did so, and tugged against the reins to follow.

"Not right now, Quickpaw," Corsair said, patting him on the head.

His ictharr growled, accepting his master's instructions, and remained where he was.

Two intense hours of fighting and rushing from one side of the courtyard to the other left all the wolves on the verge of exhaustion, still standing upright to save face. Some had their tongues hanging from the corners of their mouths, their companions still filled with enough energy to keep going. Quickpaw continued to watch the snow fall, tilting his head left and right in bewilderment.

Alpha McVarn, finishing his conversation with his subordinates, stepped out into the open.

"Thank you all for attending the Krosguard final training day. It has been a brutal two hours of pitting our riders and their ictharrs against one another during this final assessment. I ask that you show your support and gratitude to these fine wolves. They have thrown themselves at the hardest fighting force Vos Draemar has and, while some have left us, this group has fought on. Regardless of whether they enter the ranks or not, they've struggled for a month without tiring."

The audience applauded, showering the remaining trainees in praise, until Alpha McVarn raised his paw and silenced them once more.

"Before we conclude, however, we would like to close with a final duel. As tradition, we always have our best fighter of the cohort compete against one of our greatest riders in the Krosguard. Already boasting a victory against me, I call..."

He turned.

"...*Corsair Sedrid* to the arena!"

The crowd applauded as Corsair's head snapped up to look at them, ears flat and eyes wide.

"What?" he said, turning to look at Axel.

"You're on, go!"

Axel gestured for him to hurry up and Corsair did so, leading Quickpaw out into the open by the reins. His ictharr padded alongside him, scanning the faces of the crowd, eyes wide and maw agape in excitement.

"You haven't lost a fight today," Alpha McVarn said. "This hasn't happened in 30 years, son. It's a title to wear with pride."

"Thank you, Alpha," Corsair said, looking to his father with a gleaming expression on his face.

His father met his gaze with a scowl.

Corsair looked away.

"Before we end today's fighting and your final day of training in the Krosguard, you are going to face Lieutenant Maximus Verschelden."

Corsair's already faltering expression collapsed.

"W-what?"

Alpha McVarn was already walking out of the courtyard and back to his advisors, the crowds cheering and whooping for Corsair. He turned, making eye contact with Ragnar, unsure of what to do.

"Behind you!" he yelled.

Corsair heard something charging towards him and threw himself out the way, rolling towards Quickpaw and pushing himself up on to his hind paws. Thornfang shot past, plated in armour, circling around at the other end of the courtyard. She turned and stopped, her rider pulling on the reins.

In the saddle sat the Butcher of Tomskon.

With armour clinging to him and masked helmet on, the only thing Corsair could see were his two harsh eyes glaring out at him through the two holes. A moment of terror passed where he became frozen, feeling the temptation to flee rise.

But, with a growl, he steeled himself.

"Come on, Quickpaw."

Placing his helmet on his head, visor still up, he climbed into Quickpaw's saddle and drew his lance. He growled as he glared back at his opponent, clenching one paw around one of the reins while the other tightened around the shaft of the lance.

The Butcher of Tomskon stared.

Corsair Sedrid slammed his visor down.

Neither yielded.

"Ready!" a soldier yelled.

The lupine drummer prepared himself, raising his drumsticks into the air.

Silence.

We've got this. We've got this.

"*Begin!*"

The drummer rapped the drum, this time with a wild tempo.

Corsair's heart mimicked that reckless beat. With a snap of the reins, the Butcher of Tomskon sent Thornfang hurtling towards them.

"*Hyah!*"

Corsair yanked the reins to the left and Quickpaw yowled in panic, following his commands. He felt the air right next to his head split as the lancehead tore through it. The crowd groaned in anticipation, watching as Corsair rode Quickpaw around to the opposite side and turned.

His enemy charged again, aiming his lance at his head. Corsair turned and evaded the attack, speeding across to the other side.

"Stay still!" The Butcher of Tomskon yelled.

"Left, Quickpaw!"

He turned and, despite his agility, he could do nothing to stop the incoming battering ram.

Thornfang rammed into Quickpaw's side. Corsair's heart wrenched as he heard Quickpaw yelp in pain, collapsing on to his side, before he flew off the saddle and rolled through the snow. There was a pained yap from Quickpaw as the Butcher of Tomskon rode past, prodding him in the side with his sword.

"Hit!"

Corsair hurried to his hind paws, drawing his sword and looking back towards his steed. He was on his side in the snow, trying to get on to all fours while still dazed. The Butcher of Tomskon was turning around to charge him again, sword at the ready. Corsair rushed towards Quickpaw, dodging out the way of a swing, and helped his steed on to his paws. Quickpaw gave a growl of thanks while his master leapt on to his saddle, taking up the reins and turning-

Quickpaw yowled to alert him but it was too late.

Corsair's eyes widened as he saw his opponent on top of them. He opened his mouth to scream. In panic, he tried to summon his sword from his scabbard but failed, pulling it in a way that made it snag on the leather.

The crowd gasped as the lieutenant's sword *clanged* against the helmet.

The force behind the swing knocked him from his saddle, sending him spiralling down to the snow while his helmet flew from his head. He landed and grunted. The world spun around him, his head throbbing with pain, unable to understand what he was doing with his disorientated senses. He attempted to push himself up but lost his balance and fell into the snow again.

He could see his mother standing, paws to her mouth in horror of what she was witnessing. Axel held Ragnar back.

Corsair was one hit away from losing.

I'm in anyway. I win. He loses.

But that didn't matter as he realised Quickpaw was still being chased by Thornfang, Lieutenant Maximus targeting him and ignoring the vulnerable opponent on the ground.

"Hey!" he yelled. "Leave him alone!"

He pushed himself up to his hind paws, stumbling, and drew his sword. Quickpaw shot past him, eyes wide, wanting to flee from the monster but continually glancing at his master, afraid to leave him behind. Thornfang was slower, easily outmanoeuvred, but she had the advantage of greater stamina. Quickpaw was exerting himself, almost tumbling into the snow.

"Quickpaw, come here!"

In Quickpaw's panicked frenzy, he couldn't hear him nor did he have the option to. The Butcher of Tomskon used Thornfang to act as a wedge between Quickpaw and the prince, still wary that Corsair could hit him and often checking over his shoulder. Corsair tried to approach and attack Thornfang but failed, unable to rush after her.

"You're fighting me, not him!"

The audience clamoured, booing the lieutenant as he hunted Quickpaw. Quickpaw yowled and yapped, trying to call to his master for help, but Corsair couldn't do anything.

"*Stop!*"

No one dared intervene despite their passionate complaints, not willing to get between two ictharrs locked in battle. Thornfang intercepted him and rammed him down, pinning him with one mighty paw. He scrambled desperately, trying to propel himself away, but nothing worked.

Corsair knew he was too far away to get closer in time. He dropped his sword and leaned down.

As he was carrying out his plan, he heard the audience gasp.

"Someone stop him!" a wolf yelled.

"Lieutenant, what the hell are you doing?" Alpha McVarn ordered.

Corsair looked up, plan ready to be executed, and saw Thornfang's hellish maw open. Her serrated fangs were on display, open and aimed to sink into Quickpaw's neck. The Butcher of Tomskon didn't try to stop it.

"No!"

Corsair hurled the snowball.

It shot across the gap and, as Thornfang was bringing her fangs back to lunge forwards, the snowball struck the Butcher of Tomskon in the side of the helmet. Snow shot through the right eyehole and into his eye, causing him to yell out and yank on the reins. Thornfang pulled away at the last second, alleviating the pressure on Quickpaw. Eyes wide and whimpering, Quickpaw darted back to his master.

"Are you okay?"

Quickpaw whined. Corsair glanced at his opponent as he recovered from the hit, turning around to charge.

"OK, I need you to keep him distracted."

Quickpaw gave a confused growl but his master gave him no time to enquire further. The Butcher of Tomskon charged back and, with a maddened look in his eyes, aimed for the wolf's head. Corsair stood his ground, sword at the ready.

He's aggressive. He's always on the attack and always charging back and forth to prevent me from retaliating.

He dodged the attack as the Butcher of Tomskon hurtled past. Quickpaw yapped up a storm. The crowd complained and groaned, annoyed. Thornfang focused on him again, giving chase.

He's weak on defence. He's never had to defend before because there's never been a scenario where he's had to rely on that.

There was no time to doubt himself. Thornfang continued her pursuit of Quickpaw, still lagging behind somewhat.

"To me!" he yelled. "To me!"

Quickpaw yapped in response and rushed towards him, Thornfang hidden behind his body. Corsair readied his sword, holding his ground, and yelled to his steed.

"*Left!*"

Immediately, Quickpaw threw himself to the side as Thornfang leapt forwards with maw open. She was met with a yell and a strong swing, the broadside of the blade smacking against the side of her head and knocking her off course. The crowd cheered, applauding the successful hit.

"Hit!"

The Butcher of Tomskon grunted and steered around, turning on Corsair, but Quickpaw began yapping again. The Butcher of Tomskon tried to lead Thornfang forwards but she was distracted by the continuous noise. She ignored her master and turned, roaring at Quickpaw.

"Not him, get Sedrid!"

Corsair took his opportunity, yelled out, and swung at Thornfang's head. Hearing him attack, she stepped back out the way and knocked him down with a swing of her paw, opening her mouth and revealing her fangs once more.

Before he could back away, she thrust her fangs towards his tail.

"*No!*" his mother wailed.

With a snarl, Quickpaw leapt forwards and knocked the black ictharr down. She was too formidable to fall from the weak attack but the Butcher of Tomskon was caught off guard and fell from the saddle. He rolled across the snow, helmet falling from his head. He scrambled up to his hind paws and drew his sword.

The Butcher of Tomskon turned to climb up into the saddle again but Corsair rushed forwards and attacked with a swing. Thornfang turned to defend her master before she was hit across the snout by Quickpaw, taunting her. Without her rider, all she could do was endlessly chase him, bounding through the snow to sink her fangs into his flesh.

"Keep her busy!" Corsair yelled.

The Butcher of Tomskon yelled out and brought the sword down from above. He parried it and clashed his blade against his, locking them in a stalemate. They both leaned in against their swords, glaring at one another.

"One hit is all it takes, Sedrid. *One hit.*"

Snarling, Corsair shoved him away and took a step back. He watched the opponent growl and bare his fangs, ready to attack, before the Butcher of Tomskon charged forwards and raised his sword.

Now!

Corsair took his chances and stabbed forwards. The blunt tip *scraped* against the metal of the Butcher of Tomskon's torso plating, knocking him back and interrupting his attack.

"Hit! Final warning, Lieutenant!"

"What the hell is going on?" someone yelled. "Someone interrupt this thing!"

"Do you want to get in the middle of *that*?" someone else bellowed.

Yelling out, the Butcher of Tomskon unleashed a series of swings at him. Corsair weaved out the way of every slash and swing. Upon the final attack, he couldn't back away further and was forced to parry the blow, returning him to the clash with the brutal wolf.

"I'm ending this now, Sedrid. Learn your *place!*"

Corsair tried to break the clash but, before he could rear back to separate, he felt his sword get thrown upwards. With eyes widening, he saw his weapon fly into the air.

He was left completely defenceless.

Everything slowed down.

The lightning speed of the drumming was reduced to nothing more than a resting heartbeat thudding inside Corsair's head.

His eyes watched the sword's trajectory in flight, seeing it arc up above. It was destined to land a metre behind the Butcher of Tomskon.

He saw the Butcher of Tomskon draw his sword's hilt into him, bringing the sword tip back to stab Corsair.

Corsair reacted in time.

He spun around the sword, dodging the tip, and felt his body graze against Maximus. His paw rose to snatch the sword from the air, the pommel aiming down towards the ground, and there was a moment of frozen movement where everything held still.

The crowd fell silent. Not even the snowfall stirred.

Corsair caught the sword, turned, and swung at the Butcher of Tomskon's head.

Thud.

The sword's broadside struck the Butcher of Tomskon in the side of the head and knocked him down. He yelped and collapsed, groaning with a paw up to his temple.

The battle concluded with a final thundering drumbeat.

"*Finish!* Sedrid is..."

The soldier was drowned out by the sudden roaring of the crowd, all of those in attendance standing up and applauding Corsair for his victory against the cruel lieutenant. Soldiers rushed into the court-yard and formed a perimeter around Thornfang, holding their swords up and forcing her away from Quickpaw.

Corsair moved away from the hurt lieutenant, who lay dazed in the snow. He saw Quickpaw rushing towards him. Dropping his sword, he knelt and wrapped his arms around his neck. Quickpaw, tail wagging, nuzzled his master and hooked his front paws over his shoulders.

"You're not hurt, are you?"

Quickpaw growled in denial.

"Thank God. I'm so sorry that you went through that."

Quickpaw gave a forgiving growl. Corsair let go, smiling.

He looked back to his mother and met her gaze, hearing her words through the roaring of the crowds.

"I love you, Corsair! I love you!"

He held her gaze, watching her celebrate his achievement, and felt so much pride at the sight.

I love you too, Mum.

The moment, however, was somewhat tarnished when his eyes fell on his father's empty chair.

Corsair stood before the altar.

His name was one of the many called from the list those accepted into the ranks of the Krosguard. He earned the right to fight among the greatest wolves in the Clan of the Great Lupine and deserved the honour of wearing their armour. The pride in such an achievement, in not losing a single fight to any of the combatants, erased any sense of dread he had felt beforehand. All he could imagine was how proud his mother and father would be.

Alpha McVarn turned to him.

"Do you, Corsair Sedrid, willingly accept the responsibilities of a Krosguard warrior?"

"I do."

"Do you promise to defend the Clan of the Great Lupine from all who wish to do its people harm?"

"I do."

"And, finally, do you promise to serve valiantly in the name of the clan, the people, justice, and the Winter Baron?"

"I do."

Corsair stood there for a moment in silence, ecstatic in victory, unsure of what to do next.

Alpha McVarn coughed.

"Time to kneel, son."

"Oh! Right, sorry."

He knelt. Alpha McVarn leant down and, with red paint on a digit of his paw, drew that familiar scar-like streak across his right eye and to the base of his snout.

"Rise."

Corsair stood, feeling the paint dry on his fur.

Alpha McVarn offered a paw forward. He shook it, making eye contact with the alpha.

"The lieutenant is being kept from the front line after what he did and, in a few weeks, he'll be looking at a military hearing in the capital. Despite that... son, you and Quickpaw held your own out there. I'm sorry for doubting you."

Removing his paw, Alpha McVarn smiled.

"Welcome to the Krosguard, soldier."

CHAPTER FOURTEEN

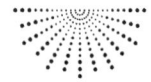

Corsair stepped out of the church and into the snowy exterior, pelted by countless snowflakes, but the cold could do nothing to chill the prince's spirits. There, to the side of the door, he found Axel and Ragnar waiting for him with newly-painted red streaks across their right eyes. Quickpaw, Harangoth and Arwenin stood beside them. On seeing his master, Quickpaw bounded forward and licked him across the face, getting a chuckle from the two onlookers.

"That must be his way of congratulating you," Axel said.

"Definitely."

Corsair made eye contact with Ragnar and that was enough to initiate a hug. He came forward and wrapped his arms around his sibling, holding him there and smiling over his shoulder as his tail wagged.

"Maximus played dirty," Ragnar said. "And you still beat him. You didn't lose a single match."

"You let me win the first one."

"I'm the older brother. It's what I have to do. Regardless of what went on, you're okay?"

"I'm fine. Thankfully," Corsair said. "McVarn told me Maximus is having a hearing in Grand Wolf Plains. He's not coming with us."

"Good. That sadist will get kicked out and sent back to prison, hopefully."

They pulled apart. Corsair found his eyes resting on the noble form of Harangoth.

"You did well today," he said, stroking his head. "Thanks for going easy on Quickpaw."

He gave an appreciative growl. As Quickpaw approached Harangoth looked down at him and nodded, a gesture that his friend returned. Arwenin observed the duo from beside Axel, allowing herself to be stroked on the side of her neck by her master.

"Where's Mum?" Corsair asked.

"She'll be somewhere around here. Knowing her, she's hunting us down as we speak."

"We'd better not keep her waiting, then. Axel, do you want to meet her?"

As he opened his mouth to answer, he heard someone call to them metres away. All three wolves turned to see three lupine maidens hurrying over, crowding round Axel with their braided tails swinging behind them.

"There he is!" one said, pinching his ear. "Our little hero with his new Krosguard marking."

"Here we go," Axel sighed, rolling his eyes. "I'm a lost cause. Save yourselves."

"That's not a way to talk to us when you're in front of the champion of the Krosguard," a second chuckled, slugging him in the arm before looking at Corsair. "Hello, Sir. I'm Moira. Axel's sister."

"Hello, Moira."

"You were really impressive, Sir," a third said. "I'm Monika, also this idiot's sister. You were a lot better than him."

"I have to put up with this all the time," Axel said.

"Arwie would have done better without you," the first one said before looking to Corsair. "I'm Eliza, Sir."

Axel sighed as the three demons clamoured, continuing to harass him. Quickpaw yapped with all the excitement, standing beside Axel to be involved in the commotion.

"I suggest you two get out of here before they start thinking about braiding your tails."

"Are you sure you'll be OK?" Corsair asked, stifling a laugh.

"Probably. I wouldn't place any Iggregoms on it, though."

"Let's go and find Mum, Corsair," Ragnar said. "We don't want to keep her waiting."

The two Sedrids began to walk away with Harangoth in tow, waving back at the sisters. Quickpaw still lingered with them, yapping in excitement.

"Come on Quickpaw!" Corsair said as he hurried after Ragnar. "Nice meeting you, Eliza, Moira and Monika!"

"Don't go too easy on him!" Ragnar said.

"We won't, Sir!" the trio said, turning on Axel as one began to pamper Arwenin.

"Thanks for that, Ragnar!" Axel bellowed as the horde set upon him.

They walked away. Ragnar chuckled, glancing over his shoulder.

"We may never see him again. After they're done with him, all that will be left will be bones and blood."

"I think Arwenin is enjoying it, though," Corsair said, looking back to see her with tummy in the air.

He was ecstatic. His tail swung from side to side. He had made it into the Krosguard. He could picture his father there, welcoming him with open arms, telling him how well he did by defeating the vile lieutenant.

They walked into the courtyard of families hugging the soldiers, congratulating them on their entrance or comforting them after their rejection. Ictharrs, both ashamed and proud, dotted the arena.

"*Corsair! Ragnee!*"

They both looked right and saw their mother rushing towards them, two guards striding after her in a dignified attempt to keep up.

No matter how hard they braced, the princes were almost knocked off their hind paws as she launched herself at them. Corsair took one step back to balance himself, wobbling for a moment, before he hugged her. He felt his brother do the same, towering over her. Quickpaw and Harangoth stayed standing side by side as they watched the reunion.

"We missed you," Ragnar said.

"I missed you both *so much*. There wasn't a day that I wasn't thinking about you two. Are you okay, Corsair? Did that monster hurt you?"

"I'm okay, Mum. He's in a lot of trouble with McVarn. I'm okay. We won't see him again."

Corsair pulled her in closer and let his mother nuzzle him, trying to catch that familiar scent of her son. He had never thought that a month away from his mother could be so painful.

She pulled away and placed her paws on both their shoulders. She looked back and forth between the two. Corsair saw that her eyes were glistening with tears, on the verge of weeping, and he frowned.

"Mum, come on," Ragnar said. "You'll make me start crying in a second."

"I'm sorry... you two know I would never mean to make a scene but... it's only been 20 years or so since you were both cubs and now *look at you*. You're both my brave warriors with your new and well-deserved Krosguard markings."

The siblings smiled. His mother focused her gaze on the gap between the two as Corsair felt someone push through. He looked left to see Quickpaw poking his head out. Harangoth was still standing where he was left, waiting to be called over.

"Oh, and how could I forget you, Quickpaw? You were such a hero today."

"He was," Corsair said. "He's fine, too. Hopefully they keep that monster somewhere she can't hurt anyone."

She rewarded Quickpaw with a scratch behind the ears. Ragnar gestured for Harangoth to come over and he did so, padding towards his master.

"Harangoth. You were so brave today," she said.

"Always by my side, huh? You never let me down," Ragnar said, reaching up and patting him on the head.

Harangoth nuzzled against him, a rare gesture from the ictharr, and the trio broke into laughter. They all petted the two steeds for a moment, showering them in praise, and it ended with Quickpaw on his back in the snow and Harangoth looking directly ahead.

Corsair looked around.

Where's Dad?

"Hey, Mum, where's Dad?"

For a fraction of a second, his mother hesitated. There was a flicker of hurt in her face, one that broke the warm and joyous attitude she was displaying, and he spotted it. She recovered before he could address it.

"He went for a walk to the back of the church. Why?"

"I wanted to talk to him, see how I did."

"You did great, darling."

"We did well, Corsair," Ragnar said.

"Yeah but... I want to see what he thought."

"I don't think he's in the mood, darling."

"Mum, come on, I just want to talk to him."

With a surrendering sigh, his mother nodded.

"You two go together. Come back though – I want to speak to you a bit more, okay?"

"Yes, Mum. Come on, Quickpaw!"

Corsair turned and rushed off to the back of the church, Quickpaw in tow. Ragnar exchanged looks with his mother, reassuring her that they would be all right, before telling Harangoth to follow him and hurrying after his brother.

∽

Turning the corner, he found his father waiting.

He stood ahead of him, peering out across a small plateau of snowy grass that stretched downwards into the rest of the town. He overlooked it, a guardian of some sorts, and the guards stood beside him facing the opposite direction. They saw the approaching prince but did not alert his father, knowing he would introduce himself on his own terms.

Corsair heard Ragnar coming up behind him, Harangoth following. He gestured for Quickpaw to follow before stepping out and approaching his father.

"Father, hey! Mum told me you were-"

"Leave us, guards."

"Yes, Winter Baron," the soldiers said, walking past Corsair and then past Ragnar as he arrived by his brother's side. The younger brother ignored this, continuing to talk.

"I think it went really well that time, Father. I didn't think I'd beat the lieutenant and Thornfang but I did! I thought I was going to lose and then they went to hurt Quickpaw and I got the snowball and hit him in the face. I was... oh, I think I did really well today."

His father remained silent.

Corsair's wagging tail stiffened and his ears twitched. Quickpaw glanced at his master, unsure of the atmosphere his father was generating, and then looked to Harangoth for advice. The black ictharr tilted his head as he gazed into the Winter Baron's back, confused and with one ear standing.

"Corsair, come on," Ragnar said, placing a paw on his shoulder.

Corsair shrugged him off and stepped forwards again.

"Father? Why are you so quiet?"

And, finally, his father spoke.

"You didn't do well, Corsair. You weren't anywhere close to doing well."

"But Father, I won all my games. I beat Maximus."

"You didn't deserve to."

Every word his father delivered cut at Corsair's spirit like sharpened steel, slashing it down from the top and working its way to the foundation. He battled on, hoping to weather the storm and receive some form of appreciation for his performance.

"But I..."

His father turned and Corsair immediately stepped back, ears flattening.

"I don't care that you won all your games. Do you not understand what I am saying to you? *You didn't deserve it.*"

"Father–" his brother tried to intervene.

"I'm not talking to you, Ragnar."

Corsair was stunned. He blinked, his face contorted in a hurt grimace, shaking his head softly. His paw returned to its usual position.

"I don't... what did I do wrong?"

His father stepped forwards.

"What did you do wrong? *What did you do wrong?* Tiberius has spent years teaching you, taking my place to educate you on proper riding etiquette and technique, but when I watched you it was as if you had *forgotten all of it.*"

"But–"

"And what the hell was *that thing* doing?"

The Winter Baron pointed a digit at Quickpaw. The ictharr's ears flattened and he shrank back, no longer willing to be part of the reunion. Harangoth stepped in front of his counterpart, staring at the wolf while Quickpaw peeked around him.

"W-what do you mean?"

"*Running away?* Crying out for you like he's still a pup? It was embarrassing to watch. You barely had control over it and God knows why you didn't get a new one like *I told you to.*"

"Father, come on." Ragnar tried again.

"Don't get me started on you, Ragnar. You don't think I noticed you going easy on your brother? You thought you could hide that? You didn't use your shield *once.*"

"I wanted him to–"

"It doesn't matter what you want. It doesn't matter if you wanted to be nice, or to let him win, or to not hurt his feelings because your ictharr is better than whatever mutt Corsair chooses to ride."

Quickpaw whimpered, receding back further.

"Because out there, *in war*, the rabbits won't be nice! They'll kill you when they have the opportunity so what you did was beyond stupid!"

Corsair's eyes stung.

"I thought I did really-"

"*You didn't do well,* Corsair. Just because you've come running to me, panting and whining for attention like an excitable pup, doesn't mean I will be any less tolerant of your inconsiderate mistakes. Seriously, Corsair, what the hell were you thinking? Did you even listen to me during training? Or were you busy thinking about frolicking in the hills with *that*?"

Ragnar glared.

"Father, you need to stop."

"I will not stop, Ragnar, until you two understand the seriousness of the situation and *don't you dare take that tone with your father!*"

Corsair didn't know what to feel. His body was taut with pain, his heart torn into pieces, and his hope shattered completely. His father had slashed the column of wishful thinking down to a stump, which he proceeded to stamp on repeatedly as if it was nothing.

He felt betrayed.

And that feeling of betrayal slowly transformed into anger. A lick of furious fire sparked inside him and, as the flames grew over the coming seconds, he felt nothing but hatred. He loathed the wolf who stood before him and belittled him as if he were nothing. As if he were an insignificant stain. As if he didn't have time for him.

Corsair growled.

His father stopped yelling and turned his head, eyes wide and ears upright.

"Are you... *growling* at your father?"

"You're not a father."

Arthur Sedrid turned and stepped forwards, Ragnar wary of the distance between them.

"What did you just say?"

"*You're not a father*. You call yourself one all the time, saying, 'I'm your father,' but you're not. You don't act like one. You *never* act like one."

"Do not lecture me on how-"

"When was the last time you said you loved me?"

Silence.

Arthur Sedrid glared at his son, stumped for an answer. Corsair took this as a cue to continue.

"When was the last time you hugged me? Do you remember when that was? When was the last time you took me and Ragnee to the tavern? When was the last time I even talked to you outside training? When was the last time you let me play with Quickpaw without you staring at him like you are doing now, as if he's something evil?"

Arthur Sedrid stared.

"We have done nothing but slave away for you since the first day we got our swords and ictharrs. We have trained day and night for you. *I* have trained day and night for you. I did everything I could to impress you, to make you appreciate me and what I can do, but it's never enough. Everything I do is flawed or stupid. I'm always the idiot late to training. I'm not good enough ever to be praised. I'm not good enough ever to be given a break. I'm not good enough even to get a pat on the back when I do something well."

His vision blurred from the tears, sniffling, but he refused to distract himself by trying to wipe them away.

"Everything... *everything*... I have done was to impress you. *This*. This stupid Krosguard training. I never wanted to do this. I never wanted to go to war. But now? *Now?* I'm going to die because of you and your stupid idea of contribution and *you don't even care*. A father cares. You don't."

Arthur Sedrid stared at him, eyes wide in realisation.

Corsair, with all the strength in his heart, said it loud and clear.

"I *hate* you!"

And, clearly, that was enough for him.

Arthur Sedrid snapped his jaws at Corsair. Corsair fell and yelled out, curling up on his side and covering his neck as he pleaded and trembled on the ground.

For a moment, everything froze.

Corsair Sedrid, 10 years old, lay curled up on his side with a paw up his neck.

Arthur Sedrid stood over him, blood dripping from his fangs. The crimson had not splattered as it would if he had shaken his head to tear flesh, only daring to cover the rows of blades within his maw.

The sting and the terror paralysed Corsair.

"You swing this thing around like an *idiot*. This is not a toy, this is a legacy. You have far more to learn before you even *dare* to do this."

Arthur Sedrid scooped up Corsair's longsword, almost as tall as the pup was, and walked back to the house.

Alone, terrified and with paw to the side of his bleeding neck, Corsair lay in the snow beside his father's betrayal.

Corsair was dragged out of his doldrums as Quickpaw leapt to his aid. He stood in front of him, snarling at his attacker, receiving support from Harangoth.

Ragnar shoved him back.

"What the hell are you doing?"

"Don't you lay a paw on me! I'm keeping him in line!"

"By trying to kill him? *Again?*"

"You watch your tone with me or-"

"*Get away from my pups right now!*"

Their mother rushed towards them, the guards watching from the corner. She wedged her way between Ragnar and her husband.

"I saw that, you horrible bastard! I *saw* you try to bite him!"

"Ophelia, this isn't your place!"

"It's my place if you dare try to hurt my cubs! If you even try to lay another paw on him or Corsair, so help me God I will *kill you,* Arthur!"

The couple began yelling at one another, causing a commotion, and a few more wolves began peering around the side of the church to witness it. The guards ordered them away, telling them it was none of their business. Quickpaw began yapping at the argument.

It was all too much for Corsair.

Tears flowing, he got up and ran.

Quickpaw padded around the corner of the church and found his master there, knees up to his chest and arms in front of his face, shoulders moving up and down.

He was sobbing.

Momentarily, he was unsure as to how to approach the situation. He tilted his head at his master, trying to conjure up some plan to lift his spirits, but felt reluctant.

After that moment subsided, though, he padded over with head lowered. Easing himself to the ground, he leaned his head forwards and gave a soft growl, enquiring as to whether his master was all right.

His master looked up, sniffling. His green eyes were red-rimmed and glistening, and he was blinking repeatedly to bat away the tears. The sight made Quickpaw shuffle forwards and press his snout into his master's side.

"Oh... h-hey, Quickpaw."

He sniffled and patted him on the head.

"I'm just... I'm a bit sad, Quickpaw. I..."

He didn't finish his sentence. He paused and shook his head, wiping away the tears, before looking back to his steed.

"Thank you... for defending me."

Quickpaw didn't respond. He continued to stare at his master, a concerned look upon his face, watching the tears fall. He was fighting it, furiously wiping his eyes, but he couldn't hold them back.

"I don't get him, I... I won. We won *all games* so what the hell is his..."

He stopped himself and looked to the left, ears standing upright. Quickpaw followed his gaze. His mother stood there with eyes focused on her miserable son. She rushed forwards and knelt.

"Corsair, are you okay?"

"I'm okay."

"You're not bleeding?"

"No, Mum."

She threw herself at her son and wrapped her arms around him, shielding him from the snow and whatever harm could possibly come his way. He hugged back, closing his eyes as Quickpaw watched.

"I'd never let him hurt you. Never."

"He almost..."

"Shush, it's okay, darling."

"Is Ragnee all right?"

"He's fine. He's making sure Arthur keeps his distance."

He nodded, sniffling.

"Mum... do I have to go?"

She squeezed her eyes shut.

"I want to bring you home. I want to keep you safe but... I can't. Only your father can bring you out and..." she stopped.

"I did this for him," Corsair said. "I did it so he'd be happy. Now I'm going to die."

"Don't say that."

She gestured for Quickpaw to come forward. He did so.

"Look to your left."

He didn't respond.

"Darling, *please*. Let go of me and look to your left."

Reluctantly, he brought himself away from her and looked to his left. Sitting there, meeting his gaze, was his best friend. The loyal steed voiced his concern with a soft growl, maw hanging open by an inch, and this brought a small smile to his master's face. Like the first time they met, his master held his paw in front of his companion. Quickpaw nuzzled against it, mewling.

"I'll always be there, Corsair. Always. So will Quickpaw. He'll protect you. You can always rely on him."

He nodded, sniffling.

"And there'll be your brother and Harangoth. You'll be safe, my love. Nothing will hurt you, I promise."

Quickpaw brought his head back and then brought it forward with snout pointed to the ground. His master found his paw gently pressing on the top of his head between the ears.

"Cheeky," his mother chuckled.

"Yeah," his master sniffled, scratching him between the ears.

He met his mother's loving gaze.

"I love you, Mum."

"I love you too. Always."

CHAPTER FIFTEEN

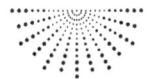

The wolves had estimated that their journey to the clan's eastern border would be a few days' ride. Now, days later, Corsair Sedrid could feel the rising dread as he realised their destination was only a single day away.

Underneath the black night sky pockmarked with distant stars, the wolves' encampment lay in a clearing. The Krosguard was to join with battalions of the army before they travelled past the defensive perimeter and launched their assault on Pothole Plains. Most wolves lay within their tents, gerbeast leather flapping in the gentle wind against the poles of their temporary shelters.

Inside one of the tents, 20 wolves dozed. There was a tangle of limbs and tails stretched out across their sleeping pads, pillowed against the bodies of their comrades. Amid the silent chaos lay Corsair, fortunate enough to have his own section in the corner (though the lupine beside him was on the brink of rolling into his territory).

Other than the whispers of the wind and the odd snore, it was silent.

He couldn't sleep. His mind was whirring with hundreds of

anxious thoughts, knowing tomorrow would be his first day of combat. And he couldn't stop thinking about his conflict with his father at Ignatius' Mount. How he had argued so brazenly.

He had never dared to speak to his father like that before.

He looked across the invasive lupine to the slumbering hulk of his brother, curled up on his side and facing the opposite corner. He slumbered, shoulders rising and falling, lost in a realm that his younger brother was nowhere near accessing. His body was so contorted that all his muscles ached. His tail was trapped beneath his right leg and complained continuously about its position. He adjusted himself in the miniscule ways available but it didn't relieve the torment.

I can't do this.

Desperate for an escape, he contained his urgency and eased himself up into a crouched position. He couldn't stand fully upright because of the low ceiling. Carefully stepping over the strewn arms and dormant tails of the slumbering wolves, he snuck his way over to the small mouth of the tent and stepped out into the open.

The environment was slightly different from how it was at home. He had noticed this over time during his journey. There was a gradual change of climate as they neared the eastern border, with the thickness of the snow melting away significantly with each mile they travelled. With Pothole Plains not too far away, the grass was barely covered by any snow at all. Mere flecks fended off the heat in isolated patches. His hind-paw socks endured the wet grass. He felt no need to pull a cloak over his shoulders. He enjoyed the warmer night air despite the occasional breeze.

Aestiom is slowly passing. Soon it won't be so warm out.

The camp was filled with many tents similar to Corsair's. Some limbs and tails spilled out from the mouths of their shelters and they acted as furry foliage to the pathway of thinly snow-covered grass that formed the aisle between the tents.

Ahead of him, down the pathway, was the encampment's bonfire. It was beginning to die, its bold flames now diminishing as its fuel was gradually consumed. He knew there were logs placed around it to act as makeshift seating so he headed in that direction. A guard patrolled past. His eyes fixed on Corsair for a moment before looking away. There was no curfew in place, seemingly unnecessary when most wolves wanted to sleep and prepare for the day of battle ahead. Reprimanding him would be unnecessary.

Finally, he arrived at the centre of the camp. As he expected, several logs were set facing the fire to allow wolves to enjoy the warmth it provided while it still burned. He spotted the closest one and approached it, sitting down and gazing into the flames.

It gave him time to dwell on things.

Before he could think about anything else, the confrontation with his father pushed itself to the front of the queue. All the things his father said. He had been humiliated, rescued by his brother from the fierce argument, fearing that his father would once more bite down on his neck and pierce the skin. Even thinking about it made Corsair's paw move to protect the scar that lay hidden beneath the black fur.

That scar, in its permanence, forbade him from ever forgetting what happened.

I don't even know what I did wrong. I won every game. Ragnee let me win the first, sure, but from then on it was us. Quickpaw and me. We did that, not anyone else.

He felt weak for crying and curling up into a ball in front of his father. He was 20 – it seemed forbidden to behave like that when he was supposed to be an adult.

I'm stronger now. I don't need to get Dad's approval any more. He's shown that he doesn't care. Now I don't.

Then he questioned the possibility of even coming home alive. He disposed of that question with a shudder.

"Up late, huh?"

A familiar voice jolted Corsair to reality and made him whirl around in his seat, ears standing and eyes wide. He saw a white wolf with a braided tail standing there, dressed in a long-sleeved shirt and pair of slacks. He saw the red streak across his right eye.

"Axel, you scared me to death."

"Sorry. I didn't mean to startle you. I saw you sitting there and... well, thought I'd say hello."

Corsair nodded.

"Like I said, you're up late. You don't feel like getting some sleep before the big battle tomorrow?"

"I'm..." he began, then hesitated.

"Having trouble sleeping, huh?"

"Y-yeah, I guess."

"Want to talk about it?"

Corsair opened his mouth to answer, wanting to say yes, but he held his tongue.

"I, uh..."

"I understand if you don't want to. Don't lose sleep over it. Well, don't lose any more of it than you are now, anyway."

Corsair snorted with laughter. Axel continued.

"If you don't want to talk, I can go-"

"No!"

He winced at how desperate he sounded.

"I mean... you've probably heard rumours, right?"

"Of the shouting match between you and your dad? It's circulated a bit."

"If it doesn't bother you, then... I'd like to talk about it. Maybe it would help me sleep better."

"No problem. Sleep's for the weak, right?"

He chuckled as the apothecary walked over and sat down beside him, crossing his arms and sitting upright.

"You're fine talking about this?"

"I want to."

"Then fire away."

Corsair sighed, nodded to himself, but hesitated again. Axel was patient, looking into the fire, ears up to listen to his story but eyes averted so as not to pressure him. He appreciated the gesture – it made talking about his father easier.

"Back at Ignatius' Mount, my father wasn't happy with my performance. He said that it was like I'd forgotten about everything he and Alpha Tiberius taught me."

"The alpha of the army taught you himself?"

"Yeah. He and my father are friends. Whenever he had a spare hour or two, he'd teach us."

"Right. But anyway, you won every game, right? Apart from your brother letting you win the first one, you did it all. Any sibling with a heart would do that for their younger sibling – even my demon sisters, as much as I claimed otherwise."

"Exactly. He got angry at me and then he started yelling at Quickpaw and then he started yelling at Ragnee and then I started arguing."

"Okay."

"Maybe it sounds normal to anyone else but with my father you don't argue back. Ever. In 20 years, that was the first time I put my hind paw down."

"And what did he do?"

"He... stopped. For a moment, he just stopped, like he didn't know what was going on. Then he tried to bite me and Ragnar held him back and then... I don't know, I ran. I just ran."

Axel turned to look at him. "Your dad tried to bite you? Where?"

"On the neck."

Axel blinked. "Wow."

"I'm not saying it's normal. It wasn't."

"No, of course. Just didn't expect to hear that."

"Did I ever tell you about my scar?"

"Your scar?"

"On the left side of my neck, look."

Corsair craned his neck in a way that exposed the scar tissue beneath the fur. Axel hissed in response, wincing.

"*He* did that?"

"When I was 10. It was... something, honestly. I almost died."

"God, Corsair, I'm so sorry."

"It's nothing you have to apologise for. Ever since I was 10, he just... became weird. He stopped being close with us. It was like we didn't know him. I tried my hardest to get his approval – I tried the hardest I could during my tournaments. I didn't win as many as Ragnee did in jousting and stuff but I still tried. And I did well in other areas."

"You told me. Longswords and races. And, regardless of how good you were, you've got to respect trying."

"Yeah. Dad didn't do that."

They sat in silence for a moment, listening to the crackling of the fire. Axel decided to speak.

"My dad has done some bad things. Not *damning* things but, you know, mistakes we all make. But, I got to say, your dad... sounds a bit like a bastard."

"We share the same opinion, don't worry."

"You've talked to your brother about this, right?"

"Yeah, I have."

"Then why am I the one hearing this? If you're still worrying, talk to him. He's your brother."

"I know but... I've talked to him five times about this since we left. He's got his own things to worry about without carrying my worries, too. Besides, he's sleeping right now."

"He's a good brother, Corsair, I can tell. You could tell him the same thing, *word for word*, and he wouldn't care if it was the thousandth time he heard it."

"Really?"

"Okay, maybe not 1,000 times, but you get what I mean. He's there for you."

"I know he is. Right now isn't the time, anyway, especially before tomorrow."

They fell silent again. Corsair growled, feeling anger mount inside him.

"I don't even want to be here, you know? I was happy living the life I had. Yeah, my father sometimes made it unbearable, but I had my mother. I had free rides with Quickpaw. I had afternoons off. I had tournaments. I had Rohesia to speak to. Now all I've got is some stupid paint over my right eye."

"You did it for your dad?"

"Not voluntarily. He made me. He even told me to leave Quickpaw and pick another ictharr and that's what got to me most of the time. He'd pick on him for doing nothing. For not being bred like Harangoth was."

"I didn't see any of the 'bred' ictharrs stand up to Thornfang like he did."

"Exactly. And now we're here because of him. I could die tomorrow."

"Hey, come on-"

"Quickpaw could die tomorrow. I don't want him to get hurt and I don't know how I'd even cope if something happened to him. What if Ragnee died or Harangoth died or Rohesia? I don't even know where she is right now and I just don't want to be in this stupid situation where..." He could feel his eyes stinging, tears trying to push their way out, but he shook his head and wiped his eyes. The fiery anger subsided.

"Sorry."

"It's all right. It's something important to you."

"Maybe I'm not the ideal Krosguard soldier McVarn thought I could be. Hell, I wouldn't be surprised if Maximus held it over my head."

"Don't worry about Maximus. That maniac is stuck in a cell waiting for his hearing so he can just be sent back to prison where he belongs. And, besides, being scared isn't something to feel ashamed about."

"How do you mean?"

"The first thing you want to know is that everyone, ultimately, wants to survive. All these wolves here – the veterans, the recruits, the eager and so on – are all going crazy with fear. As much as I hate to say it, someone here will die in seconds of the battle starting. That's the nature of it. And all of us are just waiting to see who it's going to be."

"But I see all these riders joking around and looking excited about war, Axel. *War.* They'll be killing someone tomorrow. Do they not see that?"

"They're good at hiding their fear. They act pumped and train to keep their image, maintaining their dominance. I'm not saying everyone here is as compassionate as you. Some of the wolves here couldn't care less about the rabbits and will cut them down with no hesitation. The fact you're aware of the consequence of killing someone, no matter who they are, speaks volumes."

"Right."

"I think it takes guts to be open about your insecurity. Hiding it behind layers and layers of armour only stresses the fact that you can't confront your fear. Leaving it out in the open shows you don't care so there's no need to hide it, right?"

"I guess. You seem kind of..."

Axel tilted his head.

"Kind of what?"

"I don't know. That answer seemed really well-rehearsed."

He chuckled.

"I'm passionate about it. I didn't join the army to fight or kill, I joined to save. That hasn't changed."

"But you were training like us. You were training how to kill people."

"The Krosguard don't really want apothecaries who'll ride out and die whenever someone corners them. I've got to be able to defend myself, even if it goes against what I think."

Axel leaned in.

"But you know I was talking about how not everyone is as sensitive as you about killing?"

"Yeah?"

"I want to tell you something – do not drop your guard. Maybe some of the wolves here freak you out but the rabbits aren't any more appealing than they are. A lot of them will try and kill you without hesitation either because they're scared or because they hate you. Out there, Corsair, it's about survival. *Do not let your guard down*, understand?"

"I understand."

"I know what I'm saying is probably the last thing you want to hear but you need to be prepared if you want to survive this. You're a good rider, Corsair. And a good person."

"Don't flatter me."

"Don't flatter you? Okay, maybe saying, 'You have good control,' or, 'Your ictharr is fast,' is flattery, but falling down the side of a hill and almost plummeting to your death *on the first day* and still surviving? It's impossible for that to be flattery. It is just a pure hard fact that you are a good rider."

"I almost got kicked out by McVarn because of what Quickpaw did."

"And Quickpaw stopped me and Arwie from getting kicked out. Sure, it was an accident and you didn't intend to do it, but it was still what saved my backside there."

Corsair shook his head in denial.

"And Quickpaw is loyal to you. He loves you with all his heart. He'll keep you safe. If you can survive whatever mess of a race the first day had going on, you can survive this."

"Thanks."

He paused.

"Axel, by the way, I'm sorry for not intervening when Arwenin was being... you know..."

"Difficult?"

"I guess. I should have. If Quickpaw didn't drag me out there, I don't know if I'd be having this conversation with you."

"No big deal. It's scary going up against whatever monster Maximus rode. But that's done. Don't worry about it."

They sat there for a few more minutes, silently gazing at the fire as it fizzled out and died. They were plunged into darkness. The only light left came from the lanterns marking the path between the tents.

"Is there anything else?"

"I'm scared. That's it."

"It's normal, Corsair. Everyone here is scared. You'll make it through, I know you will, buddy."

He nodded.

"Did this help? You talking to me?"

"It helped a bit, yeah."

With a grunt, Axel stood.

"I'm glad to be of service. I'll be heading to bed. Well, I say bed, but I actually mean a luxurious damp piece of padding on the ground."

Corsair chuckled.

"I don't mean to be your mother, either, but I think you should go back to bed soon. You'll need all the rest you can get. Whether you listen to me is up to you but it's the smart thing to do."

"I will, soon. Thanks."

Axel patted him on the shoulder, smiled and walked away. He was left alone in the dark, staring at the dead embers of the fire, knowing that what he dreaded most was only hours away.

I can do this. Screw Dad and screw everything else. I'll survive this war. We'll survive it. I'm strong. I'm not scared.

Solidifying his new-found resolve with a nod, he stood up and returned to bed.

THE SIEGE OF POTHOLE PLAINS

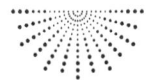

(1139, AESTIOM)

The next morning passed quickly. Corsair was awoken by the deep voice of a soldier ordering the drowsy wolves to be ready for the final part of their journey to the border. Before he knew it, he found himself on Quickpaw's back and riding towards Pothole Plains.

And, eventually, he was there.

The fields surrounding the settlement were covered with hills and bumps, with not a speck of white to be seen on the grass or the few trees. There were many small crater-like dips in the ground between the wolves and their target, some filled with clear sun-warmed water while others were empty. Corsair saw the town across the numerous hills and potholes separating them. He could see the cosy cottages and the marketplace, quaint in comparison to the one back in the capital. He could see the fields of crops around it with all the farmhouses, farmyards and barns.

He could see the specks of the enemy rushing back and forth, their cries in the Eposian tongue carrying across the plains.

It's happening it's happening it's happening–

He took a deep breath. It was nothing to panic about – he was a brave wolf. He wasn't scared. The rabbits didn't scare him. In minutes, they'd be fleeing from the Clan of the Great Lupine and abandoning the settlement. Nothing would stop him.

"Maintain ranks!" the officer yelled.

Before him, arranged in formation among shield-wielding wolves, were tens of soldiers placed in block-like formations. They were spaced apart evenly across the hill, archers arranged behind them and with bows ready, waiting for their signal. On his left and right were his Krosguard comrades, many of them veterans that mingled with the recruits who graduated with him. Ragnar was to his left, lance at the ready, visor up and shield held.

Quickpaw whimpered again.

"We'll be fine," Corsair said. "I won't let anything happen to you. Listen to what I say and we'll be fine."

The ictharr gave a trembling growl, one that understood what he was saying but still doubted it. Quickpaw glanced left and right, looking at the brave faces of his fellow soldiers, trying to muster up the courage they had. Harangoth growled to get his attention and then nodded, a reassuring gesture that he appreciated.

"*Alpha is present!*"

Whatever murmurs circulated the ranks, whether excited or anxious, fell silent when they saw Alpha McVarn ride out in front of them. He turned, putting his back to the settlement.

"The Land of the Sun and Moon have overstayed their welcome in *our* settlement. They have driven our people out from their homes and into the cold to freeze to death. They have taken advantage of our hospitality and kindness sealed by the Raskartz-Amien pact. The Winter Baron wants to remind them of the consequences of threatening our people and jeopardising the safety of the Clan of the Great Lupine."

He drew his sword.

"Today, we reclaim Pothole Plains. You are to advance towards the settlement and send the rabbits running. Raise our banner in the town centre and demonstrate to them exactly how the Clan of the Great Lupine deals with those who stand against us. Krosguard, wait for my signal to charge. Soldiers, prepare to march. Archers, ready your bows!"

"*Ready bows!*" a subordinate yelled.

Corsair heard stretching bowstrings as the archers nocked their arrows and aimed up into the sky, preparing to launch a volley. The soldiers before him formed walking boxes of armour, with the shields raised to form a front-facing wall and ceiling. The Clan of the Great Lupine's insignia glared at the settlement, taunting the rabbits.

Oh God it's happening...

"*Volley!*"

A hundred bowstrings snapped forwards, followed by the sound of arrows whizzing through the air. Hundreds of silhouettes shot across the ground, approaching the settlement, some embedding into the soil whilst the rest began to hit the buildings.

"Catapults!" Alpha McVarn yelled.

"*Catapults!*" a subordinate relayed.

The siege battery behind them flung their destructive ammunition into the sky, hurling them towards the town. They struck buildings and crushed silhouettes, sending rubble flying.

"Drums!" Alpha McVarn bellowed.

"*Drums!*" a subordinate yelled.

A steady beat thundered through the air as several painted wolves battered the drums, heads down in concentration.

"Shield walls, *advance!*"

"Forward, soldiers!"

The giant steel insects began to crawl forwards, moving down the hill and advancing towards the fields. Arrows flew back in their direction, deflecting off the shields and landing unheeded in the turf. Another volley was fired by the lupines, soaring into the sky and flying over the advancing soldiers.

"Corsair."

He turned his head to see Ragnar looking at him.

"You'll be fine, all right? Stay focused, don't panic, and there'll be nothing to worry about."

"Ragnee-"

"Krosguard! Visors down!" Alpha McVarn yelled.

"I love you," his brother said, slamming down the helmet's visor and looking away. Corsair focused his gaze on him, hoping it would not be the last time they spoke, before looking forwards and pushing his visor down. He felt the steel plating cover his snout and face. Vision was limited to the eyeholes. His breathing was loud inside the confines of the helmet, bouncing off the walls and into his crushed ears.

Stay calm stay calm...

"Ready your weapons!"

Corsair gripped his paw tighter around the shaft of the lance. Another whimper came from Quickpaw, beginning to shy away from the front rank.

He gasped as he saw boulders fly up into the sky, launched by rabbit trebuchets, and watched them come crashing down into the dirt. One struck a metal insect and crushed the warriors within it, their brief, interrupted screams of pain echoing back across the plains.

"For the Clan of the Great Lupine..."

Alpha McVarn thrusted his sword towards the settlement.

"*...attack!*"

With a chorus of triumphant yells, howls and the rapid beat of the war drums, the Krosguard propelled themselves down the hill. Banners attached to the necks of lances fluttered in the wind, displaying the clan's emblem that howled in unison with them. Quickpaw charged forwards, leading his rider into the enemy. They were gaining on the shield walls, distracting the archers from their targets, and Corsair could see the distant figures begin to fire on them instead.

"Keep going, we're doing well!"

And then the first arrow hit.

A rider ahead of him, metres off to his right, was struck in the chest by an arrow. The force behind the hit punctured the armour and he yelled out, collapsing sideways off his ictharr and rolling away. His companion squealed and turned, chasing after its rider, almost knocking down one of its comrades.

"Don't stop!"

They arrived beside the shield walls and surged past, giving the archers cause for concern. Their aims shifted from the advancing insects to the beasts of war, firing volleys towards them.

"*Incoming!*"

Corsair gasped as the ictharr in front was shot in the paw, making it squeal in pain and trip over. It began barrelling towards Quickpaw, rolling towards his legs at surprising speed.

"Leap!"

Quickpaw leapt into the air, narrowly avoiding being knocked down and sent sprawling. More and more riders went down around him, dying alongside their ictharrs and collapsing on to the grass.

"Javelins!"

Nearby riders drew their javelins and hurled them towards the archers, watching them arc through the air and impale some of the rabbits. More wolves were shot down, left injured or dead in the grass.

"Keep moving!"

Corsair's heart was thundering inside his chest, his mind racing as he processed the chaos raging around him. He heard the dying scream of an ictharr nearby. Quickpaw went taut in terror.

"We'll be okay! Just-"

He saw a pothole up ahead, too wide to jump over. A body of water sat inside, tranquil in the middle of the conflict, and he yanked on the reins.

"Stop!"

Quickpaw skidded to a halt, a metre short of the hole, and his master directed him away and back to the shield walls. His fellow riders kept doing circles around them, throwing javelins and drawing the enemy's fire. Infantry began running down the hill to support them, more volleys flying through the air.

"Bridges!" a soldier yelled. "We're here, get the bridges!"

"*Bridges!*"

As the shield walls arrived at the side of the potholes, their faces opened up and allowed teams of wolves to hurry out and place down reinforced planks of wood. Each one was wide enough to allow the shield wall to cross it and strong enough to hold its weight, preventing the soldiers from falling into the waters below.

The soldiers scurried back into cover.

"Onwards! Over the bridges!"

"Krosguard, keep moving!" Alpha McVarn yelled. "Across the bridges, protect those shield walls!"

Corsair, as reluctant as he was, directed Quickpaw towards the bridges without hesitation. He sprinted towards one, eager to cross and conclude the battle.

"Stay with me, Quickpaw, come on! Faster!"

He neared the bridge, only a metre away from the side of the water-filled hole, until Corsair saw a wolf's face peering up at him.

Then he saw the long ears.

Then he saw the short and stubby nose.

And then he realised that face did not belong to a lupine.

The waters tore open as the rabbits emerged from the concealment of the pond's reeds, rising up with swords and spears at the ready. With the shield wall's flanks unprotected, the lupines could only turn and yell out in panic as the rabbits closed in on them and forced them into the water, dismantling the shield wall in seconds. The sounds of ambush came from around them, with the waters churning as the rabbits rushed out from their concealed positions.

Corsair tried to yank on the reins as Quickpaw continued to travel towards the pond but it was too late. He pushed out his paws to bring him and Corsair skidding to a halt but he was travelling too fast. The ground disappeared from beneath his front paws and Corsair felt Quickpaw pitch forwards, seeing the surface of the water rise up towards him with frightening speed.

With a scream of panic, he fell from the saddle and plunged into the pond.

Water seeped in through his armour and drenched his clothes, penetrating the material and soaking the fur beneath it. It poured in through the holes in his helmet and blinded him. He squeezed his eyes shut, trying to endure the sting. Sightless, he thrashed and struggled, wrenching his helmet from his head and discarding it in the water. He clawed his way up, hearing the sounds of combat grow louder and louder.

With a gasp, he broke through the surface and coughed up the water he had swallowed. He furiously scrubbed his eyes and tried to get his bearings. His ears flattened as the world roared around him – all he could hear were screams of pain from wolf and rabbit alike, interrupted often by the sounds of soldiers calling to one another. Metal clashed against metal, screeching and clanging, disorienting him.

Then he heard it.

Quickpaw.

He turned left and saw his steed thrashing in the water among the battling wolves and rabbits, eyes wide in panic as he struggled against the reeds. The fact the pond was shallow did nothing to calm him – he kept clawing frantically at the water, turning his head left and right to find his master but splashing water into his eyes and blinding himself.

"Quickpaw!"

To his right, he heard a scream in Eposian and turned. A ginger rabbit dressed in a reinforced leather vest, with leather pads over the shins and forearms and shoulders, rushed through the water. A black metal helmet sat on her head, a short ridge running along the top until it protruded down and rested between her eyes like a spike. She raised her one-paw sword to slash at him. Corsair stepped back while reaching for his own weapon. He tried to draw it from its scabbard.

The hilt caught on his belt.

Oh God I can't fight back I can't-

Fear driving him, he abandoned his efforts to arm himself and dived under the water, narrowly avoiding the sharp blade as it cut through the air. He swam forward, despite the weight of his armour, hoping the soldier would not persist, before he pulled himself up again.

He turned.

She had stopped pursuing him, unable to track his shape through the exploding surface of the water, but instead set her attention on the vulnerable Quickpaw, trapped in a state of terror. She waded forward, sword held by her side and ready to slay the beast.

"No!"

Corsair hurried forwards, crashing through the water, eyes set on the back of the rabbit. Panic fuelled him to keep running forwards, to defend his best friend, and he fumbled for his blade as he advanced. It refused to come free, its hilt still snagged on his belt.

Don't lay a paw on him don't you dare lay a paw on him...

Another enemy stepped out and brought her blade back, ready to swing at him, but Corsair shoved the rabbit and sent her falling backwards into the water. Dying screams and cries of pain sounded from all around him, accompanied by the *snips* of arrows cutting through the air as they flew past. The distance between him and the rabbit was closing.

Quickpaw was oblivious to his approaching demise, unable to see the rabbit bring up her blade over his neck.

Not him please not him don't touch him-

She prepared to carve Quickpaw's head from his body.

Quickpaw, with wide eyes and flattened ears, looked up at the rabbit and yowled in panic.

"Get away from him!"

The rabbit looked over her shoulder, eyes wide and mouth slightly open in surprise, but couldn't react in time as Corsair crashed into her. The sword fell from her gloved paws and splashed into the water beside Quickpaw, sinking to the bottom.

Corsair slammed the rabbit into the bank of the pond, pinning her there with one arm pressed against her chest and the other pulling back to punch her in the face. He felt his clenched metal paw connect with his target. She yelled out as the blow knocked her helmet off. He brought back his paw to strike again but she shoved him off and threw him into the edge of the pond. Corsair was momentarily stunned.

He came back to his senses as he saw the rabbit yank a dagger from a sheath by her hind paw and charge him, aiming the blade for his throat. Before he could think, Corsair's paws were up to intercept the rabbit's swinging arm and he caught the wrist, pushing it away from him.

They struggled against each other. The rabbit used her other paw to support her arm, forcing the blade closer to his jugular. Corsair's arms trembled, desperately enduring the rabbit's strength.

I'm going to die no please not like this I don't want to die please...

"Ragnee! Help! I need help! Someone!"

No one came to his aid.

His arms were giving out, unable to hold back the rabbit for much longer. His mind whirred, knowing death was moments away.

He made a bold move.

He abandoned his efforts to hold the blade back and, instead, pushed it down to the side. The dagger shot down towards the surface of the pond, still held in the rabbit's paws, but brought the soldier forwards into a disadvantageous position. Corsair turned away from the rabbit, pressing his back against her front, and positioned his elbow in front of her nose. He brought it forwards and then slammed the metal elbow into the rabbit's face.

She let out a scream as the metal broke her nose on impact, dropping the dagger and reeling back. It disappeared with a *plop* but Corsair swung one paw down into the water and caught the hilt.

He heard that familiar cry and knew the rabbit was charging him.

Corsair turned, bringing the dagger up from the water, and swung it around with arm extended to confront his opponent.

He realised the rabbit was a lot closer than anticipated.

With one panicked swipe of the knife, he slit her throat.

Blood sprayed out from the slit, hitting him in the eyes and across the bridge of his snout. He dropped the blade and tipped backwards, crashing against the edge of the pond, green eyes wide in shock as he realised what he'd done. The rabbit clutched her bleeding throat, eyes wide in pain and fear, stumbling back away from him. Blood poured on to her gloves and she gargled, struggling against fate.

With a dying gurgle, her eyes dimmed and she pitched forwards into the water. Corsair's gaze transfixed on the floating corpse.

A mist of crimson bloomed around her.

I killed her.

He looked to his left.

He saw a wolf slash down a rabbit, his dying shriek cutting through the rest of the soundscape.

I killed someone.

He looked to his right.

He saw a rabbit stab a wolf in the back. His howl of pain was interrupted as she shoved him down into the water, stabbing again and again.

This isn't right. This can't be right.

A lupine comrade turned and retaliated, cutting the rabbit's head from her shoulders and kicking her corpse down. He reached for his wounded fellow wolf, dragging him to the surface.

This can't be right! This isn't right! This isn't right!

What little resolve he had at the start of the battle disappeared in a fraction of a second, throwing him into a chasm of hysteria.

"Help!" he screamed, shaking his head and beginning to cry. "I can't do this! I'm going to die! I'm going to die, someone help me!"

His wolf comrades ignored him, clambering out of the pond and continuing to charge forwards. Arrows flew by and embedded themselves in the flesh of his comrades, followed by their dying screams and howls.

"Please! I'm going to die! *I'm going to die I can't do this anymore!* Ragnee! Rohesia! Axel! Quickpaw! Someone, please, do something! Save me! *Save me!*"

He heard the sound of something rushing towards him, just loud enough to be heard over Quickpaw's persistent panic. He was hyperventilating, eyes trained on the floating rabbit corpse amongst many, watching the water turn crimson.

"Save me!"

Something dropped down into the water beside him and he bellowed in surprise, falling on to his rump in the water and pushing himself away.

"Get away from me!"

"Hey, hey, take it easy!"

Axel helped him on to his hind paws and hurried him under the bridge. Arwenin dropped down and rushed over to Quickpaw, offering yaps of reassurance and helping him out of the reeds. Quickpaw steeled himself and padded through the water with her, ducking under the bridge for refuge.

Axel positioned Corsair against the edge of the pond.

"Are you hurt? Where are you hurt?"

"I-I killed someone," Corsair stuttered. "She was going to kill Quickpaw so I attacked her and we struggled and she tried to stab me and I killed her I killed her I killed her..."

"What?"

"I killed someone, Axel! I killed someone and I can't do this anymore! I can't see people die, I can't kill anyone! You need to take me home! You need to get me out of here!"

Corsair winced as Axel growled.

"Are you kidding me, Corsair?"

"P-please, Axel, I can't do this! I can't go out there! I'm going to die or kill someone else and I've got blood on my face! I don't want to die, Axel, please!"

"You can't be wasting my time like this, Corsair! Other people need help!"

"But…"

The ground trembled as a boulder hurtled into the earth and they both ducked down. Screams and howls followed, accompanied by the *thuds* of bodies hurled into the air by the impact crashing back into the ground.

"Apothecary!" someone wailed. "My leg! I can't move!"

"Oh God, it hurts! *It hurts!*"

Axel stepped away from Corsair, moving to leave the pond, but the prince caught his arm.

"You can't leave me alone here! Please! I'll die!"

"You'll die if you stay here," he said, shrugging him off. "A boulder from a trebuchet could hit this pond and then you're done."

"But-"

"If you get caught deserting or running away, you go to jail. Keep moving forward. I don't have time for this. Come on Arwie!"

Axel rushed out into the open and began to clamber out, his ictharr heaving herself on to dry land with dripping-wet fur.

"I can't kill anyone again!" Corsair yelled.

But the apothecary didn't answer. He mounted Arwenin and sped off towards the screams as another trebuchet boulder crashed down into the wolves. Corsair cowered under the bridge, the bodies of his enemies floating beside him while his comrades lay at the bottom by his hind paws, their armour dragging them down. He shook his head and stepped back, kneeling into the water.

"I can't. I can't do it. I can't do it."

Quickpaw growled and he turned his head. His ictharr was as terrified as he was, lowered down to shy away from the edge of the pond, unsure of what to do. The wolf continued to kneel there for a moment, listening to the yells of pain coming from all sides.

I can't do it again. I can't. It's another person. I'm killing another person.

Then he remembered what Axel had said. Jail. He'd be locked away. How long? He didn't know. A month or a couple of years behind bars for cowardice. If he continued to stay there, he faced a harsh sentence from which his status wouldn't save him.

All the blood. The bodies. The dying howls. The dead ictharrs.

He knew that, much to his dismay, he had to advance. Even if he weren't found, the bridge wouldn't deflect a trebuchet boulder flung towards the pond and would crush both him and Quickpaw in a second. His best chance was not to remain stationary but to keep moving.

He turned to meet Quickpaw's reluctant gaze.

"W-we have to go forwards."

Quickpaw gave a growl of fearful protest, shrinking into the bank of the pond.

"Trust me... okay? I won't let anyone hurt you. I promise you."

Quickpaw remained unsure for a following moment, tempted by the idea of staying where they were, but forced out a growl of agreement. Corsair led him out from beneath the bridge and, after scanning the bloodied and muddied landscape, dragged himself out from the water. He got to his hind paws as Quickpaw pulled himself out of the pond. He mounted him, sitting down in the saddle and turning to face the settlement.

I can't do it.

He froze again.

I can't do this.

With nothing but the desperation to survive left in him, he snapped the reins and charged forwards after his comrades.

In the town centre of Pothole Plains stood a newly-erected triage centre, consisting of dozens of leather tents. The banner of the Land of the Sun and Moon, a circle that was half-moon, half-sun, flew high above them. One side was bright yellow, glowing with light, while the other was dark purple. It reminded the soldiers of their faith and devotion – of their duty to defend their land from the lupine invaders.

Beds and cabinets of medical supplies filled the tents of the triage centre. A line of trebuchets stood several metres away, showering the enemy with boulders. Teams of rabbits heaved the ammunition into position, readying it to fire.

However, minutes after the wolves launched their assault, the officer could see how dire the situation was.

Every bed was filled with wounded, crimson staining the white sheets of the beds and the stone paving beneath them. Some soldiers were laid out on the ground, given thin sheets to lie on as scant comfort. She watched doctors rush to and fro from tent to tent, tending to the wounded as best they could.

She knew offering to help would only complicate the doctors' job even further.

"Make way!"

She turned to see two soldiers rushing past, paws holding either end of a leather stretcher. Blood was splattered across their armour and faces but they pressed on, carrying the wounded to safety. The officer followed the stretcher with her eyes and saw a rabbit lying there, eyes barely open and moaning weakly with several arrows protruding from his chest. Blood stained the leather sheet holding him up, pouring from his wounds.

Help them recover, merciful moon.

"Officer!"

She turned back to face the entrance to the town centre. A lone rabbit ran towards her, pumping his legs forwards to close the distance as quickly as he could. When he arrived by the officer, he keeled over and panted, shaking his head.

"You have news?" she asked.

The messenger opened his mouth to speak but hesitated, unsure of how to deliver his message. She didn't need to ask what was troubling him to know how the battle was faring. She suppressed her rising fear, knowing what defeat would lead to.

"How badly are we losing, soldier?"

"The lupines are advancing on the crops. It will be moments before they are upon the outskirts and minutes before they besiege our base camp, officer. They number too many."

She stood there, mouth agape.

"They are already nearing the crops? What about the ambushes?"

"They attempted to cross the ponds with their bridges and our soldiers leapt at them from the shallows but they were overwhelmed within a minute, officer. The sun's ferocity was not enough – the lupines are simply too vicious. The soldiers need orders while they still have beating hearts in their chests or all will be lost."

The officer looked over her shoulder and towards the west. Cries of battle echoed from the front lines, growing louder with every passing second. The enemy would be overrunning them before long, no matter how many rabbits she sent to slow their advance.

"Any attempt to defend the settlement further will only lead to a slaughter. We must prepare to retreat from Pothole Plains."

"Retreat? Officer, the reinforcements may still-"

"Do not let pride cloud your judgement, soldier. We have been abandoned. The wolves will keep charging, howling and snarling in bloodlust, cutting us down without hesitation. We are outmatched despite our preparations. Pothole Plains is lost."

"Then what do you propose, officer?"

The officer pointed to the series of carriages lined up on the road leading to the eastern exit of the settlement, used a month ago to ferry cargo from their homeland to the front. Adeuns - creatures of formidable muscle - were connected in pairs to each carriage, waiting for their drivers to lead them.

"Help the wounded on to the carriages and prepare to make haste for our land. When the wounded are accounted for, summon all our troops back to the town centre and ensure they make it on to the transports."

"What about our supplies? Our weaponry?"

"Abandon everything except for the essentials – medicine, food, water. Spread the word as far as you can."

"What if there isn't enough time, officer?"

"Don't worry about that! Go!"

Not arguing, the rabbit rushed into the tents. She listened to his frantic cries as he spread the news, hoping the vulnerable would be shielded from harm.

She turned to face her subordinate.

"Acier?"

A white rabbit in standard dress stood before her – golden robes over the dark trousers and white service shirt beneath the reinforced black-leather armour that was clamped over her torso, shins, forearms and shoulders. Black hind-paw socks and gloves covered her paws. Dangling from her shoulders and neck were strips of black cloth, reaching down from the headdress she wore. They concealed every-thing except her eyes, revealing the single black spot on the right side of her face.

The officer looked down at Acier's *Caeli* sword, the one-pawed engraved blade hanging at her side.

"The wolves are upon us. We must keep the enemy occupied. Rally the troops."

The white rabbit nodded before she rushed off towards the triage centre. The officer looked back towards the west. Towards the enemy.

Grant us fiery vengeance, sun. Let us slay every last lupine.

"Charge!"

"Into the fields! Cut them down!"

"Take back Pothole Plains – for the Clan of the Great Lupine!"

"For the Winter Baron!"

Quickpaw bounded towards the wooden fence surrounding the crops, his master guiding him there while making sharp turns to avoid knocking down their slower comrades.

"Leap!"

Quickpaw jumped the fence and landed on the other side without an issue, taking a few steps before coming to a stop. Quickpaw growled, unable to see through the crops, looking left and right for directions.

"We need to keep moving, Quickpaw! I'll lead you, come-"

A howl of pain sounded metres to his left and he looked up. His position on Quickpaw's back allowed him to see over the tops of the tall crop plants, watching as a Krosguard rider lurched back with three arrows protruding from his chest and another from his throat. A cut-off yelp followed as his ictharr died, a stray arrow striking it in the face, and Corsair looked towards the source of the projectiles.

A number of farm buildings loomed ahead, the windows broken for the archers to fire at the wolves and their mounts.

Corsair saw the rabbits target him, drawing back the strings of their bows.

"Down!"

He dived out of the saddle and crashed into the ground, his armour clattering as it came against the soil. Quickpaw lay down, ducking his head away from the path of the arrows that whizzed through the air where they had just been standing.

"Archers!" a wolf yelled.

"They're in the huts! Charge! Kill them!"

"Forward!"

"Keep moving, keep moving!"

"In the buildings! Move the archers, get the ranks to the fence and fire into those buildings!"

"*Archers!* Someone get the archers!"

From every direction, the plants rustled as wolves rushed past. Corsair caught glimpses of them as they charged, watching as they wove out of the way of arrows and advanced with swords and shields at the ready.

Then his eyes fell upon a body.

A wolf lay dead in the middle of the crops. She was sprawled out on her front, blood pooling from beneath her. Her head was turned so her lifeless eyes gazed into his.

Corsair froze, green eyes wide and body taut, unable to move.

No. I can't stop. I need to keep going.

His will faltered.

We need to keep moving. If we don't, we could both die.

He nodded, coming back to reality.

"We need to run. Fast. Come on, stay close!"

He charged forwards, knocking aside the plants as he advanced. He could hear Quickpaw behind him, padding along at a similar pace, following his master towards the edge of the field of crops. He couldn't see ahead of him so he followed the yells of his comrades, assuming they knew in which direction they were travelling. He wove around blades of wheat, moving as much as he could to dodge incoming projectiles, eyes swivelling in their sockets as they scanned for flying arrows. As he ran, Corsair looked up. He saw the farm-houses ahead.

He saw one of the rabbits aiming out the window.

At him.

"Quickp-"

Before he could react, he heard the *snap* of the string being released and felt something crash against him.

He screamed, falling to the side, curling up into a ball and shielding where he was hit. Quickpaw yowled and rushed towards him, whimpering and mewling for him to get up. Corsair couldn't. His tears blinded him, the screams deafened him, and he couldn't concentrate.

I'm dying I'm dying oh God the arrow got me-

He looked down and investigated the wound, wincing with every move, and placed a gauntleted paw against the arrow. He expected pain to shoot through him, to summon another scream.

But he felt none.

Confused, he pushed it with his paw.

The arrow fell out, the tip untainted by blood. Quickpaw growled in concern. The armour was dented inwards where the arrow had struck him but, fortunately, had held fast against the projectile.

Corsair let out a small sigh of relief but didn't stop for any longer.

"I'm okay... I'm okay."

Knowing he wasn't injured, he got up and rushed forwards, leading Quickpaw ahead. His heart thudded inside his chest, his body beginning to burn from the exertion, but the idea that a rabbit was aiming for him again kept him moving.

At last, he reached the edge of the fields.

Corsair rushed towards the fence and went to jump over it, fuelled by adrenaline, but felt his hind paw smack the top bar. He fell. He yelled as he did so, landing on his front and rolling before coming to a halt. He spared no time. He shot up to his hind paws and threw himself down by the base of the building, gesturing for Quickpaw to follow. The ictharr leapt over the fence and rushed towards him, ducking down by his side and looking up. Copying his steed, Corsair gazed up at the windows, panting with his pink tongue hanging from the corner of his mouth. He could hear the clashing of metal above him, accompanied by the shrieks of slain rabbits.

"The archers are down!" a wolf yelled. "Forwards! To the centre!"

"Raise our banner and kill them all!"

A roar of adrenaline-fuelled bravery came from the wolves as they rushed out from the fields, emerging from the rows of wheat and pushing down the road between the buildings. Corsair watched them from his position. They were all snarling, growling, barking and howling as they advanced. Krosguard riders shot out and darted forwards, lances ready in paw.

Keep moving keep moving...

"Up, Quickpaw, come on!"

He stood and mounted his steed, settling into the saddle, before he took up the reins and snapped at them. Quickpaw shot forwards and around the bend, racing past his comrades and following after the front line that was advancing into the town. Soldiers charged after a detachment of rabbits down the pathway leading to the centre, flanked by shrubbery and bushes.

"They're on the run! After them!"

"Leave no rabbit standing! Onwards!"

Seeing the rabbits before him, he drew back on the reins.

Quickpaw eased to a stop in the middle of the road, questioning his master's decision with a growl. He didn't respond – he watched as his comrades rushed after the rabbits, beginning to catch up. He knew what would follow – the sounds of combat, the despaired screams of the dying, the siren call of metal clanging against metal that would fail to tempt him.

He was scared. He could see the rabbit again before him; throat slashed, blood pouring. He could feel it clinging to his face. The blood he spilt. The blood of the person he murdered.

I can't keep doing this. Get it together and keep moving. Get it together and keep moving! We're going to survive this!

"*Hyah!*"

He snapped at the reins and Quickpaw bound forwards, shooting after his comrades. The wall of rabbits continued to rush back to the centre of Pothole Plains, yelling to each other in their native tongue. They turned and fired arrows as they ran. Corsair ducked out the way of each one, wary that his head was exposed.

Just survive just survive just survive...

Then the bushes moved.

Rabbits poured out from the undergrowth, giving a courageous battle shriek as they charged weapon-first into the flanks of the wolves. Archers stepped out and fired at the Krosguard soldiers, knocking them from their saddles or firing into their steeds to bring them to a sudden halt. Corsair saw a fellow rider collapse from his dead ictharr, still alive, before rabbits swarmed him and slashed him to pieces.

"Back, back, go back!"

Quickpaw turned, hoping to retreat, but saw rabbits charging from behind. They aimed their swords and spears at Quickpaw and sprinted at him. With nowhere else to retreat to, the cornered beast snarled, bared his fangs and leant down on his front paws.

A foolhardy rabbit came forwards, bringing his spear back to thrust into Quickpaw's neck. Quickpaw intercepted his attack by springing forwards and knocking him to the side. He yelled out, stumbling away and crashing into another rabbit. Another enemy followed, stepping to the side to swing, but Quickpaw swiped across the area in front of him with his paw. Even if he didn't possess Harangoth's brawn, he was strong enough to send the rabbit flying back a metre.

Corsair winced as he heard the *screech* of metal scraping against metal, coming from his left. He looked down to see an enemy's sword resting against Quickpaw's side, trying to cut through the armour.

"Kick!"

Quickpaw turned and his rear legs shot out, striking the soldier in the stomach. He was sent flying back into the battle, unable to resist the formidable force.

We're being mobbed. They'll overwhelm Quickpaw.

Pushing through the fear, he swung one leg over and dropped down from his companion. His steed looked over his shoulder, asking for orders with a growl of urgency.

"I'll help hold them off! Focus on yourself!"

He readied his longsword, the weight of its implication bearing down on him.

It's me or them. It's me or them.

Corsair looked left and saw a rabbit charging forwards, a spear in his paws with the head aiming straight for his stomach.

"Stay back, I don't want to-"

The rabbit thrust his spear forwards. Instinct taking over, Corsair dodged left and slashed at his stomach.

He felt the blade eat through the reinforced leather.

The soldier choked, dropping his weapon, paws clutching his stomach and the blade in it.

Corsair froze. His green eyes stared at the face of the rabbit, recognising the look of fear and despair on his face. Seconds of pain passed before his eyes closed and his body slipped sideways off the blade. Corsair remained there, towering over his foe.

It's me or them. It's me or –

"Clan of the Great Lupine!"

Heads turned, but combat raged on. Only those who were unengaged focused on the voice, distracted from the inferno of war.

Ahead, a line of rabbit reinforcements stood tall. They wore the same armour as their counterparts – golden robes, black leather armour and a black metal helmet. While all the rest had helmets without any decoration, the central soldier (a brown rabbit) enjoyed the privilege of a white sun painted on one side and a moon painted on the other.

"May the moon forgive your corrupt and covetous souls!" she yelled in Lanzig, thrusting her sword at them. "By the sun's bright fury, *prepare to die!*"

A terrifying shriek came from the soldiers, drawing weapons and rushing forwards. Corsair backed away, looking at Quickpaw. The ictharr was still keeping the attacking rabbits at bay, snarling and yowling at them with a ferocity that could only be summoned by desperation. He turned to aid him, sword at the ready.

"Behind you!"

Corsair didn't know if he was being spoken to but he didn't take any chances. Turning around, he saw a rabbit with her face hidden by dark fabric charge with her sword's blade held downwards. As she arrived by his side she swung up with tremendous speed and strength, unleashed within a fraction of a second. The strike knocked him back as he deflected.

"I've got her!" a wolf bellowed.

A wolf clad in chainmail lunged at the rabbit, attempting to attack the mysterious warrior, but the masked assailant spun away and slashed at his back. The sword cut through the armour and left a nasty gash. Hissing in pain, the soldier retaliated with a swing.

With almost no exertion, the masked rabbit leapt up into the air and curled into a ball. She shot up above the swing, arcing over the wolf, and unfurled in mid-air as she swung her sword at the soldier's throat.

Shnick.

She landed, blood dripping from her sword.

The wolf fell to his knees. Blood pouring from the ravine carved across his throat, he clamped his metal paws over the wound and choked. He struggled against death, falling on to his side and kicking. He lasted seconds in that battle. His legs became still and, relaxing, his arms fell by his side. The soldier lay there, face contorted in shock, fear and confusion.

What the hell was that?

The masked one turned on Corsair.

"Wait, I-"

Without a sound, she spun forwards and sliced downwards, chopping the air. Corsair, held back by guilt and terror, dodged out the way. He shook his head to plead but, whether it was through lack of understanding or deliberate ignorance, she refused to pay any heed. She unleashed a barrage of fluid swings from all sides, attacking from every direction. He struggled to keep up. He dodged back but the masked one persisted, targeting him, and he looked around for any way of escape.

Corsair kicked at his foe. As she was so aggressive in her offensive, she did not expect the sudden counterattack and stumbled back. However, what Corsair expected to be a few seconds' break was drastically shortened. She advanced again and rolled, ducking past Corsair, before stabbing backwards. He yelled out, feeling the blade clash against his armour, but was saved by its strength once again. He was only forced back a step.

"I don't want to-"

She brought her blade down, quick and hard, but Corsair's survival instincts leapt into action. Bringing his sword up, he parried the blow and slashed down, aiming for her front. He felt the tip catch the front of the armour but knew it hadn't cut any deeper.

The masked one stepped back, blade at the ready.

"I just want to live! Please! We don't need to fight! I don't want to kill you!"

She spun her blade in defiance of his refusal. He prepared himself to slay yet another rabbit. His conscience protested and rioted inside him, spreading chaotic guilt all throughout, but he knew it was his life or hers.

A loud cry in the rabbit's native tongue came from his right. Both combatants looked towards the voice.

The rabbits' leader strode forward, the blood of Corsair's comrades still on her sword. Corsair quickly turned to aim his sword at her. He switched continuously from target to target as she approached, unsure of who he would be fighting, and kept his wits about him. He glanced over his shoulder, looking for Quickpaw.

Quickpaw, come on.

The leader spoke rapidly in a foreign language, surprisingly soft and delicate to Corsair's ears. She gestured back to the centre while keeping her eyes on him. The masked one stood there for a moment, seemingly reluctant to follow her superior's orders, before a shouted command from her officer made her listen and she did as she was told. She rushed away, disappearing into the crowd.

Corsair's eyes focused on the leader in front of him.

"You will suffer for this attack," she said in Lanzig. "Your Winter Baron will have his proud warriors slaughtered and desecrated."

Corsair shook his head, taking a step back.

"I don't want to kill anyone else. Please. Just go away."

"There is no refusing this, wolf. Your blood will turn that white banner of yours to crimson."

After the venomous threat, filled with hate and loathing, she took up battle stance.

"Prepare to perish, *invader*."

She walked forwards slowly with a confident gait. Corsair could only back away with his sword up to his snout in face-on stance.

Cornered. Surrounded. Confronted. Trapped.

There was no alternative. He had to fight.

Breaking his reluctance with a yell, he stepped forwards and stabbed at her chest. She knocked it away with her blade and slashed, a swing that was blocked by his sword. Corsair attacked and she blocked. They repeated the encounters several times, both attempting to stab at their opponent, before he broke the cycle and evaded backwards. He took a moment to draw breath, to assess the situation, but that time was cut short as the enemy stepped forwards and swung down. He blocked the swing and felt his weapon hold back the blade, his snout inches away from the officer's determined face.

"May the moon have mercy on your evil soul, lupine!"

Corsair pushed the blade down to the left, bringing the clash away from their faces and towards the ground, before he tore his blade away and knocked his sword's hilt against her helmet. She grunted. Persevering, he attacked again, slashing at her head. She deflected the attack with her blade and riposted. Weaving his right side out of the way, he spun to the side and brought the sword around as he did so, snarling.

He felt his weapon collide against her armour and tear through the leather, ripping into flesh. She yelled out as the sword cut through her body, blood pouring from the fissure in her defences.

"*G-gadour!*" she swore.

Corsair stepped back, hoping that would drive all her will to fight away, but she shook it off and swung. He ducked beneath her attack and rose again, stabbing towards her face. She jerked her head out the way of the jab, saving herself from a quick and brutal death, but Corsair continued and sliced downwards. The blade sent up sparks as it scraped against the helmet, sliding down and crashing against the shoulder plating.

"You're going to die, wolf!"

The leader swung down and his sword leapt up to defend its master, supported by Corsair's strength. They held each other there, grunting and pushing back, each trying to keep the adversary's blade at bay. He could feel his strength waning, knowing the rabbit was wearing him down.

I can't keep this up – she'll tire me out and kill me I need to end this...

As if he heard him, Quickpaw tore through the thinning crowd and leapt at the leader, fangs bared and front legs outstretched towards her.

She heard the oncoming battering ram and decided against being torn apart by an ictharr's maw. She pushed away from him, swinging as she turned to strike Quickpaw. Agility prevailing, he darted out the way of the attack and drew her attention away from his master, granting him the prime opportunity to strike. Mind racing, Corsair didn't hesitate as he brought the sword back and rushed forwards, thrusting it at her back.

She swatted away the ictharr with her sword, deterring him from attacking again, and turned with blade held up in the air. She ignored the pain of the wounds inflicted upon her, ready to slay Corsair in one downward blow.

Both let out a battle cry as they collided with each other.

Crunch.

Both froze.

Corsair stared at the soldier's leather torso, eyes wide with paws clenched around the hilt of his sword. She did the same, eyes focused on him, sword still held above her head in shock.

Trembling, her paws slackened and her blade fell to the ground, clattering against the path.

She choked and looked down.

Corsair's sword was rammed through her torso.

Corsair looked up at the leader's face. Despite her stern expression, he saw a glimmer of fear behind it. Blood dribbled from the corner of her mouth.

"I... I tried to tell you that... that..."

The rabbit, with some strength left in her, placed a paw on his shoulder and pulled herself into him. She exhaled, her breath trembling like her body, and stared into the prince's eyes.

"The Clan... of the Great L-Lupine... will crumble into... dust... before the glory of the... the sun and... the... the..."

Struggling to finish her sentence, her eyes dimmed and her body stopped trembling. A final sigh came from her, the last of her life vacating the body. She slumped forwards against him. Corsair took a step back, supporting himself against the weight of the corpse, before standing there.

He stood still.

I killed her. I did this.

Restraining his disgust, fuelled by guilt, he pushed the corpse off his sword. He looked away to avoid the horrid pupils, life drained from her eyes, and winced as she hit the ground with a *thump*.

Around him, the battle was over. Rabbits retreated from the wolves while their allies lay slaughtered around his hind paws. There were plenty of wolves and ictharrs to accompany them, cut to pieces.

No longer in danger, he dropped his sword and fell to his knees.

It's over.

He looked down at his gauntlets. The padding beneath and between the metal plating was coated in crimson. He trembled at the sight of copious blood on his paws. It was spattered over his white tabard. It was over his face, over his chest.

I killed three people. Three people with...

With families.

With stories.

With lives, like his own.

Corsair mourned his innocence in frozen silence, crying over its corpse that now lay among the bodies of wolves and rabbits alike.

Quickpaw whimpered as he saw the corpses of fellow ictharrs strewn across the roadway. He sat, ears folded down, and bowed his head to mourn the loss of his brethren.

It was a bloodbath.

CHAPTER SIXTEEN

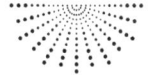

"*E*asy, easy."

Corsair eased back on the reins. Quickpaw slowed to a halt, stopping metres behind the eastern gate. He threw one leg over the side and dropped down to the ground, landing with a crunch in the snow. He removed his bag of belongings from Quickpaw's saddle and slung it over his shoulder, stepping forwards and taking his companion's reins in one paw.

The gates shut behind him. He breathed in the cold night air.

He was home.

Grand Wolf Plains was blanketed by the darkness of nightfall, with mantled lanterns placed to provide weak illumination for the main pathway. At this hour citizens were too busy sleeping to be walking about the town.

He was alone. He was thankful for that.

His mind drifted to the idea of returning home immediately, retiring to his bed for the rest of the night, but he knew his father would be surprised first and angered second. He couldn't bear to see him again, not after their fierce confrontation. He needed time to think, time to prepare.

Mr Duncan.

The tavern owner most certainly preferred the sight of his older brother to him, but he didn't care about his personal opinion. A strong drink and a few hours of contemplation would be enough to clear his mind.

He hoped, anyway.

He let out a fog of breath.

"Come on, Quickpaw."

They set off. He looked up as he walked, watching the delicate snowfall. He never thought he would long to feel the icy embrace of the cold after such a short period of relief from it.

It was only four days since the horror of Pothole Plains.

Minutes after he killed the rabbit officer, Pothole Plains had fallen. Those who tried to fend off the unstoppable waves of wolves were slaughtered, blood spilled across the fresh grass of the settlement, but most fled in a convoy of wagons drawn by adeuns. The air was filled with celebration and triumph, wolves howling up to the clear blue sky as the banner of the Clan of the Great Lupine flew high in the town centre.

Corsair, however, had not got up from his knees. He remained there, blinking away the tears, trying to cope with the brutality of the battle he had experienced.

So many had died around him. He wished he could forget.

Had it not been for the kindness of Alpha McVarn, he would have been trapped on the front for months on end.

The town hall's interior had been ransacked, ornaments and trophies torn down from the walls as an act of reclamation. The hall, where meetings would have been held, was long empty. It was devoid of any decoration and instead housed the wounded. Ragnar and Corsair sat in the entrance hall on a bench spared from the ransacking. Corsair could hear the moans of the injured from deeper within the building.

Axel was among the staff seeing to the wounded, lost amongst the chaos, but Corsair felt too disheartened to find him. Quickpaw and Harangoth were left in the temporary stables, given time to rest and recover from the fierce battle they had endured.

He felt miserable.

He wanted to leave. All those false hopes he'd had for himself before the battle, all those promises to be a strong warrior worthy of Krosguard service, were gone. He was not a warrior. War was not for him. It never had been. He had never wanted it to be. He had deluded himself into thinking he could charge headfirst into the carnage of battle.

Yet, there he was, sitting beside his sibling.

Corsair wiped at his eyes and sniffled.

"We'll find a way through this," Ragnar said. "There's got to be-"

"There isn't. There isn't a way through this, Ragnee. I... killed three people and... I've got to do it again until this *stupid* war is over."

"We need to stay strong."

"I can't stay strong anymore. I'm tired of staying strong. For once, I want to cry and go home – curl up in my bed and rest."

Three wolves walked into the entrance hall, on their way to the door opposite, but stopped. Neither of the siblings looked up initially, lost in their woes, until Ragnar lifted his head and Corsair followed. Alpha McVarn stood in the doorway, helmet tucked under his arm to reveal the three tied-off strands of black fur hanging from the back of his head. Two Krosguard soldiers stood on either side of him, swords in scabbard, with blood spattered across their armour and garments.

Alpha McVarn spotted them.

"Son, is that you?"

Corsair looked away. Ragnar stood to attention.

"At ease. Is he wounded?"

"No, Alpha. It's... been a burden for all of us. It's bothering him."

"Well, it's good that he's not hurt. I'm glad to hear that. How about you, son?"

"I'm fine, Alpha. I'm holding it together. Just."

"And your ictharrs?"

"Sleeping off the stress in the stables, Alpha."

"No doubt. You can sit."

The older sibling sat down beside his brother. Corsair didn't look up as the alpha knelt in front of him, placing a paw on his knee. The guards lingered behind their superior.

"Are you okay, son?"

No response.

"Son?"

"I saw so many people die today. So many wolves, so many rabbits, so... so much blood. I... killed three rabbits."

Corsair was so overwhelmed with emotion, barely holding the tears back as they stung his eyes, that he made an appeal to his alpha.

"Alpha... I'm begging you... I can't do this anymore. *We* can't do this anymore."

"Son, I'm sorry, but you took an oath. You promised to serve the Krosguard at least until the end of this war."

"I never wanted to be in the Krosguard."

Silence followed. He was crying silent tears, trickling from his eyes and becoming lost in his white fur with cunning stealth. He didn't care.

"I did it because I didn't want to argue with Dad. I did it because he wanted me to join this stupid thing..."

"Corsair," his brother said warningly.

"And I did. I hate this. I hate *all* of it and I can't do this anymore."

"Son-"

"That night in the church, Alpha, is a moment I regret. I should have gone home. Ragnee and I should have taken our ictharrs and gone home. I was out of my depth here, I always was. I lied to myself. We don't belong here."

He sniffled.

"I hate my father with everything in my heart. I *hate* him. He got me into this. He got us into this."

As he cried, he felt McVarn gently rest his paw on his shoulder, an act of comfort that he appreciated.

"Corsair, son, I can't let you go. It's wartime – under any other circumstance, I would. I would let you both go. But I can't. I know it's hard to hear, son, and I understand-"

The prince growled and shoved him off. Stumbling, the alpha took a step back and his guards drew their swords, wary of Corsair as he shot up from his seat.

"Don't lie to me! Don't stand there and tell me you understand when you have no idea what I'm talking about! If you're going to stand there and tell me that you're sending me back to fight them and kill more people, to spill more blood and watch more of my people die, then you don't understand *anything*!"

"Corsair!" Ragnar said.

"You told me back at Ignatius' Mount that you were a good judge of character, McVarn, you said that to me! If you're such a good judge of character, look me in the eyes and tell me that you think I belong here!"

"Corsair, stop!"

"I said look me in the eyes, McVarn! Look at me and tell me you're sending both of us back out there to die, to-"

"Corsair, shut up!"

The younger Sedrid turned, wincing in response to his brother's fierce reprimand. Ragnar glared at him for a moment before jerking his head back to the bench, ordering his brother to sit back down. Corsair did so, silenced.

Two soldiers rushed out through the doors of the main hall, paws on the grips of their swords.

"Is everything all right out here, Alpha?" one asked.

McVarn kept his focus on the younger Sedrid. Corsair could see him in the corner of his eye but kept staring at the tiled floor, not willing to meet his gaze.

"Yes. Everything's okay out here. Sorry for the noise."

The two soldiers nodded and disappeared back inside. Ragnar sighed.

"I'm sorry, Alpha. He's stressed."

"I can see that, son," the alpha grunted, unamused.

"I... I know we both took an oath. We swore to fight for the clan and the Winter Baron. But we can't-"

"I cannot send you both home and force others to stay. I warned your brother that his privilege as the Winter Baron's son would not be considered in the Krosguard. You are not better than anyone else."

"But you see how my brother is right now. You see what a heavy toll this has taken on him. He lied to try to prove himself and he realises it was a mistake. A big mistake."

"Do you not understand me, son? I can't let two soldiers walk away, especially because we are in the middle of a war and especially because you two are members of the Krosguard. We need the skills you two possess more than ever."

"Then send Corsair home. I'll stay."

Corsair's ears stood to attention. He shook his head, standing.

"No, Ragnee..."

His brother silenced him, holding out an arm for him to not draw closer. Ragnar held the alpha's pensive gaze.

"I can endure this. I can stay. But he needs to go back home. War isn't for him."

"I feel horrible treating him differently from all the others who want to go back to their families, too."

"I ask that you make an exception this once. Let him go home. He doesn't belong here among trained killers, you can see that."

Alpha McVarn looked at Corsair. The prince stood there, waiting for him to deliver his verdict.

"We'll have a wagon heading back to Ignatius' Mount to deliver the severely wounded along a trail back to their homes. It'll be heading back tonight. If he's ready to follow them on his ictharr, I'll permit him to leave. *Only* him."

"I understand, Alpha, thank you."

"You can't be serious, Alpha," one of the guards said.

"If I wanted your input on my decisions, I'd ask for it, son."

The soldier grumbled, shaking his head and looking away.

"T-thank you, Alpha," Corsair said.

Alpha McVarn patted him on the shoulder, giving him a soft smile and shaking paws with Ragnar before walking past them and towards the main hall. He turned as he left.

"Wash that paint off your face when you get back. Safe journey, son."

The alpha turned into the hall and vanished, his guards following. Corsair confronted his brother.

"Ragnee, come with me."

"I can't."

"Just ride back with me. He doesn't need to know."

"I could go to jail if I deserted, Corsair. You heard what he said – we don't get treated any different from the rest of them."

"Please, Ragnee. I can't go home alone. I can't leave you here to get hurt."

His brother sighed.

"I'll look after myself. Harangoth will look after me. I can survive."

"Promise me you'll come back unharmed."

"I will."

"*Promise.*"

"I promise, Corsair, that I will come back as you see me now."

The younger Sedrid hugged his brother, pulling him in, and Ragnar hugged him back.

"Stay safe."

"I will. Tell Mum not to worry about me. Make sure she doesn't get stressed, okay?"

Corsair nodded, stepping back out of the embrace.

～

With the desperation now gone, part of him felt guilty.

There were many others who were as scared as he was, who had seen friends and comrades cut down and pierced with arrows, bleeding to death on the ground and screaming. Unlike him, they had the bravery to carry on for their clan.

And there Corsair was, a little pup who ran home because he was too scared of the big, bad rabbits.

I looked like such a coward.

Miles away, his comrades might have been engaging in another battle. They were out there dying while he was there safe and sound, shielded and protected from what his clan considered a duty.

A patrol of two soldiers walked past him, one of them holding a lantern in his paw. Corsair saw the lantern holder turn.

"Uh, excuse me, Sir? What are you doing out at this hour?"

The prince turned.

"I've come home."

For some unknown reason, the guards' eyes widened. They glanced at one another, suddenly unsure of him, and Corsair shifted his eyes from one guard to the other.

"Uh, Sir, something has happened."

"I don't want to hear it. Leave me be."

"No, Sir, it's urgent."

"Just do your stupid jobs and leave me alone!"

Corsair didn't want to hear it. He didn't want to be disturbed by anyone. He didn't care if it was their job – he needed time to himself, he needed time alone. Whatever was going on could wait.

He arrived at the town centre. It was unnerving to see what was always a bright and lively trading space barren and desolate, left to the devices of the dark. Even though he knew it would be filled with life the next day, the deathly silence of the place felt unnatural and eerie.

He looked up. The silhouette of Julian Krosguard loomed over the desolate town centre, remaining vigilant during the hours of the night. The imposing monument looked terrifying in the dark, as if its eyes were following him as he moved, and Corsair shuddered.

He led Quickpaw down to the entrance of Mr Duncan's tavern, turning into the stables and taking the first free stall. One lone ictharr was positioned further down, staring at the stall in front of it, but the rest were empty.

"Have a rest. You've been walking all day."

Quickpaw was too tired to argue. He padded into the pen and turned as the door shut, curling up on the ground.

"If anything happens, yowl. I'll come out."

Quickpaw mewled, exhausted, and Corsair let him be.

As he neared the doorway to Mr Duncan's tavern, he glanced over at the Great Hall of Wolves. He stopped as he saw light shining through the windows, with an entourage of guards positioned outside.

Dad must be holding a meeting.

He was tempted to return to the house and sneak into his room now that he knew his father was away, but he had already covered the distance and passed his home already. Deeming it useless, he turned back to face the door and pushed it open, stepping inside the tavern.

Corsair expected Mr Duncan's to be empty. He was partially correct. At the bar he could see a drunken wolf slumped over his drink, barely conscious. A pair of lupine maidens were drinking together at a corner table, whispering, and the owner of the tavern stood behind the counter with arms crossed over his chest.

Mr Duncan's eyes fell on Corsair, his face immediately softening.

"Corsair?"

He didn't answer. He approached the bar and took a seat, face drained of all energy, and met the bartender's worried gaze.

"A pint of Stronbeniz, please."

"But why are you-"

"I'd rather not talk about it, Mr Duncan."

Mr Duncan kept his eyes on him but Corsair looked away.

Sensing that he was not in the mood to talk, the barkeep turned and proceeded to prepare his drink. The prince leant back in his chair and let his eyes wander. Thankfully, he found that the drunk was too distracted with trying to remain awake to care about him, and the two female wolves were too busy talking to notice.

Mr Duncan turned back to him, a full pitcher in paw. He lowered it on to the counter and slid it over, golden liquid swishing from left to right, and Corsair concluded the transaction by passing an Iggregom to him.

"No, no, you keep that. On the house."

Without a word, the wolf tipped back the pitcher and drank. He felt the strong alcohol purge his throat, making him wince, but he kept drinking until he needed to breathe and placed the pitcher back on the counter. He let the fur around his mouth drip for a moment, not bothering to wipe it, before he lifted one arm and cleaned away the beads hanging from his maw.

Mr Duncan was still looking at him.

"Is your brother all right?"

"He's fine."

Corsair couldn't meet the barkeep's eyes. In truth, he didn't know how his brother was. He left him behind to run away, to hide from the war they faced, and for all he knew Ragnar and Harangoth were charging headfirst into swords and arrows.

"Why are you back? Is the war over?"

"Mr Duncan, I said I don't want to talk about it."

Mr Duncan nodded.

"Okay. I'm sorry. I'll leave you alone."

Another swig and the wolf felt the bite of the mead, enduring it and drinking down every last drop until his pitcher was dry and he was sipping at air. He placed it down and gestured for another drink. Mr Duncan nodded and turned away without a word.

There was a temptation to drink away the worries he had, to forget about it all and let himself float away into the ecstasy of drunken fatigue despite inexperience at doing so. He had never been drunk, never felt the surge of jovial energy he had seen other wolves experiencing, never felt the ache of the aftermath the next day.

The door opened behind him and he looked over his shoulder.

Two soldiers stood at the door, both in chainmail shirts with flecks of snow decorating them. Corsair immediately felt irritated, grunting. They had followed him even though he told them to leave him alone. He hoped it was by coincidence that they arrived there.

Don't talk to me. Leave me alone, don't talk to me.

"Uh, Sir?"

Corsair growled and this was enough to get the barkeep to turn around. The growl imposed silence on one of the soldiers, taken aback by his aggression, but the other persisted.

"Sir-"

"I told you two to leave me alone, didn't I?"

"But, Sir, it's-"

"Oh, it's important, it's important! If it's so damn important, go and bother my father! He's the stupid Winter Baron anyway, why are you here talking to his son about it if it's so important?"

The two guards glanced at each other again. Corsair had disturbed the peace of the tavern and now the few occupants were focusing on the commotion at the counter.

"Why do you keep looking at each other like that? I just want some peace after being out on the front. Can't I have that?"

"Sir, it's about your father."

Corsair let out a wry laugh, one that was scornful and sarcastic and at the expense of the sincerity the two soldiers showed.

"Let me guess – he wants me to run over to the Great Hall of Wolves to listen to him rant about how he's disappointed in me and how I'm a disgrace to the Sedrid lineage? How I'm not a wolf? If he wants to do that so badly he can come over here and say it himself, in front of everyone so they get to see exactly what he's like with me."

Silence.

"Go on then, spit it out. That's what he wants, isn't it?"

The soldiers looked uncomfortable, disheartened in response to the unwarranted level of his outburst. The air was tense. The atmosphere was hostile.

Corsair looked from one guard to the other.

"I'm sorry, I just... is something wrong?"

The lantern holder stepped forward to whisper in his ear, one that Corsair willingly lent him as it stood.

"Sir... Sir, your father is dying."

Whatever fragile and sombre peace was held over the interior of the Great Hall of Wolves shattered as Corsair barged through the door with the two guards trailing behind him.

He didn't even need to ask where he was.

At the front of the hall, with the podium cleared to make room, his father lay on whatever comforts the guards and servants could bring. A pillow rested under his head while sheets were folded beneath his body to form thicker padding. A doctor was sitting next to him, his instruments laid out to one side, but the look of defeat on his face told Corsair that his efforts were fruitless.

His mother leant over her husband, crying tears of misery, holding a paw under his head and with the other resting on his chest. Peter and the servants stood metres away, watching the Winter Baron they had served for years die, and the guards stood farther back. All eyes but his mother's were on the new arrival, surprised at the sudden entry.

Corsair rushed forwards, barging past Peter, moving around the wide benches and mounting the steps to the stage.

He fell to his knees by his father's side, opposite his mother.

"Dad, Dad, what happened?"

His father croaked, too pained to speak. Corsair looked up at the doctor.

"What happened to him?"

"He was on his way to a meeting with the King of Opulus, Sir.

On his way there, the ictharrs leading the wagon lost control and caused a collision with another carriage. His side was pierced, and I removed the shard, but there's some manner of internal bleeding beyond repair. I tried to offer him a pain relief remedy to ease his suffering but... he refused to take it."

Corsair looked down and saw the bandaging wrapped tightly around his father's abdomen where the shard had punctured his side, a futile attempt to remedy his wound. He looked up.

"Do something, you idiot!"

"Sir, I cannot-"

"It's your job to save his life so save him! He's dying, *save him*!"

Corsair could feel tears rushing from his eyes, choking him, and he had to keep swallowing to even have a chance at speaking. He was trembling and verging on hysteria, acting on intense emotion as his father died in front of him.

As he opened his mouth to berate the doctor further, he saw the pained look on his mother's face. The dying moments of his father weren't to be filled with arguing and conflict.

He should die peacefully.

Corsair restrained himself, looking down at his father.

"Arthur?" his mother whimpered. "Arthur, please... you can't leave us. I need you. Your cubs need you."

Corsair watched his mother cradle her husband's face in her paws, keeping his head up. He tried to make eye contact with his father, to try to say goodbye, but he couldn't connect.

For a moment, he thought he was too delirious even to realise what Corsair was doing. But, then, he saw how much his father was struggling against his wife's paws.

He's trying to look away from me.

"I love you so much, Arthur."

His father tried to reply but his words caught in his throat as pain ruptured whatever thoughts he had in his head. His face contorted, agonised, and Corsair could only watch through tear-filled eyes.

Look at me. Dad, look at me.

He wouldn't.

Corsair placed a paw on his father's chest, feeling the sputtering heartbeat beneath his ribs.

"Dad? Dad, don't go."

He never thought his father would have enough energy remaining to push his paw away. It wasn't hard or with any force but Corsair saw his father raise his right paw and heave against the weight of his son's. He watched in horror as his paw was eased off his father's chest.

"Dad?"

His father was looking away from him again, eyes focusing on his wife, and Corsair called out once more.

"Dad, please."

Seconds passed. His mother held her gaze with her dying husband, eyes rimmed with red, until she looked up at her son.

She shook her head.

Corsair knew what that look meant. She didn't have to say anything.

Other than the wailing of Ophelia Sedrid, there was no sound. The guards and servants remained still. The snowfall outside was non-existent. Every soul in Grand Wolf Plains was at rest.

Corsair Sedrid focused on his father's corpse, cradled by his mother, and let his tears hit the floor without a word.

CHAPTER SEVENTEEN

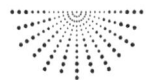

$\mathcal{A}$ few days later, thousands gathered in Grand Wolf Plains.
News of the Winter Baron's untimely and unfortunate
death reached all frontiers of the Clan of the Great Lupine. It
wouldn't have been a surprise to Corsair if the Land of the Sun and
Moon knew it too, celebrating the death of their enemy's leader in the
hopes that it would lower the troops' morale.

Corsair sat inside the Great Hall of Wolves, on the front row to
allow easy access to the podium. His brother and mother were sitting
to the left of him, each one holding a parchment in their paws, and
the pews behind them were filled with friends and colleagues of the
Winter Baron. Outside, hundreds of wolves surrounded the building,
watched by solemn guards who had to do little work. None of the
wolves would have dared make a ruckus, or yell, or shout, or cause
disruption.

Everyone was silent.

The priest, a white-fronted wolf swathed in his religious robes,
stood behind the podium. His paws were placed one on the other in
front of his lap, head down in respect, holding the silence intact.

Corsair looked left towards his brother.

Ragnar's eyes were on the priest, right paw repeatedly tapping against his knee. The other paw held his parchment, which quivered and trembled. It was barely restrained by his will.

It was a rude awakening for his brother. He was brought home from the front to be given the news and Corsair watched his older brother cry and wail in the living room, comforted by his mother like a cub.

In all his years, Corsair had never seen his strong, resilient and determined brother cry.

Corsair's eyes moved past Ragnar and focused on his mother. There sat the widow, her eyes shut and head bowed, mumbling a prayer underneath her breath. He had not seen her shed a tear since the death of her husband but she had become withdrawn, never talking to anyone, and sitting on the bed with one paw placed on the side where his father had slept.

She looked empty, vacant. As if she had lost some part of her.

Beyond her was Mr Duncan. The large wolf sat there in silence, staring pensively at the wall in front of them. As the good friend he was, he had come to say his goodbyes to his companion.

And, finally, Corsair.

The younger Sedrid had tried to be supportive to his sibling and mother. He tried to converse with them, told Peter to keep an eye on them, offered to go to the tavern, to go on a walk, to do *anything* as long as they talked to him.

They were never prepared to do anything other than grieve. In reality he didn't wish to go out on a walk or go to the tavern either, but he needed a distraction. He needed something to conceal the fact that his father ignored him, even on his deathbed, by pushing away his paw as the light finally left him.

I'm such a disappointment.

Yet he did not know how to feel.

Hatred and misery threw him to and fro, rebounding him off one and towards the other. One moment the grief would root him to the spot, the next it was alleviated by an uncompassionate void that resented the wolf they had gathered to remember.

Head rising slowly, the priest addressed the hall.

"It is here, today, that we have come to say our goodbyes to Winter Baron Arthur Sedrid. In a series of misfortunes, our great leader was killed a week ago, a victim of a tragic accident. But, today, we look past the unfortunate events of his passing and we dwell on the good and warmth Arthur Sedrid brought to his family, his friends, his colleagues and his clan."

He gestured to the front row.

"If she wishes, Ophelia Sedrid may come up and speak."

Corsair watched his mother open her eyes and nod, rising up from her seat and walking to the stage. Mr Duncan whispered his condolences to her as she moved. A servant followed, not ordered to do so, and Corsair appreciated her concern.

The priest stepped aside and let the widow step forward. She cast her gaze to the back of the room, scanning the faces in the seats and above in the viewing galleries. With a shaky sigh, as loud as a shout in the silence of the hall, she looked down at her parchment and began to read.

"At the age of 25, I saw Arthur Sedrid for the first time. It was at a tournament all the way to the west in Gredstok. When I saw him afterwards at a celebratory dinner I just..."

She stopped.

"He was the most handsome wolf I ever laid my eyes on. He was kind, caring and... we got along so well. We were soulmates. We were even more than that and we spent years and years together. *Thirty* years. My life has been so great with him in it, and it's... I can't believe that..."

Tears began to brim over but she raised a paw to hold the servant's assistance at bay.

"Apologies. I... can't believe that he's gone. He was an entity of kindness, of love, of courage and loyalty. His heart was so big and his company was always welcome and... now, he's gone."

She paused.

"I ask that all of you remember him for the wolf he was, and that we don't shed any more tears over our loss. Whether you knew him as a colleague or had the pleasure of knowing him as a friend, I ask that you keep him in your prayers and memories. He's a strong wolf, but... after this life we need all the help we can get."

She paused again before nodding, confirming that her speech was over. Not a sound was made as she stepped down and sat back on the front row, wiping her eyes.

"If Ragnar Sedrid wishes to speak, he is welcome to come up and say a few words."

Ragnar's response was almost immediate. He got up instantly and padded over to the podium while Corsair looked down at the floor and readied his speech. Unaccompanied by any servants, considered strong enough to speak without a threat of emotion breaking through, Ragnar began.

"Ever since a young age, I've looked up to my father. When I was a pup, all I could do was dream of being a brave warrior like him and being as courageous and strong as he was. I think that's a dream most wolves have about their fathers. I don't think, however, most people get to do that. It's all lost as we get older, probably because we have jobs to do and lives to lead that are too busy to let us remember the dreams we wanted to pursue as pups."

He looked up at the viewing galleries.

"My father, Arthur Sedrid, is someone who managed to do that for me. Even though he had constant meetings, even though he was always busy leading the clan for his people and what he believed was just and right, he had time for me. Because of him, I managed to become as strong and courageous as he was. I managed to hold my own all because he showed the love and effort for me to do so."

He looked back down to the audience.

"When I heard that the one figure in my life that I looked up to was gone, killed in an accident, I... I cried. I couldn't stop crying. I'm thankful that I had such support from all of you and my family.

Without you all, I would have curled up and lost all of what my father trained and taught me to be. But I know now that I should never lose sight of who I am. To honour the time and love he gave to me, dedicated to my life, I will never forget what my father helped me become."

He paused.

"I love you, Dad."

He let the final phrase hover in the air before he stepped down and returned to his seat. Corsair felt his brother pat him on the back, a way of comforting him, but it only awakened him to the realisation that it was his turn to speak.

He didn't know if he could do it.

I'm lying. I'm lying through my teeth.

"I now invite Corsair Sedrid to speak a few words, if he wishes."

Corsair looked up and found all eyes in the hall to be on him.

There was no chance he would refuse. He would not wish to dishonour and disgrace his father in front of all these people, during the final time he would have to commemorate him fully. But, as he stood, he found that every step towards the podium was heavy. His body repelled him from the stage, his heart drumming away, but he forced himself up. He muttered thanks to the priest before he took position and looked out to see the whole hall looking back, soft and considerate gazes made into harsh and judging glares by the number of them.

I'm lying. Everything written here is a lie.

Pushing through it, he looked down and began to read.

"My father has always been a loving wolf."

That sentence alone made him question his own memory, as if he had been living half of his life with another family, but he pushed through.

"As a pup, I always wanted to be a great fighter. I always wanted to become skilled with a sword, to ride an ictharr into my battles, and no one enabled my dream more than him. He was a great teacher, and he was disciplined enough to never give up on me and always helped me through my training. Even when Alpha Tiberius took over, he was always there to help us."

He continued.

"Every day of my life has been great with my father in it. Every hour, every minute, every second has been so fulfilling with his love and care. Now that he's gone... I don't know what to do."

I'm lying.

"My father was a wonderful wolf. He always looked out for others and cared for us and..."

Did he?

Did his father care for him? Arthur Sedrid willingly sent him and his brother off to war, to be exposed to the sights of bodies and blood and severed limbs and dying screams. Was that caring? Was the bite that almost killed him caring? Were the ceaseless days of lectures and yelling filled with love? Did his father even care? Did Corsair even–

"And I love him."

Silence.

"I love you, Dad. I miss you."

He said it again to confirm it. To prove it. He wanted to show that he loved his father, that he missed his father and felt the sting of his eternal absence.

But he couldn't forget the sting of the bite 10 years ago, eternally stamped on his neck. That loomed in his head as he sat back down and covered his face with his paws.

Did he love me? Did my father even care? Would he have cared if I had died out there, alone and scared?

Before he could finish that thought, he heard the priest begin to speak.

"Before we move on to our concluding sermon, I would like to read out the will of the late Winter Baron Arthur Sedrid."

In the silence that followed, all that could be heard was the sound of a scroll being unravelled and parchment being pulled taut. Corsair peered up at the priest, along with everyone else, listening to what his father had left behind for them, but already knew the answer.

Nothing for me. Ragnee will be Winter Baron. I'll be left as nobody. An outsider. A stranger.

"To the people of our great clan – if you are reading this, it must be in the event of my passing. If my demise was brought about through natural means, I ask that you all put your sorrow and grief to rest and set about on a new day as soon as you can. Dwelling on my passing will never bring me back. If I have been killed through foul play, I ask the soldiers of my clan to bring the culprit to justice for my family's wellbeing."

Silence.

"In the event of my passing, I ask that my title as Winter Baron be passed on to..."

The priest cut himself off. A face of confusion came upon him, and he blinked twice to challenge the reality of what was written. A low murmur of uncertainty hovered over the hall.

What's wrong?

"It appears that... it says here, that in the event of my passing, I ask that my title as Winter Baron be passed on to... Alpha Dominic Tiberius of the clan army."

"What?" Ragnar said.

Everyone turned to look at the front row, where the large shape of Alpha Tiberius sat. The hulking brown wolf didn't look left or right, watery eyes focused on the priest while everyone clamoured around him.

"I am aware that my eldest son, Ragnar Sedrid, is next in line for my leadership. However, until he is believed to be of a responsible and mature age, I ask that my loyal advisor Alpha Tiberius acts as provisional Winter Baron until that time comes."

That sealed it.

Minutes later, as a result of his father's act of contempt of the maturity of his eldest son, Corsair witnessed Alpha Dominic Tiberius of the clan army being crowned as Winter Baron of the Clan of the Great Lupine.

The next hour, following the declaration of the new Winter Baron, was filled with a wealth of condolences and sympathies for the young Sedrid. He met friends and colleagues of his father, names he vaguely recalled hearing months and years ago. He was unacquainted with the majority but, knowing better than to question their identity, he nodded and thanked them.

Now, however, the two brothers knelt before the memorial.

A new inscription had been added to the timeline of Winter Barons and Baronesses, stretching back to the origins of the Clan of the Great Lupine with an ornate engraving of the first Winter Baron. Corsair's eyes scanned each row left to right, reading every inscription in his head, before he finally arrived over his father's name.

Winter Baron Arthur Sedrid. A great leader taken from us by unfortunate circumstances. May God bless his valiant soul. 1079 – 1139.

All Corsair could do was stare at the one thing he could remember his father by, with his body stowed away and his helmet given over to his loyal colleague. It came as a surprise to them all, particularly Ragnar, but it was for no reason of material gain. His brother was a kind person. He was not the type to put his loss of leadership, something so material, over his father's death.

He glanced to his left. His brother was kneeling beside him, still facing the wall, inhaling and exhaling with a steady rhythm. His shoulders rose and fell with every breath. Corsair sensed an unusual calm over him.

I should say something.

His brother beat him to it.

"I feel like you want to say something."

Corsair hesitated. Ragnar turned his head.

"I know it was difficult to go up there and say those things about Dad. After all you've been through with him, the toughest thing to do would be to save face for everyone."

"Did you mean it?" Corsair said. "What you said?"

"Some. Part of me wanted to bring up Ignatius Mount and 10 years ago but... I don't know. I didn't want to unearth all of this knowing you'd be the focal point."

"Yeah. Thanks, I appreciate it. I just..."

A pause.

"Go on," Ragnar said.

"I... a part of me feels bad for saying this. Especially as it's the day of his funeral."

"I think that's the best time for you to say what you need about him. No one else is listening. Say it if you want to."

Corsair waited. He glanced back to the front podium, the place where his father declared war a month ago, and back to the engraving. His eyes focused on the chiselled letters, feeling a paw move up to the side of his neck.

"I hate him."

A pause. Ragnar didn't interrupt, eyes focused on his brother.

"Before what happened, I loved him like nothing else. He was the greatest father I could ever ask for. He played with us. He talked to us. He tucked us into bed every night when we were little. But then it all changed after what happened. A little bit before then, even. It was probably the change in his attitude that led him to bite me."

Ragnar listened.

"And for the last 10 years, I've never resented a wolf more. I've never felt so much anger towards someone for the way they've treated me. I've never felt so much disgust for a person who would dismiss me and everything I did at every turn. I thought I'd feel this about someone else, someone like Maximus. Not Dad."

He sighed.

"And... now I'm confused."

"Why are you confused?"

"I'm confused because, all this time, I've told myself I hated him. For years, I've let these thoughts brew over and over again but last week, when I saw him die... I cried. The person I hated the most made me sprint from Mr Duncan's tavern to be by his side. I... don't understand why it hurt so much."

Corsair looked over at him.

"You felt it too, right? That pain? That feeling of being pulled in two?"

Ragnar sighed and looked at him.

"Maybe... maybe we've been mourning for the last 10 years and it's only come to a head now."

Looking back at his engraving, Corsair couldn't help but agree.

Both Sedrids' ears stood as the door opened with a creak, looking over their shoulders.

At first glance, he knew that the new arrivals were more than regular visitors. A team of eight soldiers stood there, all dressed in master-crafted steel armour that was so highly polished it was as if they were walking mirrors. Every panel of metal was engraved and etched with insignias and symbols, from their shin guards to their helmets' cheek pieces. Corsair was dazzled. Each soldier had a helmet placed on his head, consisting of a mask that covered their snouts and faces. The fronts of their torso pieces were shaped into the outlines of abdomens, metal muscle shielding the flesh beneath the armour.

At the centre of the entourage were two figures and Corsair's eyes were immediately drawn to the stature of the schnauzer.

The figure was dressed in the finest of clothing, with every thread of his red cape embroidered with an affluent needle. His body was clad in royal robes, laden with silk and velvet, and his hind paws were shielded from the snow by thick leather hind-paw socks. The black schnauzer, his fur greying beneath his short snout, wore a glorious gold crown encrusted with countless jewels and diamonds of values Corsair could not fathom.

"Ah, there you are," the schnauzer said, his grand and wavering voice bearing the trace of an accent. "You must be Ragnar and Corsair Sedrid, are you not?"

Both Sedrids stood, Ragnar leading the way to the front entrance with Corsair following.

"Uh, yes, I'm Ragnar. This is my brother, Corsair."

"I see."

The two lupines stopped before the schnauzer.

"Apologies for the sudden intrusion. Your mother directed me to the Great Hall of Wolves to offer my condolences regarding your terrible loss. I am Damien Farramor, King of Opulus."

The two wolves stood there, mouths agape.

"You're the King of Opulus, Your Majesty?"

"No need for the astonished look. A hound of my age still has enough spirit inside them to lead a kingdom. Isn't that right, Valour?"

As the king turned to his right, Corsair's eyes fell upon the second figure. A hound dressed in gold-tinted armour from hind paw to neck, with every inch of fur covered by interlocking plates of metal, stepped into the hall. A laurel crown of black metal reached around from the back of his helmet to the front, the ends stopping just above the eyes. A longsword pointing downwards, its blade wrapped in a chain of black laurel leaves from hilt to tip, was painted on his right shoulder guard. From the waist hung two blood-red garments, one covering the front of each leg. The Kingdom of Opulus's emblem was emblazoned on each standard. It was that same downwards-pointing longsword once again, the golden crown beaming from above its grip. Protruding from the left side of the blade, face carved into one half, was the black head of a cat – from the right, the black head of a dog peered out.

However, as the knight lifted his helmet, it wasn't the armour or intricate decorations that got Corsair's attention.

It was the wearer.

Before him stood a doberman, just as tall as he was, with his helmet tucked beneath his arm and his longsword sheathed in his buckle. Two golden eyes.

Corsair remembered those two eyes. He remembered how he had

been knocked down, defeated, and stared up into them as the tip of the victor's blade was pressed against his neck.

Corsair saw the doberman offer a paw.

"Corsair Sedrid," he said in a kind voice with a shade of an accent. "I am Valour. We fought a while ago."

"You beat me."

"I did, yes. I have to admit, though, that it was luck. I was prepared to have you kick my arse back to Opulus."

Corsair chuckled along with him. He appreciated his modesty, hiding the fact that he had demolished the wolf, and it made the sudden meeting less awkward.

"Valour is my personal advisor," the King of Opulus said. "And commander of the *Militaria* chapter of the Royal Order – the finest hound knights in all of Vos Draemar."

"Thank you, Your Majesty."

"But, anyway, I have come here to offer my sincerest condolences for your terrible loss. Your father perished on his journey to my kingdom and I cannot help but feel partially responsible."

"Don't, Your Majesty," Ragnar said. "It... it wasn't your fault. No one could have seen it coming."

"Indeed. The future holds bizarre events – it is the unfortunate way of reality. Was your father buried here, if I may ask?"

"His body is buried in the church graveyard but it's tradition for us to remember them here. They commemorate the Winter Barons and Winter Baronesses back where we just were."

Ragnar turned, pointing to the back wall of the hall.

"I can show you, if you want."

"That would be kind. It would be good to have the opportunity to pay my respects to your father. Legionnaires, stay here."

"*Dominus patria regis, Rex,*" the legionnaires said in unison, taking up positions by the door. Corsair narrowed his eyes in confusion, an expression Valour saw.

"New Opulusian," he said. "It means 'loyalty over all, King'. It's the Opulusian Legion's motto. Excluding the word 'king', anyway."

Corsair nodded, appreciative of the explanation. They walked in silence up the aisle and towards the memorial site, arriving as Ragnar pointed to the engraving.

"Here it is, Your Majesty."

The king knelt and placed his paw on the space beside the engraving, eyes scrutinising every curve and dot of his name.

"It is a great shame. I would have enjoyed meeting him."

"He was a good leader."

"I can imagine. This capital is a thriving community – the people I have spoken to were delightful. It is a product of a good rule."

The king stood and turned to face Corsair.

"I apologise if I seem too conversational in a time of grief. I don't mean to be insensitive."

"Not at all, Your Majesty," Corsair said. "Some wounds can't be healed, no matter what. It doesn't matter if you're polite about it, I guess."

"Wise words, Corsair, wise words. I will shut my maw and leave you two alone. Commander, I believe it is time we took our leave."

"Of course, Your Majesty."

As Valour relayed the orders to the legionnaires in New Opulusian, the king turned and shook paws with Corsair.

"It has been a pleasure meeting you."

"You too, Your Majesty."

He turned and shook Ragnar's paw.

"It has been a pleasure meeting you."

"The pleasure's all mine, Your Majesty."

The king stepped back, addressing both of them.

"Please know that you have my best wishes for your family during these dark hours."

"Thank you, Your Majesty," the two wolves answered.

Corsair turned to Valour to shake his paw and met his eye as they exchanged farewells. There was a sorrowful look there, apologetic, and – while Corsair didn't say it outright – he appreciated the sensitivity shown.

"Maybe we'll meet again over a pint?" he said.

The prince only chuckled, a non-committal response, and the doberman sensed it was best to leave it at that. They turned, the king signalling the guards to march out the front of the hall. Corsair turned back to the wall.

Why didn't you love me? Why did you treat me as you did?

Why does it hurt if I hate you so much?

CHAPTER EIGHTEEN

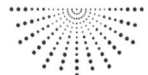

*N*ights later, Corsair turned down the breeding ground of nightmares that was his bed and decided to walk through his home town.

He was becoming more accustomed to the silence of Grand Wolf Plains. There was a time, merely days ago, where he had preferred the comfort of strong daylight over the dim light of lanterns, but now it had all changed. He could hide in the dark, circumvent the horrible thoughts that would chase him in his sleep, and dwell on what had happened. It would give him the opportunity to try to clear his head.

He couldn't endure sleep any more. He couldn't survive the harsh memories that flashed before his eyes. The memories of his father dying and shunning him, of his father biting him in the side of the neck. All the bad memories had resurfaced and they were searching for him, lurking in his dreams.

Not tonight.

Walking through the town centre for the fifth time, Corsair stopped to listen to the silence of the night. No ictharr stirred, no trader badgered him, no playful cubs scampered past.

All was silent.

He looked up at the monument. Julian Krosguard stood forever vigilant, watching over the citizens with a careful yet miserable eye. Misery hovered around the statue, despaired at the loss of a great leader. However, it still stood ready to defend its people with shield and sword in paw.

Corsair looked to his left and saw the Great Hall of Wolves. Its bleak shadow loomed in the distance, left in darkness. He remembered all the times he would see his father at the front of the hall, addressing the public with the Winter Baron's helmet on his head. Those golden wings glinted in the sunlight streaming through the windows.

He couldn't think of anyone else who wore that helmet better than Arthur Sedrid.

But, now, it rested on Alpha Tiberius's head.

His father would have never chosen Corsair as the next Winter Baron. He knew it after their fierce confrontation with one another yet he never expected him to pass it over to a non-Sedrid. Ragnar was the rightful heir – he was respectable, disciplined, mature. Harangoth even matched him perfectly. For what reason would his father decline him the right to the helmet?

Maybe his father had been blinded by anger, believing that if such insubordination arose in his younger son, then it might have originated with his elder.

He felt his eyes water.

I have to move on from him now. He's dead. It's been a week.

He shook his head and fought back the sting of tears.

I need to move on from him now.

But Corsair didn't know what he would even be able to move on to. All that was left of his father's legacy was a bloody war being fought in the east and that wasn't under Sedrid control any more. It was in the paws of Alpha Tiberius, not even a relative of his father, and his family was left barely relevant to the leadership. All that was left was Ragnar, who was waiting until he was 'mature enough' for the helmet to be passed to him.

He partially understood it. Neither he nor his brother was experienced in leading an army during wartime. That was a hefty responsibility, one that could not be placed so easily upon a wolf's shoulders. But it was their birth right. They were Sedrids, the next in line to leadership. Having it denied seemed wrong, almost as if they had been teased with the idea of it for 20 years.

It's a lot of pressure. Maybe, right now, it's for the best.

That's all he could conclude about it.

He strode down the main pathway, moving towards the east wall. The snowfall was light, drifting down from the heavens, and it was so soft that Corsair didn't even notice it landing on him. He was scanning the surroundings, looking at the skeletal shadows of the trees that covered the south of Grand Wolf Plains.

"Stop right there!"

He turned his head.

Three Opulusian legionnaires approached him, their leader with a lantern in his paw while the other hovered over his sheathed short sword. They converged on him with intent but, upon realising who it was, the ferocity behind the eyes relented.

"Oh... apologies, Sir. I thought you were someone else."

"It's all right."

"Any reason you're wandering around at this hour?"

"Just thinking. Enjoying the quiet."

"I'd recommend that you return home, Sir. If that's not possible, then keep your eyes open – you never know who's wandering around at this hour."

"I'll be careful. Thank you."

The leader turned and jerked his head in the opposite direction, leading them off past Corsair. He watched them leave, the small orange radius of light disappearing down the pathway as the hounds continued their sweep.

Some form of agreement had been reached between Alpha Tiberius and the King of Opulus. Days before, Corsair had seen a convoy of Opulusian legionnaires arrive at the heart of the town, disembarking from their vehicles and taking up residence in the barracks to the north. They arrived to the welcoming arms of wolves content with their support against the Land of the Sun and Moon. Their sleek steel armour and stoic facemasks were sights to behold, particularly en masse.

They were certainly sterner than the lupines who came before. Some wolf patrols still roamed around but they were in the minority. In a short space of time, the Opulusians replaced the lupine soldiers patrolling the streets until the sight of armed wolves became a rare occurrence.

Corsair walked on for another minute before he saw a figure up ahead, standing motionless to the side. There was someone shrouded in a dark cloak, facing away from him and peering out towards the south. He took two steps towards the figure before he stopped, eyes focusing on the cloaked back.

His paw shifted on to the pommel of his longsword, tucked away into its scabbard.

"Is everything all right?"

The figure turned, surprised by the sudden sound of the voice, and Corsair's paw clenched over the sword in anticipation. A millisecond later, his paw relaxed as he saw the six strands of black fur shooting down from the wolf's jaw. He felt relieved when he saw paws gloved in white fur and that familiar strip of white running down the snout. A silhouette of a bow hung over her shoulder by the string.

Rohesia stepped forwards.

"You're home?" Corsair asked.

"Most of us were brought back after your father..."

She stopped herself.

"I'm... so sorry, Corsair."

His immediate response was to dismiss it as nothing, but the polite retort seemed hard to conjure in his current state of mind. Instead, he nodded, using silence as a way to cover up his emotions.

"Are Ragnar and your mother okay?"

"Mum is... quiet. She doesn't talk much – she usually sits by the side of the bed where Dad used to sleep. Ragnee has the servants watching her all day, every day. And he's holding it together but... he's torn apart inside, I know it."

He paused.

"I came out here to walk. You want to tag along?"

She nodded, stepping forward from the side of the path and arriving by his side. They began to walk, advancing slowly, focused on the conversation between them.

"Are you okay?"

"I'm... I'm all right, Rohesia. What are you doing out here, anyway?"

"Same as you – I came out here to walk."

"Why were you looking off into the trees?"

"I was enjoying the quiet. I usually come out at night and listen to the silence – it's not something you get to hear often in this city."

Corsair glanced behind him. Rohesia stopped, paw reaching for her dagger.

"What is it?"

"Nothing. I saw Opulusian legionnaires earlier."

"Did they stop you?"

"They stopped me because they thought I was someone else. When they saw me, though, they left me alone."

The archer nodded, allowing the duo to walk forwards again.

"I was thinking about Tiberius. He must have made some sort of deal with the King of Opulus to have all these hounds walking around in Grand Wolf Plains."

"They must be here to help us with the war."

"Which means the chances of peace are pretty slim now, huh?"

Rohesia didn't answer.

"I feel sorry for all the soldiers still out there."

"We'll be going back soon."

He felt his heart sink as he registered what she said, turning his head to make eye contact.

"You're going back to the front?"

"They still need soldiers to fight against the Land of the Sun and Moon. You can't fight a war without soldiers. I'm not going, though."

"They won't notice you're gone?"

"Maybe they won't, maybe they will. Right now, though, I don't think they'll be chasing up runaway recruits after all that's gone on."

"Right. As long as you're not getting into bad trouble."

A lapse in the conversation was exposed, a gaping wound that widened with every silent second, until Rohesia broke the silence.

"Corsair, I know something's bothering you."

"My father's dead. Take a lucky guess."

He realised how harsh his tone was and stopped, bringing the pair to a halt in the middle of the pathway. He sighed and shook his head.

"Sorry. I don't want to be rude to you."

"It's okay. It's a sensitive time. I just don't want you to feel alone in this."

"Thank you. I..."

He paused, unsure of himself.

She's trustworthy. Rohesia is trustworthy.

"I think Dad hated me."

Rohesia didn't say anything.

"Sorry, I just sound like a spoilt brat for saying that."

"Are you kidding? Corsair, just say it. I'm not going to judge you."

He stood there, trying to conjure up the words, but gave up with a defeated sigh. Instead, he reached his paws up to the left side of his neck and parted the fur, revealing the scar. He turned his head to the right and leaned back.

"See that?"

"See what?"

"My neck. There's a scar on my neck."

She leaned in, squinting, before she noticed the scar tissue beneath the fur. They were standing not too far from a building, a lantern glowing directly on to them, so it made seeing the scar easier.

"It looks like a bite."

"Dad gave me that scar when I was 10."

Her eyes widened.

"He *bit you*?"

"He almost killed me. I don't know why he did it. He told the doctors it was an accident, that Ragnee was being rough with me and bit too hard. My family are the only people who know it was him."

"That's horrible. You were so young."

"And I feel like that was the main moment that set everything into motion with him. After that...I don't remember a time in the last decade or so when he was a father to me."

Rohesia didn't speak. Corsair continued.

"He sent me out to fight in a war where it was... horrible. I don't need to describe it because you saw what I saw but... it terrified me. It still does. Then, when I come back, a guard tells me he's dying. I run to the Great Hall of Wolves and I'm crying over him with Mum and I rest a paw on his chest. He sees me and... he pushes it off him. He ignores me. He doesn't even look at me."

Now that he had talked about it, now that he had willingly opened the chest of misery, he felt the tears penetrate his defences and brim over in his eyes. He wiped them away, sniffling.

"I don't know what I did. I wanted Dad to love me and appreciate me and approve of me but every time I did anything it was never enough. Every tournament was flawed, every lesson was at best okay, every mistake was amplified and... I went to war for him, only to have him kick the snow in my face on my last training day. He..."

He gave a trembling sigh.

"He tried to bite me. Again. I've spent all the years of my life looking up to him and I've been so... so *pathetic*..."

"No, Corsair-"

"So pathetic that I've crawled back to him after every kick in the side to try and get his approval. I didn't get the message, even after 10 years. I was just an annoying pup. Nothing more."

He sniffled.

"And you'd think, after all of that, I'd get the message. I'd realise he didn't care and I'd hate him. I would know for sure that I hated him. But... I'm confused. I don't love him. Everything I said at the funeral was a lie but when I was sitting in front of his engraving, I missed him. I *missed* the wolf who almost killed me. Why?"

"I don't know, Corsair. I honestly don't. Maybe it's not him you're missing."

Corsair grimaced, shaking his head as he felt the dredges of regret sink in.

"I'm sorry, I shouldn't have dumped all of that on you."

"It's fine. You need to get this off your chest and out into the open. It helps you to cope."

"I feel like-"

A shout echoed from further down the pathway.

Both the wolves turned, ears up and eyes wide, peering down the path. In the distance he could see the light of a house stretching out on to the road, door left wide open and more shouts rising from inside.

That's when he realised that it was his house.

Without a word, he shot off towards his home, Rohesia not too far behind him. They were by the door in seconds, stepping through it and scanning the room.

"Get off me! *Get off me!*"

Ragnar was on the ground, pinned down by five Opulusian legionnaires, all armoured and using both paws to restrain him. His brother writhed, grunting and growling, snapping his jaws at them as he tried to throw them off.

"Get off my son!" his mother yelled, pinned in the corner of the dining room. "Get off him, you vicious mutts!"

"Hey!" Corsair yelled, drawing his sword. "Get off him!"

He came forwards, snarling as he approached, but then a wolf stepped out in his path. He saw the tip of a longsword being pushed towards him and he stopped, taking a step back.

He looked into the attacker's face and recognised that insane grin immediately.

"It's been a while, Sedrid," Lieutenant Maximus Verschelden said with a smirk. "You're probably eager to talk about how I didn't get sent to jail, I know, but that'll have to wait while we talk to your brother."

He gestured to Corsair's sword with his free paw.

"Drop it."

Corsair, without room to retaliate or take up a defensive stance, dropped his blade.

"Now kick it away."

He kicked it. It slid towards Lieutenant Maximus's hind paws, and he kicked it away further. It slid over to the fireplace.

He saw the blade stop by another set of hind paws and looked up. Alpha Tiberius stood in front of the fire, reading through a leather-bound journal. He flicked through the pages of the book in silence. The servants were sitting on the landing, facing the wall as three legionnaires guarded them with swords drawn. Peter was muttering words of comfort to his fellow servants, donning a hardened expression in the face of danger.

"What are you doing?" Corsair growled. "Let him go! He's done nothing wrong!"

"That's not mine! That's not mine!" Ragnar yelled. "You're a liar!"

Alpha Tiberius looked up at Corsair and lifted the book in one paw, gesturing to it.

"This book here was found by a tavern worker. It was left by Ragnar Sedrid, son of the deceased Arthur Sedrid, and this proves that your brother was planning to collaborate willingly in a scheme to seize power from me and have me killed."

Corsair recoiled.

"He what?"

"Let me read it to you. Dear Lieutenant Francis Ziedik of the army, I am able to inform you that I will do anything in my power to help you overthrow Winter Baron Tiberius. Why my father passed the leadership to him I will never know, but it must be some form of mistake. That winged helmet is Sedrid property and Sedrid property alone. Yours sincerely..."

He looked at Ragnar.

"...Ragnar Sedrid, the *true Winter Baron*."

"That's a lie! Corsair, don't listen to him, I didn't write that!"

"Please, let him go! Take me! Take me, please, don't hurt him!" his mother wailed.

Corsair stood in horror, unsure of what to do in the situation. With Lieutenant Maximus standing before him, his brother pinned and restrained on the floor, his mother trapped and the servants under surveillance, there was nought he could do.

Lieutenant Maximus sneered.

"Nothing to say, Sedrid? No brave words to defend your brother?"

He ignored the taunts. Alpha Tiberius sighed and closed the diary.

"That's one of *many* excerpts going back and forth between him and this lieutenant, going back to the day after I inherited the Winter Baron's helm. They have been using this journal to communicate and send letters in secret."

Ragnar struggled against the legionnaires, but their cumulative strength was too overwhelming to resist.

"This kind of betrayal is high treason. Ragnar, if you're found guilty of high treason in front of a court... you'll be executed."

"*No!* No, don't you touch my son, don't you touch him!"

Ragnar kicked and yelled out. One of the legionnaires removed a muzzle from his belt while the other four held him down.

"Get off me!"

Taking advantage of a momentary lapse in the legionnaires' united strength, Ragnar swung his left elbow back. The blow struck the legionnaire holding the muzzle in the side of his snout and sent him reeling back, helmet slipping from his head and clattering to the floor. The husky swore in New Opulusian before diving back on top of Ragnar, clamping the muzzle down over his snout with a *snap*. Ragnar let out a muffled yell, eyes wide in terror. Corsair met the Winter Baron's eyes.

"Alpha Tiberius-"

"It's Winter Baron Tiberius now, Sedrid," Lieutenant Maximus said.

"Winter Baron Tiberius... please don't kill him."

"He's guilty of high treason, Corsair. The rules apply to all of us." Winter Baron Tiberius said.

"He did something stupid. We're still emotional and irrational after Dad's passing. He knows what he did was wrong – this won't happen again, *ever*. Please, Winter Baron, don't kill him. Don't kill my brother. We've already lost our father. Please."

Winter Baron Tiberius looked back to the large wolf fighting for his life on the ground, his mother staring at him with pleading eyes. Lieutenant Maximus trained his eyes on Corsair, sword still thrust out towards him.

"I think you must have been influenced by the wrong people. Groomed, to a degree, Ragnar. With your mind in such a fragile, emotional state, I can understand you giving in to their whispers of conspiracy. I will have you charged as an accomplice, not an orchestrator, so you don't face execution. You're too young, too rash, and it would weigh on my conscience to have you executed."

Ragnar didn't relax fully. He remained tense, ready to struggle again if necessary.

"But repercussions have to be faced. You are an accomplice nonetheless and, if found guilty before a court, you will be exiled to the *Deuvick Feldanas*."

Corsair, upon hearing that name, knew what it meant.

The Derelict Plains of the North.

"*Let him go!*"

Corsair's mother pushed and punched feebly at the guard

holding her. The hound responded by grabbing her by the arms and shoving her back.

"Milady, you need to desist now."

"Let my pup go!"

As she charged forwards again to berate the legionnaire, the hound slapped her hard across the face. She fell down to one side, shielding her head, whimpering and crying as the legionnaires restraining Ragnar lifted him up.

"Mum! Touch her again and I'll kill you! You hear me? If you lay a paw on her-"

"You're not in any position to make threats, Sedrid," Lieutenant Maximus said. "If I was you, I'd shut my maw and stop resisting before anything gets worse."

"Take him to jail," Winter Baron Tiberius said.

Ragnar was dragged toward the door, his hind paws kicking out from behind as he tried to catch some form of friction underneath him, but he could do nothing. He cried out, trying to deliver his final words to his family, but could only do so in incomprehensible muffled sounds.

"Ragnee!" Corsair cried.

"No, Ragnee!" his mother cried, reaching out from where she was lying on the floor.

His older brother was dragged out the door and from sight, Rohesia watching them disappear down the pathway.

"I'm sorry it had to come to this. You need to understand that-"

Corsair pushed past Lieutenant Maximus, knocking the sword out of the way, and brought his right arm back before thrusting his clenched paw forwards. He struck the Winter Baron in the side of the snout. He reeled back, both paws shooting up to where he was struck.

"You disgusting-"

Lieutenant Maximus recovered and grabbed Corsair from behind, throwing him down to the floor. He scrambled to get back up but was pinned by the lieutenant straddling him, one leg on either side of his body. He leant back into the floor as he felt the longsword's blade being pushed up against his throat.

"Give me one more excuse, *deserter*."

"That's... that's enough, Lieutenant. Leave him be."

Adhering to his superior's orders, he alleviated the pressure from Corsair's neck and stood, sword still in paw. Vulnerable, Corsair made the mistake of trying to get up on to all-fours. Lieutenant Maximus brought his leg back and kicked him hard in the side.

Corsair yelled out, falling back on to his front, paws clutching his body.

"Lieutenant, I said stop!"

Corsair anticipated more but was relieved to see the lieutenant restrain himself.

"We're done here. Make sure Ragnar ends up in a cell for the night and that he is tried as soon as he can be."

Grunting in response, the lieutenant rolled his shoulders as he strolled through the door. He barged past Rohesia, growling as he did so, and disappeared into the night. The legionnaires monitoring the servants rushed down the stairs and jogged out, leaving the Winter Baron alone with the distraught family.

He walked to the door and lingered there, turning. Corsair sat up, slouched forwards with his paws pressed to the side where he had been kicked.

"I'm sorry for-"

"Get out of here *before I kill you*," Corsair snarled.

The Winter Baron stood there, a look of regret upon his face, before he turned and walked away. Rohesia rushed inside as he left, hurrying over to Corsair and kneeling.

"Are you okay?"

"I'm fine."

She helped Corsair to his hind paws. He exhaled gingerly as he stood up.

His mother still lay on the floor, her robes spread out around her as she heaved hot tears of anguish. Corsair arrived by her side with Rohesia in tow, Peter leading the servants down to them.

"Mum? Come on, sit up."

He eased his mother up into a sitting position, the servants gathering behind him, before she threw herself forward and wrapped her arms around his shoulders. He hugged back, feeling his mother cry against him.

"Not Ragnee! Not my... *beautiful R-Ragnee!*"

"It's okay, Mum. It's okay."

She began to wail, somewhat muffled by her face being pressed against his chest, but it was loud in the silence of the night. Corsair looked to the servants, gesturing for them to find her a drink and something to eat, before turning his attention back to his despairing mother.

"Ragnee will be fine. He's strong."

"They're going to kill him."

"They won't. I know they won't. He'll be fine."

She pulled back, leaving the stains of tears against the material of his shirt and cloak. Her eyes were red. She placed both paws on the sides of his face.

"Don't you leave me. I-I can't lose you, too. I'll *die* if I lose you."

"I'm right here, Mum. Okay? I'll always be right here."

She hugged him again, continuing to cry. All he could do was nuzzle his snout against her neck. He tried to comfort her as much as he could but it was futile even to try.

Feeling completely helpless, all he could do was hold his grieving mother and resist the desire to cry for the loss of Ragnar Sedrid.

CHAPTER NINETEEN

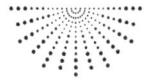

*R*ohesia saw the two legionnaires drag a wolf from his home, throwing him down into the snow of the main thoroughfare. Bystanders backed away, forced to do so by the imperative barks of the hounds surrounding the house. Some aimed crossbows at the crowd while others threatened them with their swords.

"Nothing to see here! This is official clan business and it does not concern the general public! Carry on!"

"What has he done?" someone yelled.

One of the two legionnaires descended on the wolf with the pommel of his sword, striking him over the head. The victim yelped and curled up, left helpless as the legionnaires continued to batter him.

"What are you doing to him?"

"There is nothing to see here!"

The legionnaire beat him one more time before he lifted his limp body up, barely conscious. Aided by his partner, he began to drag him away towards jail. A third legionnaire joined them while the rest of the cohort held a perimeter.

"Arnold!" his wife cried, rushing out the door. "*Arnold!*"

Rohesia could see the small shape of a cub behind her, standing there with eyes wide and mouth agape in a face of confusion. He had no idea what was happening. Her heart sank as she knew the meaning of his father's arrest would be lost on him, deflected by his cubhood innocence.

"Since when has Opulus had authority here? You can't just arrest people for no reason!" someone protested.

"This is a matter regarding Winter Baron Tiberius and individuals who wish to disrupt the peace and integrity of this clan. Move along!"

"You dragged a father away from his cub and his wife! You're disgusting!"

The crowd of onlookers began to yell at them, a chorus of barks and snarls. Some civilians edged closer. The leader did not fall back – instead, he yelled to his comrades in New Opulusian. The legionnaires behind him stepped forwards, short swords at the ready, while their comrades levelled crossbows at the crowds.

"We have orders to ensure the clan is secure and that all co-conspirators of Lieutenant Ziedik are punished! If you do not disperse immediately, we will use force and arrest those who resist! This is an unlawful gathering! *Disperse!*"

None of the wolves dared challenge the array of swords and crossbow bolts aimed at them. Many turned and hurried away, looking over their shoulders at the site of the arrest, but Rohesia lingered. She watched the mother.

She hugged her pup, shielding him from the conflict outside, whispering something to him. His face retained that same bewildered expression, unchanged, without a trace of understanding.

Poor pup.

She saw a legionnaire turn his sights on her.

"Final warning! Disperse or be met with the consequences!"

Rohesia knew she was no longer welcome and continued on her way towards the Sedrid household.

Days had passed since Ragnar Sedrid was dragged from his

home, kicking and yowling as the rest of his family watched in horror. Raids on households across the town increased in frequency with each passing day. To her horror, Rohesia had witnessed many such assaults. Mothers and fathers were torn away from their families, restrained by cruel dogs. Anyone who tried to resist or intervene was beaten ruthlessly until they were barely conscious.

Everyone is being accused of trying to overthrow Tiberius.

Something wasn't right in Grand Wolf Plains, and she imagined that the same regime of terror and punishment was being imposed across the clan territory. The order that the Sedrids had brought before was torn apart by the new leader.

Her face fell as she thought about Corsair.

There's no reason for Corsair to be arrested. He's done nothing wrong.

But Ragnar hadn't done anything wrong. He wasn't the kind of wolf to become a revolutionary. She had not spent as much time with him as she had with Corsair but knowing him for so many years had allowed her to develop a moderate understanding of his brother's character.

Conspirator wasn't one of the words she'd use to describe him.

She hoped no further action would be taken against the Sedrids.

"They just dragged someone away to jail!"

Rohesia saw a group of citizens surrounding two wolf soldiers, complaining in bulk as they gestured in the opposite direction.

"We can't do anything about that," a guard said, crestfallen.

"Why not? It's your job to protect us, go help him!"

"Our orders are to make sure Opulusian raids go on unhindered. There are a few people who Lieutenant Ziedik knew that are still unaccounted for. Once this is over, the raids will stop."

"He's not even the real Winter Baron. That helmet belonged to Arthur's son and they exiled him."

"I don't understand why you don't intervene," another civilian said.

"Because we can't," the guard said.

"Why can't you?"

"Our orders are-"

"Why the hell do orders matter when those dogs are arresting people in front of their pups and beating them to death? Do something!"

"I have pups to feed, I can't afford to disobey!"

Rohesia walked on past the debate.

If our own soldiers can't protect any of us... are we safe? At all?

"I am not smuggling anything!"

Rohesia looked ahead. On the left side of the road, surrounded by a team of legionnaires, was a carriage that had been halted. The ictharr roared and yowled in panic as the driver was forced on to the ground. Legionnaires turned the interior upside down, hurling boxes and crates out of the door. A trio of legionnaires dragged the boxes to the side of the roadway and tore them open, rummaging through the contents.

"What are you doing?" the carriage driver bellowed. "Those are my goods! You're ruining my business!"

"You are suspected of smuggling contraband," a legionnaire said. "We have orders to investigate."

"Contraband? What contraband? I just got here!"

Rohesia quickly left the scene, walking down the road. She stepped in front of the Sedrid door, lifting her paw to knock, but stopped when she heard a whimper from around the corner of the house. Her ears stood and she looked left, taking a step back.

Quickpaw and Harangoth.

She looked back to the door.

I can spare a minute.

Padding through the snow, she rounded the corner and arrived in front of the three stalls that formed the stable. A lone servant stood in front of a stall, heaving a bag of food and dropping it to the ground. Quickpaw's snout rested on the door to his pen, whimpering in boredom, until his eyes fell upon the black wolf and he began yapping in excitement. He stood and rested his front paws on the top of the door, eager to rush out and greet her.

She looked to the stall on the left.

Harangoth did not display the same excitement as his friend. He stood upright in his stall, staring past Rohesia and towards the main pathway in front of the house, not averting his gaze for a moment.

She stopped in front of Quickpaw's stall and scratched the scruff of his neck. He turned his head and craned it forward, eyes closed to enjoy the pampering Rohesia provided. After a few seconds she brought her paw back and patted him on the head, calming him down.

"I bet you're feeling really stuffy in there."

Quickpaw yapped.

"I can't take you on a ride. You might have to wait a little bit longer."

He whimpered in disappointment, sitting down and resting his snout on the top of the door again. She patted him on the bridge of his snout a final time before moving on to Harangoth's stall, stopping beside the servant. She watched as they poured some fodder into a small metal trough, lifting it up and lowering it into the pen. She placed it beside the door, right in front of the stoic ictharr's body.

He didn't move.

"Has he been eating?" Rohesia asked.

"He ate a little this morning," the servant sighed. "He's smart enough to eat so he can keep going every day but... that's it. He doesn't stop staring at the pathway."

Rohesia murmured in response, stepping past the servant as she moved on to feed Quickpaw. Harangoth was unresponsive to her movements and seemed almost catatonic. She leaned in and rested a paw on the side of his neck, stroking it gently.

"Ragnar will come back. You won't have to wait much longer."

Harangoth gave a small whimper, one so quiet and short that she wondered if she really even heard it, but did nothing more. She gave a sad smile, admiring his undying loyalty to his master before picking up the trough and moving it towards him.

"You need to eat. You can't be strong without food."

Harangoth, as expected, ignored her. Knowing the servant would look after them well enough, she turned and walked away from the stables. Arriving back in front of the door, she knocked three times and waited for it to be answered. She heard hushed whispers on the other side and then heard someone approach it. The lock clicked.

The door creaked open and a green eye peered out through the crack, identifying the individual.

"It's Rohesia. I'm back with ingredients for dinner."

Recognising her, Corsair widened the gap and allowed her entry to the house. She stepped inside and let the door shut behind her.

Silence.

The calm of the house was unusual. When she had visited the house before Arthur Sedrid's death, it was filled with life. Servants had bustled from room to room, Corsair and Ragnar held loud conversations in the living or dining area, and the atmosphere was joyous.

Now, apart from a few servants carrying out tasks in deathly silence, there was not a sound to be heard. It was as if the spirit of the house had been dragged out through the front door with Ragnar. All that was left was the emotionless, soulless carcass of the building.

"You got everything?" Corsair asked.

"Yeah, I got everything. I checked in on Quickpaw and Harangoth before I knocked on the door."

"How are they?"

"Quickpaw is anxious to go on a ride and Harangoth is just... staring."

He didn't answer. The effects of his brother's arrest were visible on him. His eyes were dull and lacking the energy they once had, more deprived of life than they were before Ragnar's exile. His fur was ruffled and unkempt, ears twitching, tail flicking back and forth with paranoia. He held his sword tight in his paw, ready for an encounter that Rohesia hoped would never come.

"Put it on the table."

She followed his instructions without hesitation, placing down the sack of goods. A servant, remaining silent, took the purchases and carried them into the kitchen, the door opening and shutting without making a sound.

"Thanks," Corsair said.

"Everything was okay while I was gone?"

"Nothing happened. You?"

She opened her mouth just as she heard the kitchen door open. She looked over her shoulder.

Ophelia Sedrid was not attempting to look presentable any more. Grief had made her indifferent to the condition of her tail, the fur standing up in places and flattened in others. Her usually flawless dress was covered in crinkles and crumples, lines of age showing on the material, and Rohesia noticed that her paws trembled somewhat.

"Thank you for bringing the ingredients in, dear," she said, a forced smile upon her face.

"I'm happy to help, Lady Sedrid."

"Are you going up to bed, Mum?" Corsair asked.

"Yes. You'll be okay?"

"I'll be okay."

"Can you fetch me a pitcher of water from the kitchen pail?"

"I'll do it, Mrs Sedrid," Rohesia offered.

"No, darling, it's fine."

"I can do it, Rohesia."

Corsair walked off towards the kitchen and disappeared through the door, retrieving her drink.

"I'm so happy you're living with us," she said. "You are a delight to have around. You always were. I wish we had invited you years ago! So polite."

"Oh, thank you," Rohesia giggled. "I'm happy to hear I'm not annoying company, Lady Sedrid."

"Not at all, darling, not at all. Is your bedding comfortable? If not, there is always…"

She winced.

"There is always Ragnee's room."

Rohesia glanced over at the fire. Laid out on the carpet before it was a rectangular sheet, a pillow placed at the end with a folded blanket at the other. While many would turn their nose up at the accommodation, Rohesia regarded it with gratitude.

"No, no, I am completely fine, Lady Sedrid. I appreciate the hospitality and I wouldn't want to disturb the room."

Ophelia nodded, understanding.

"I have something to ask you, darling. I apologise for its severity."

"Of course. What is it, Lady Sedrid?"

"I need you to make a promise to me."

"A promise?"

"A promise to keep Corsair safe from harm."

She didn't know how to answer.

"He's my cub. He's all I have left now – my husband is dead, my eldest son has been exiled, and now all I have left is him. If he were to be taken away from me, I… I wouldn't be able to cope. He's my treasure, the most precious thing in this world to me, and I can't bear to see a wolf or dog touch a *hair* on his body. So… I'm asking you to promise me that you'll protect him no matter what. That you'll make sure he stays safe in this house."

Rohesia nodded.

"I promise, Lady Sedrid. I'll look after Corsair."

"You'll protect him?"

"With my life. You can rely on me, Lady Sedrid."

Ophelia sighed and hugged Rohesia. She hugged back, feeling it was the right way to respond, and could hear the tears in her voice.

"I don't want to lose anyone else. He's all I have."

"You won't, Lady Sedrid."

She felt her tighten her grip.

"*Thank you,*" she whispered.

As Corsair entered, she stepped back and wiped away a tear.

"Here you go, Mum. Do you want me to carry it up?"

"I'm fine."

"Okay. Take as long as you need."

Rohesia watched Corsair and his mother hug, remaining in the embrace for several seconds, before the bond was broken and his mother disappeared up the stairs. She listened to her walk across the landing, the wooden floorboards creaking above them, and then heard her door shut.

Not another sound came from above them.

Corsair turned and walked in the direction of the fire, sitting down on the carpet and resting his sword beside him. Rohesia remained where she was for a moment, glancing up at the ceiling, before she followed and sat down beside her makeshift bedding.

Corsair stared into the fire, eyes focused on the flame.

She knew what he was thinking about.

"Ragnar is strong," she said. "He'll be fine. Even if it is the north."

Corsair didn't look at her.

"I hope to God he is."

"He is. I promise you that he is."

Silence reigned supreme throughout the house, not a sound coming from the servants as they continued to work. Rohesia let Corsair speak at his own speed.

"The last thing you expect to see is your brother being arrested in the middle of the night, your mother crying in the corner, every servant fearing for their lives on the landing. When I walked in that night, I... I didn't know what was happening."

He continued to stare into the fire.

"He was so scared. Ragnee's always been the big, tough brother. He's never let his guard down, never allowed anyone to best him, and there he was – eyes wide open and struggling for his life. He thought he was going to die. I did, too."

He paused.

"I've never heard Mum scream so much in her life."

275

Rohesia kept her eyes on the wolf. The lively spirit he used to possess, the jovial character that she used to play with in the snow as a cub, was gone. What sat before her was a person filled with despair and misery, unsure of what further torture the future held, a being living in fear.

"I'm going insane in here. I've checked that door repeatedly every day since Ragnee was taken. I don't know how many times I've thought, 'This is it, they're here to take Mum away,' when someone just walks past the house. I'm... I'm so scared. What will they do to her if they drag her away, kicking and screaming? They could kill her, Rohesia. Those monsters could *kill* my mother."

"You'll be okay, Corsair. I'll make sure that you'll both be okay. And maybe, if it makes you feel better... pray? God will listen."

"God doesn't care. God hasn't cared for days now. What has he done for me? What has this great, all-powerful God done for me other than kill Dad, have Ragnee taken from me, and left me with a despairing mother who won't stop..."

He shielded his face, body trembling.

"She won't stop calling out for Ragnee in her sleep. I can hear her. When I check on her she's reliving that nightmare every night, trying to protect him, and all I can do is watch her suffer."

Rohesia remembered the look of terror on his mother's face, terrified not for her own wellbeing but her son's. She had watched her crumple and curl up on the ground, reduced to a sobbing hysterical mess.

"What can I do? I'm trapped in this situation and I can't see a way out. We're not safe. The guards who were posted outside were ordered to go somewhere else. We can't take any carriages out of here without being stopped and sent back. I can't ride Quickpaw because they'll stop me. We can't go *anywhere*."

Rohesia wanted to say that some people could travel freely, that they could smuggle themselves aboard a carriage, but she remembered how legionnaires ransacked a transport on the side of the road.

They get caught and they'll be in a lot of trouble. There's no leaving through the gates if they're checking everything that comes in and out.

"You know Ragnee didn't do it, right?"

"Do what?"

"He didn't write what Tiberius said."

"No, of course."

Corsair nodded.

"Ragnee isn't a revolutionary. The cruel monster said it himself – it wasn't like him. He's been framed. He has to be."

"But why? For what reason would they have to attack your family?"

"I don't know, I'm... I just know it wasn't him. Others may think he might do it because he wanted to take the helmet back but that's not Ragnee. He's not vengeful like that. I mean, think about it. Remember when I told you the legionnaires stopped me?"

"Yes?"

"The moment they realised it was me, they let me go. I didn't think anything of it at the time, but now... I can't help thinking that they thought I was Ragnee. They were searching for him and it just... it just feels like they were searching for him before they'd found anything."

Rohesia nodded. She lowered a paw on to Corsair's shoulder, her friend turning his head to look at it before raising his eyes to look into hers. Those green eyes shimmered with tears, rimmed with red.

"Maybe I could have stopped them."

"Corsair."

"Maybe I could have... I could..."

And then he cried.

He lowered his head into himself and began to sob, tears falling from his eyes and on to the carpet. Rohesia could only stare for a moment, her heart shattered by the sight of the wolf weeping in despair and hopelessness, trapped in a horrible situation with no visible exit. She leant in and wrapped her arms around him, allowing her friend to hug back and cry on her shoulder.

"What... what did we do? W-what did we do to deserve this?"

"Nothing, Corsair, nothing."

"Why us? *Why us?*"

She shushed him.

"It's okay, it's okay."

He continued to heave up and down as he wept, mourning the loss of both his father and brother. She could only whisper hollow comforts into his ear as he grieved. The feeling was horrible – being confined to the role of bystander, unable to help or mitigate the damage dealt.

All she could do was hold her friend tight and remember the promise she made to Ophelia Sedrid.

A promise to keep Corsair safe from harm.

CHAPTER TWENTY

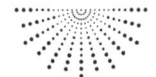

*C*orsair needed to leave the house, otherwise he would go insane.

He was aware of how bad the circumstances were – they came for his brother and, for all he knew, they were waiting for the right opportunity to take one more from the Sedrid family. It was safer for him to be in his home where the servants kept a lookout for any approaching Opulusians.

But he couldn't cope. He was growing increasingly paranoid at home – every time anyone walked past his door he was convinced that they were coming to barrel inside, swords drawn, and beat him to a pulp before dragging him away to jail.

Or, even worse, pinning him down as they stole his mother away.

I need to clear my head. I need to breathe in some fresh air. After that, I won't need to leave. I'll stay inside. It's only a few minutes' walk.

Corsair, sure he was prepared for his expedition, slid his sword into his scabbard. It sat there, loyal and ready to defend its wielder, waiting to be summoned at a moment's notice. He gave it a reassuring pat, resting his paw on the grip, before leaving his room and crossing the landing to the top of the stairs.

Peter stood by the door, a fellow servant beside him. They were both quiet, listening for any sound of an approaching party despite chatter emanating from the kitchen. Corsair could see Rohesia's makeshift bedding on the floor, left tidy and vacant with clothes folded on top, which was a sign that his exit would go unhindered.

He glanced down the landing towards his mother's room. The door was shut, his mother having retired for the afternoon. Satisfied with this knowledge, he turned his head back and proceeded down the stairs, the servants' eyes on him.

"Sir?" Peter asked. "Are you going somewhere?"

"For a walk."

"In this situation? Sir, that doesn't seem smart."

"Corsair?"

Corsair winced as he heard Rohesia's voice from behind him, turning to face her. The black wolf stood by the kitchen door in a gown his mother had lent her, glaring at him with pitcher of water in paw.

"What are you doing?" she asked, coming forward.

"I need to get out of the house."

"What?"

"Rohesia, please, I'm losing it in here. I told you – I can't stop fearing that they'll be coming through the door at any moment."

"And what makes you think out there is any better than in here? Don't be an idiot, Corsair."

"It's only a few minutes. A walk down to the centre and back, that's it. I need some fresh air."

"And what do I tell your mother?"

"She doesn't need to know anything, Rohesia, that's the point."

She was silent, hesitant.

"It'll cause her unnecessary stress. She'll get worried and the last thing I want is for her to come out looking for me. I'll be fine."

"I've seen those legionnaires raid houses and drag people out.

They don't mess around. They could easily grab you out there where none of us can protect you."

"I'll be fine. I'll be in the middle of everyone – they wouldn't think of grabbing me without starting a commotion."

"They did that to other wolves in broad daylight, Corsair, are you not understanding me?"

"I'll be fine. I need to go out and refr-"

"No," Rohesia said, stepping in front of him to block the door. "You can't go out."

"Rohe-"

"At least give me a moment to get dressed and come with you."

"No, Rohesia, I want you here protecting Mum."

"What about the servants?"

"You have a bow, they don't. Please. She won't even be awake in a few minutes – keep a look out and I'll be back, I promise."

Corsair held her gaze, making her glance away towards the fire, before she sighed and stepped aside.

"Down the main pathway and back. Nowhere else."

"Got it."

He turned back to the door and stopped next to Peter, resting a paw on the wooden panelling.

"You'll hear me when I come back. I'll knock, I'll speak, I'll do something. But if it isn't me, *do not open the door*. You do everything you can to protect Mum if they come for her, okay?"

"With my life, Sir," Peter said as his fellow servant nodded in agreement.

"Good. I'll be back."

With that, he pushed open the door and stepped out into the cold. The snow was strong, carried forward by whistling winds, and he jerked his grimacing face away from the direction of the gust. Shielding his face with one paw and placing his other on his sword's pommel, he began to walk forwards in the direction of the town centre.

Town centre and back. That will be enough.

He could see the shapes of other figures walking back and forth along the path, huddled in groups as they conversed with one another. He could only see their squinted eyes and cringing faces as he passed by, battered by the frosty wind.

He continued forwards, trudging down the path, when he saw a group of Opulusian legionnaires on the side of the road. They weren't moving, guarding the entrance to a house with cloaks shrouding their armour. Corsair watched out of the corner of his eye, paw tightening around his sword's grip, but none of them noticed his presence. Whether or not this was intentional was beyond him – as long as they weren't approaching him or moving towards his house, there was no reason to care.

Keep moving forward.

Forcing himself through the swirling snow, he arrived at the town centre minutes later. Despite the ferocious weather, the market was still packed with customers and traders, money and goods changing paws before his eyes. He could see the odd patrol among the crowds, remaining vigilant for any thieves, so he decided to remain out of their line of sight.

As he was turning to walk back, his eyes fell upon Mr Duncan's tavern. Its doors and fiery warmth beckoned him, a place where he could rest for the time being. He felt inclined to answer its call.

He looked back down the main path, in the direction of the eastern wall.

It'll only be a few minutes more. A drink would be nice for a change.

Convinced, he hurried forwards through the barrage of snow and entered the tavern. The usual cheery sounds of wolves laughing and drinking filled his ears as he shut the door. Some sat around the fire for warmth. He felt much safer among his people in such a small space. There was no way any legionnaire would try to arrest him here, not when some drunkards would be willing throw a few swings at anyone who disturbed their drinking.

He walked to the bar and sat on one available stool, taking his place next to an old brown wolf murmuring to himself over his empty tankard.

"Corsair?"

Corsair looked up to see Mr Duncan approaching, stopping on the opposite side of the counter.

"Are you okay?"

"I'm fine. As fine as I can be, anyway."

Mr Duncan nodded, exhaling.

"Well, that's good to hear. I'm sorry about your brother... it's a shame what happened to him. And, for the record, I don't believe a word of it. None of us in here do."

Corsair grunted, unsure of how to respond.

"You want a drink on the house?"

"It's fine, I have money."

Corsair offered an Iggregom up in return for a pint and the bartender nodded. As Mr Duncan turned to provide him with a beverage, he looked down at the counter and sighed.

There's got to be some way out of this.

He had already ruled out their only option – escape. He knew they'd be identified and immediately turned back by the legionnaires but there was nothing else. He couldn't do anything other than wait for them to come. He and his mother were on limited time and they had to find something before they heard that fateful knock on the door.

Maybe we could leave through the south. It's guarded but there would be a chance we could slip through if we used the trees. If it's dark and we're quick enough, we could leave and never be spotted. We'd create enough distance by morning.

But where would they go? Travelling south would only lead them to more occupied territory and closer to the Kingdom of Opulus. Travelling north would lead them into the barren wasteland of *Deuvick Feldanas*, a desolate tract of snowy nothingness where they wouldn't survive. Travelling east would lead them towards the war he was trying to get away from and he doubted the rabbits would grant the family who had declared war on them safe sanctuary within their territory.

Maybe the west. The Kingdom of Wyndr isn't in conflict with the clan. They'd have no reason to attack us, at least.

He knew journeying to the west meant he'd be accepting the fact he would never see Ragnar again. He didn't know if he had it in him to abandon hope in his survival completely. There was a chance he was out there, waiting to be rescued.

We'll find him and live somewhere else. A smaller country somewhere on the other side of the land. We'd be safe. We could live.

His thoughts were interrupted by the sound of his order landing on the table with a *thud*, making him recoil.

"There's your drink. Let me know if you need anything else, okay?"

"Thank you."

Mr Duncan turned and walked back to the other side of the bar, tending to the orders of three female wolves. Corsair watched the bustle of the tavern for a moment before taking a swig of his drink. The familiar taste of bitter alcohol made him wince but he drank half of it before placing the pitcher down on the counter.

He heard the door open behind him and looked over his shoulder.

Through the door came two legionnaires dressed in cloaks and armour. They were conversing casually, helmets held under their arms as they entered, and all eyes followed them as they approached the bar. The chatter persevered but Corsair saw the glares the legionnaires received.

His eyes fell upon the face of the first.

He felt it.

A slow boil building in his stomach.

He recognised the husky who helped arrest his brother.

He turned away, gripping the bar hard.

Stay calm. Stay calm.

He considered leaving but knew that his sudden exit would only attract more attention to himself. His best bet was to hunker down by the bar and act as if nothing was wrong, to blend in among the other patrons.

He faced forwards and kept his eyes focused on the back of the bar, hearing the conversation of the two legionnaires get louder and louder, before they stopped behind the elderly wolf.

"Excuse me," the husky said. "Can we just slide in here?"

The old wolf looked over his shoulder and saw the two legionnaires standing there, steel armour glinting in the light of the fire. He grumbled, shaking his head, before getting up.

"Sir, you don't have to..."

The husky's voice trailed off as the elderly wolf slid past them, hobbling towards the exit. The two legionnaires exchanged looks, shrugging, before the husky sat down.

Corsair didn't dare to glance in their direction.

In the corner of his eye, however, he could see the husky frantically patting his pockets. Sighing, the legionnaire turned to his compatriot and spoke in New Opulusian. The other legionnaire, a labrador, carried out the same investigation before turning to his colleague and shaking his head.

Corsair tensed.

If he turns to me to ask for a coin, I'm finished.

Fortunately, the legionnaires decided otherwise. The husky muttered in New Opulusian before he stood and walked back towards the door. Corsair peered over his shoulder as they left, watching them carve a path between the tables.

That slow boil had risen into a fierce bubbling concoction of rage in the pit of his stomach, summoning a low growl from him.

He remembered how the husky had forced the muzzle on to Ragnar's snout.

He remembered how the husky had helped whisk away and banish his brother.

And now he just gets to walk in here and play innocent? He gets to be all polite and friendly?

Caution was no longer a concern. The pure hatred he felt in

every ounce of his flesh, from head to hind paw, overpowered any consideration he had to not risk confrontation. One paw did its best to crush the grip of his longsword, ready to summon it from its sheath.

He shot up from the bar and turned, storming towards the door.

"Corsair?" Mr Duncan called. "Corsair, where are you going?"

He ignored the barkeep and pushed out through the doors, stepping back into the icy cold of the day. He saw the two legionnaires strolling ahead of him, only a few metres from the entrance.

Glaring at the husky, he did not allow them to go any further.

"Hey!"

The duo stopped and turned, the labrador's paw instinctively moving to the sword on his belt while the husky remained calm.

That relaxed demeanour faded as the legionnaire realised who he was looking at.

"Corsair Sedrid?" the husky said.

Corsair stepped towards them.

"You helped frame my brother."

The husky frowned.

"Frame him? Sir... with all due respect, we had evidence of-"

"*Don't give me that.* The only evidence you had was the forged journal that bastard gave to you."

"It isn't our place to question the authenticity of it. We had our orders, Sir, from the Winter Baron himself."

Corsair took another step. The labrador winced, nervously glancing at his comrade.

"Just because you were told to arrest him and condemn him to death doesn't make you innocent! You still did that!"

"Sir, I understand you hate me."

"You don't understand how much I hate you right now."

Corsair unsheathed his sword.

The husky reached for his, stepping back.

"Sir... if come any closer then we can't help you."

Corsair snarled, baring his fangs.

"I don't want your damn help..."

He twirled his sword, taking up face-on stance.

"*I want you dead!*"

Corsair shot forward with a yell. He sliced downwards. The husky yelled a command in New Opulusian before he drew his short sword, darted right and swung with his free paw. The blow struck Corsair in the side of the head, sending him stumbling. With no armour to protect him, he knew that he could only rely on dodging and blocking – failure to do so would lead to his death.

The legionnaire came forwards, swinging from multiple directions with the pommel of his sword. Corsair knocked it away and swung back, snarling as he did so. The longsword clashed against the short sword's steel. Corsair jabbed forwards from an angle, aiming for the husky's head, but the husky deflected it and kicked forwards. The bottom of the dog's hind paw struck Corsair in the stomach and he staggered, maintaining his balance.

"You need to desist, now!" the husky yelled. "Do not make me hurt you!"

"So what? So you can just arrest me and exile me? So my mother is left vulnerable and defenceless? Nice try!"

Corsair swung forwards. The husky weaved and made an attempt to rip the weapon from his paws, grappling from the side. The labrador moved towards them, sheathing his sword.

"Get off me!"

Corsair turned and swung upwards with the hilt of his sword. The hilt struck the husky on the underside of his snout, left exposed by the metal of the helmet. The dog yelped. He stepped away, teetering backwards.

Corsair aimed the sword for his flank.

As he thrust it forwards, Corsair caught a glimpse of a gauntlet swinging at him from the side.

The world spun as the labrador intervened with a punch to the side of the head, knocking him down to his knees and causing his sword to slip from his paw. He grimaced, his head aching from the blow, but the pain quickly ebbed away when he saw the husky returning. Arms outstretched, the legionnaire rapidly approached to tackle him.

Corsair shot up and wrestled against the legionnaire, frantically trying to pull his sword away.

"Sir, you need to stop!"

The labrador arrived behind him and wrapped his arms around Corsair's midsection, using all his strength to attempt to rip him away. Corsair struggled and writhed, fighting a battle on two fronts, before he swung an elbow back in desperation and struck the labrador in the jaw.

Clang.

It was an awkward angle, only landing a glancing hit on the side of his snout where the armour protected him. Corsair tried again.

This time he hit his target.

Thump.

"Ow!"

The labrador reeled back. Corsair snatched the labrador's short sword from his sheath as he fell backwards. The husky kicked forwards, Corsair barely dodging left and swinging. The short sword was awkward in his paw, the size and weight alien to him, so the collision against the armour only left a scratch along the surface. A snarl came from his enemy and the dog swung back with his closed metal fist. Corsair ducked down.

Without hesitation, he jabbed the short sword forwards.

He felt the tip break the surface.

The husky yelped and stumbled back, keeling over with metal paws pressed against his abdomen.

Corsair stared.

The husky eased one trembling paw away from the gash and looked down at the dribbling crimson, cursing in New Opulusian.

But Corsair's rage was hardly exhausted.

"You'll pay for what you did to us!"

Fangs bared and sword pointed at the wounded legionnaire, Corsair yelled out and tackled the husky.

The force behind the attack launched both of them through the doors of the tavern, landing with the legionnaire on his back and Corsair on top of him. A gasp came from the tavern's customers as they froze, eyes on the brawling duo.

"Hey, what the hell?"

"Break it up, break it up!"

"Hit him, Sedrid!"

"Get him, go on!"

Corsair growled, determined to teach the hound a lesson. He pushed himself up on to his knees, looking down to reach for the grip of the short sword.

He froze.

The crowd gasped.

In a moment of clarity, a lapse in the fog, he realised what he'd done.

The sword protruded through a crevice in the armour, tearing through the metal muscle over the stomach and penetrating the feeble flesh beneath. The legionnaire lay there, twitching and gagging, eyes wide in pain. His arms trembled as he reached up towards the wound, finding the blade embedded in his abdomen. Corsair saw a line of crimson dribble from beneath the mask and down the side of his neck, coming from the corner of the legionnaire's mouth.

Corsair pushed himself away and stood, wide-eyed. The sight immediately washed away all rage that had consumed him.

"I-I... oh G-God... help..."

The legionnaire coughed and choked, trying to reach out for help. He attempted to continue speaking but, with the pain racking his body, was interrupted by the blood that he was coughing up.

The labrador barged past Corsair and dropped to his knees, paws hovering over the wound in reluctance.

"*Medicalis, medicalis!* Get a doctor!" he yelled. "Get help, someone!"

Wolves shot up from their chairs, hurrying over to the dying husky's side. A group of them jeered and cheered, congratulating Corsair.

He did not share their pride.

Corsair backed away, walking out the doors with his eyes still focused on the bloodied dog. Crimson slowly pooled beneath him, crawling across the wooden floorboards and towards the door as if it was trying to point to him. Some wolves glared at the young Sedrid in horror, looking from the victim to the culprit.

"No," Corsair muttered, shaking his head. "I didn't... I didn't mean it, I didn't. He... he..."

And then a new wave of horror arrived.

He had given them an excuse.

He had murdered an Opulusian. He gave them a reason to arrest him. He gave them a reason to come and drag him away.

No no no no no...

With the tavern focused on the dying legionnaire, Corsair wasted no time.

Picking up his sword, he turned tail and fled.

Back down the main pathway he sprinted, muscles burning as he tried to distance himself from the husky. His eyes stung, his mind whirred, and his heart thundered.

Oh God, what have I done? What have I done?

He came against the door and berated it with clenched paw, glancing back down the main pathway with panicked eyes.

"Let me in! Please, let me in, *let me in!*"

"Sir?"

"Let me in, oh God, please!"

The door swung open and Corsair rushed into the house, shooting up the stairs and across the landing. He ignored Rohesia's calls from the kitchen, alerted by his frantic behaviour, and barged into his mother's room. His mother was sitting on the side of the bed, a servant next to her with a book in her paws, and both looked up at Corsair. Rohesia rushed in behind him.

"Mum, Mum!"

It only took his mother a fraction of a second to see the expression on Corsair's face, shooting up to her hind paws and coming forward.

"Corsair, what's wrong?" she asked.

For a moment, he struggled even to get a word out, left speechless by the experience.

"Corsair?"

"I... I... I killed someone. God, Mum, I killed someone."

Her eyes widened.

"What?"

"I... I went for a walk and I saw one of the legionnaires who arrested Ragnar and... I killed him."

He saw his mother's face harden.

"I told you not to leave the house, Corsair! I told you not to leave the house!"

"I couldn't cope!"

"I can't cope with any of this, Corsair, but you don't see me running around Grand Wolf Plains looking to get into fights with the *bastard Opulusians*! What kind of *idiot* does that? Why would you do that?"

"I know but, Mum, we need to go. We need to get on the ictharrs and leave. Or find a carriage. O-or we can run through the woods and-"

"Get a bag ready."

The servant nodded and rushed out the room.

"Mum, I didn't mean to-"

"That doesn't matter now. We have minutes before they get here after finding the legionnaire. Rohesia, get a bag ready to leave and get changed. Only the essentials."

"Of course, Lady Sedrid," Rohesia agreed, nodding.

She turned and hurried down the stairs, leaving Corsair alone with his mother.

"Corsair, Dahlia will be making a bag for you. You're dressed, you have your sword – all you need is food and water to last a few days travel. Take Harangoth and Quickpaw with you."

"What about you?" Corsair asked.

"Now's not the time."

"No, Mum, I'm not leaving you here to be arrested. You're coming with me."

"Corsair, go downstairs and leave me. I'm not letting them capture my son. If we leave together, I will be unable to stall them. They will be upon our trail in an instant."

"No, Mum, you can't leave me. M-Mum, come on, I need you."

"You need to hurry."

"Mum-"

"Go!"

She pushed him out the room and stood in the doorway, a barrier to prevent him running back inside. The young Sedrid turned to face his mother, eyes red with tears and ears down.

"If you die, Corsair, it will kill me. If I die, you'll be able to keep living. You're young. You have your life ahead of you."

"No, Mum, please. Mum, don't leave me."

His mother came forwards and wrapped his arms around her son, Corsair hugging her back and hiding his face in her neck.

"I love you so much, Corsair," she said, nuzzling him. "You can do this. I will always be with you, no matter what."

"Mum, please. I can't do this alone."

"Rohesia will look after you."

His mother forced him off her and stepped back, paw on the door.

"And God will keep you safe."

"Mum, no!"

Corsair came forwards to barrel into the room but his mother slammed the door in his face, locking it and leaving him outside. Both paws resting on the door, he stared at the wooden panelling through red-rimmed eyes.

"Mum?" he whimpered. "Please let me in...Mum?"

No response.

"Corsair!" Rohesia yelled. "We need to go!"

He continued to stare for a moment, locked in a trance. He knew he would never see his mother again, that he was being sent away so he could live, and he resented himself for his stupidity. He shouldn't have let his anger get the better of him. He shouldn't have let his rage damn them.

"*Corsair*, we haven't got time!"

I love you, Mum.

He wiped away the tears and stormed back down the landing, taking his bag from Rohesia and rushing away through the door.

CHAPTER TWENTY-ONE

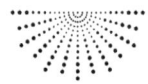

Ten minutes later, Ophelia Sedrid was sitting on her side of the bed, Peter standing by the door in silence.

One paw rested where Arthur once lay.

She stared longingly at the empty place where he used to sleep. Transfixed by the memory of her husband sleeping there, snoring, she felt at peace with herself.

I did the right thing.

She didn't care if he killed someone – Corsair was her son and that fact came before anything else. She would never pass him over to the brutal hounds that patrolled Grand Wolf Plains, never betray the intangible bond between the two, and she was ready to die hundreds of agonising deaths to protect him.

She remained silent and closed her eyes. She bowed her head in prayer, one paw still resting on the bed with the other on her lap, before standing and walking to her dresser. On its surface was a single letter, held shut by a black wax seal with the Clan of the Great Lupine's insignia stamped on it.

She loved and, simultaneously, loathed it.

She lifted it up.

Should I have given this to him?

Sighing, she looked down at the dresser drawer. She didn't know to what extent her room would be ransacked. There were no loose floorboards for it to seek refuge beneath.

She looked to Peter, who made eye contact with her.

"This is... something I wanted Corsair to have."

"Milady?"

"I wanted to give it to him but... it felt wrong. It felt insulting. I want him to find it one day but... now? This cannot be at the forefront of his mind."

She held it out to Peter.

"These hounds are ruthless. They will search me, certainly, and they will search my room. Perhaps they will not be so thorough with you. Hide it on yourself or somewhere they will not search."

Peter hesitated for a moment, unsure of himself.

"You will see them yourself, Milady, I am sure."

"I wish I could be so certain, too," she chuckled. "Please."

Peter sighed and eased it out of her paw. He slid it into his uniform, stowing it away from sight.

"If you ever come across Corsair or Ragnee then I ask that you give it to them."

"I'll protect it with my life, Milady."

"Thank you. Peter?"

"Yes, Milady?"

"Was it wrong of me to have kept it hidden? What Arthur did?"

"Perhaps, Milady, but I can hardly vilify you for complicity when I have been silent. The love we had for him, the respect we had for him, blinded us. Perhaps... as wrong as we are to have not spoken, he was the one who placed us in such a troubling situation. The onus is on him... wherever he may be now."

And then they arrived.

Ophelia heard the door fly open, followed by the yells of fake surprise from the servants. Voices filled the room as the legionnaires spread out throughout the household, already rushing into the kitchen and coming up the stairs with terrifying speed.

"*On the ground!*"

"We have the right to search this property under the authority of Winter Baron Tiberius!"

"Resist and you will be met with force!"

Ophelia, as she heard the squad of legionnaires barge into Corsair's room, stood and composed herself. She considered herself quite the actor – she wasn't beyond playing the fool if she needed to.

"Ready, Milady?" Peter asked, paw on the door.

"I am ready."

Stay safe, Corsair.

With that final thought echoing in her mind as the door was opened, she took a deep breath and stepped out.

The interior was besieged. Five legionnaires scoured the ground floor, with two of the five tending to the servants lined up against the wall. A single figure, adorned in golden armour, stood by the fireplace whilst watching the raid ensue.

"What is the meaning of this?" she bellowed.

She yelped with shock as she felt one strong paw land on her shoulder, already directing her towards the stairs. It belonged to a legionnaire guiding her down towards the other marauders. Another legionnaire grabbed Peter and marched him towards the stairs, sword held in his other paw.

"Ophelia Sedrid, we are searching this residence for a fugitive," the legionnaire said. "We would appreciate it if you cooperated and did not interfere."

Aware of the Opulusians' aggression, she did not dare to resist. Instead she donned a look of confused anger, shooting glares at one legionnaire and then shifting her gaze to another. She saw four other legionnaires ransacking Corsair's room, searching under the bed and in the corners before filing out to search Ragnar's room. She hid her satisfaction. They would find no one there.

The idiots.

She allowed herself to be escorted to the dining table. Peter was forced on to his knees alongside the other servants, paws placed on the back of his head.

"Sit."

A legionnaire pulled out a chair and forced her down, making her snarl in response. The legionnaire stepped back, short sword sheathed, and lurked behind her.

Ophelia looked back to the lone soldier by the fireplace.

He watched his fellow soldiers. His golden armour indicated that he was of another military position, probably of higher rank than his fellow legionnaires. A golden variant of the same helmet masked his identity.

He looked up to the landing above. An exchange in New Opulusian passed between him and a legionnaire on the landing, the latter relaying information of their findings to their superior. The leader spoke in that same tongue but something was peculiar about it – it was a seemingly more informal dialect than she had heard the king speaking.

The leader looked down from the landing and towards Ophelia. A pair of strong gold eyes met hers through the holes in his mask. She looked away.

Ophelia heard the legionnaires filing out of the rooms and making their way down the stairs, taking up positions along the walls, while a few walked outside to guard the door. She could hear them outside, urging some people to move along, until the sound was muffled by one of the guards shutting the door to hide the activity within.

Silence.

The leader glanced at the door, waiting a moment, before he looked back and approached Ophelia. He stopped by the head of the table, looking down at the wolf, before he reached up and removed the helmet from his head and placed it in front of her.

"I'm sorry for the mess," Valour said. "We have met before. I'm sure you remember."

"I don't care if we've met before," Ophelia said. "I want to know the meaning of this invasion. This is an unwarranted attack on my privacy while I'm still mourning the loss of my husband. What is happening?"

"We're looking for your son."

She flinched.

"Corsair? For what reason?"

"We–"

"Are you here to take him away as well?"

"Milady–"

"Tiberius has the audacity to come and take another son from me, just like he did to my precious Ragnee?"

"Milady, I will explain all in due time if you let me speak."

She scowled at the doberman, turning her snout up at him, before crossing one leg over the other.

"Speak."

"Thank you. Your son was witnessed stabbing a member of the Opulusian Legion in the stomach before fleeing the scene of the crime as his victim lay in the middle of Mr Duncan's tavern bleeding to death.""What?" she gasped.

"His partner attempted to treat the wound but the legionnaire was dead by the time an Opulusian Legion doctor arrived on the scene. Your son killed one of our legionnaires. This is a very serious matter and we are to arrest him at once. We were hoping you, if we did not find him here, would be able to tell us where he could be."

She was silent, mouth open.

"Milady?"

"I... I don't know where he is."

He looked unimpressed.

"I respect your loyalty to your son but we know he came home right afterwards."

"He did no such thing. He left home this morning and then didn't come back. I thought you might have snatched him off the street."

"Milady, as a parent myself, I don't need any evidence or witnesses to know he returned home after the incident because the first thing my daughters would do in a terrible situation like that is come to me or my husband."

Ophelia was caught off-guard by this information. She quickly steeled herself, growling, before retorting.

"Corsair isn't like your daughters."

"Your son killed him."

"My son did not hurt that legionnaire."

"A lot of people say otherwise, Milady. I know he killed him."

She opened her mouth but found that she could not provide any evidence. Cornered, with Valour seeing through her lies, she felt the urge to confront him directly grow inside of her, emitted through a rising growl.

"He was here on the night Ragnee was taken."

"Who?"

"This legionnaire you are speaking of. He helped take my son away. Corsair saw him and... that is when the altercation started."

"Altercation? He killed him, Milady."

"Only after you killed his brother."

"Ragnar Sedrid has been exiled -"

"To the *Deuvick Feldanas*. He will freeze to death if he doesn't starve."

Valour was silent. She continued.

"So if you think you can walk in here and expect me to bark up an answer as to where my son went, you're a fool. You're all idiots if you believe that for a second. I'm not letting you kill my second son."

He remained silent for the next few seconds, held back by Ophelia's outspoken love, and tried again.

"Your son is responsible for the death of an Opulusian and it's my duty to my kingdom to assure that those related to the deceased receive justice as compensation."

"Justice? Justice for what, being related to a hound who would tear a son from their family without question?"

"Ragnar Sedrid was conspiring to overthrow the Winter Baron."

"He was *framed*. He would never do such a thing. He has no lust for power, unlike that monster you work for."

Valour scowled.

"Milady, maybe you do not understand. This legionnaire had sons. This legionnaire had a husband. He had a name. Sigil Longvidas. He had a family. If he were a monster for supposedly tearing a hole in yours, what does it make Corsair for doing the same to another?"

"Maybe you should tell his adoring husband and sons that he helped punish an innocent person."

"Maybe it's your careless disregard of life that put Corsair on the path of murder."

Whether or not it was intentional, Valour struck a nerve.

"Don't you *dare* lecture me on poor upbringing! I have raised that pup with nothing but love and care! You have no right, *no right*, to walk in here and tell me how I have raised him!"

She was slightly out of breath, drawing in air quickly to recover from her rage. The doberman maintained eye contact with her.

"I am being lenient here, Milady. If you don't tell us where he is, I'll have to bring you down to the Great Hall of Wolves for further questioning."

"I have *nothing* to say to you. Take me to Tiberius – you're a fool if you think anything will change."

"Don't make this harder than it actually is, Milady."

She glared at him. Valour sighed and turned to the legionnaires. He delivered a command in New Opulusian. Without hesitation, the legionnaires stepped back from the servants, sheathing their weapons. Valour gestured to the hound behind Ophelia and the legionnaire nodded, stepping forwards and placing his gauntleted paw on her shoulder again. She did not flinch – instead, she stared defiantly at her captors, unfazed by the helmets and swords before her.

"Do you need a cloak?" Valour asked.

"Upstairs, in my room."

He turned and made eye contact with the nearest legionnaire, who nodded and raced up the stairs to retrieve her apparel. Valour stepped towards her.

"Milady, we will find him with or without your help. I can't guarantee it will be as pretty without. If you are as compassionate as you seem, you should tell me where he is. For his wellbe-"

"And if you were any less of an idiot than I think you are, you would consider my words. You'll never find him. You all stand here in your suits of armour and wielding those sharp swords, kicking down doors and trying to drive fear into us. But my son will outsmart *all* of you dumb mutts, and he'll make you look like nothing but a few pathetic pups in oversized suits of armour, tails between your legs."

The legionnaire returned. She snatched the cloak from him and pulled it over herself.

"Drag me away, then. You'll get nothing out of me."

"Oh God oh God oh God..."

"Corsair, *be quiet.*"

The duo hid within the snowy woodlands of the south, concealed behind a fallen tree trunk. Knowing that patrols would spot them as they fled, Rohesia suggested waiting for a good moment to make their way through the forest. Even with the speed of Quickpaw and the strength of Harangoth, they were no longer protected by their armour – a stray crossbow bolt would risk bringing either beast down if well placed.

Rohesia was hunkered down beside Corsair, bow at the ready, with leather armour strapped over her torso and black slacks pulled hastily over her legs. Harangoth lay on his front beside her, ducked down behind the log, while Quickpaw lay next to Corsair with his concerned eyes trained on him.

Corsair was a wreck.

Sniffling and whimpering, he sat with his back up against the trunk. He held his paws over his snout, trying to muffle his cries and whines, but he couldn't stop the fierce oncoming emotion.

Mum's dead Mum's dead Mum's dead...

They heard yelling from the house only minutes ago, carried along by the frosty winds. Rohesia told him where his mother was being led to, having spotted her en route to the Great Hall of Wolves while she was scouting the area. He couldn't help but feel responsible. He had left the house to go on a walk. He had allowed himself to be tempted to go to the tavern. He had stabbed the legionnaire in the stomach, killing him in front of tens of witnesses.

It's all my fault! Why did I do that? Why?

"Rohesia?"

"Quiet."

"R-Rohesia-"

She turned.

"You're going to get us caught, *be quiet.*"

"I've killed her, haven't I? They'll kill Mum in my place. And then it's just... it's just..."

Then it's just me.

That thought scared him. The idea that he was the last Sedrid standing made him let out a whimper. Quickpaw mewled in sympathy with his master, pushing his snout into the side of his leg, but he ignored him.

"What do we do?"

"We go."

"No, Rohesia, we can't-"

She gestured for him to lower his voice.

"She told us to go."

"And there's no way I'm doing that. We can rescue her and-"

"I'm not sure I should even listen to what you're saying."

"Okay, Rohesia, I-"

She punched him in the arm.

"Stop being a pup for five seconds and *be quiet.*"

She glanced over the tree trunk, checking for any nearby patrols, before turning back.

"I told you to not go out. I told you it wasn't smart but you still went out there. God, I should have stopped you. You went out there and *killed* a legionnaire."

"He arrested Ragnar."

"And now his friends are coming *to kill* you, you idiot."

"And I can't let Mum suffer because of my stupidity."

She was quiet. Her eyes focused on the shimmering, red-rimmed eyes of her friend, pleading with her to cooperate. Quickpaw and Harangoth's eyes were trained on the distraught Corsair.

"She's all I have left. Dad's dead and I can't even guarantee Ragnee is still alive. If I lose Mum, I won't be able to cope. She's all that I have. I can't turn my back on her and leave."

"This is even assuming they'll kill her, Corsair. Do you know how unstable the clan would become if they found out the legion had executed her?"

"But that still doesn't make it right. She's doing it because she doesn't want me to die."

"I understand her."

"So do I. But I don't want her to die, either."

"Even if we're assuming they'll hurt her, Corsair, if you go back you could both die."

"And I'd rather be dead than be alive in a world where I'm all alone."

"What are they gonna do, Corsair? There's no way they'd kill her. At worst, she's an accomplice."

"*I can't afford to take that chance.*"

He glared at his friend, her eyes holding his gaze.

"Rohesia... please. Please."

She hesitated, looking away for a few seconds, before looking back.

"My gut is telling me this is a bad idea... but okay. Okay, we'll rescue her."

He let out a sigh of relief.

"Thank you, Rohesia, thank you. We'll do it – we'll save her and get out of here."

"She was being taken to the Great Hall of Wolves. That's heavily guarded."

"We'd need to distract them somehow."

"How?"

Corsair was left stumped by the question. He descended into thought, conjuring up different solutions to the problem before him. She reached an idea, looking back up.

"The church's belltower."

"You could ring it?"

"Maybe. Or I could howl. I could do something to get their attention and make them head my way."

"That sounds as if it would work, but you'd need to get out of there as soon as possible."

"I'm more worried about you. If I mess up the timing-"

"You won't."

"But I could."

"Rohesia, trust me, you won't. I'll be fine."

She held his gaze, lacking confidence in the idea, but nodded.

"I'll get ready near the hall tonight. You'll head off to the tower and howl or ring the bell, which will make them run over towards the sound thinking it's me. I'll go in and get Mum and then we'll meet up in the woods to escape. We'll leave Quickpaw and Harangoth here to lead us away from Grand Wolf Plains when we get back."

"What about Quickpaw and Harangoth? A patrol could find them out here, alone."

"We'll hide them in bushes or something. We have to take that risk. And they're smart."

Quickpaw mewled in agreement. Harangoth remained silent.

"And there'll be soldiers inside the Great Hall of Wolves, Corsair."

"I'll go in from the gallery above, see how many legionnaires there are before I try to rescue her. I can do it."

"There's a risk that-"

"It doesn't matter. If I can get out of here with her, it's worth it. She'd do the same."

Rohesia looked worried by the idea of his death lurking in the shadows, waiting to claim him, but she complied with a nod.

"Okay, okay," Corsair said. "We can save her. We can do it."

"Just be careful, Corsair."

With that, the two cubhood friends waited in silence for dusk to arrive.

A BRAZEN RESCUE

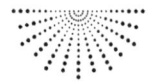

(1139, AESTIOM)

Ophelia sat on the bench with a perfect posture and stern expression.

The hall was empty except for the five legionnaires standing in the room with their backs pressed against the wall. They each held a crossbow, bolt loaded with sharpened tip, and each had a sword in the scabbard on their belt. None of them spoke or made a sound. The only ones who dared speak were the two people in front of her, a half-metre away.

"Ophelia," Winter Baron Tiberius pleaded. "You need to understand that there is a family on the other end of this. The law is the law, the rules apply to everyone. He killed a legionnaire. You need to tell us where he is or you'll be tried for being an accomplice to murder."

"I'm not telling you a thing."

Valour stood a metre behind the Winter Baron, both arms down by his side with one paw holding his helmet. Sympathy lurked behind his eyes, visible on the other side of the icy layer, but Ophelia could tell the hound valued his duty more than he wished to help her.

"Your son killed that legionnaire," Winter Baron Tiberius repeated.

Ophelia remained silent.

"You are not helping Corsair here."

"I'm not helping him?" Ophelia scoffed. "If I tell you where he is, he dies. I'm not stupid. You've taken Ragnee from me in the middle of the night and you think I'll be willing to let you do the same to Corsair? Do you take me for an idiot?"

"I take you for someone rational, Ophelia. Someone who knows the right thing to do."

"Flattery won't work with me."

The Winter Baron shook his head and looked to the commander standing behind him, who also shook his head.

"Damn it, Ophelia, you are making this situation escalate further than it has to."

"You and your band of legionnaires have made this situation escalate, not me. You have kicked down my door and stormed my home *twice*. You have robbed me of one son – you will not rob me of the other."

"And I'm sure by this point you know what repercussions you face. You're complicit by hiding a fugitive, Ophelia. You could go to jail."

Ophelia stood.

"I do not care what happens to me. Jail or death I do not fear. My husband is dead. My eldest son is exiled and left to die. If I can defend the last thing in my life that I love, I will do it in a heartbeat. So go on. Remind me of the punishment I face. Remind me of what will happen if your mighty little soldiers can't find Corsair. I can assure you that you will never, *never*, overcome the love I have for my son."

She shook her head, scowling.

"To think we once let you train them. We once let you into our home. We treated you like a friend. Arthur *trusted* you. If only we knew what lengths you'd go to spit on his grave."

Winter Baron Tiberius held her strong gaze, one that was filled with passion and pride for her youngest son. Eventually, he looked away and began conversing with Valour, communicating with him in a whisper Ophelia couldn't overhear.

She sat down and bowed her head.

Stay safe, Corsair. God's watching over you.

Corsair crept up to the corner of the building and stopped. He peered around the house on to the main pathway and saw the lights of the Great Hall of Wolves further along, bathing the surrounding perimeter in warm light.

There it is.

He knew his mother was inside that building, sacrificing herself to allow him to escape. He hoped that nobody dared to lay a paw on her.

Please be safe.

He moved his focus on to the front of the building and saw several soldiers standing guard outside. To his surprise they were not the canine warriors he had expected – instead, Krosguard soldiers were posted on watch around the building, each holding a lantern up in the air to illuminate their surroundings.

While he felt more comfortable with the idea of his lupine brethren being nearby, he couldn't risk being spotted. Orders were orders – he would be arrested or killed on sight.

He glanced to the opposite side of the path. There, around to the back of the building, was a rear staircase into the viewing gallery above where he could survey the interior. Looking down, he gave his sword a reassuring tap on the hilt before raising his head.

Now all he had to do was wait for the signal.

He crouched to conceal himself in the shadows further, wary of the possibility that a patrol could head down the path from the east and spot him as they moved. The snowfall wasn't as thick as it had been earlier, which he would have appreciated at that moment, but waiting for it to become more ferocious was out of the question.

I'm coming Mum. I'm coming.

Then, he heard it.

At first, the bell sounded like a usual component of the night soundscape. The soldiers, at most, gave a casual glance towards the church before looking away. Then, however, a howl rang out across the silent town. It echoed down the main pathway and caused the soldiers to turn, peering over towards the bell tower.

"What the hell?" one said.

"Is that him?"

"Probably."

"What's that idiot doing? He's going to get himself caught," a familiar voice said.

Axel?

He didn't focus on it. Corsair's eyes shot over towards the door as a legionnaire stepped out.

"Where's that howling coming from?" they asked.

"From the church."

A Krosguard soldier pointed up towards the silhouette of the tower in the distance, the bell continuing to toll as Rohesia howled again.

"That could be him," they ordered. "Converge!"

The Krosguard were reluctant, only some beginning to move.

"I said *converge!* Move it!"

The whole squad hurried off in the direction of the tower, yelling to one another as they did so. The legionnaire watched them rush off in the opposite direction, eyes lingering, before disappearing back inside and shutting the door.

Corsair looked towards the tower and nodded.

Thank you, Rohesia. Now get out of there.

Hoping the archer would know when to make her quick getaway, he crept across the road. Looking left and right, he assumed the coast was clear and advanced, moving to-

The doors flew open as a legionnaire stormed out the Great Hall of Wolves, four others following behind them. He gasped and ducked behind the corner of the building, heart pounding in his chest, ears strained to listen for any indication they had seen him.

As the doors shut again, all he could hear was the sound of the legionnaires' yells fading into the distance.

That was too close.

He waited a moment, allowing his frightened heart to calm down, before looking towards the next corner and advancing. Carefully, he peeked around it with one eye. One paw rested on the grip of his sword as he did so, ready to dispatch any threat before him quickly.

To his relief, not a soul was visible by the stairs.

He checked over his shoulder. With no one behind or ahead of him, the coast was clear for Corsair to creep up the stairs and stop by the door. He placed a paw on the panel of wood and gently pushed it open, peeking through the growing gap between the door and the frame for any sign of a legionnaire. Fortune favoured him – there was no one in the gallery. He hurried in before easing the door shut.

"One of the legionnaires told me that there's howling at the bell tower," a familiar voice said.

"So that's him?"

"It very well may be a diversion of some kind – a fugitive on the run wouldn't stand on a bell tower and call everyone to them – but we'll see."

"My son wouldn't be so stupid."

Corsair froze as he heard his mother's voice, strong and firm. It brought him relief that she was well enough to speak with such an authoritative tone.

She's not injured, thank God.

"You'll have a chance to say your goodbyes when he is escorted here."

As they argued, he edged towards the banister and peered over.

He scanned the walls.

There was no legionnaire in sight.

He looked down.

He saw his mother and Winter Baron Tiberius directly beneath him. Valour stood near them.

He looked back towards the door. He had little time before the legionnaires realised the howling from the tower was a diversion and returned to the hall, sealing his fate if he was still inside. He had to act.

Adrenaline pumping, Corsair leapt over the bannister. The fall wasn't great enough to cause him any harm and he landed with a grunt, bending his knees before rising to his full height and drawing his sword. Valour and Winter Baron Tiberius whirled around, caught by surprise, and his mother froze.

"You let her go now!" Corsair growled, taking up face-on stance.

Valour darted back and slammed his helmet on to his head, drawing his own sword and taking up the same stance as the wolf. Winter Baron Tiberius stepped away, Corsair's mother standing.

"Corsair, what are you doing? I told you to go."

"I'm not leaving you here. I'm here to rescue you and if either of you two try to stop me I'll kill you here and now!"

"Don't be stupid!" Valour warned. "Drop your weapon! Neither of us want this to get ugly!"

"Let my mother go or I'll kill you!"

"Too much blood has been spilled today already, Corsair! Do not make a second mistake!"

"The only mistake I'd be making is leaving here without her!"

The golden armour of the canine glinted in the light of the lanterns, matched by the golden eyes of the doberman. He stared through the holes in his mask.

Both combatants knew that neither would back down.

"You are guilty of the murder of an Opulusian legionnaire. I'm giving you one last chance to drop your sword and surrender."

"I'm not leaving here without her."

"Corsair... don't make me kill you in front of your mother."

"Step aside!"

Both warriors growled at one another, trying to get the other to lower their weapon, but neither yielded. Valour twirled his sword on either side of him and Corsair did the same.

With a yell, the prince came forward and –

The counterattack was unexpected. Before Corsair could attack, Valour shot forwards shoulder-first and rammed him in the chest, knocking him back. He stumbled, wide-eyed. Valour swung down from above and sliced from the left and right in quick succession, Corsair barely able to keep the sharp blade away from him. He tried to riposte, jabbing at the doberman's face, but the commander knocked it away and kicked him.

"You lay a paw on him and I'll kill you!" Ophelia yelled as Winter Baron Tiberius held her back.

Corsair rolled underneath a swing, arriving behind the doberman and stabbing at his back. Valour dropped to one knee while turning, knocking the stab upwards from him and slashing back. Corsair staggered away, barely out the arc of the swing. He rebalanced just as the commander surged forwards. A flurry of blows ensued, metal clashing against metal with a crisp *clang* upon every strike. Corsair was being overwhelmed, lacking the confidence to strike back, until he randomly attacked to alleviate the pressure.

Corsair attacked with the hilt of his blade, knocking the side of Valour's snout as he advanced. The commander reeled back from the shock, shaking his head to mitigate the blow, but recovered quicker than Corsair expected. He charged forwards with a slash. The wolf blocked the attack from the left, pushing it away, but Valour swung the sword around from the right and knocked his blade out of his paws.

Corsair watched as his weapon slid under the benches, leaving him defenceless.

He dived underneath the benches as Valour's sword struck the ground where he had been standing, advancing on Corsair as he scrambled under the seats. Corsair looked up to see Valour on top of the benches, sword positioned to stab downwards. He rolled before the doberman's longsword struck the floor. Valour yanked it back up for a second attempt. Corsair advanced before rolling again, narrowly missing being impaled against the wooden floorboards.

Corsair dodged one more stab before rushing forwards and feeling his sword's grip in his paw, clambering on to a bench and standing. Valour leapt on to his bench and swung as he did so. Corsair parried his blow. Overpowering the commander, he pushed him over the side of the benches and into the aisle.

"*Die!*" Corsair yelled, leaping at Valour with a swing.

The doberman yanked his body away and gradually retreated towards the podium at the front, blocking swing after swing from the prince. Corsair grunted with every blow he dealt, rage pulsing through him with the assistance of his adrenaline rush.

Valour swung at his neck. Corsair dropped to one knee and stabbed at his stomach but his blow was deflected by the dog's quick reflexes. Corsair blocked his swift counterattack. Both blades were held in a stalemate directly above his head, Corsair struggling with the combined force of his opponent's strength and the gravity assisting him.

Valour yelled out and kicked him in the chest, knocking the wolf backwards. He rolled down the aisle and got back up to his hind paws, backing away from the canine as he advanced. Their blades clashed repeatedly against one another, neither combatant giving ground, until Valour smacked Corsair in the side of the head with his hilt.

He yelped and crashed into the benches to the side, seeing his opponent raise his blade up high and bring it down. His blade leapt to his aid, clanging against the other sword a small distance away from the wolf's body. Both struggled there for a moment, gravity assisting Valour, until Corsair kicked at his stomach. The slight recoil from the canine was enough to allow him a chance to push away the blade and slash at the commander, forcing him back a few steps.

"Stop this!" Winter Baron Tiberius yelled. "Corsair, lower your weapon! We can reach a deal!"

Valour dodged back from Corsair's swing, remaining motionless a metre ahead of him. The prince remained there, panting with his pink tongue hanging from one side of his mouth. He welcomed with open arms the chance to recover his stamina, waiting to cut down the doberman, and rage caused him to overlook the enemy's uncharacteristic lapse in offense.

Without any second-thought, Corsair yelled out and charged forward, bringing the sword down from above with all the force he could muster.

It was a mistake.

Valour, without any sign of exertion, parried the blow perfectly. The repelling force knocked Corsair off-balance, making him stumble backwards with his sword away from his body. He had a fraction of a second to see the gauntleted paw hurtling towards his face.

A clean hit.

The blow struck the side of his snout, raising a pained yelp from him as he tumbled back. His sword fell from his paws once again, landing behind Valour. He landed on his back hard, groaning as he hit the floor.

"No!" Ophelia yelled. "Don't you dare! Don't you dare touch my son!"

Corsair knew he was unarmed and vulnerable. Desperate, he shot up to his hind paws and charged Valour, snarling as he did so. The commander kicked him back as he lunged, creating distance between him and the attacker, before striking him in the side of the head. Corsair fell back down.

"No!"

"Ophelia, no!"

World spinning, Corsair saw Valour raise his sword up to deliver the killing blow. He raised a paw, a futile attempt to beg for mercy, but nothing could be done for him.

"Wait!"

With a yell, Valour stabbed the sword downwards.

Corsair clamped his eyes shut.

He let out a yelp in anticipation, expecting to be left in agony as Valour's sword tore into his body before he succumbed.

But he felt nothing. There was no excruciating sting or agonising burn.

What?

He opened one eye.

The hall was still around him. He lay on the floor, breath heavy and panicked. Nothing made a sound and, for a moment, he thought he was dead.

Then he looked up.

Valour's sword had torn through the back and the bloodied tip emerged from the front. Blood oozed from the fatal ravine left in the torso, drenching the clothes in crimson, and the surrounding fur was turned from white to red.

Valour's eyes were wide.

Winter Baron Tiberius was silent.

Corsair's ears folded back.

Ophelia Sedrid's face was taut with pain, eyes bulging and mouth wide open. She gasped and, trembling with agony, moved her paws towards the exit point. She coughed once and blood dribbled from her mouth, staining the white fur by her maw.

She looked up and made eye contact with her son.

"M-Mum, what..."

Her eyes shimmered, tears dripping from her eyes, and then all life disappeared from them in an instant. Her arms dropped, her tail went limp, her mouth slackened and her face relaxed.

The disgusting sound of Valour's sword being dragged out through the lacerated flesh and bone was the last sound Ophelia Sedrid made, her lifeless corpse flopping forwards on to her front.

The commander backed away, gasping. His paw's grip slackened in shock and the bloodied sword fell, landing with a *clang*.

Corsair's eyes remained on the body of his mother. The details overwhelmed him; the blood, the bulging eyes, the stiff tail, the taut face, the motionless limbs.

315

"M-Mum?"

And then he screamed.

"*No!*"

He scrambled forwards towards the body of his mother and turned her over, revealing the cruel wound in her torso. He placed his paws on the wound and applied pressure, tears rushing down from his stinging eyes. He shook his head, pleading and begging.

"No, Mum, no! No, you can't! You can't leave me here! Mum! Mum, I need you! I need you! You can't leave me here – *Mum!*"

No response.

He shook her as hard as he could, trying to rouse her from her sleep, but her eyes remained vacant and she did not stir. Whimpering and pleading, his throat was choked with tears and the words he uttered became unintelligible. He shook his head again.

"You can't. This wasn't meant to happen. This wasn't how it was meant to be. I was... I was meant to save you. I was meant to escape here with you. I was meant to find Ragnee with you."

Closing his eyes, he sobbed and brought his head down, nuzzling his mother. He tried to coax her to wake up, to feel her heartbeat through the fur of her neck.

Nothing.

"Please, Mum, *wake up! Wake up!*"

Ophelia Sedrid was not waking up.

Corsair threw his head back and let out a miserable howl, the sound of a soul being extinguished in a single puff. Valour and Winter Baron Tiberius stood there, watching the young wolf grieve as he caressed his dead mother, trying to deny it was even happening.

Corsair didn't even care when he heard the door open, followed by the gasps of the returning legionnaires.

"It's him!"

"He killed Sigil, *get him!*"

He grasped his mother tightly.

It did nothing against the torrent that ensued.

He was struck on the back of the head and his grip loosened, more paws grabbing him by the shoulders and dragging him back. He screamed and struggled, trying to fight his way back, but the team of legionnaires surrounded him and separated him from the body. No matter how much he screamed and begged, they did not let him crawl back to his dead mother.

Instead, they let go of him and began to kick. He yelped and whimpered, reaching out as he was beaten and pummelled, suffering the harsh torture of the husky's vengeful comrades. A feeble attempt to push them away rewarded him with a greater barrage of blows. All he could do was yell and writhe in pain on the ground.

The young Sedrid was left alone in the world, his mother's corpse lying a metre away from him, blood still pouring from the sword wound in her chest.

CHAPTER TWENTY-TWO

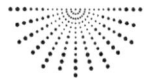

*C*orsair found that the only way to resist the endless pain was to curl up into a ball and cover his head, enduring the agony of the relentless blows dealt. The legionnaires swore and beat him, taking turns to avenge their dead comrade.

Seconds passed before Winter Baron Tiberius called them off.

"That's enough, that's enough!"

Corsair remained in his ball and he was smart to do so. One legionnaire got a final kick at his stomach, making Corsair groan in pain as the air was driven from him, before stepping back and rolling his shoulders.

"Get him up."

Two legionnaires sheathed their swords and came forward. They grabbed one arm each and hauled him up on to his knees, Corsair's body was limp with pain. Everything ached – his side, his back, his front, his legs, his tail, his head. He didn't dare move a muscle for fear of sparking a chain reaction of agony through his body. Only the two hounds gripping his arms held him upright. His head dangled down-wards and he closed his eyes, squeezing two lone tears from them.

Winter Baron Tiberius came forwards and knelt in front of him.

"Corsair?"

Mum. Please wake up. Mum.

He felt one paw touch the bottom of his snout and gently tilt his head up, his stinging eyes opening to see a blurred Winter Baron before him. A blink revealed the look of sympathy on his face, eyes soft and ears down, but Corsair couldn't see through the cloud of misery that engulfed him.

Mum, please... I can't do this alone. I can't be the last Sedrid. Please get up.

"Corsair, I'm so sorry. This was never meant to happen."

Corsair didn't care. Sniffling, he didn't move or react. His eyes lingered on the corpse of his mother behind the Winter Baron, willing her to get up, willing her to rise and hug him.

But no matter how much he tried, Ophelia Sedrid was not coming back.

Winter Baron Tiberius lowered his paw, allowing Corsair's head to droop, and stood.

"What happened here today is beyond tragic. Ophelia Sedrid was a caring mother and a loving wife to her husband, Arthur Sedrid, while he was alive. This is..."

He couldn't finish. Corsair continued to stare at the corpse, unable to avert his gaze.

"What do we do, Winter Baron?" a legionnaire asked.

He gave a sorrowful glance to the despairing wolf.

"If the public finds out Ophelia Sedrid was killed by an Opulusian blade, there would be outrage. The Clan of the Great Lupine would be torn apart. We need to keep this secret. If it gets out, the security of the clan will be at risk. We cannot have our nation torn apart – especially while we're in the middle of a war. It'll be all the rabbits need to invade us further."

"We can't just hide her," a legionnaire said. "Ophelia Sedrid is a well-known figure. People will start to suspect something is wrong if she doesn't turn up again, Winter Baron."

"And that's..."

A pained pause.

"And that's why I propose we make it so Corsair appears to be the culprit."

Corsair clamped his eyes shut, weakly shaking his head to deny the false account, but was too feeble to react with rage or anger. He continued to dangle from the arms of the legionnaires, a shell of a person.

"No one can know the true nature of Ophelia's death. We must tell the public when the time comes that Corsair was hiding nearby and, when he knew his mother was telling us his location, he attacked her and killed her."

"Understood, Winter Baron," a legionnaire agreed, nodding.

"For the time being, speak nothing of it. You two, escort Corsair to the jail. Take two of the Krosguard posted outside with you."

"Will he not be trialled?" a legionnaire asked.

"If we make this an official case as we did with Ragnar, then what truly happened could be revealed. We can't risk it. He goes to jail and..."

He sighed.

"And we execute him. I'll deal with all the logistical and legal aftermath."

"Yes, Winter Baron."

Yanked up to his hind paws, Corsair was turned around and escorted out through the large doors of the Great Hall of Wolves. Even though he lacked the strength to look over his shoulder, he could feel the murderer staring into his back, the victor in their second conflict.

The doors opened and Corsair was thrown out into the snow.

He landed with a whimper, the freezing cold of the snow making the numerous bruises across his body sting. He feebly turned on to his front, trying to push himself up while sobbing, but slipped and fell back into the snow.

"Corsair?"

The despairing wolf pushed himself up onto his forearms and

cried, looking up at the owner of the voice. He saw the braided tail before the face. Axel looked down at his friend with a look of bewilderment, eyes connecting with his, his helmet held by its rim in one paw.

"Axel..."

He tried to reach out for the apothecary but heard someone crunching through the snow towards him. He turned his head and found himself staring at a pair of armoured hind paws.

"Well, well, well."

Corsair knew that voice.

A steel blade eased down from above, its tip pushing against the bottom of his snout and forcing him to look up.

The Butcher of Tomskon's grinning face met his gaze, his free paw resting on one hip. His hellish companion was nowhere to be seen, slumbering in a stable somewhere, but it didn't make the situation any better for him.

"There you are. We've been looking everywhere for you, deserter."

He removed the blade as one of the two canines kicked Corsair in the side. He yelled out and rolled on to his back, clutching his body, clothes and fur soaked from the snow.

"He needs help," Axel said, stepping forward to help him. "He's-"

"Take another step and you'll be in as much pain as he is, *Auryon*."

Corsair locked eyes with Axel again. The apothecary displayed the urge to intervene in his face, left hesitant by the repercussions he would endure. One paw dangled dangerously close to the grip of his sword. Corsair shook his head at him.

Axel, grudgingly, understood the message and moved his paw away from his weapon.

"I knew you wouldn't be too far behind your brother," Lieutenant Maximus said. "Apples and trees and whatnot."

Another sharp kick and Corsair let out a scream of anguish,

321

groaning and grunting as he curled up again to shield himself. He was denied this defence, the two legionnaires each taking an arm again and forcing him up to his hind paws.

"Where are you taking him?" the lieutenant asked.

"To the jail. Per the Winter Baron's orders, Lieutenant."

"What else did he say?"

"That we take two Krosguard soldiers out here with us."

The lieutenant grinned.

"Well, how convenient. I'll lead you two there. Fedellis, come with me."

Axel stepped forward.

"Lieutenant, I'd like to volun-"

Lieutenant Maximus gave him a firm shove. He fell down into the snow, landing on his rump.

"If I catch you following us, Auryon, I'll break your stupid tail off."

Lieutenant Maximus gestured for the apothecary to take his leave. Axel glanced at Corsair. The wounded prince hesitated, fearing the idea of being left in the company of the lieutenant, but nodded for him to comply.

Knowing it was best to listen to the prince, he got up and hurried away.

"Let's get this traitor moving."

Lieutenant Maximus strode ahead of the restrained wolf, leading the legionnaires towards the jail. One canine looked over his shoulder, gesturing for the other wolf to follow. Fedellis complied. Corsair tried to make eye contact with him, to try and signal him for help, but he refused to meet his gaze.

Both canines dragged him in the direction of the jail, Lieutenant Maximus leading the way. Fedellis brought up the rear.

Despair clung to the last Sedrid.

This is it. I'm going to be thrown in a cell, locked away and killed.

There was no strength left in him to fight back or resist. There was no one to help him. All his mind could focus on was the idea that he was going to die in front of everyone else, made out to be his mother's killer, when the true culprit was in the Great Hall of Wolves next to the Winter Baron.

The image of his mother lying dead in the aisle, crimson pooling beneath her as a result of her sacrifice, appeared before his mind.

He closed his eyes again and let his head droop.

Mum, I'm so sorry. It's all my fault. I should have killed him. I should have beaten him. Because he was about to kill me you had to get involved and...

He couldn't bring himself to think of it. He couldn't remind himself of the fate that befell his loving mother. Even if the image were sitting right there before him, he couldn't utter the words that she was dead. It seemed impossible. It seemed like it was beyond any chance of occurring.

And, yet, it had happened.

The escort team dragged him down the empty streets of Grand Wolf Plains, heading north towards the jail where he would be left to reflect in anguish.

Eventually, with minutes passing in silence, they passed the Lupine Halls of Justice and arrived.

The grey brick building was relatively small, only a little smaller than the Sedrid house, and the single wooden door into the prison was chipped and weathered. Lieutenant Maximus stopped at the entrance.

"Throw him in a cell for the night. Me and Fedellis will wait around until some more guards turn up."

The legionnaires nodded. They brought him towards the door, intent on walking right through, but the lieutenant put out a paw.

"Wait a second."

He lowered himself down so he was in front of Corsair, holding his weak gaze.

He grinned.

"I'll see you on that chopping block soon, *Sedrid*."

And with that, the canines dragged him into the jail.

The first room was small and bare, made of stone and with the only piece of furniture being the jailer's desk on the right side of the room. The jailer, a grey wolf with a belly bulging through his clothes, looked up and saw the three individuals standing there, eyes focusing on the young Sedrid.

"Corsair Sedrid?" he said, standing. "Sir, why are you-"

"On orders of Winter Baron Tiberius, you are to ask no questions. He has committed a crime against the current leadership and the Kingdom of Opulus. He is to be imprisoned and punished."

The jailer hesitated before nodding, getting up and leading them through the wooden door into the next chamber. The far wall was lined with several cells, the prisoners separated from the free world by a wall of iron bars. Only one cell of many was occupied, a lone drunkard lying asleep in the corner of his cell with the small comfort of his clothes.

Corsair was led to the farthest cell. The jailer opened the door and he was thrown inside. Corsair landed and yelped, left sprawled out on the floor, and he could barely raise his head to see the metal door shut with a painful squeal. Both legionnaires took up positions by the cell and the jailer backed away, glancing over his shoulder at the captive, before disappearing through the door and shutting it.

In his cell, Corsair lowered his head back on to the cold stone floor and stared at the ceiling.

Mum... why you? Why you? What did you do? What did we do?

Eyelids growing heavier and body weakening, Corsair let out one last sob before closing his eyes and passing out.

Rohesia could tell by the commotion outside the Great Hall of Wolves that the plan had not worked.

She managed to evade capture when the Opulusians and Krosguard converged on the church bell tower, scrambling to the top to arrest the culprit who was no longer there. She then rushed to their rendezvous in the woods and waited in a tree near Quickpaw and Harangoth's hiding spot, awaiting Corsair's return.

But Corsair and his mother never arrived.

Telling the two ictharrs to follow, she walked back to the Great Hall of Wolves to investigate further. She hoped the outcome she dreaded had not come to pass, but her heart sank when she saw several legionnaires and wolves standing vigilant outside the building.

If he had escaped, they would have arrived in the woods. The soldiers would be running around searching for them.

He must have been captured.

Or killed.

After she returned Quickpaw and Harangoth to their stables beside the desolate Sedrid household, safe under the careful watch of Peter and the other servants, she began to search the town. She wandered down the main pathway and gazed into the darkness for any sign of her friend. Remaining vigilant for any nearby patrols, she continued to whisper Corsair's name and survey the area, hoping that she would come across the lupine.

Please be okay.

She looked up and immediately felt something crash into her.

Yelping, she hit the ground and scrambled back. She shot up, drawing her dagger and pointing it towards the person who had tackled her. He stepped back, paw moving to his longsword while the other extended out to reason with her. An ictharr growled by his side with a bundle of rope discarded by her front paws.

"Whoa, take it easy. It was an accident, all right?"

Rohesia kept her arm extended, the dagger sitting in her paw. She noticed a braided tail dangling behind both the wolf and ictharr but didn't focus on it.

"Where is he?" she asked.

He moved his paw away from his sword.

"Are you talking about Corsair?"

She paused. She lowered her dagger and sheathed it.

"You know what happened to him? Is he dead? Is he-"

"He's alive. Who are you? How do you know him?"

"A cubhood friend."

His eyes widened in realisation.

"You're Rohesia?"

"It doesn't matter who I am. Is he okay?"

"He's been thrown in jail."

She winced.

"Did they hurt him?"

"From what I saw, he's in bad shape. I couldn't get a proper look at him but he could barely walk or speak. They threw him out the Great Hall of Wolves and kicked him in the stomach, then dragged him away."

The jail. He's in the jail.

She turned, drawing her dagger from her sheath again. She had taken one step, determined to free Corsair from capture, when the braided wolf placed a paw on her shoulder.

"I know what you're thinking and..."

"*Get your paw off me,*" she growled, shrugging his paw off and pointing the dagger at his throat. He stepped back, paws up in surrender, his ictharr snarling beside him.

"All right, I get it, but can you put the dagger down? I'm trying to help you."

"Then why are you stopping me?"

"Because you'll die if you go over there. Every single soldier in Grand Wolf Plains is out on patrol right now or guarding the jail."

"I need to help him."

"And how are you going to do that if you're dead, genius?"

Rohesia paused, considering the sincerity of his warning. He seemed to have no reason to deceive her – he was a wolf, after all. His allegiance to Corsair would make sense, unlike the image of an Opulusian trying to help her.

Then again, Tiberius was a wolf.

And Tiberius was no ally.

She lowered her dagger, still wary.

"Are they going to kill him?"

"From the way they're acting, probably. That's why I bumped into you – I was running to Alpha McVarn to tell him."

"Who?"

"Leader of the Krosguard. He was our alpha."

Corsair was in the Krosguard.

"*Our* alpha? You know Corsair?"

"We fought at Pothole Plains together. I spent a whole month training with him. I'm Axel. I'm a friend."

"And you're not lying to me when you say that he's been captured?"

"No, I'm not, and I need to get going. If you want to come with me, fine, but I need to talk to him now. Come on, Arwie."

He moved past Rohesia, rushing off in the direction they had been running in before. Arwenin clamped her fangs over the bundle of rope and trotted past the archer, snarling as she passed. Rohesia's gaze lingered on the braided wolf. She hesitated, tempted by the idea of trying to rescue her friend, before seeing sense in following the Krosguard and sprinting after him.

"I already know why you're here and I don't know what to tell you."

Rohesia and Axel were sitting in the drawing room of the alpha's accommodation, a temporary living space while he was carrying out work in the capital away from his home town. Arwenin sat in a pen in the stables outside the house, heartily chewing the bundle of rope she had been carrying. The hardened Krosguard sat before them in his chair next to the fire, his strong face softened with remorse.

"He's in trouble," Axel said flatly.

"I know he's in trouble. I've seen plenty of wolves stuck in trouble and I can assure you that he's up to his neck in it. Killing a legionnaire tends to do that."

"Can we do anything to help him?" Rohesia asked.

The look of defeat upon his face did not bode well.

"My power as of right now is limited. I don't know what the hell Tiberius is doing with the Opulusians but I know it's not long before I'll have nothing but an empty title left. I have little to no authority over the legionnaires and I wouldn't be surprised if my authority over the Krosguard started to fade."

"But with the power you have now you can do something, right?" Axel said. "You can't just let him sit there – there has to be a plan or... something."

"Honestly, son, I'm trying to think of one and I can only come up with some form of jailbreak attempt. How it would end is beyond me."

"We have to try," Rohesia said. "They'll kill him. All that will be left is his mother and then-"

"Ophelia Sedrid is dead."

Silence. Rohesia and Axel glared at the alpha, silent.

"You're kidding," Axel said.

"I wish I was, son. I was told 20 minutes ago when I was called down to the Great Hall of Wolves. They showed me her body. Tiberius told me Corsair killed her."

"How did I not know this?"

"I don't know – all the Krosguard soldiers there saw the body and they're probably spreading the word throughout the barracks right now."

"But you don't believe that, do you?"

"Do I believe that the wolf I found crying and begging to be sent home after Pothole Plains, a wolf left in hysterics after one battle, is guilty of murdering his mother? Not for the life of me, son."

Rohesia kept staring ahead, mouth slightly agape in shock. The elegant and dignified Ophelia Sedrid, the wolf who had become nothing but a shell during the last few days of her life, the wolf she made a promise to, was dead.

I promised to protect Corsair. I told her that he would be kept safe.

And now the person she had vowed to protect sat in a cell, waiting to be executed.

"We know for sure he won't be exiled?" the Axel said.

"Tiberius was lenient with Ragnar. He got lucky, from what they told me – even if the judges sent him to the *Deuvick Feldanas*. Now that another Sedrid has crossed the line..."

He exhaled.

"His odds aren't great. He'll be executed. Even if Tiberius wanted to spare him, I'm sure the King of Opulus or that Royal Order commander wouldn't feel the same way."

Rohesia could imagine Corsair lying alone in a cell, the last Sedrid standing, left with the images of his dead mother in his head. He was lying there, waiting to be executed.

I can't let him die. He can't die.

"This'll be the end of Sedrid rule as we know it," McVarn said. "With the rest of his family dead, his execution will lead to the Tiberius bloodline."

"This seems all too coincidental," Axel said. "They're bumping off Sedrids, they have to be."

"It seems that way. Why? I don't know. I don't know what Tiberius is up to with the Opulusians but all we can focus on is-"

"We have to save Corsair," Rohesia said.

"And that's easier said than done."

"You have your Krosguard here, right?"

"Some of them."

"We can organise some form of rescue. We could raid the prison or-"

"What is it with you and that jail?" Axel interrupted. "The capital is covered by the legion. We lead an attack on that jail, it's over. We'll be surrounded."

"There's no way we could attack the jail," McVarn said. "Besides, when I say 'some of them', I mean 15. Fifteen Krosguard, as good as they can be, won't last long. There's at least a whole regiment of the Opulusian Legion stationed here – that's at least 100 of them. Not to mention that Lieutenant Maximus is back and won't want Corsair's execution going awry."

"What?" the Axel said. "How? I thought he was imprisoned for what happened on final training day."

"I did, too. Somehow, he wriggled free of the whole thing. Tiberius most likely got him out of it. Why he should want to help that lunatic, I don't know."

"So we can't raid the prison?" Rohesia said.

"No. It's not an option. It's suicide."

"Then... then..."

She stammered, desperately grasping at straws for a solution, when it came to her.

"If they execute him, when will it be?"

"Usually he'd be trialled and, if found guilty, given a few days to live before being executed. But they told me he was being executed tomorrow morning without delay. We haven't got a lot of time."

"Can Tiberius do that?" Axel asked.

"Legal or not, he's doing it. They want Corsair dead as soon as possible."

"So why aren't they killing him now? Framing him after he's dead?"

"Because then the Winter Baron's entire remaining family would have been wiped out within a week without anyone seeing anything and there's no way anyone would buy it. They need a public execution to create some semblance of legitimacy to the whole charade."

"Where will it be?" Rohesia asked. "The execution?"

"Down at the market centre by the Julian Krosguard statue."

"Then we can attack there. We can ambush the execution and rescue him – if we get Quickpaw and Harangoth ready, we can rescue him and escape."

"Same problem – too few soldiers."

"What about the public? You thought of spreading the word to them yet?" Axel asked.

McVarn looked at him for a moment, narrowing his eyes.

"You want me to turn the public against the legionnaires?"

"You wouldn't need to," Rohesia said. "They already hate the hounds as it is. If they were told that Corsair Sedrid was being framed so he'd be executed, there'd be uproar. They'd turn against the legionnaires in a heartbeat."

"Then they'd hear that he murdered an Opulusian in cold blood. One who, from what I'm hearing, a lot of the other legionnaires liked."

"Who was he?" Axel said. "The legionnaire Corsair killed?"

"A husky called Sigil. He wasn't an officer or a leader, just a rank-and-file soldier. Whether he was a bastard or not is hard to determine now. Look, point is that they're not gonna let this hound's killer get away easy. They want him dead. Even if you make it to the ictharrs, then what? Krosguard riders will pursue you."

"Alpha, I know it's your job to think things through," she said, standing. "But right now all you need to know is that we have a city filled with wolves that don't like the legionnaires being here enough as it is. You've seen them dragging out other wolves, exiling them to the north. Everyone has seen it – if you can convince them enough to help us free Corsair at his execution tomorrow, they can riot. We'll have the numbers. We have to take this chance."

He hummed in thought, nodding his head as he mulled things over. She kept her eyes on him, feeling them sting with the idea that he would deny the aid they wanted.

As she opened her mouth to plead, he spoke.

"We'll do it. The Krosguard will agree to help – I know some riders here who'd be trustworthy. You two could also help spread the word tomorrow, get the crowds riled up. I'm sure you'll be happy to help, son?"

Axel hesitated. A troubled look was upon his face.

"I mean... I don't like the idea of so many innocent people being in the heat of it all if it kicks off but... I haven't got a choice, have I? It's this or let Corsair die."

He exhaled.

"I think... I can't stand by and watch this happen. I'll help."

"It's not an easy decision, son. And you? Your name?"

"Rohesia."

"I can see you want Corsair to make it out safely. You know him?"

"A cubhood friend, Alpha. I can't see him die."

"I don't expect you to. I don't expect either of you two to see him die tomorrow. If this goes well, we can evacuate Corsair from the clan to wherever the hell we think of taking him. I know for a fact it can't be in the Clan of the Great Lupine's territory, that's for sure."

"Yes, Alpha," the two wolves agreed, nodding.

McVarn leaned forward, resting his elbows on his knees.

"I can promise you this, though. Tomorrow, when we decide to start the riot, there'll be a lot going on. If we get the public involved then... I know for a fact some people might die. Those dogs are ruthless. You two need to make sure Corsair makes it out alive. If he dies during the escape then all of this will be for nothing and a lot of people will die in vain. At the very least make their deaths matter."

Rohesia and Axel nodded.

"And when you get to those ictharrs, *run*. They will chase you, no doubt, and they will throw every javelin and crossbow bolt at you to make sure Corsair doesn't make it out of here alive. Your ictharrs better be ready to run until they collapse."

"Quickpaw will be more than ready," Rohesia said.

"And I'll keep them off Corsair as best I can. Arwie's capable," Axel said.

"I don't doubt it. You two can stay here for the time being, rest a little. I'll head to the barracks and give the troops I trust the rundown, let them know what the plan is, and make sure we are prepared for tomorrow."

Rohesia watched the alpha get up and disappear up the stairs, moving into his room to retrieve something. Axel sat back down, exhaling as he did so, and rubbed his face.

She glanced out the window.

She could see the distant glow of the sun dawning on the horizon, rising to mark a new day. She focused her eyes on it. She knew that the moment the sun rose, the snow would be stained crimson with the blood of many wolves, all sacrificing themselves to preserve Sedrid rule.

A promise to keep Corsair safe from harm.

"I will," she muttered. "He'll make it out of this alive, or I'll kill every last hound that lays a paw on him."

THE END OF A LIFE

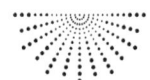

(1139, AESTIOM)

*C*orsair was, agonisingly, awake when the sun rose over Grand Wolf Plains. He trembled and shivered on the floor, tucked away in the corner where he had managed to drag himself, eyes flickering open and shut. Throughout the night he had repeatedly wavered in and out of consciousness, every part of his body aching. Even the most minor movement was a taxing undertaking.

The experience was worsened by the persisting memory of his mother's death. He kept seeing her body over him, Valour's sword through her back and chest, her eyes wide as she fought for life. He kept remembering how she had thrown herself in front of the sword to save him.

He remembered how he lost the duel.

He remembered that, because of him, his mother intervened.

Why didn't I kill him? Why couldn't I just kill him?

He heard the door to the prison chamber open and shut. He slightly tilted his head to focus his eyes on the jail door, wincing as he did so. Four guards now stood in front of his cell, the two original captors reinforced with an additional pair of legionnaires. He knew there would be further hounds waiting outside, securing the building to make sure no one would try and break in.

Not that anyone would have any reason – only Axel had seen what had happened to him. Rohesia would have no idea where he was until his final moments, about to be executed in front of everyone.

He was going to die alone and with his people thinking of him as a monster. As a traitor.

Someone padded over from the door to the cell. The four guards stood upright and ceased their conversations, snouts aimed up high. Corsair let out a shaky breath and kept his eyes on the cell door.

Commander Valour, leader of the Royal Order's *Militaria* chapter, stepped into view with helmet tucked under arm and sword sheathed.

Neither said a word.

Valour focused his eyes on him. Corsair returned the glare. He could only lie there, sickly like a pup, waiting for it all to be over.

The commander muttered something in New Opulusian. The legionnaire responded before he turned and unlocked the cell. The keys jangled in his paws as the other three walked out of the room. Valour patted the remaining legionnaire on the shoulder as he left, leaving him alone with the injured wolf as the door shut.

He remained there for a further moment, eyes on Corsair, before he pushed the door and stepped in.

"I know that I'm the last person you want to see. I..."

He hesitated.

"My apologies will never be enough. I know that."

Corsair murmured something, mouth wide open as he raked in breath.

"Pardon?"

"If you were... really sorry... you'd tell everyone you killed her."

He hesitated, considering it, before shaking his head.

"I... I can't. More people would die. I have a duty."

An ember of fury sparked inside of Corsair. He snarled.

"Then... y-you're not sorry..."

If he weren't trapped in such pain, he would have thrown himself at the doberman. But the ember fizzled out. He was too weak to go beyond the snarl. He lay there, glaring at the murderer, knowing that if he were strong enough to stand he would kill the doberman where he stood. He would avenge his mother and kill the commander with the blade that he used to kill her.

"I didn't want it to be like this."

"I don't... believe that for a... second."

"Cors-"

"S-shut up, just... *be quiet.* I d-don't...want to hear...you try t-to ease your... *conscience...*"

Valour stood there in silence, uncertain, before he turned to the door.

"Come in!"

The door opened again and the four legionnaires strolled back into view, glaring at the wolf. Corsair tried to prop himself up on his arm but failed, slipping back on to his side.

"Forgive me, Corsair. I didn't want it to be like this."

He hesitated again, troubled, before he shook his head and issued a command to the legionnaires in New Opulusian. He stepped back as the four legionnaires walked in, cornering the Sedrid and immediately setting upon him. Two pinned him down while the rest tore away his top and slacks, leaving him only with his undergarments. His lack of clothes only revealed the severity of the bruises left upon his body, the skin beneath the fur black and purple.

Corsair shivered on the ground, still curled up on his side, shielding his chest with his arms and shifting his eyes from one guard to the next in sequence. He noticed that they kept their distance from him, one of them stepping back out of the cell.

He saw the legionnaire step around the door with a pail of water.

"Hope this hurts, bastard!"

The legionnaire threw the contents over the wolf and the icy water stabbed at him with frozen daggers from every side. Corsair gasped and strained on the floor, coughing up some water that splashed into his mouth and blinking his eyes clear.

"Get up."

Two legionnaires grabbed him, one for each arm, and hauled him up to his hind paws. Corsair struggled but the attempt was so feeble that his strength petered out within a second. He dangled from their arms as they dragged him from the cell and through the jail, Valour and the other legionnaires following.

As soon as the door opened, Corsair was blasted with a freezing hell. The snow was vicious, beating his exposed body as he tried to shy away from the cold winds. The soaked fur clinging to him and the lack of clothes made the once tolerable bite of the wind unbearable.

The two hounds stopped by a pile of snow and threw him into it. He howled as he landed, the bruises being attacked by the dreadful cold, and was left shivering viciously in the snow. They grabbed him, dragging the prisoner away to his doom.

"I hope it hurts as much as it did for Sigil," one of the legionnaires growled.

"Count yourself lucky Sedrid," the other snarled. "Some of our friends wanted to do a *lot* worse."

The path to his execution was lined with legionnaires and lupine soldiers, all standing guard to prevent any interception while he was being escorted. A group of citizens argued with a squad of Opulusian legionnaires to the left as they turned right, being held back by the presence of sharpened swords.

Corsair saw him.

Lieutenant Maximus stood off to the side, grinning at him as he was escorted past.

"You'll be joining mummy soon enough, Sedrid."

Too weak to reply, Corsair was dragged away. Valour overtook them, leading the way, ignoring the shouts of wolves nearby as they pointed out the convict.

Finally, they arrived at the base of Julian Krosguard's statue.

The centre had been cleared, leaving the market stalls empty and desolate. A perimeter of steel-clad dogs held the line from all sides of the town centre, some Krosguard supporting their defence as they patrolled the lines of civilians watching.

They all think I'm a monster. They all think I killed Mum.

He closed his eyes.

Ragnee, Mum... Dad... I'll see you soon.

Not too far from the east side of the main path was an execution block, hastily placed. Corsair was escorted to it and forced down to his knees. A weak growl came from him in protest of the pain shooting up his legs.

"Down."

One legionnaire placed a paw on the back of his head and forced it down on to the block. He whimpered, his head resting on its side. He could still see the area in front of him by moving his eyes, not given enough leeway to turn even by the slightest angle.

Valour drew his longsword.

"Citizens of Grand Wolf Plains!"

The crowds fell silent, the yells dying down to murmurs and the murmurs finally dying altogether. All eyes fell upon the sight of Corsair Sedrid being held down, seconds away from his demise.

"Today marks the day where justice is brought down on the wicked! Today, Corsair Sedrid meets his just punishment for the murder of Sigil Longvidas, a devoted member of the Opulusian Legion who fought for the security and safety of both the Kingdom of Opulus and the Clan of the Great Lupine! He had his life snuffed out by this wolf yesterday for no reason – not that *any reason* could justify such an outrageous crime!"

Corsair could do nothing but listen to the lies and wait. How the doberman could don such a fake face and spew lies was beyond him, even after he murdered his mother. He knew it didn't matter. Before long he would have his head separated from his body and be taken from the world he knew, thrown into the inky darkness or glorious heavens that awaited him.

"He claimed, not one, but *two lives!* The second life that was taken from this world before her time was the life of Ophelia Sedrid, his own mother!"

Some of the crowd gasped, a conflicted cloud of muttering hanging over the audiences on all sides, while others continued to stare.

Corsair frowned at the lack of reaction.

Valour persisted through the chatter, riding the controversy.

"His mother, a wolf who loved him more than her own life, died as a result of his endless rage! Because she tried to bring him to justice, to bring peace to the family of the deceased, she was killed! Now is the day that Corsair Sedrid pays for his crimes and seeks forgiveness from the departed souls above us in heaven."

Valour gradually turned from the onlookers, passing the longsword to the nearest legionnaire. He took it, muttering a New Opulusian phrase to his superior, and took up position on Corsair's right. The wolf winced as he felt the sword's edge rest on the back of his neck. His breathing increased and his heart thundered, knowing death was coming up behind him.

He closed his eyes, squeezing final tears from them.

"May God forgive your crimes in heaven and may you find the error of your ways after this life!"

The sword was moved from his neck.

I'm so sorry, Mum. It's all my fault this happened.

"Stop!"

The cacophony that had built up was torn down by the sudden cry of a voice, one that interrupted the death of the Sedrid lineage. Corsair opened one eye and peered out.

Alpha Jonah McVarn stood by the line of legionnaires, dressed in Krosguard armour and with gauntleted paw resting on the hilt of his sword. The nearby Opulusians stepped away, swords at the ready, taken aback by the sudden protest.

"Alpha McVarn, you have no right to be here."

The alpha gave a wry laugh.

"And you have a just reason to kill him? All of you – you're executing him because it lines up with whatever secret agenda Tiberius has agreed to with your king!"

"Corsair Sedrid killed Sigil Longvidas, he must pay the-"

"We all see through your lies! We see through the lie you, your king and Tiberius are weaving! You stand there, telling us that Corsair killed a legionnaire without saying that Sigil Longvidas was one of many legionnaires who arrested and exiled Ragnar Sedrid because he was framed! This is all orchestrated to get rid of the Sedrid family!"

The legionnaires looked to Valour, waiting for the command. The doberman stared.

"McVarn, you need to step back."

"And his mother? None of us believe he killed him! We all know it's something to do with you Opulusians skulking about our clan! Maybe framing Corsair as guilty would allow you to justify his execution without anyone noticing? Maybe it was just another way for Tiberius to gain full control!"

The crowd began to yell and growl, pushing forward at the legionnaires. The Opulusians were distracted, their attention divided between the agitated crowd and the vocal Krosguard alpha.

"That's why you exiled Ragnar! It was a way to get rid of the Sedrids!"

"If you do not desist we will respond with force!" Valour yelled, following the warning with a command in New Opulusian.

The legionnaires repeated the order to the civilians, pointing their swords at them to push them back, but the wolves didn't back down. Some began to back away, sensing some form of conflict was about to break loose, but the majority remained.

Corsair looked up. The sword was lowered, the legionnaire wary of the situation's increasing tension.

"You killed Ophelia!" a voice yelled.

"Murderer!"

"Foul mutt!"

"Death to the mutts!"

"Death to the mutts!"

"*Death to the mutts!*"

The crowd chanted, the voices coming from all directions. A rock flew out from the seething mass and barely missed a legionnaire.

"You've taken away Ophelia and Ragnar Sedrid! You've taken away our control over our own country! You've taken away many of our brothers, sisters, wives, husbands and pups to make sure you dominate our clan!"

Alpha McVarn drew his sword.

"But you'll never take away *the spirit of the Clan of the Great Lupine!*"

Valour turned.

"*Tu morta!*" he yelled, thrusting his paw towards Corsair.

Corsair gasped as the legionnaire raised the sword, yelling as he did so, when an arrow shot out from the crowd and struck him in the side of the throat. The legionnaire gurgled and choked, throwing the sword down and clutching his neck as he collapsed on to his side.

"*Death to the mutts!*"

The crowds pushed forwards, overwhelming the frontline legionnaires and beating them down relentlessly while a barrage of bricks and rocks flew overhead. The Krosguard nearby turned and attacked the canines, slashing at them while driving forwards with the rioting crowds.

The legionnaire behind Corsair let go of his head and hurried to the side of his companion, placing his paws on the wound. Corsair slumped to the right and landed on his side, grunting as he did so.

What's going on?

He began to push himself up, his muscles burning as he exerted himself, when he saw Valour approaching. Snatching up his longsword as he moved, the dog kicked him in the side and knocked him to the ground. He yelped, trying to get back up, but saw Valour aim his sword for his chest.

Clang.

McVarn deflected the blow and knocked the doberman away, turning and hurriedly helping Corsair to his hind paws.

"You have to run! Keep moving down the path! Don't..."

Corsair's saw Valour running back, swinging as he charged, and the alpha saw this look of terror. McVarn spun around and blocked the swing, fighting back against the doberman and looking over his shoulder once more.

"*Run*, son! *Run!*"

With a surge of energy, he looked to the east and staggered from the town centre in that direction. Fighting raged around him, groups of civilians pummelling legionnaires while Krosguard soldiers provided armoured assistance to the fight. One saw the approaching wolf and stepped forward, directing him ahead.

"Keep going! You'll be safe, just go!"

He nodded but struggled to persevere, the world around him spinning as he stumbled left and right.

"*Death to the mutts!*"

A legionnaire lost in the chaos grunted as a rock struck him in the side of the head, knocking him down. The crowd set upon him with punches and kicks, some attacking the downed legionnaire with wooden batons.

A command in New Opulusian echoed across the town centre and, in an instant, the legionnaires retaliated.

Groups of legionnaires pushed into the crowd, slashing left and right to bring down the rioters. While most of the sword blows cut through the air, threatening enough to send the wolves fleeing, some struck flesh. Howls of anguish filled the air as wolves perished, cut down. Nearby wolves pushed the injured prince past, spurring him through the chaos as their line receded.

"*Look out!*" someone yelled.

Corsair looked over his shoulder and saw a legionnaire racing after him, knocking wolves aside as he advanced. He fell backwards and tried to scramble back, shaking his head and raising his paws up to shield himself.

"Wait!" he pleaded.

A wolf darted across and stabbed the dog in the side, puncturing through his armour plating and making him yelp. Before the legionnaire could react, she drew her dagger out and slashed the legionnaire's throat, causing blood to spurt from the wound. The legionnaire reeled back and fell. Corsair's eyes rested on the convulsing corpse of the legionnaire, panting, before he looked up at his saviour.

"Up, get up!" Rohesia bellowed, offering a paw.

He took her paw and pulled himself up, the archer steadying him before putting his arm over her shoulder and guiding him down the path.

"How did you-"

"No time, Corsair, we need to move!"

He nodded weakly and looked over his shoulder at the chaos. The Opulusians were forging a path after him, stepping over dead bodies as they carved their way into the wolves. More and more legionnaires rushed in behind them, arriving from their posts to reinforce. Corsair watched as one wolf was struck by three crossbow bolts, going down with a shriek.

Then his green eyes saw the Butcher of Tomskon break through the crowd, rushing after the duo at astonishing speed. A female wolf stepped out, a stone in her paw to attack the butcher. Without hesitation, he sidestepped the swing and slashed her down. She screamed in anguish, collapsing on to her side as crimson began to pour.

"*Where do you think you're going, Sedrid?*" the Butcher of Tomskon screamed.

"Rohesia, behind!" Corsair said.

She looked over her shoulder and saw the incoming monster. Grunting, she pushed him off her and further down the path.

"Keep going, don't stop!" she ordered, drawing her bow.

Corsair lingered there for a moment, looking down the path. There, not too far away, he could see a squad of ictharrs waiting. All but two of them waited with a rider in the saddle. A few wolves were standing in front of it, guarding it, and one waved vigorously at the wolf.

"I said don't stop!"

He began to move forwards, advancing towards the ictharrs, before he looked over his shoulder again. He saw the Butcher of Tomskon charging towards Rohesia, sword ready to swing. She fired. The arrow deflected off his chest, leaving a small dent where the head had struck the plating. He recoiled and slowed momentarily, caught unaware by the shot, but prepared himself for the next projectile. Rohesia fired again and he dodged to the right, pushing towards her. Drawing her dagger, she stabbed forwards at the Butcher of Tomskon's throat only to have her attack deflected.

"Out of my way!"

He shoved her to the side, knocking her down into the snow, and approached Corsair.

"I should have known you'd run away from a fight, Sedrid!"

Corsair raised his paws to shield his head, stumbling backwards, but could do nothing as the Butcher of Tomskon brought his sword back to swing from the side.

Rohesia charged him, attacking with the dagger. It sparked against the armour and failed to penetrate. He yelled and turned, swinging at the archer and missing as she dodged back.

"You're a persistent one, aren't you?"

She lunged, snarling as she did so, but he kicked her down on to the ground and brought the sword down. Rohesia jerked her body to the side, the blade eating through the snow beneath her, and she snapped her jaws at the butcher. Without any exertion, he knocked her face away with one gauntleted paw and then placed it over her throat. She gave a cut-off yelp, kicking and struggling against him, her eyes bulging. He attempted to finish her with one swift swing into her side but the archer's paw shot out and grabbed his wrist, struggling without air.

"All that flair and you can't even fight back," the Butcher of Tomskon chuckled.

Rohesia was dying.

"Corsair, come on!"

He looked back at the wagon – he could make it while he was distracted with Rohesia, evading death once more and escaping capture.

But she'll die.

And that was enough of a reason for him to turn around and tackle him.

He flung himself at the Butcher of Tomskon, knocking him off Rohesia and to the side. Both rolled through the snow, separating, but the butcher quickly got to his hind paws and grabbed his sword from the ground. Corsair scrambled back as the assailant approached with sword raised high.

"I'm not done with you, *bastard!*" a voice screamed from behind the wolf.

McVarn, bleeding from the head, charged from behind and swung. The insult alerted the Butcher of Tomskon to his presence and made him turn, metal meeting metal.

"I never liked you, you sadistic piece of shit," McVarn growled.

"Likewise, old timer. *Likewise!*"

They engaged, swinging and slicing at each other, giving Corsair the distraction he needed. He saw Valour breaking through the crowd, charging towards the alpha.

And, not too far behind him, Thornfang was hurrying towards her master.

"Come on, come on!" Rohesia gasped, helping him up.

The two wolves hurried towards the ictharrs, leaving the raging battle behind them. He heard Quickpaw yap to him as they approached, urging them to move faster. The other wolves rode forwards towards the fleeing duo and enveloped them, eyes peeled for any approaching cavalry.

"We need to move, now, hustle!" Axel yelled from Arwenin's saddle.

"I'll help you up, come on!" Rohesia yelled.

They helped Corsair up into Quickpaw's saddle, Quickpaw lowering his body down to make it easier. He snatched the reins and pulled himself up, feeling Rohesia clamber up behind him. She drew her bow again, fetching an arrow from her quiver.

"We're ready!" Axel yelled. "Let's go, come on!"

He looked over his shoulder.

Within a minute, the battle was lost. The remnants of the rioters fled in droves down alleyways and paths, leaving many dead and wounded behind. Squads of legionnaires jogged down the main pathway, converging on wounded rioters to arrest them whilst others chased after the escaping wolves.

Corsair could see Alpha McVarn fending off both Valour and the Butcher of Tomskon. The black wolf struggled under the pressure of defending two sides, shifting his focus from one side to the other repeatedly.

Come on, McVarn.

But it was too much for the alpha to handle. As he fought off the lieutenant, Valour reached forwards and ripped the sword from his paw. The commander tossed it away, forcing him to turn around and surrender with sword aimed at his throat. The alpha froze, confronted by a sharpened blade.

He forgot about the one behind him.

The Butcher of Tomskon, despite seeing him surrender, rammed his sword through the alpha's back. The blade shot through and protruded from his front, summoning a scream from McVarn.

No!

The Butcher of Tomskon shoved him off the blade. He ignored the commander's reprimands and hurried away, gesturing to someone.

Then Corsair saw him jump up into Thornfang's saddle and chase after them, slamming his visor down over his face and drawing a javelin. Three riders broke free from the crowd, joining the pursuit.

Rohesia noticed them, too.

"Corsair, ride! *Ride!*"

346

Adrenaline gushing through his veins, he snapped at the reins. Quickpaw bounded forwards, Harangoth to his left and Arwenin to his right. The Krosguard riders around them followed, looking over their shoulders as they rode.

The Butcher of Tomskon hurled a javelin.

"*Look out!*"

A javelin thudded into a rider's back, powering through the armour and pushing its way out through his chest. He yelped and slumped off one side of his ictharr, rolling away as his comrades rode on.

"Fire back!" Axel yelled. "Fire back!"

Rohesia fired an arrow back at the Butcher of Tomskon. He didn't even flinch as it flew past him, reaching for another javelin.

"Weave! Move around!"

Corsair drew the reins left and right, ignoring the burning pain of his arms and legs. He felt the air tear beside him as a javelin missed Quickpaw, embedding itself into the snow. Rohesia returned fire alongside the other riders accompanying them, trying to deter the pursuers.

"There's the gate!"

The eastern gate stood wide open, leading out into the open plains of the Clan of the Great Lupine. Hope burned inside Corsair's heart at the idea of surviving the ordeal, of escaping his fate.

"It won't stay open for ever!" Axel yelled.

Another Krosguard soldier went down, his ictharr killed beneath him and sent sprawling into the snow. Corsair peered over his shoulder to see Thornfang drawing up close behind, her rider glaring through the holes in his helmet.

"Hit him!" Corsair yelled.

"I'm out of arrows!"

He felt that hope begin to extinguish as he saw Thornfang accelerate up behind him, maw opening slowly as he neared Quickpaw's hind legs. Those serrated fangs glistened with saliva, prepared to shred through flesh.

Thornfang brought her jaws back and thrust them forwards.

Arwenin's rear legs shot back as she ran, striking Thornfang in the side of the face. The beast yelped, caught off-guard by the ambush, and stumbled. The Butcher of Tomskon yelled out as he flew forward over his steed and into the snow, rolling across the ground and coming to a halt. Quickpaw glanced over to his saviour, making eye contact as they ran, before looking ahead and continuing to run for his life.

"The gates are closing!"

Corsair looked ahead.

Opulusian legionnaires stood on the east wall, one pulling back on the mechanism to close the large doors. They began to swing shut, creaking back into place.

If those gates close, we're all dead.

"Faster, Quickpaw! Faster!"

He snapped at the reins.

"*Hyah, hyah!*"

Quickpaw yowled as he pounded forwards as fast as he could, leading the remainder of the squad towards the door. Corsair closed his eyes as he saw the doors begin to shut, expecting to be squashed as they ran through, but felt the doors breeze past as they barrelled out into the open. The rest of the rescue team were right behind him, barely making it through before the gates shut with an earth-shaking *thud*. Their pursuers were trapped on the other side, barred from giving chase by their Opulusian comrades.

"Look out!"

Crossbow bolts began to rain down on them from above, legionnaires leaning over the side to take shots at the escapees. Not needing to be urged to do so, they accelerated away from the chaos of Grand Wolf Plains and disappeared into the winter fields of the Clan of the Great Lupine.

CHAPTER TWENTY-THREE

*V*alour's eyes lingered on the closed east gates, knowing that by the time they were reopened Corsair and his rescuers would be out of sight. Cursing under his breath, he slid his longsword back into its scabbard and let his eyes linger on where he had last seen the escapees.

"*Comosol!*" the legionnaires behind him yelled in New Opulusian.

"What is it?" he turned.

"We've dealt with most of the rioters and the others have fled. What are our orders?"

His eyes glanced over the legionnaire's shoulder and rested on the distant sight of the town centre. Bodies were strewn across the ground, the blood of the wounded mingling with the blood of the dead. Howls of pain echoed along the path, coming from hound and wolf alike.

"How many are wounded?"

"We haven't got a clue, *Comosol*."

"Search the town centre and look for survivors. Get them help from our doctors."

"And the wounded rioters?"

"Them, too."

"But they helped Sedrid escape, *Comosol*," another legionnaire said.

"Punishing them won't change anything right now. All that matters is that we save as many lives as we can – go!"

"Of course! *Dominus patria regis, Comosol!*"

Saluting, the legionnaire turned and beckoned for his fellow soldiers to follow as he rushed back towards the aftermath of the battle. Valour watched them for a moment, wincing as he heard a wail of despair echo from the town centre.

He heard something padding towards him and turned.

Lieutenant Maximus of the Krosguard rode in the saddle of his hellish steed. He came to a stop just before the commander, the trio of riders behind him following suit.

Valour growled.

"You killed him."

"Is that what you're concerned about? McVarn?"

"He was surrendering. I had his sword. He didn't need to be killed."

"The old fool helped Corsair escape."

"He could have given us information and, even if he couldn't, he was *surrendering*."

"He tried to kill both of us. He got what he deserved."

The lieutenant's expression betrayed him. A look of pride sat upon his face, made ever so annoying by that smirk, and this eliminated any chance that he killed the alpha out of necessity. Valour knew he killed him out of choice.

"Corsair got away thanks to you."

"I'm not going to shift blame like a pup. I think you should return to your duties and report to your Winter Baron. Do something useful with your time instead of waste mine."

Lieutenant Maximus growled. They held each other's gaze, the other Krosguard soldiers waiting behind their superior, before the lieutenant muttered something under his breath and snapped at the reins. Thornfang padded away, grunting at the commander, with the other Krosguard in tow.

Valour, following them with his gaze, focused on the distant chaos of the riot.

This wasn't meant to happen.

He looked down at the Krosguard alpha's body, the crimson pooling from his stomach as it oozed from the grievous wound he had sustained. The snow was stained with the black wolf's blood, blossoming beneath him. His eyes stared up to the sky.

That's when he saw the lupine's eyes move, his eyelids slowly closing and opening.

Valour gasped and dropped to his knees, placing a paw on his shoulder.

"McVarn, can you hear me? Can you see me?"

Alpha McVarn let out a wounded wheeze.

Sounds like he's hurt bad.

But then, a second later, Valour realised something.

He was laughing.

The commander knelt in silence, listening to the scorned laughter of the black wolf, his head slowly turning to look into the doberman's eyes.

"I call... myself a good... judge of character... but I let that sack... of twisted shit kill me..."

"You're not gonna die, Alpha, don't worry!"

Valour looked back down the path.

"*Medicalis! Medicalis!*"

Alpha McVarn patted Valour's leg.

"S-save it. I don't want...any charity from you. I'd rather die... than let you Opulusians...be the one to save me."

"Why, Alpha? Why all of this? All of this bloodshed for one wolf?"

Alpha McVarn met his gaze.

"You're one to talk... all of this bloodshed... for one legionnaire."

Valour didn't respond. Alpha McVarn spluttered and retched, blood dribbling from the corner of his mouth. Valour could see his life leaving his body. It ebbed from him like the blood from his stomach, the brave heart in his chest slowing.

The dying Krosguard alpha held eye contact with him, meeting the dog's pair of golden eyes. He moved his paw up and closed the gauntlet around Valour's paw, trying to squeeze it with all his might. He used this to lift himself up slightly, leaning in to his face.

"Long-"

He coughed.

"Long... live... the Sedrids."

With that, Alpha Jonah McVarn of the Krosguard let himself drop back to the ground.

He lifted his vacant eyes up to the sky and, with a final breath, died.

Silence.

Valour stayed crouched by his side for a moment, still holding the alpha's limp metal paw. With a deep exhale, he lowered it on to the snow, standing and looking back to the east gate. The doors were now open, a group of Krosguard soldiers rushing out on the backs of ictharrs, but he knew their search would be fruitless.

He looked down at the corpse of the alpha.

"I'm sorry."

He closed the alpha's eyes. Giving one last look at the deceased body of Alpha McVarn, he turned and hurried in the direction of Julian Krosguard's statue.

An hour later, the ictharrs trudged along after the adrenaline-fuelled sprint had depleted their stamina, pink tongues drooping from the corners of their mouths. Their riders were equally tired, weathered by the cold winds.

There was nowhere in the clan where it was safe to take refuge.

After the escape, Rohesia knew that orders would be given out to scour the clan's territory until Corsair was found. She couldn't risk trusting the people to hide them, yet, she struggled to think of where to go next. War raged in the east. The south led towards the Kingdom of Loxworth and the Allied Procyoni States – countries that wouldn't hesitate to paw them back over to their clan. There was no guarantee the west was any different.

They couldn't trust anyone – they had to travel to the barren wastelands of the *Deuvick Feldanas*, where few people would dare to go.

Quickpaw panted with every step, heaving himself through the snow. Arwenin was in an equally exhausted condition and Harangoth was only a bit better, wincing as he carried his weary body forwards.

"We need to stop," Rohesia said. "They're exhausted."

"No one's following us?" Axel asked, pushing up his visor and looking over his shoulder.

"No. We're okay."

Nodding in agreement, the apothecary eased Arwenin to a halt. Corsair, grunting as he pulled on the reins, brought Quickpaw to a stop. Harangoth trotted forwards a further step before he fell down into the snow on his front, his body heaving with every breath.

"You did good, guys," Axel said, dropping down and removing his helmet. "You got us out of there alive. Take a break."

All the ictharrs, including the ones belonging to the Krosguard soldiers that followed, groaned in response before lying down in the snow. Rohesia stepped out of Quickpaw's saddle, scanning the area around her as she did so. They were on a long snowy road flanked by two walls of trees, acting as barriers to prevent them careening off.

"We're safe, Corsair. We lost them."

She expected some response, a 'yes' or a mumble, but she heard nothing.

She turned.

Corsair was slumped forwards in the saddle, raking in breath as if he was struggling to breathe, viciously trembling as the cold snapped its jaws at him. The only protection he had was the spare cloaks they had thrown over him, all threadbare and thin. Quickpaw could sense how fragile his master was, giving Rohesia a look of concern.

"Corsair?"

She placed a paw on his shoulder and almost yanked it away. The wolf was freezing, jittering frantically as he clutched the reins. His green eyes stared forwards, focused on something in the distance, but when Rohesia followed his gaze she saw nothing.

"Axel?"

Then she felt him slump against her and fall from one side of Quickpaw. Rohesia caught him in her arms and lowered him down, feeling his body shudder and quiver in her paws. Fogged breath plumed out from his maw like smoke from a fire.

"Hey, what's wrong?" Axel said.

"He's really cold!" Rohesia said.

The apothecary rushed over, the two soldiers following. They all knelt beside the prince, clamouring over him while allowing space to give the medical expert access.

"He needs another cloak. Take yours off, Rohesia."

The archer hurriedly tore her cloak from her and wrapped it over Corsair's shivering body. He winced as her paw came against the numerous bruises laid out across his trembling frame.

"What's wrong with him?" a soldier asked.

"He's in shock. It's the cold – we've been riding with him almost naked. Cloaks can only do so much."

"We didn't bring spare clothes?" another said.

"I didn't know the bastards were gonna strip him down and cover him in water."

Axel rested a paw on his cloaked shoulder, leaning in.

"Corsair, listen to me. You're going to be okay, all right? You're just cold, that's it. We're going to get you warm and find somewhere to rest."

Corsair tried to speak, opening his mouth an inch, before that determination was blown away by the wind.

"What?" Rohesia said, leaning in.

"I think... I-I... am... dying..."

"You're not dying, buddy," Axel said. "You hear me? Don't quit on us now – we've come all this way."

"I'm... s-so... cold..."

"Get him up against Quickpaw, come on!"

They all eased him up despite his yelps of pained protest and guided him over to his steed, laying him down by Quickpaw's side. Quickpaw growled in concern for his master, shuffling over to shield him with his white fur.

"He'll be okay, right?" Rohesia asked.

"We need to keep him warm," Axel said. "How we're going to keep moving when he has no clothes, I don't know."

"We could carry him into the trees," one soldier said.

"Maybe. But we need to find something quick. This cold is freezing enough to..."

Axel didn't say it, conscious of Corsair hearing him.

"Regardless of our position, we need to find a way to shield him from the cold. It won't be comfortable but... I'll take off my armour and give it to him. He'll at least be covered that way."

"Are you sure?" another soldier said. "I can do it."

"I wouldn't be doing my job right if I let you do it. Don't worry – as much as I hate this weather, I can survive it."

Axel stood, reaching for his breastplate to tear off, before all the wolves' ears stood to attention. Ictharrs and lupines alike looked down the road, eyes peering through the snowy barrage.

The shape of a figure could be discerned in the distance, moving towards them, waving and yelling frantically for help.

"*Help us! Help!*"

"Who's that?" a soldier said.

"Not someone we know," Axel said, moving his paws from his chest to the grip of his sword.

Rohesia stood, signalling for the soldiers to stay by Corsair's side, and drew her dagger from her belt. Her bow could only sit over her shoulder idly, acting as a mere bystander beside her empty quiver.

"Hey! You okay over there?" Axel yelled to them, metres ahead of Rohesia.

"You need to help me! My husband, my husband... oh, God, *why?*"

"What's happened to your husband?"

"I require assistance, please! Come over here!"

The figure drew closer, beckoning for the wolf to approach them. Axel stepped back, drawing his sword.

"Hey, hey, keep your distance!"

The figure came to a stop.

"Tell me what's happened to your husband if you want me to help you! If he's hurt, I can heal him!"

"He is injured terribly! You must aid him or he shall perish!"

"What happened?"

Something twitched in the trees to Rohesia's right.

She turned her head, eyes focused on the space where she thought she saw something flicker. Concentrating her gaze on the spot, she saw that nothing stirred.

It's the snow.

Then she saw a shadow flicker to her left.

She took a step back, looking over her shoulder. The two soldiers had noticed the same movement as well, peering into the forest with paws resting on the grips of their sheathed swords. Corsair remained curled up by Quickpaw's side, somewhat sheltered from the snow. All the ictharrs looked at the left side of the road, gazing into the bushes.

Harangoth, the closest ictharr, snarled and stood. He backed away, sensing something inside the snowy foliage.

"Axel!"

The apothecary looked over his shoulder. His eyes fell upon the sight of Harangoth growling at the woods to the left, fixated on a presence they couldn't sense. He looked back to the figure, drawing his sword.

"Come a step closer and I'll cut you down, you hear me? Quit whatever it is you're doing and turn around!"

Before the figure could react, Rohesia heard a chilling cry of anger come from behind her. She spun, swinging her dagger as she turned, but the blade deflected off the sturdy armour of the charging figure. Rohesia couldn't dodge out the way and was knocked down to the ground, her dagger flying from her paws.

"*Ambush!*"

"It's an ambush!"

Screams arose from all sides, figures breaking from the trees and charging out into the open space of the snowy road. Rohesia reached for her dagger but felt a metal hind paw pin her arm down, leaving her helpless.

"I advise you not to retaliate," they said in an accented voice.

She growled and looked up into the mask of the tall warrior. The armoured figure wielded a massive war hammer with ornate designs along the metal shaft and hammer head. Powerful eyes met hers through the holes in the mask, confronting Rohesia's defensive glare, and the archer couldn't help but look away.

"Get off me!" Axel yelled, being tackled to the ground by several attackers. "What the hell is this? Who the hell-"

"Shut it!"

A perimeter formed around the stalled convoy. The attackers closed in on the ictharrs, aiming an arsenal of weapons at the steeds. Harangoth backed up towards Quickpaw, turning his head left and right to deter the approaching threats. Arwenin rushed to Quickpaw's side, standing her ground and baring her fangs at the enemy. Harangoth and Arwenin defended Quickpaw and his wounded master, snarling. Quickpaw lay there, craning his head down over his master as if he was protecting his young. The two soldiers took up positions alongside the steeds, drawing their swords.

"Tell these lot to turn on to their backs or I'll kill them!" one bandit yelled with the same accent as the armoured soldier, readying her spear.

"Don't touch him! Hurt them and *I'll kill you!*"

"I said tell them to get on to their backs and not to move!"

Rohesia saw how outnumbered they all were. Dozens of people had poured from the gaps between the trees, armed to the teeth with protective armour and weaponry. Some were mounted on ictharrs of their own, aiming bows and crossbows at the cornered wolves. Despite their ferocity, the ictharrs would all be slain regardless of how valiantly they defended Corsair.

"I recommend you listen to him," the tall warrior said. "We will use force if necessary."

Grudgingly, she did as she was told.

"Harangoth, Quickpaw! Everyone, on your backs!"

The ictharrs questioned her decision with inquisitive growls, tilting their heads. Harangoth puffed out air through his flared nostrils, preparing to charge at the attackers.

"Listen to me and get on to your backs! Do it!"

"Do it, Arwie!" Axel yelled.

Submitting, Arwenin lowered herself down and rolled on to her back, paws dangling limp in the air. The two other ictharrs, growling, followed suit, their owners lowering their swords and putting their paws up in the air. Quickpaw whimpered, glancing down at Corsair's shivering form, before he did the same.

Harangoth lingered, fangs bared.

"Harangoth!"

He growled, telling the archer to shut up.

"They'll kill you, stop!"

Quickpaw yapped at him, trying to convince the behemoth, but he didn't listen. With a roar, Harangoth lunged forwards at the perimeter, hurling himself at the sharpened tips of swords and spears that awaited him.

"*Harangoth!*"

There was the *snap* of a crossbow firing before a net shot out and wrapped around his paws, binding them together. The net threw him off his lunge entirely, causing him to land short of the vast array of weaponry aimed at him. He landed on his side, confused as to how he had missed, and didn't have time to fight back as the bandits leapt on him.

"Pin him!"

"Get the muzzle!"

While 10 bandits held Harangoth down, one unclipped a large muzzle from his belt and knelt in front of the beast. With a *snap*, he clamped the muzzle down over the ferocious ictharr's maw and stepped back, watching him writhe on the ground to resist the hold of the restraints. Seconds passed before Harangoth gave up trying, lying still in the snow while growling at his captors.

Rohesia looked in the direction of where the shot came from.

A figure, swathed in a brown hooded cloak like the tall warrior's, approached. The bottom of the cloak was torn and ripped. Rohesia caught a glimpse of a canine adorned in blackened Opulusian legionnaire armour. There were numerous scratches and dents in the plating, particularly over the abdominal area, which had been left as souvenirs from blades and arrows. An unusual contraption akin to a crossbow sat in his paws, larger and loaded with a different kind of ammunition.

"Get that wolf up!"

While the other bandits tied the four paws of the other ictharrs together, restraining them, two grabbed Corsair by the arms and dragged him away from Quickpaw. Quickpaw growled, glaring.

"Hurt him and I'll kill you!" Rohesia yelled.

"Rather unlikely," the tall warrior said.

They moved his hind paw off her, using their free paw to pull her up. Restrained and unable to fight back against the warrior's strength, she was guided into the middle of the open road where Axel and the rest of the wolves were already held captive, kneeling in the snow with brigands looming behind them.

"Apologies."

The tower of metal shoved her down and she growled. Rohesia couldn't even attempt to get up before two of the mysterious attackers grabbed her and held her there, keeping her on her knees.

"Move it, wolf!"

Rohesia looked right to see the two bandits guiding Corsair towards them. The brigands' paws were the only things stopping him from falling, his legs rendered unreliable from the harsh bruising.

"We ain't got all day, pal!"

They shoved him down hard and Corsair didn't have the strength to balance himself. He fell on to his side, shivering with nothing but his undergarments and a few cloaks to shield him against the cold.

"Hey, stop that!" Rohesia yelled. "He's hurt!"

"Shut up!" the guards behind her ordered, shaking her.

Rohesia obeyed but kept her eyes on Corsair, ready to intervene if necessary. Two brigands brought him on to his knees, holding him up. His head drooped and one of the duo forced their other paw under his snout, holding his head. Eyes barely open, Corsair was on the verge of passing out, trembling from the cold.

"You need to keep him warm, he's-"

The guard smacked Rohesia on the back of the head hard and she yelped, leaning forwards to move her head away. The duo yanked her back up and held her there, forcing a paw beneath her snout.

She could see that the rest of the ambushers had formed a small group opposite them, with both the crossbow-wielding canine and hammer-carrying juggernaut at the front. She noticed that each bandit had a metal plate on their shoulder painted blue, a uniform characteristic among all their differing armours and appearances. It was that sense of uniformity among bandits that struck her.

What kind of group of bandits is this? And this far into the clan?

She began to notice something else. Despite the array of masks, made of both metal and fabric, she saw felines standing before her. All of them spoke with the same accent and muttered to one another in the same tongue – most likely Sikkharan.

Are these Silverclaw thugs?

The juggernaut glanced to the right and then turned to face the crowd, silencing them with a mighty roar.

"Silence for Lady Riskar!"

It was eerie how quickly silence fell upon the crowds. All the bandits looked to Rohesia's left, and the archer followed their eyes to the approaching figure.

The individual that had been calling for help sauntered down the space between the hostages and the ambushers. Rohesia was close enough to see that Lady Riskar was a small-eared grey cat. A blue gown of some fabric engulfed her, swishing with every step she took and, where the dress was tight around the waist, Rohesia could see a rapier dangling from the belt, well-kept and polished. Lady Riskar gave off an air of authority, potent enough to quell the rowdiness of the bandits in the crowd.

She stopped before the five hostages and let the silence rule for a moment, casting her gaze from one end of the line to the other before turning around to her band of criminals. She then cast her gaze over to the five restrained ictharrs lying on their backs, eyes focused on her.

"Well, this is most certainly a disappointing haul," she said with that same Sikkharan accent. "Nothing else? No supplies?"

"Naught of what was expected, Milady," the juggernaut said. "Five riders and five ictharr steeds."

She tutted.

"Well, this just shall not do. Why would the clan even send a group out here with no supplies? It seems a rather pointless venture."

She pointed to Corsair on Rohesia's right.

"And what is the value of sheltering a homeless wolf?"

A chuckle rose among the crowd, one which Axel interrupted.

"And what about it?"

"Hey, shut it!"

One of the guards drew a dagger and pressed it against his throat, making him lean back to alleviate the pressure on his neck. Lady Riskar came forward, kneeling in front of him.

"Would you care to tell me why you are journeying north?"

Axel panted. The guard pushed the blade further, making him yelp.

"Well, maybe I could say something if touchy-feely here got the knife away from my throat!"

"Ah, how rude of me. Kilik?"

The bandit removed the blade and Axel let out a gasp for air, leaning forward with a paw against his throat.

"Is that better, darling?"

Axel didn't answer, blinking as he desperately tried to come up with a believable lie.

"Would you care to answer me now?"

"We're... we're traders."

"Traders? Without supplies or a carriage?"

"Yeah. We sold all of it. Sold all our produce in Grand Wolf Plains."

"My, you are most certainly prepared to trade, aren't you?"

Lady Riskar tapped the plating of his armour, panic rising in the wolf's eyes. Axel hurried to answer.

"It's for protection-"

"Kilik?"

Lady Riskar got up and Kilik brought Axel's head back, pressing the knife against his throat again. He growled, swearing under his breath as the cat moved on to Rohesia.

She snarled at her.

"Oh my! How terribly defensive you are. Little pup far from home?"

Another chuckle arose from the crowd, the bandits watching as their leader toyed with their captives. Rohesia remained silent, knowing it was better not to talk.

"Care to suggest a reason as to why you are heading north?"

She did not answer.

"Darling, refusing to speak shall not help you."

She did not say a word.

"I must admit, it is *adorable* that you are so determined to serve this vow of silence."

The cat ruffled the fur on Rohesia's head and Rohesia resisted the urge to bite her, knowing that she would only end up in a more uncomfortable situation than she was already in. Lady Riskar moved on towards Corsair, whose eyes were barely open.

"A drunkard? A drifter? What is his purpose out here?"

"We picked him up. We were taking him north to his family," Axel groaned.

"Is that so? I never thought your clan was particularly charitable. Then again, years have passed by."

She knelt in front of Corsair, her face inches from the wolf's snout. His eyes were half-open and his breathing so heavy that Rohesia could hear it from where she knelt.

"I find his lack of clothes rather... primitive."

"Ronny ain't got no clothes beneath those slacks!" a bandit said.

"Shut it, Simon!"

The crowd broke into roaring laughter and Lady Riskar joined in with them while Rohesia's eyes focused on Corsair. She wanted the wolf to turn and meet her gaze, to show some form of sign that he was with them, but he didn't move.

Corsair's in bad shape. I have to do something.

"Any reason why you are journeying north?"

He didn't answer.

She waved a paw in front of his face.

"Hello?"

Corsair let out a weak groan of exhaustion, not moving. Lady Riskar gave a snort of derision and looked back towards her crowd of minions, shaking her head and leaning in.

"Come on, pup, time to wake up. It is rude to ignore people speaking to you."

The grey cat placed a paw on the left side of Corsair's neck.

In a second Rohesia witnessed Corsair become overwhelmed with a new surge of energy. With a terrifyingly loud bark and snarl,

Corsair snapped his jaws at the bandit leader and sent her reeling back from the shock, falling on to her rear. The group of minions all drew their weapons and the two guards behind Corsair pulled him back, one drawing a dagger.

"Don't you hurt him!" Rohesia yelled. "Don't you touch Corsair! Touch him and I'll make you regret it!"

The onlookers gasped condescendingly, some patronising her further in Sikkharan and applauding her defiance. Laughter spread from bandit to bandit as her captors hauled her back, smacking her across the head again.

"Speak when spoken to," the bandit warned.

Rohesia looked back up at Lady Riskar, expecting her to antagonise Corsair further, but was surprised to see an expression of confused shock upon her face. She stared at the archer, eyes and mouth wide, still sitting in the snow.

"Milady?" the canine said. "What's going on?"

"Whose name did you just utter?" she asked.

Rohesia remained silent, cursing herself for speaking. The cat's followers shared the same bout of confusion, murmuring to one another.

"What was his name?" she asked, getting up. "*Corsair*? Did you say *Corsair*?"

Rohesia was reluctant to answer.

"It is a simple enquiry, wolf. Is his name Corsa-"

"Yes, for the love of God!" Axel yelled. "Corsair Sedrid, son of Arthur and Ophelia Sedrid, next in line for Winter Baron! God, was it that hard Rohesia?"

She didn't care about the apothecary's outburst. She watched the cat turn to face Corsair again, looking up to the guards with a bewildered look.

"Let them go," she said.

"Milady, what is-"

"I said let them go."

The bandits, confused, stepped back from the captives. Kilik removed the dagger from Axel's neck and the others took their paws off the captives' shoulders. Corsair somehow remained upright on his knees, body trembling.

"I should have remembered those green eyes."

Lady Riskar focused her gaze on Corsair, eyes wide in amazement.

"Corsair Sedrid. It's been 10 years."

EPILOGUE

*V*alour walked through the doors of the Great Hall of Wolves, helmet under his arm and bloodied sword slid into scabbard. His ears perked up as he entered, stopping by the door so as not to disturb the meeting between the Winter Baron and his numerous advisors. He saw a soldier standing up ahead, leaning against one of the benches with arms folded across his chest and an uninterested look on his face.

"The judges are outraged," one advisor said. "They are claiming there was no trial to speak of. That Corsair was sentenced to death without having his case given a proper review."

"I understand there is a lapse in protocol regarding Corsair but, right now, we can't focus on that."

"When shall we focus on it?" a second said. "You defied clan law, Winter Baron. You are meant to uphold it – not bend it to your will when you see fit!"

"I assure you that this was a mere lapse in protocol. Nothing more. As I said, we must find Corsair. Have messenger birds been sent out?"

"Many. Other towns are carrying out searches as we speak, Winter Baron," one said.

"And our neighbours to the south?"

"Official envoys have been sent to warn them of Corsair. There's no doubt that our allies will comply."

"What do you think our chances of finding him are?"

The advisors all hesitated, unsure of how to calculate the odds. One spoke for them.

"There is every chance he is already miles and miles away, Winter Baron. Those who rescued him may have taken him south, east, west or even north to the *Deuvick Feldanas.*"

Winter Baron Tiberius shook his head.

"They wouldn't journey south into more allied territory. Nor would they go east towards a warzone. Either they've gone north or west, which means we cannot pursue them. The Kingdom of Wyndr will not heed our words and I will not send soldiers into the north. We focus on searching our land and the south for now."

"And if we don't find him, Winter Baron?"

"Let's not focus on that. We will find him, one way or another. If that is all, I would like to adjourn our meeting."

"*We* adjourn meetings, Winter Baron," one of the advisors said as they stood. "Do not forget your place."

Without another word, the group of advisors stood and walked away. None acknowledged the commander as they left, not uttering a word.

"There he is," the soldier scoffed. "Our murderer in shining armour."

"Quiet, Maximus."

Lieutenant Maximus sneered and pushed himself off the bench, glaring at the doberman. Valour ignored him, focusing on the Winter Baron.

The brown wolf sighed and stepped down from the podium. Weariness clear in his face, he turned and sat down on the front bench, placing his head in his paws. Valour stood for a moment, watching in silence, before he decided to come forward. The metal plating over his hind paws caused each step to echo through the empty hall, emphasising how vacant it was.

He stopped by the end of the bench Tiberius sat on. Lieutenant Maximus watched.

"I take it the situation is under control?" the Winter Baron said, rubbing his face.

"Dealt with to the best of our ability, Winter Baron."

A pause.

"How many people died?"

"Fifty-two, Winter Baron."

"How many of them were civilians?"

"Forty-two, Winter Baron."

"And wounded?"

"Seventy-eight, Winter Baron."

Winter Baron Tiberius sharply inhaled and gently let the air out, leaning back against the bench and looking up at the Opulusian commander.

"You dogs have royally messed this one up, eh?" Lieutenant Maximus said. "Couldn't even catch the little runt while he ran to his friends."

They ignored him. The Winter Baron continued.

"What did McVarn do to-"

"He's dead, Winter Baron."

Valour glared at Lieutenant Maximus from over his shoulder.

"Your trusted lieutenant here made sure of that."

Lieutenant Maximus chuckled.

"For a commander, you're way too hung up on one dead wolf."

"He was surrendering."

"He was a traitor, Winter Baron," the lieutenant said to Tiberius. "I did you and this clan a favour killing him. He would have just been more trouble down the line."

"Because killing a military leader during wartime is anywhere close to a smart move? Don't act like you know what you're talking about, Maximus, you killed him because you wanted to. There was no need for it."

"Don't talk to me about killing as if you know nothing, mutt. You don't think I know about Ophelia?"

Valour stopped. The lieutenant grinned.

"You slaughtered an innocent wolf. She was in custody – *your* custody. Unarmed. She couldn't have even put up a fight."

"Lieutenant," Winter Baron Tiberius warned.

"At least I killed someone who had it coming. Someone who wasn't innocent. You just went and murdered the late Winter Baron's wife for no good reason, even though she was unarmed. She had already surrendered. And yet *you killed her*."

"*Lieutenant*."

Silence. Winter Baron Tiberius stood and turned to the quarrelling lieutenant and commander.

"This situation is already enough of a mess without your antics getting in the way. Make sure everything is under control outside and that all the corpses are being disposed of."

Lieutenant Maximus sighed.

"Fine, *Winter Baron*. All I'm saying is that McVarn is dead and buried for good reason. That vacancy is gonna need to be covered. I mean... *Alpha Maximus Verschelden* has a better ring to it, doesn't it?"

The Winter Baron ignored his claim of succession in the Krosguard, glaring at him. As the lieutenant turned to walk to the door, he stopped by Valour's side.

The wolf held eye contact with the doberman for a moment. In that look, Valour saw a disturbing concoction of intense maddened excitement and furious anger, all brewing behind his terrifying gaze.

"You'd think with all that polished gear and all those markings you'd know how to make sure an execution doesn't go wrong," Lieutenant Maximus scoffed. "Guess they make just anyone commander nowadays."

Valour didn't waste his breath on him. They held each other's gaze before, eventually, the lieutenant padded out of the Great Hall of Wolves.

"I apologise for the lieutenant," Winter Baron Tiberius said. "His bitter and cruel attitude can be disturbing for most people."

"Disturbing is a hell of a way to call him a soulless bastard. How the hell is he even a lieutenant?"

"He is a skilled asset."

"*Skilled asset?* He is a detriment and a liability. He should not be within a mile of military leadership."

"Decisions were made to have him in the army as a result of his sentence and he proved himself during the war."

"Well I hope nothing comes of that 'Alpha Maximus Verschelden' suggestion."

The Winter Baron didn't answer.

Valour snorted in contempt.

"You can't seriously be considering it."

"That decision is my prerogative, not yours."

"He kills without second thought, Winter Ba-"

"I said that decision is *my* prerogative. I do not want your input."

Silence. Valour held his tongue. He watched as Winter Baron Tiberius bowed his head in thought, thinking of what to say.

Finally, he spoke.

"Jonah McVarn. He was never the one to let orders get in the way of what he thought was right. A blessing and a curse."

A silence fell between them. Neither dared to break it, the events of the past day too tragic and unfortunate to comment upon for the moment. Valour bore a great deal of this guilt and he cast a shame-faced look down at his sword. The blood was still spattered along the blade, reminding him of the life he had taken in a vain attempt to kill Corsair.

"I failed you, Winter Baron. You and my king."

"The blame is not yours to bear," Winter Baron Tiberius said. "You can only do so much as an outsider to this clan. It was my responsibility to have coordinated this process better."

"I killed her."

The Winter Baron paused, caught off-guard by the sudden mentioning of her demise.

"Not intentionally. That was... that was Ophelia's own unfortunate and tragic choice."

Valour didn't answer. He remembered what Ophelia Sedrid had said to him in defiance, standing up to protect her son.

I can assure you that you will never, never, overcome the love I have for my son.

"Those who have been wounded are being treated by apothecaries and doctors, Winter Baron. We've decided to give amnesty to those who were involved in the riot. The last thing we need is to punish them – it won't do anything but widen the divide between my people and yours."

"I can agree to that. Make sure they're well-kept, well-fed and looked after."

The Winter Baron met Valour's gaze, eyes sullen with misery. He sighed.

"It's a black day for the Clan of the Great Lupine."

Outside, in the centre of Grand Wolf Plains, stood Julian Krosguard. Forever frozen in stone, the founder of the clan could only weep in silence as he gazed down on the slain bodies of the innocent, listening to the howls of despair echo across the plains.

...

The figure stood in the silence of the cave.

The cavern was illuminated only by a single torch on the wall opposite, casting light over the shattered relics of their imprisonment. Nature's architecture formed mouths in the walls that lead into adjacent dimly-lit rooms and chambers.

Nothing stirred.

The figure stood there, motionless and patient, facing the wall.

Silence all around.

The end of the year was still far away.
They needed to be patient.
They needed to wait.
For everything would be as it was in the beginning...
...erased and renewed.

Dear reader,

We hope you enjoyed reading *The Sharpened Fangs Of Lupine Spirit*. Please take a moment to leave a review, even if it's a short one. Your opinion is important to us.

Discover more books by H.G. Sansostri at https://www.nextchapter.pub/authors/hg-sansostri

Want to know when one of our books is free or discounted? Join the newsletter at http://eepurl.com/bqqB3H

Best regards,
H.G. Sansostri and the Next Chapter Team

ABOUT THE AUTHOR

Harrison Giovanni Sansostri is a 19-year-old student from North London presently studying psychology at university. HG is also an actor and has done film, theatre and commercials for many years. HG started writing at a very early age with his first book published at just 12 years old, *The Little Dudes Skool Survival Guide*, and his second book, *The Chronicles of Derek Dunstable*, published at 14 years old. He spent many years touring primary schools and promoting his books. He was also invited to participate in the Manx Literary Festival on the Isle of Man. He then took a creative break to focus on improving his writing skills and created the *Vos Draemar* series, writing the first in the seven-book series, *The Sharpened Fangs of Lupine Spirit*.

CPSIA information can be obtained
at www.ICGtesting.com
Printed in the USA
LVHW030920291221
707364LV00005B/70